IN SOMEONE'S HANDS

ROSE KAUSER

This story is neither the beginning nor the end.
Enjoy.

PROLOGUE

Medisa
07/09/2021 (Tuesday)

I used my body as a barricade. My nails gripped onto the door frame as my feet slipped on the floorboards, trying to keep the door from coming in. The door began to break out of its hold, the screws became loose and I was starting to give up. My body was starting to give up.

"Open the fucking door, Medisa!"

The voices outside the door could be heard so clearly, like there was nothing in between me inside the room and them in the hallway. Once it clicked that I couldn't hold my back to the door for long, I gave up and let them in. What was going to happen was inevitable anyways.

Ayaan stormed into the room.

There wasn't anywhere for me to go, but I knew the quick scared backsteps I took away from him would put some distance between us, hopefully doing something to the intensity of the next blow.

Maybe it was a punch, and a slap delivered by the floor when I had dropped onto it? Or it was a slap so hard it felt like a punch that had blocked out any feeling of my body hitting the floor—

'It doesn't matter what it was, point is, you got hit so hard it confused your senses for a bit.'

"Prick." I'd managed to get out even with a lump forming in my throat, tears blocking my view and needles stabbing my face from where his hand last touched.

I knew as soon as the word left my mouth he wouldn't be satisfied until he'd done some more. Something else. And although I'd known better than to say anything (from years of experience), I didn't give a flying fuck. I knew that my brother, the so-called man, couldn't stand me fighting back, couldn't stand him not being able to scare or beat me into listening to him. Deep down, I knew that even under all his delusions, all his acts, he knew that he was no man, he wasn't even close to being one. He knew that he was a prick, he just didn't like hearing it from a mouth he despised.

I quickly pulled my legs towards my chest to prepare to either get up and move, or to turn into a ball with my head protected. Not being able to decide in time, I am picked up with ease and chucked back onto the floor, only this time it's across the room. I'm guessing that was his attempt to open up my undecided version of a hedgehog ball.

Although my eyes were squeezed shut from before I was thrown, they stayed that way because of the new pain introduced by the impact. It was like I was being compressed between the floor and someone's boot, and I felt it down to my lungs.

As if it would heal me faster, I grabbed a hold of my shirt where the pain gathered the most whilst he stomped over to me.

I took a few more hits in the process of trying to breathe. I hadn't had the time to properly inhale or exhale, my sight continued to be blocked by thick tears forged with anger rather than sadness, and there was no point in even acknowledging my vocal cords.

"Ayaan stop! What are you doing stop! You could kill her stop it!" Ammi, as usual got involved too late. "<u>Look at the size of her and the size of you!</u> Stop it *now*!"

He gave in to her pleas then stormed out the room. Probably to take the rest of his anger out on the cat, or the walls.

Ayaan's mood swings have always been shocking. One minute he's laughing and throwing jokes at everyone, next minute my presence alone would be enough for him to throw anything but a joke at me. I never fully understood why he hated me so much, or why Ataya had so much jealousy and anger stored up towards me. What did I do that was so bad everyone in this house only saw evil when they looked at me? Dramatic-yes, but true.

I needed to leave.

I've learnt whatever lessons I could from the people I'm supposed to call family. Does being blood related even matter if this is the treatment I got for it?

Now that the room was empty, my tears refused to be held back. I tried to stop myself from being so weak and vulnerable but my self-sabotaging habit knocked me down. I thought about all the bad things that have happened to me over the years—you would think that I found a way to cope after all this time of abuse but no, the thoughts *always* reoccur.

As I laid on the floor, not quite ready to get up and act like nothing happened (meaning I ignore the family until enough time had passed for me to 'act normal' again) the same thoughts ran across my mind. '*Why me? Why wasn't I born into a family that would build me up? Why was I born into a family that broke and teased what I tried to build?*' Why? Why? Why? Depressing and filled with extreme self-pity—I know. But I only felt like that after some sort of abuse and <u>Thank God</u> for that. I couldn't stand being one of those people who pitied themselves twenty-four-seven. But those thoughts *are* what got me up. It's what made me see things differently and what made me more than meets the eye. You see, self-pity almost always led to anger—hate. And if you're strong enough, you can use that as motivation. Motivation to get up, motivation to do something about your situation and for some people those '*why me?*' questions gave them motivation for revenge. How far they go with said 'revenge' is based on many things, the most important one being how much they have left to care.

And I'm close to having none.

Anyways, we don't need to get into that because before I act on any vengeful thoughts, I always tried to make myself see straight by reminding myself that I'm in a better position than a lot of people around the world. Not in the sense that I look at those who have problems I cannot relate to (although I do that too), I actually think about and compare myself to others who also go through abuse but genuinely cannot escape. However—respectfully, but also not really—I've found that method to be shit, absolute shit. Yes, it's sad that there are people in unfortunate circumstances, but thinking of them in attempts to make myself feel better is bullshit. It doesn't make me feel better. It just shoves my problems to the side, or to the back of my mind, or to a dark corner. And not only does that take away any sense of comfort or validation, it just piles up my emotions. And those emotions wait, they wait for me to be abused again so that they can come back as a reminder of how shitty my life has been. Which leads to the infiltration of my next method, '*the good things in my life.*' I push, and I mean *push*, for my mind to remember the good experiences I've had, but that always snowballs into thinking about the traumatic events they led to. And believe it or not, that's happened enough times for me to recognise the pattern and half-develop something called 'cherophobia.' I say 'half' because I don't refrain from having fun, but I do *sometimes* anticipate 'the bad' making an appearance. I think it's some sort of mental quick-draw situation. Anyways, an example of the snowball thing is my ninth birthday. After having all the girls in the year show up to my house, I made the mistake of calling one a pussy (something I overheard from someone outside, *obviously* not knowing the meaning—sue me) and even though we all laughed at the word, Ayaan felt the need to humiliate me in front of everyone (the usual '*throw across the floor*' move). I ended up quietly sobbing and was forced to put on an act until everyone was collected—which happened quickly after the live wrestling move. I know that was 11 years ago, but pretty much every other good memory played out like that. It's as if every happy moment has to be linked to a sad one.

But hey, '*God does not burden a soul beyond that it can bear.*' I understood that, I did, I still do, but I couldn't take it anymore, I wouldn't. I had to get myself out. Clearly beatings will be prescribed until I've taken the hint with a bag full of necessities to actually leave this damn place. And I took the hint, *several* times, but I've never had the right amount of drive—apparently the emotions abuse invoke aren't enough—to actually attempt to get away. Usually in these situations I planned to leave, but then my mind begins to play devil's advocate and convinces my body that it's being irrational; running away would not solve anything, it would only bring new problems in, like money and finding a place to stay. My *own* mind turns against me as it constantly breaks and repairs its own cage.

What a joke.

Internet advice and Amana would say to pray, to turn to God and to keep a kind-open heart, but I couldn't, I struggled to. The last thing I wanted to do after my family provoked negative feelings was get on a prayer mat. I mentally wouldn't be there even if I had got to one. My mind would be filled with betrayal (from those who are supposed to love and protect me), anger (for those who are supposed to love and protect me), hurt (from those who are supposed to love and protect me) and definitely self-pity. So instead of doing what my soul needed, I turned to music.

I never listened to sad songs, my life was sad, I didn't need a woeful soundtrack to go with it. What I needed and what worked was the lively, rebellious, heart pumping type of music. With them, I pictured myself dancing anywhere and everywhere, or running out in the middle of the night doing something defiant. Any sort of lively scenario that would make me feel alive, I was in them—the main character, all in my mind. If I couldn't change my reality, my environment, I thought of a world, a scenario, where I could—where I did.

After years of living in my mind with a personalised playlist, I finally came to realise music was not what I needed. Music was not my friend, it's just something that gave me an illusion, a fantasy life. It convinced me that my lively thoughts were enough. It distracted me from anything that actually mattered and anything that would actually help. For example, praying. I could have been praying for inner peace and all that, but no because every time I tried, someone in this house pissed me off enough for me to—for some reason— turn my back. Not completely, but at a tipping point. And though I know serenity can be achieved (I've had a taste), it for some reason is not as seductive as the 'free-spirited' ways of the west. Which—trust me, I know—sounds stupid. It is stupid. Another example of music being an opp is how it took my focus on doing something that would actually help get me out of this place, like a job. Though, to be fair, that one was not that hard…who dreams a working life for themselves?

Music in a way was something that sided with my family, it did what they did, it let me dream, dream so that I was never actually awake to focus on my life. I thought that I was using it to benefit me, block out the noise and memories of my life but no, it just drugged me up whilst taking my minutes, hours, months and years, and with them unlived memories, lessons and opportunities.

Just like many other not so noticeable bruised nights, I drifted off and began to feel myself letting go off reality once more, only this time I closed my eyes with new intentions that I *will* see through. Crumbs and fantasies were no longer enough.

Chapter 1

Medisa
4/10/2021 (Monday)

"Is there an alien inside you or something?"

My face questioned Amana.

Although I knew that she was joking, I also knew that she would never quickly sweep away the possibility of me being pregnant because she genuinely fears pregnancies, sexually active or not.

Despite her method of choice, she obviously knew something was up, and this was her way of slightly lightening up the mood whilst simultaneously opening up the doors to a much-needed conversation.

"I'm just sayinggg, you missed the first week of Uni and been acting strange for the past month and said that you had something you wanted to talk about…sounds a bit suspicious to me." Amana spoke with her shoulders frozen in a shrugged position as her bottom lip spilled out. Her hands were spread out as if to say *'I have a point.'*

She did have a point, but I was too distracted by the memories of Ayaan beating my arse, and the little itch my finger had to flick her protruding bottom lip down, to both hear and see it go back up into position.

I decided against it.

"I can't stay at my house anymore, I'm twenty years old and I haven't really accomplished anything for myself. I'm old enough to do things without a parent or guardian, I just need money—"

"Don't we all."

"I'm serious…We need to leave, but then I just think about their feelings and then I'm automatically back in the cage thinking about everyone but me."

"Let's go then." Amana's words were casual, maybe even a little fed-up.

"What?"

"What? You said it yourself. *We're* old enough. We don't have to live like this anymore, we can make money as we go along. We don't need to be set from the start."

I froze for a few seconds, taken aback. Usually in these matters, Amana is the one to hold back—to come up with a plan—so the sudden switch to being spontaneous caught me off-guard.

"Hear me out. Then after that, if you still want to leave, we'll go." I managed to say without letting too much time pass.

'Did she just use reverse psychology to get me to stay?'

"Proceed wifey." Amana got comfortable, propping her feet up onto the seat in front of her.

After she elegantly pushed her hair back and away from her face, I knew that I had her undivided attention.

"Long story short. I emailed this place asking if they were still hiring and sent a smaller version of a CV, slash personal statement. They emailed back saying that they would get in touch soon and I was hoping that they would've by now so that I could come to you with something that's been confirmed rather than something that's inconclusive." I rushed through my words but made sure to not be too incoherent because I did not want to repeat that all again.

"You bitch. You know that you don't have to wait, you can tell me whenever, even if it's just an idea, I don't care."

I laughed at her sudden outburst and spoke between her points with '*I know, I know,*' like I was a child being reminded of a life lesson or something.

"<u>If God wills it</u>, you will hear back from them soon, don't worry."

"Ah-meen." I responded. "The pay is *high*—as in we would have enough by the time Uni ends." My eyes grew large to emphasise how big this could be.

"What are they called?" She whipped out her phone, obviously wanting to research them herself.

"Bar…Ba-Baronial?" I focused on Amana's eyes as though it would help me say the name correctly. As I struggled to get the name out, her face was like I had shot her unborn baby. I couldn't help but smile at her expression and what I made of it.

"Co-come again?" She mocked after recovering from momentarily pausing.

"Shut up." I swatted her away without making physical contact.

"What jobs are they offering?" Amana questioned like I didn't know what I was doing. Granted, I didn't know what jobs they were offering, but she wouldn't know that.

'*Her eyes say otherwise.*'

I almost mentally beat myself for not coming to her with this after doing some rigorous research, but to be fair, I was on a '*beggars can't be choosers*' vibe.

"Some sort of service job or receptionist role or something." In person, I had answered at the right time (I didn't let too much time pass) and I spoke casually as if I had all the facts down. But in my mind, I knew that I panicked and said '*service job*' as if every job isn't a service to something.

Amana continued to look at me like she were trying to

figure out if I had any working brain cells. I took it as an opportunity to quickly speak before she completely, but slowly, annihilates me with some passive aggressiveness.

"I looked it up. It looks legit, and if they accept me, I'm doing something that I've never done before, which is actually sticking to an escape plan."

Whilst I wondered if my guilt trip was changing the way she would deliver how stupid I am in this matter, her huge cat eyes switched between which eye of mine to look into.

"Let me look for some more jobs before you sign up to something you would end up hating."

'And the guilt trip lands.' The tip of my brows and lips twitch up to my succession.

"So don't finalise anything, okay?" She continued. Her voice laced with a gentleness that only made an appearance when she felt the need to comfort.

"Okay." I nodded, taking my eyes off Amana to look into the distance, scoping the students out whilst our next topic of conversation came about.

Other than the two of us, no one else really wore nice outfits. There were a few international students who were decked out in brands, but I didn't really like the look of that. Then there were students from the UK who did that, but you could tell when someone got excited with their loan and when someone has been living a certain lifestyle.

I don't look to judge, I looked to take inspiration from and to compliment, but there's no one who has an aesthetic that catches my eye. If anything, we were the ones inspiring people, even on our off days.

Out of nowhere, a few feet away, a group of boys started to cheer for someone as they were greeting them. Normally I wouldn't care, but they made me jump. I didn't recognise the boy they greeted, but then again, I haven't really been sociable this year, or updating my brain on campus faces—something I naturally did in case of an emergency. You never know when you need to give a report or approach someone familiar for help.

When he was done with the greetings, he came into our view. From what I'd managed to see, he was already easy on the eyes, but now, now he had more of an appeal. He had to be foreign or something, I've never seen a guy from the UK dress like that. To find a guy who had the ability to put things together that actually went, felt like finding some sort of national treasure or world's wonder or something.

"His name's Kade." Amana revealed after following my gaze. I would argue and say that I wasn't actually looking at him, just his clothes, but she would take the piss and milk it.

Failing to ignore her expression, I went back to stalk him with my eyes, repeating his name after Amana, only when *I* echoed it, it was as he approached us.

"Shit." I let out quietly.

Times like this convinced me the beatings I got were truly deserved because what the hell possessed me to do that?

"Yeah?" Kade's eyes flickered between us then settled on Amana.

"I was just telling her about you. She was saying your name not knowing that it's yours because A: She likes the name and B: She likes your clothes." Amana explained as if my behaviour was completely normal and reoccurring. Still, I would rather her say that, than chat-shit and say that I was in awe of his looks.

Kade had a face on. He's entertained, but he also seemed to be a little alarmed.

Before things got more awkward than needs be, Amana

let him know that they'll talk later, to which he responded with a nod to her and a polite smile to me.

As he walked away, both me and Amana—as if it were a survival instinct—stared at his arse, looked to each other, then spoke with our expressions. It was at this point that Amana decided to take it upon herself to fill me in with the details I somehow missed.

I'm taught that Kade is known by a lot of people for his sense of style and looks—mostly looks—and that no one actually chills with him. I also learnt that Kade is twenty-three years old, *not* a student, and his reason for coming here every now and then is unknown, but there are rumours, because when people are given blanks, they tend to fill them in with fiction. They had to, how else were they going to survive? By focussing on their own lives? No, don't be ridiculous.

No one knew the details about Kade but because he attracts attention, they've given him a story, the popular one, liked by the majority of the girls of course, is that he's a mafia leader and launders money through the university. Obviously the girlies came up with the most typical (most wished scenario) but after seeing him and how he acts, I could see it being a thing.

I almost want it to be a thing.

"How do you know all of this?" Honestly, I'm impressed.

"Because he's slept with some of the girls."

"*Damn*. No way."

"Yeahhhh." She stretched the word as if to say 'you better believe it.' "He's a secretive hoe."

"Yeah…he's secreting *something*." My eyebrows flicked as I made a double entendre. And Amana, like I suspected, tried not to laugh too hard (she likes to claim that I'm not funny), whilst pretending to throw something at me. "The

only concrete thing that you guys have on him is his age."
I said as I flinched at the phantom object Amana threw at
me. "Imagine it comes out that he's a head of departments
underaged son. The look on everyone's faces would be the
funniest thing."

"Don't laugh too hard. He's fucked me over."

I stopped finding my thought funny.

"'*Over*' what?" I joked, but also wanted a quick confession.

Amana tilted her head as if to say '*really?*'

"No, but seriously, did he do something stupid?"

"No I was joking, wanted to humble you real-quick. Just
because he can't sleep with us, doesn't mean he can't do us
over."

"Fax." I respond.

"No Printer." Amana finished. "Here look at these." She
hands over her phone, revealing pictures she's been sneaking
of Kade. I laughed at the randomness before looking at him
properly this time and not just his clothes.

He was intimidating, but attractive, but scary, but attractive. His body was built, not enough for him to look like Hercules, but enough for you to know that he could stand his
ground in a fight if needs be. And he didn't have a skin-fade
like every other boy in this Uni, which added so much more
to his looks. His wavy-curly hair was like how the actors
had it in the 90s (without the grease), shorter at the back and
longer at the front. His curls don't exactly hide his forehead,
but some do come down and stop before touching his brows.
A middle part might even make an appearance depending on
how his hair fell after he ran his fingers through. His eyes
were coloured and matched perfectly with his dark curly-
wavy hair. Basically, he looked like every villain with a sob

story and I couldn't tell if I gave a shit or not. If I wasn't careful, my mind would turn Kade into something like music; a fun distraction I couldn't afford.

After a long day of learning pretty much nothing, I somehow ended the day exhausted. I would be ready to go home, as shocking as that is, but Amana had texted during class that we should spend some time together after our classes, and I agreed.

A session was very much needed.

My phone lit up in my hand.

'Going to be late DON'T GO HOME WAIT FOR MEEE'

I chuckled at the message.

'It was nice seeing you today' I waited a few seconds before adding, 'Nah I'm kidding, I'll just walk around for a bit.'

Before putting my phone away, I read her response.

'Know best bitch x'

Walking around campus, I realised how there wasn't much to do when you're by yourself and have no work. Well, when you have work but you can't be arsed to do it. Praying and going to the library wasn't an option either. I'm on my period and it's too early to go to the campus library, there would still be large groups of people being unnecessarily loud and vaping as if they aren't sitting directly under a fire alarm.

Eventually, I found my way to the Gardens. It's placed away from the ongoing traffic of London city, and the university's structure wrapped round, alienating the garden, which verbally sounds suffocating but it's actually pretty open and quiet.

The Gardens were beautifully accessorised with twisted wooden arches that split in all sorts of directions, creating benches here and there along the path. And since the sun's nowhere to be seen, they've turned on the dim lights which created an orange hue here and there.

I made myself and my belongings comfortable on the bench, then took in the sky. A calming habit.

I had a few minutes to myself before the door into the Gardens had opened and closed. I gave it no physical attention, my head still faced up to the sky. It was clear today, more stars than usual, I think? I was about to close my eyes and take a deep breath in of London's finest polluted air before someone coughed. And it wasn't a normal cough, no. It was the type of cough done to clear ones throat, but to also get another's attention.

I peered towards the barely lit figure in the archway and thought with extreme sarcasm, '*Ahh there he is, the male of the Uni, the fashion icon, the mafia boss who will rescue me and save the day with his looks and skills whilst only telling me his age.*' I almost dramatically reached out to add to the scene.

Suppressing my laugh, I took a closer look at the figure. As my eyes made their way up and down his body several times, I realised he wasn't moving to explore the Gardens, he was staring at me, almost as if he had said something and was waiting for me to respond.

How I kept pulling myself from reality and having animated responses to my thoughts, I did not know, but I wanted to throw myself off a roof because of it.

"I've done two rounds in this campus trying to find you, I ended up asking some students and they said that they saw a girl walk into the gardens." He spoke whilst trying to hold in any reaction to the performance he just saw on my face.

His deep vocals were soothing, I liked the little husk it held, but I couldn't let it mute me, so like the idiot I am, I said what others would've kept to themselves.

"Are you laughing at me?" I spoke through furrowed brows and a smile, clearly faking how offended I am. "I was making faces 'cause I saw you and started to take the piss in my head."

Kade pushed his head back into his neck, creating the smallest, almost non-existent double chin I've ever seen.

"You were making fun out of me in your head? What were you saying?" He moved closer with devilish curiosity.

"Don't worry about it." I get my answer out the way. "Why were you looking for me anyways?"

"Amana texted, letting me know that you're here alone and that she has another half hour to an hour to go, so she—"

"She wants you to keep me company." I gasped as I raised my hands to my mouth in sarcastic surprise. "Look at that we're already besties, finishing each other's sentences 'n all."

Kade gasped to match my sarcasm, then, he let out a little laugh as he positioned himself to be directly in front of me on the other side of the arch. Whilst he made himself comfortable and made conversation, I couldn't help but think about how Amana blindsided me with this. I didn't know that she knew him well enough for her to have his number. Thoughts of them going out and skipping down roads and into restaurants to then feeding each other, flood my brain and I know if I don't manually interfere, I will end up with vivid scenes of intimacy.

She trusts him enough to let him be around me, she's given him her number, that should be enough for me to know that they have some sort of relationship—should be. So, maybe I should drop a bit of my sarcasm and start to be a little nicer.

Can't let him think Amana is friends with a cow.

Bringing myself back to reality, I see that he's still here. To a normal person, I'm sure his looks would be enough to hold their attention and attentive ear, but for some reason I couldn't seem to get past the male part. I really can't help but associate them with everything that's wrong with this world.

'Just pretend that he's Amana.'

"Sooo…" I got his attention. "Where you from? You Brish?" I tried asking in my best cockney accent, even though it was probably the furthest accent from his.

He sucked in air through his teeth as he angled his head up to the sky. After a few seconds pass, not enough for there to be an awkward gap, but enough for me to notice, he answered. "I'm made up of almost every country in the world."

"O-kayyyy." I looked around.

'What the heck is that supposed to mean?'

Again, I heavily breathed out through my nose to prevent an actual laugh from escaping, not knowing if it was his answer that got that reaction or my humorous thoughts.

"Alright that's it. You need to stop having conversations with yourself and let me in on the jokes."

I gave in, there was no point in lying.

"I know this don't make sense but the word 'slag' came to mind." I smiled through my words, my hand given the role of waving around.

It took about a second for me to realise it wasn't funny and didn't make sense, but Kade had his brows furrowed and looked amused, almost like the face he made in the morning.

"Hear me out-hear me out. You said every country in the world and my mind just flew to the word 'slag.'" I tried explaining my conclusion but failed, I guess it was a stupid un-explainable thought that should've remained a thought.

"Are you calling my mum a sla—" He spoke with hu-mour behind his words when my phone lit up beside me.

Someone was calling and I answered immediately. In the past I never answered my phone if it was from an unknown number. In fact, I never answered my phone. But this time, other than the fact that I had to get out of this situation, I had a feeling it was someone from Baronial. Who else would it be? So, I answered the second, second, I saw the 'No Caller ID' on my screen.

It was a woman from Baronial.

I told her I was ready and could start as soon as possible. As I paced, I glanced at Kade here and there and saw that he wore no expression. It was eerie. He should play some sort of psycho stalker, he would make *money*. I was going to enter-tain that thought until I remembered why he looked like that. Maybe I had taken it too far with the whole slag thing?

After I said my thanks and hung up, I turned to Kade who One: was way too close to me. And Two: scanned over my face several times.

"Is everything okay?" He spoke with a slight accent which was weird as it's the first I heard it, but I had good news so I almost instantly booted it to the back of my mind.

"I got the job." I whispered so quietly I was unsure if he had heard me or not. I positioned my head in an angle it's nev-er been in before to face him. "I got the job. I actually got the job." I announced a little higher the third time round. Moving around in circles I quickly found Amana's name and sent her a voice note. "They want me to come in to sign a few things but scream for me baby 'cause I got the job!" I whooped as Kade loosened up with his best proud impression.

"Whooping instead of screams. Interesting."

I stopped moving and tried to maintain eye contact with this 6'3—I'm guessing—male.

"Is it?" My tone and words, too quick for my brain, come out and smack him with some attitude. "*Sorry*, sorry, that came out rude." I tried to fix how I presented myself to this stranger and *not* someone that knows and understands my sense of humour. I think of a summarised explanation. "Er, yeah, fun fact, for some reason I can't scream. Don't think my vocal cords are strong enough or something."

It's cold out, yet this interaction has made me sweat, another thing that didn't consult with me.

Kade responds with a *'fair enough'* expression but continued to monitor my movements with darkened eyes. Not knowing what to say, I sit down and distract myself with the arches in the distance and then with the sky. He then sat down on the part of the bench that provided no back support, adjusting himself as he spoke. "Bet I know a few things that would make you scream."

His response being so out of the blue during the noticeable awkward atmosphere, had me whipping my head to look at him with a smile filled with disgust.

"How original. What, are you 10?" I stared at him. My eyes traveling up and down with more *'the nerve of this guy,'* than admiration.

There's no way he's not the son of someone important. The way Kade made himself comfortable, resting back while his elbows supported his body, you would think he owned this part of the University. His head's flopped back into his neck, allowing him to have the view of the sky as well as the option of looking down his nose at me. Using his tongue, he took in his bottom lip as he smirked. He had one prominent dimple and I'm too slow, slash not bothered enough to figure out if it's on the same side as mine. The more I observed, the more details I began to pick up on his appearance. His scrunched-up sleeves exposed his somewhat muscular, tattooed, veiny forearms and hands. Even with the obvious scarring here and there—obviously a fighter, or someone who has anger issues—his skin looked soft. Soft enough that it served as a reminder to moisturise the heck out of myself when I got home. His tattoos weren't black, there were white looking, or at least a few shades lighter than his skin colour (his skin colour on the honey, light golden-brown side) making them look more like scars then actual patterns. I liked them. He didn't have anything basic tattooed onto him, they just looked like thorns in some places, and like smoke in others. His eyes were another thing I found I liked. Not just the shape and the thick brows, but the colour. The colour wasn't in my face, they had brown—maybe even a little gold in them towards the centre and when he smiled, so did his eyes. His slight open mouth also gave away his teeth, and he's got canines— vampire canines, for fucks sake. Before I realised it, he had me smiling back at him, even if it was with a little disgust.

It's that damn James Franco type of smile, with the crows feet and dimple.

"Astaghfirullah." I said a little lower than my usual volume whilst scooting myself away.

Who the hell was this guy (to Amana)? From what I know, boys don't just go around doing favours for girls because they feel like it. There's always something attached. Unless of course, Amana forgot to mention a miniscule detail in her lesson of Kade, that he actually is a friend.

A good one.

It's the only thing that does, but doesn't, make sense.

Amana wouldn't let me be around some stupid, perverted boy and not just because we're Muslims. Which can only mean that they know each other. But how? And since when? And why am I only just finding out now?

"I was thinking of things like spiders and clowns, what were you thinking of?" His eyes were innocent but paired with the slow binks, smile and the tone of his voice, he was anything but.

"Oh, you know, slowly torturing me and then eventually ripping my heart out." I answered casually after remembering what he was talking about. "What else would I be thinking of?" I hit him back with the same slow blinks, smile and tone of voice.

Kade gives in, letting out a quick short of breath type of laugh. "How am I doing?"

"You got points for matching my energy, points for the sarcasm, points for being somewhat interesting, and then you lost some for the first sexual comment and then trying to be smart about it."

"Amana had said you liked innuendoes and such."

Once again, he had my head snapping to view him. I guess I could scratch out them just being acquaintances.

"I do like innuendoes and…such."

"Too early then?"

"Way too early for the kind you went for."

"Apologies. I'll wait a bit for the next one."

I gave a smile that hid 98% of my lips whilst slowly nodding my head and turning away, feeling the awkward silence making its way to the next part of our interaction.

"So, what lucky place gets to have a special character like you?" It didn't take long for him to ask out of what seemed like genuine curiosity.

"Baronial?" The name of the business came out more like a questionable suggestion than a confident answer. "Don't ask me what they do because honestly I have no idea, I just need the money and they offered plenty."

Kade didn't respond so I checked his face, expecting him to laugh at my pronunciation, or my reasoning. Wouldn't take a genius to figure out that he's loaded, he's wearing brands I haven't even heard of and has a style I've only seen on Pinterest or something.

"If good money is what you need, I can get you a job at my workplace. You'll be more comfortable and there's a lot of benefits that come with it." He spoke as if it was his dad's place.

"Say a benefit."

"Me. You'll get to see and spend time with me."

I scoffed, well, I heavily huffed through my nose, and like it were a signal, rain began to fall through the gapped roof.

"This better not be some sort of pathetic fallacy, my life is already shit thanks." I lazily saluted with two fingers then pretended to leave.

Kade grabbed my forearm, gently tugging me back. The distance between our bodies shortened, but before it got dangerously close, he let go and busied himself with our belongings.

I stood dumbfounded in the rain watching him put everything under the bench whilst the droplets increased in quantity and weight.

"We're not leaving until you take the job!" If he didn't raise his voice, I'm sure that I wouldn't have been able to hear him.

"You're crazy! Did Amana put you up to this?!" I tried to grab my things and leave but he'd blocked me with his body.

"Oh, you have no idea!" He laughed the words out as if he were itching to show me just how crazy he could be… weirdo. "You taking the job or not?"

Before I could have said anything, another voice entered the conversation. "What the heck are you guys doing!"

I twisted the upper half of my body, allowing myself to see Amana at the doorway into the Gardens. She squinted as her hands shielded her face from the rain.

Maybe the rain's a sign that I *should* take the job, not decline it?

Almost instantly after seeing her face, I remembered the promise I made in the morning to wait for a better opportunity. If she asked Kade to give me a chance, I shouldn't waste it. God knows what she did to make this happen.

I looked back to his tall built figure.

"Fine!" I yelled aggressively with a slight attitude. "I'll take the job." I gave in, lost the attitude and sounded more desperate than I wanted.

No more words were said.

Almost as soon as I agreed to take the job, Kade picked up our things then took them inside. He walked past Amana and headed straight to the library, moving slow enough for us to catch up, but fast enough for him to avoid any comments.

'*Odd.*' Why would he approach me all buddy-buddy, offer a job, then remove himself?

We followed him up the stairs to the library whilst conversating with expressions two steps behind his back. As we exchanged looks Amana wiped off her blood red lipstick.

I don't think I've seen her wear that shade before.

If I had to read out some of our expressions it would be, '*What's his problem? What happened?*' on Amana's part and then, '*I don't know? I like the lip shade,*' on mine.

We made our way to the libraries private rooms section then walked into the one we had booked. Me and Kade took the faux leather cushioned seats against the wall whilst Amana sat opposite us on an office chair. She didn't want to sit next to our soaking bodies so she kept her distance.

"I'm going to go get you guys some tissues, hot chocolate and maybe some food?" It didn't take long for her to feel uncomfortable and try to escape a conversation we will be having.

"Take my card."

My head snapped to Kades thigh. I'm way too cold and tired to rotate it up to his head.

He's a gentleman? The bar continued to be in hell for me to be amused.

On cue—as I assumed Amana felt as though she owed us for whatever transpired in the Gardens—she speed walked away, ignoring his demand. I didn't have a problem with her paying, I had her bank details so I could easily transfer money for the both of us. Kade on the other hand, sat slightly annoyed, making me think about them some more. They're close enough for her to trust him with me and her number, but not close enough for them to have each other's bank details? What kind of relationship was this?

My body would not stop shivering and if I didn't have my jaw clamped shut, my teeth would've been tap dancing. Not making it too bait, I side-eyed Kade, focusing on his thigh to see if he was shaking too, only to feel his eyes on me. I angled myself with the mission to look straight into his eyes, but instead got distracted by his cheekbones and his clamped jaw.

"You don't have to be so tense you know? You can allow yourself to shake. It's not every day sit like a model."

He half rolled his eyes then looked back to where Amana would be sitting.

"Yeah no, you don't get to do that. If I can't have conversations in my head neither can you."

Kade's eyes lowered themselves back to me. "You need to take your clothes off and be given heat. Since we don't have towels or blankets and the radiators not working, you need body heat."

I wouldn't even be able to describe the facial expression made in response to his blunt honesty. How was I supposed to process that?

"Errr?" I extended the word until I could come up with more. "You're still taking the jokes a bit too far."

"I'm not joking."

"Oh, then I suppose you would prefer it to be your body heat, no? We're not living in the bloody ice ages. Coming at me with some sort of medieval method of survival." I picked myself up and moved to the chair next to Amana's, trying to process what he just said. I didn't care if the chair soaked up the water from my clothes, it's better that than his body heat.

As I plonked myself down, I clocked his face. He was smug, and his eyebrows gave away him holding in a laugh. Once he saw that I noticed his expression he spoke again, letting me know what humoured him.

"Ice ages and medieval methods huh? Your history teacher needs to be re-evaluated." He leaned amused, dimple exposed.

"Ugh. What a piss-take. You know what I meant." I have to tell myself that he knows and is teasing, otherwise I would have to respond and try to explain, and that would only result in furthering my frustration and slight embarrassment.

After throwing him a dirty look, I tried to concentrate on

whatever the window allowed me to see. I knew I was visibly annoyed, but I didn't care, and I could see from the corner of my eyes that he's opened his mouth to talk.

"I don't know what you me—" He stopped himself from digging a bigger hole. After a second or two, he continued. "I wasn't trying to offend you. I was trying to help you. I was going to keep it to myself but you wanted to know—"

"So, you decided not to lie and gave me what I wanted?" Frustratingly, he's not in the wrong, I did ask and he did respond. I'm not sure why I got so defensive, but now I'm annoyed that he's mocking me and breaking things down like I'm a child.

"I do enjoy giving females what they desperately want." He stated so casually as if I could give a fuck.

My eyebrows automatically pulled together so hard that even with the emotions I was feeling, I was a little worried that they would leave deep wrinkles.

"I wasn't desperate you bastard." My voice raised and my frustration towards myself for not holding my words in, were taken out with them as my tone.

"No, but you do deserve the truth." His voice was flat, and things quickly became quiet, minus the muffled sounds of other students conversating elsewhere.

I couldn't help but feel that he was talking about something else and for some reason I felt bad about calling him a bastard.

'Am I being emotionally manipulated right now?'

Things seemed to go from 0 to 100 whenever I spoke to Kade, almost as if we both had multiple strong personalities mixed into one. And this is just based off the conversations in the Gardens and now. There has to be a reason why Amana trusts him. There's no way she would introduce me to him if she thought that he was an idiot.

I continued to look at him confused as though his face would answer all questions…until his eyes met mine.

"You're so weird." I managed to blurt out before looking outside again.

"At least take your socks and shoes off, you could get seriously ill." He obviously couldn't get past me being cold and wet.

"What about you? Why aren't you taking things off?"

Not bothering to say anything, he went straight to stripping like I had money to throw.

"Okay, okay! I don't need to see all that."

'He has no shame.'

He walked out the room as if I had commanded him to do so. And since his things were still with me, I knew that he'd be back and didn't just leave out of some sort of unjustified frustration.

I didn't know how to react to any of this.

'What is Amana doing? Where even is she? She needs to stop taking her time and come back here right now.'

I pulled my phone out to text her but then Kade walked back in. He held a hoodie out to me—I gave it a hard pass—as he put what I assumed was his wallet back into his pocket.

Since I politely declined, he began to go back to stripping the top half of his body to wear it himself. Once he was done, he pulled out a pair of socks from his bag for me to wear, but I continued to say no to anything he had to offer. Not because I'm immature and trying to be annoying or stubborn, but because I didn't want to add to my debt to him if I did get this job.

"So, let's just say I get the job at your workplace—"

"You will."

"O-kay then. When I get the job at your workplace, you can't be touching me the way you did in the Gardens. It's haram."

"I'm sorry, I forgot you're a Muslim."

'He forgot? So they have spoken about me.'

"It's okay. The next time you go to touch me just remember that you're not my husband, so you don't have them privileges, but, if we're ever in a serious situation feel free to get me the eff out."

He laughed and it was like he were trying to bring up whatever was in his throat. "Is saying *'eff'* you trying to be a good Muslim?"

"Yeah. Well, a better one than before."

Right, because God doesn't know that means *'fuck'*."

My face made a *'are you serious?'* expression.

"But He does know that you're trying."

"He knows I'm trying." I spoke almost at the same time as him.

It's only been about two hours and in them we've already had a range of emotions explored. This forced friendship or whatever it was, is either going to die as quickly as it started or be till death do us part. Sounds like an exaggeration but so far that's how all my friendships have been, Amana is the only one that has 'survived' thus far.

"I'm sorry for calling you a bastard." I apologise after some time. It's only fair since I was the one who behaved poorly in the Gardens. He was just being a good whatever-he-is to Amana. I should've waited a bit before unleashing the sarcastic cow.

"And I'm sorry for offending you...multiple times."

Actually being surprised and happy with our apologies and responses, I took it as a reset button.

"I'm Medisa by the way." I smile like an idiot after realising how cheesy this late introduction may seem.

"Hello Medisa." His charming smile makes an appearance and though I've seen it in the Gardens, something about this one seems more genuine. Something else about it sends shivers across my body.

Just as I was about to ask Kade if he was religious, Amana walked in with tissue rolls on her arms like bangles, hot chocolates in one hand and a bag of hot food in the other.

Before handing anything out, she pointed out the separation and wasn't shy to show her confusion. Giving me a look, then eyeing Kade up and down, Amana grabs the chair next to me. She doesn't allow anything to be taken until she's made it clear that one way or another, she would find out what happened. Kade was threatened. If he had touched me inappropriately, she would chop his fingers off, and I couldn't let the boy lose his fingers, even if she wouldn't go through with it, he just offered to get me a job, and I really, really, needed hot chocolate, so I spoke up.

"I didn't want to get gunaah so I just moved away from him." I glanced at Kade. "Gunaah meaning sinned." I turn back to Amana who took in my words and expression, then sat down satisfied with my response.

Whilst passing us each a tissue roll, Kades drink and all of our food, she continued to stare at him intensely just in case there was something else. Kade took this as his cue to try and move the conversation away from him, to something more normal, something people who just met would talk about.

"I know that Amana's from Pakistan, but where are you from?"

Instead of asking him the usual '*where do you think I'm from?*' Me and Amana answered him at the same time, letting him know that I'm also from Pakistan.

Kade slowly moved his head back and forth, so slow I thought I imagined the slow wobble. I assumed he was thinking about how our relationship made more sense as we're both Pakistani, which *obviously* meant that we've had similar upbringings.

"Pakistan's quite diverse huh."

"Aren't all countries?" My lips pressed together as I tilted my head as if to also ask *'are you dumb?'*

"I suppose most are."

'Diverse.' I never really compared mine and Amana's looks. I've probably only done it about twice. The first time being when we first became friends, when I knew she wasn't going anywhere.

Amana's a mouth-watering being. Not only was her personality top-notch and better than anyone I knew, but her features were something else as well. When we first met, she wore a hijab, which just added to her 'mysterious beauty' vibe. And it went well with her brown skin, dark arched brows and big hazel green cat eyes. My eyes and skin on the other hand are completely different, I'm basically a light skin Asian with brown eyes. Our noses are also different. We both had what the west had deemed 'ugly' and 'undesirable,' but I just couldn't see or think that to be true when Amana looked the way that she does—Jaw droppingly, enchantingly beautiful. She had a Roman-Greek nose (I think that's what it's called) which elevated her beauty, and I had one of those weird slightly droopy button noses that honestly looked much worse when it was swollen in the morning.

<u>Thank God</u> I met Amana at just the right time. Before her, I never really saw myself, I kind of just lived life away from mirrors and cameras. I knew that I didn't look like my

sister; I never got a compliment let alone the same amount as she did on a daily basis. But then, when me and Amana got close (which happened almost instantly, if 'almost' meant we had a stage where we disliked each other), she would think the opposite and take pictures of me—of us—and instead of hating the pictures—even if I really did look bad, I thought of the memories that came with it, the mischiefs that we got up to that day, the laughs and inside jokes, not the forced backhanded compliments I received in the past. Eventually, as time went on, my confidence grew and so did hers.

We were *almost* identical in other ways, mentally, not physically and extra emphasis on the 'almost.' There were days when my mind scared Amana in the sense that she couldn't believe the things I came up with, and the fact that I would actually see them through. *Some* plans of mine took things too far so there were days where she would have to talk some sense into me, *or* if it wasn't too bad become a partner in them—to help me see it through, or more realistically, to help me out of it—an escape goat if you please. Amana came up with adventurous things too, but they were safer and involved less people compared to mine and usually had zero to a few consequences.

I watched Amana now; she was busy throwing my scrunched up wet tissues at Kade. She definitely had something against him and for some reason I'm in the dark about it.

I zoned back in and laughed at the both of them, earning some wet tissues myself. I don't even know how it began but now I'm also throwing some, mainly at Kade which Amana saw and teamed up with me on

"Wait, think of the cleaners!" He tried to get us to stop when it got too much.

"Cleaners?" Me and Amana synced, looking to each other confused and amused. She then went on to mocking him, echoing his words and pairing it with funny but disgusted expressions.

"Kade, we're going to clean this up ourselves." I shook my head, I still don't know much about him, but at least now I know for sure that he has that kind of level of privilege, other than being somewhat white passing.

After picking as much as she can up, Amana goes to bin the tissues whilst I busied myself with taking off large chunks of fluff and tissue from my damp clothes. As I was doing this, I could sense Kades eyes on me and I just knew to prepare myself for whatever he decided to throw at me next.

"Medisa, put my jacket on, it was covered from the rain so it's not wet."

It takes everything in my power to not let out the biggest sigh.

"There's no point in wearing something dry on top of something wet." I spoke with a matter-of-fact tone.

"I'm not *telling* you to wear it with that wet top, I'm telling you to take your top off and wear it." He practically demands with a *'are you dumb?'* tone.

I took a deep breath, trying to rid my thoughts of any insults for this boy, then I looked to the side at what he wanted me to wear. It's not ugly, it's what I saw him wear in the morning… I actually liked it.

"You got issues." I said. Is it a trauma related thing? Is it OCD or something? Amana isn't even bothering me with it and she's always the first one to care for me. Whatever it is, I pick his jacket up and head out the door. *'You don't have to fight all your battles,'* or whatever that saying is.

"Where you going?" Amana asks.

"To wear this ugly jacket." I hold it up knowing damn well I loved that I could wear it, then we both walked over to the toilets so that he could finally move away from the topic of me being wet.

We began walking towards Kade's car at 22:50 after going back and forth on how we were getting home. We insisted that he didn't have to drop us home but lost the argument as soon as he started to walk off with our stuff.

By the time we'd reached his car it was 23:15. I let Amana sit in the front, she's a big fan of cars and something about the shape, colour and tyres made me think that she would enjoy the ride if she was seated in the passenger seat, if not the drivers.

As we set off, Kade let me know of the position I now had at his work place. He must've glossed over how I managed to get the role without meeting anyone, but at the same time I wasn't really paying attention as my mind was running through different thoughts at speeds too quick for me to process. In the end, I assumed they had a vacancy and were desperate. I shouldn't question it too much anyways as '*beggars can't be choosers*' and questioning felt like it was something that came from a place of privilege rather than gratitude.

As he took one of the scenic routes along one of the main roads, I processed everything from today and couldn't stop smiling. The dumb smiles quickly turned into some sort of psychopathic giggle, getting Kade and Amana to have mirroring expressions as the car slowed to a stop at a red light.

"You know, you look at me like that a lot you know." I spoke to him through the centre mirror. "Which is weird because if anything I should be looking at you like that. I literally just met you today, the girls think that you're some sort of mafia man and now you're here with your fancy little car and accessories telling me that you got me a job with high pay *and* it's more convenient for me. Well shit, I might just start believing the rumours."

During my little rant Kade appeared to be captivated-if not slightly shocked by the many words I managed out, whilst Amana's expression changed with every point made until she finally let out her psychotic—slightly embarrassed, but proud laugh.

"Little? That's not a word I would use to describe myself. And I *know* you've heard rumours that nothing about me is '*little*.'" He stared through the rear-view mirror as someone's red light reflected off him. I don't even want to let my mind *think* about how good he looks.

Amana's left hand flung back between her seat and her door, aggressively wiggling, smacking the side of her seat and the car, impatient for my hand. I grabbed onto it and we both shared the same mini fits, hidden to Kade's eye.

"I'm not in the mafia." He ended our mini hand fits, making us squeeze onto each other's hand.

"Let a girl dream." I held his gaze through 'sleepy eyes' as I leaned my head towards the middle seat.

The conversation swiftly moved on to the car. Amana and Kade spoke like they were going to tear it apart and put it back together again. From what I heard, they had way too much knowledge on the topic of vehicles and I had little to none, causing me to fall in and out of sleep. After a couple minutes of fighting to stay awake and embarrassing myself by slamming my head onto the window and giving myself whiplash, I finally let myself drift away. It didn't take long for me to think his car was my bed and it took even less for me to snap out of it an hour and forty minutes later.

I recognised the weakly lit road almost instantly, then mentally thanked him for parking up opposite my house and slightly to the side.

<u>Thank God</u> he got me home, they would never let me hear the end of it if I had stayed out all night—to complete Uni work of course—without telling them in advance. I had excuses of the trains being delayed and then having to call an uber, so in terms of the time and why I'm so late, I was good, I had an army of excuses to help.

As I got my things and left the car, I apologised for accepting the car ride and it being so late, but he just reassured me by saying he was okay with dropping both me and Amana off.

Amana.

She trusted him enough to leave unconscious me in his car for him to drop off? As dangerous as that was, I'm too occupied with how late it is and how I actually made it home safely and roughly around the same time I had worked out in my head. Ergo, he didn't do anything to me whilst I was asleep. But still, she shouldn't have done that.

"Text Amana when you get home so that we know you got home safely." I turned to him before shooting off.

"Or you could give me your number and I can text you?" He leaned against his car.

'Don't react.'

"Get it off Amana. I don't have time to pull out my phone to give it to you." I needed to get inside before someone looked out the window. "And you better text me when you're home."

"Yes ma'am."

Before I crossed the road, ending the adventures of the day, I turned to Kade one last time. It was like he wanted to say something but instead, he paused, then shook his head with cheeky embarrassment.

Did I fart? Snore? Bang my head some more onto his window? I would never know, because he kept it to himself, giving me the final reason as to why I should plant myself in the middle of the road and wait for the next car.

Chapter 2

Medisa
12/10/2021 (Tuesday)

First day working somewhere that's not my house. I guess the feeling of nervousness and being excited, as well as feeling like a bunch of responsibility was just dropped onto my shoulders, was the norm in situations like this.

According to Kade, his boss trusted his opinion enough for him to choose an additional team member. Personally, I think Kade's decision wasn't questioned because the position I got was more short term than long. That, and, he's someone's son (I continued to assume).

I did ask if Kade could get Amana involved too, but apparently it would take some time before his boss let anyone else on. When I first heard him say that, I was going to turn it down, but Amana lectured me on how that would be the dumbest thing to do, so here I am, on my way to my first ever job.

From the moment I stepped out of the train station, the train even, my heart wouldn't stop making itself known. It's annoying, especially since it's making me feel as though I have something to be nervous about.

'Like the lack of experience...'

Despite it being towards the start of the month, my data ran out. So, I had taken screenshots of the map and what should be my journey since I had no idea where the building was. Taking screenshots of my journey online was the next best thing, until I took a few wrong turns and was in an area outside of the screenshots.

'Idiot.'

I walked around a bit, first trying to get back into the screenshots, then trying to muster up the courage to ask a stranger to point me in the right direction. Trying to find a friendly face led to finding a man watching me from across the road.

"Hmm, maybe he's racist?" I spoke under my breath to comfort and fill in the lack of music or friend on the phone.

The male began to approach me, dropping my heart a few centimetres. I took out my earphones as my body prepared itself to fight, or flight, or to simply shit itself where it stood.

"I'm not a racist, I'm your boss." The way he spoke reminded me of a teacher.

He looked young, but old, but young, and I presumed had a hobby of scamming new people in the area. I heard scams were growing both in numbers and intelligence. I'd watched some videos on it.

"What?" I responded as though I were saying *'don't be stupid,'* then carried on with disbelief and word vomit as if it's been proven to self-comfort in the past. "No offence but that's hard to believe. Haven't you been stalking me since the station? What? Did you decide that now's the perfect time to pull off your little scam." I accompanied my speech with hand gestures, multiple facial expressions and a tone of voice which definitely let him know that I knew what was up.

"Miss Menaal." He interrupted before I carried on, then peeked at his watch.

'*Miss Menaal.*' That was enough to shut me up. He knew my name. Whatever he said after was blurred into background noise as I had a moment of realisation, piecing together how I just spoke to the man…who was my superior in the workplace hierarchy—the man in charge of me—the man who worked at the place that will offer me the life that I so desperately needed. The man who could take it all away. I zoned back in time to hear it was organised for me to be collected, but I had walked past the car outside the station and ignored his calls.

<u>Thank God</u> I wore a cute oversized balloon sleeved white shirt, otherwise he would've spotted the amount of sweat my pits secreted and added some more negative points to his tally.

"I'm sorry, I don't answer numbers I don't have saved. If I was really late and was receiving calls, I would've answered as it would make sense that someone from Aros was calling. But as it's only been a few minutes and the calls happened from before I was supposed to arrive, I didn't answer."

He didn't say anything to my waffle-apology. He just gave a small nod and ordered me to follow him back to the car that I now noticed slowly stalked us.

After several apologies and awkward small talk, I thought about the information given to me whilst the driver found a place to park. The male sat beside me is called Bellamy, and he can lip read. He also happens to be the CEO of the business, Aros. He's twenty-six (my brother's age), is a friend of Kade's *and* they have similar bodies although he's slightly larger, so it's possible they trained together. Maybe they're related?

My work timetable consisted of evenings after Uni and some mornings on the days I didn't have anything. My weekends were left free to allow me to rest from both Uni and work. *If* I made it pass the trial week which Kade lovingly left out, the timetable will be made permanent and I got to keep my office. I might even be able to decorate it.

I turned my head back to Bellamy to take in his looks since I couldn't think of anything else to do to pass time. They would be something Amana would want me to report back to her with. The main things I could retain was his buzz cut, his brown-borderline-hazel eyes, tan skin and beauty spots planted here and there. Overall, the man sitting beside me was pretty good looking, so I mentally gave him a thumbs up. As I made mental notes and remarks, Bellamy catches me staring and my automatic response was to enlarge my eyes and give a polite constipated smile, because apparently that makes things less conspicuous and normal.

Quickly turning my head towards the window—risking whiplash—to look at something else to distract myself with, I realised we were parked up somewhere. I mentally slapped myself as I pieced together what just happened whilst wondering how long we'd been parked for.

As we awkwardly rode up the elevator together, I started to sweat more buckets than before. I hated situations like this, especially when I've just made a fool out of myself.

Softly sniffing myself so that he couldn't hear, I got a whiff of the rotten smell my body produced. My sweat and the thought of Bellamy being able to smell me made me sweat even more. '*If you can smell yourself, people around you can smell it times one-hundred,*' or whatever the saying is.

I was about to add to my panicking when the elevator doors opened.

A male stood in front, blocking the floors entrance and my eyes quickly made their way up his body thinking, '*what or who now?*' only to see Kade. A smile grew so fast and big at the familiar face that I started to overthink my reaction, so I dropped it as quick as it grew.

Bellamy excused himself after telling Kade to explain

whatever he had missed in the talk I wasn't really paying attention to on our way here.

"C'mon, let me show you around." Kade spoke before things got too quiet.

"Wait. Take this." I tried to give him back his jacket.

"You can keep it."

"Just take it."

"You don't want it?"

"No, I have a lot of jackets."

"Don't you want one of mine?"

I rolled my eyes even with my lids lowered.

He's so annoying.

"Fine. I'll hold it for you." He took his jacket back then began the tour.

I was shown the specific room I could use to pray and my own washroom where I could perform wudu. Everything else that was shown was cool, but I couldn't get past how Kade must've done some research because his pronunciation on some terms were better than me.

Any other thoughts were on the interior design of this place. The whole floor was like some sort of expensive, stylish hotel, maybe even a cool-vintage café or hang out point. I don't know, it wasn't what I expected (the usual boring modern look). It wasn't too stuffy but it wasn't too plain either. It was the right amount of randomness and space, whilst also looking professional and out of this world. White bricks on some walls, red on others, large expensive marble tiles, adjustable lights and lamps, the random gold and colours here and there and to top it all off, there's large plants and expensive looking furniture and beverages. It was almost like someone lived here when we weren't around.

On the tour, Kade moved and spoke like a professional.

A dumb statement to make (I know) but it's weird to see and process as I slept in his car, we argued in the rain and we even had jokes with him in a private library room a few days ago. He did drop his intimidating professional act every now and then to crack a joke when things got too quiet, which I appreciated, but for some reason it wasn't enough to get me to start engaging in conversation. In my defence, my mind hadn't stopped thinking a thousand things at once so it was hard for me to give my undivided attention, but I got the gist of everything. Aros basically invested in businesses, slash plans with potential, gave them support and advice as well as a good reputation, connections etc. All they had to do was agree to several things, one of the main deal breakers being an annual charity trip, where the business—and sometimes Kade—would go to countries to personally see things through and to help out where they could.

We ended up back round to where we had started, near the elevator. Apparently, the elevator could only be accessed by Bellamy, Kade and me, everyone else had their own way to their floors. Which made me think that maybe my job role was more important than I thought. I didn't think too much into it of course, as I didn't want to trigger the sweats, but still, scary.

Our last stop was our offices. They were opposite each other which was cool, but they could've had more of a distance between them. These offices practically let its occupants look into the others space with its large arse window-walls.

Reaching the offices—barely getting to the doors—was basically the end of the tour. I *was* about to ask questions when Kade began to aggressively sniff and exaggerate—I hoped—his reaction towards my body odour.

"*Damn* Medisa what do you eat?" He moaned whilst

swatting the air directly in front of his face, squinting as if the smell was affecting his eyes.

"Leave me alone." I laughed out the words, turning my giggles into a fake cry.

He gestured for me to follow him into his office which I'm convinced had the best view, it would distract *anyone* upon entering. I myself ignored where he stopped to stand to walk towards the floor to ceiling window instead.

I was about to properly observe the outside world when I heard Kade's attention seeking cough.

I slowly turned my head, which was then followed by the rest of my body when I saw his cologne collection. All of them had rich vintage looking bodies, some with jewelled animal heads, some with glass shaped figures and some mimicking whiskey or some sort of expensive alcohol bottle in miniature form.

"You might as well try them all to see which one covers up the stank." He instructed, blocking his nostrils as his eyes jumped back and forth from the collection to me. His frown smile was barely covered by his hand and his crow feet grew to be more intense with each take he took from my eyes to the scented liquid.

"That's it." I muttered.

To retaliate I simply began to pick up each and every one of them, trying them *all* out and not with just one or two puffs. In my head this was revenge, I'm wasting his collection which I'm sure was expensive, all whilst I looked directly into his eyes. However, Kade did not seem bothered by this, in fact he was hysterically laughing, the type of laughter one would hold their belly, and bend themselves backwards to try and let out.

Bellamy entered the office as soon as I clocked that wasting the cologne's was not affecting Kade. He stood still as if someone had murdered his partner and now, he was being forced to watch us dance with the body. His eyes switched between me, Kade and the expensive collection between us.

"A word Kade." Bellamy's words came from behind gritted teeth as he stopped to stare at the windows to my soul.

'Oh, he's pissed-pissed.'

I chose to leave the office as fast as I could, no questions or requests needed to be made, I was out of there in the blink of the eye. Well… that's what I wanted to happen anyway. I actually tripped on my way out—my laces had come undone—knocking over some things placed on the shelf. Also, half my body walked straight into the glass door frame making a thump along with the bangs of the things still dropping.

I didn't dare turn around and I definitely didn't need to look at them to know how they reacted.

Hours later, Kade entered my office with food. A few hours before, I had come to the conclusion that Bellamy has a soft spot for Kade because there's no other reason for him or me to still have a job. Throughout the day, when I 'glanced' up to be an audience to their interactions, Bellamy looked like he was picturing stuffing Kade into the boot of his car, and Kade looked like he was asking for it. Every now and then, they briefly stared in my direction, forcing me to look away and act busy. I assumed they didn't trust me to be alone yet, since most of their interactions were taken on our floor rather than Bellamy's.

"Bellamy is coming down to join us."

My face drastically changed and I didn't need a mirror

to see it.

"Think of it as tradition." Kade continued to talk whilst placing bags on the desk. "The food is halal so don't worry about it when you see meat."

Wasting no time, I helped out with the food and not just because it's a common courtesy thing, but because I wanted to see what he had gotten before it was placed in front of me. I'd like to think I'm not a picky eater *but* I do have preferences I would rather not stray from.

I prayed that the smell of the meals was enough to drown out the cologne's that had attached themselves to me and every bit of this office.

It wasn't.

When Bellamy entered the room, he appeared to be every bit of excited for this lunch together as me.

He wasn't wearing his blazer anymore, so I could see his muscles through his unbuttoned shirt—an exaggeration, it's like three buttons not done. Also, he didn't have tattoos like Kade, his skin was like new. And now, as I looked at him, I actually see more of his beauty even though he currently had black cat energy. It's probably what elevated his look.

I could feel Kade observing me observing Bellamy, but I ignored his presence until he did his little cough.

"So, how's the day been so far? Enjoying it?" Kade spoke with multiple innocent blinks as Bellamy took a seat beside him, and opposite me.

"It's okay, nothing I can't handle." I watched Bellamy who was sat up straight with no emotion. His whole look is stern, it's like me and Kade were being babysat. "Since when did Kade start working here?"

The question being directed towards Bellamy cleared the room of any noise except the crunch of the chips Kade put in his mouth.

Bellamy paused for a second. I wouldn't have caught it if I wasn't deeply staring at him. He chewed, then slowly swallowed his food, buying some time.

"Since a bit before my nineteenth birthday, isn't that right Bells?" Kade winked at his boss before stuffing some more chips into his gob. And Bellamy, he nodded like a child who was being forced to interact with his parents' friends, no longer being perceived as someone with authority.

"Isn't that right Bells?" I mocked, putting on an annoying voice as I picked up some of my own chips, realising too late I had said that out loud.

Kade's face replicated the smile of the Cheshire Cat as his brows raised, whilst mine risked pushing out my eyeballs to a point of no return.

"Isn't that right Bells?" Kade mocked himself as he mocked me, distorting the words even further as he twisted his face to match his deliverance. I took it even further, so much so that it was just noises rather than parts of the words. Before completing the sentence, I noticed Bellamy's expression and quickly went back to seeing him as someone who somewhat scared me.

Clearing my throat, I tried to move the conversation away and hide from what just happened, momentarily pulling a look towards Kade like he was the one being immature.

"I'm sorry if this question is rude but, do you come from money? It seems like it would take a lot to start Aros, or at least get it to where it is right now." I regret talking as soon as the words leave my mouth. Sometimes when I'm uncomfortable, I make situations worse by spewing out my thoughts in a way that's not been reviewed and edited. I suppose the question can also be seen as a compliment?

Kade's face dropped but in an amused and entertained way. He must've not expected that, but then a cheeky smile grew exposing his dimple. He turned his tilted head towards Bellamy, like he was saying *'yeah Bells, do tell us how Aros came about.'*

Bellamy gave a quick side eye to Kade before responding. "I inherited some money and put it towards investments. Then I met Kade who helped create Aros and then stayed to see it grow. He had the idea to have multiple divisions and—"

"Next question."

Kade interrupting Bellamy after he finally started to talk, slightly pissed me off. I was genuinely interested in what he was saying. Also...he just interrupted our boss?

"Medisa, what are your plans after graduating?"

Another round of silence makes an appearance.

This time I was the one crunching the chips. This question has been asked by many people and each time I did not know what to say. It's not that I don't have goals, I do, but when it comes to choosing a career path, I can't decide. Then I just want to do everything (too much) at the same time, which just stresses me out to the point where I end up doing nothing.

"Put it this way." I tried to think of a way to word it. "Aros's success was due to its multiple divisions, right?"

Kade gave a single nod paired with a frown smile.

"Well, like Aros I don't think that I'm going to get far if I stick to one thing. I want to have multiple things happening at once. My problem is that I don't know which one to start with, and my problem *used* to be being able to fund it, but now, hopefully I get to stay here a while longer while I figure things out and save money up." I gave Bellamy a *'please don't fire me'* look whilst digging my shoulders into my neck, cringing at the fact that I'm trying to guilt trip him into letting me stay.

Bellamy got up and excused himself.

I turned to Kade, my face no doubt showing the horror I felt whilst also questioning if I made a mistake, but he was quick to say that Bellamy was having a bad day, and even though it's difficult to see, he actually liked me.

"Come, let's go get some fresh air." He suggested and didn't have to repeat.

Immediately, I packed the food and got to the elevator before him, pressing the elevator call button a hundred times more than necessary.

Soon as the doors opened, I eagerly got in whilst Kade took his time striding towards me, holding his hand out for the bag of food.

"You're twenty, you've got time, just focus on yourself and stop looking at how everyone else's life is playing out." He spoke as if he's been in my position.

"I know not to look at others progressions but I feel like I've wasted my youth, you know? I had so many ideas and goals when I was younger but I kept shutting myself down before I even began—"

"Don't you think looking back at the past, like the way you are, is repeating your mistakes? You're wasting your time, bringing your mood down. What's happened has happened, what are you doing today to change the course of your life for the better?"

His whole demeaner changed, making me feel a little awkward in this 'tight' space.

Kade switching up how he wants himself to come across was confusing, but he's right, there is time to work on my goals. In fact, I'm already working towards them.

"But one life isn't enough to achieve *all* my goals." My thoughts became external.

"It is now that you have me." Once the doors opened, Kade motioned for me to walk besides him. "C'mon, I know a place where you can tell me about your goals, then I'll figure out a way to make them come true." He doesn't move until I am by his side.

When I was sure he wouldn't look down, I quickly opened Amana's messages.

'How is everything now?? Are they still not talking to you?'

'Girl this boy is taking me out somewhere refgnvowujhvoeurh'

She read my message instantly.

'WHAT? WHER?'

I thought I felt his eyes on me so I quickly hid the screen.

'Hello why are you ignoring??? Medisa you <u>bitch</u> do I need to come over there??'

'LOOOOL nono im good.. I'll call you and tell you everything later yeah?'

'You tryna get rid of me so tht you can be a sket in peace?'

'yeah basically' I joked.

Chapter 3

Medisa
14/10/2021 (Thursday)

I tried, and continued to try to independently get whatever information I could from the boys—the boy and the man. And from what I've seen so far, any interaction between Bellamy and Kade was strange. Sometimes, when I looked out from my office, into Kade's, I couldn't tell what was going on between the two, and as I'm still the new fish, I feel as though I'm not in a good position to question or even get involved.

I do have my theories though.

During the day, I'm pretty much left alone to get on with my scouting duty. I haven't really been given a target number of potentials to spot, but I do want to try and get at least one or two a day. I also didn't want to be pushing the number of times I annoyed, slash interrupted Kade—who stayed away from my office for almost all hours, minus lunch—so if I had any questions, I would write them down to ask when I would show him the people I found.

During lunch, Kade would come and ask if it was okay for us to spend it together, and since Bellamy showed no interest in being my work bestie, I've had to settle with him.

When the weather was tolerable, we had options, we could go out to eat, we could choose to stay inside, we could eat whilst walking around the area, or eat on a random bench or patch of grass without a blanket or any other cute picnic things. All options were good and Kade proved to be a decent work buddy, so I didn't really mind.

"Are you Bi?" I ended the silence.

Kade struggled to swallow his drink. "What?"

"Do you like Bellamy more than a friend? More than a boss? Do you want him to order you around in other rooms other than the office? Do you—"

"Please stop." Kades expression gave him away. He thought I was funny but he was also disturbed by what I was saying. Well, that's what I read off him anyways.

"Because if you do, then I hope you know that he groomed you, eighteen or not when you met him, it's still a little fresh from being a child don't you think? I mean, I'm twenty and I still kind of feel like a kid. And I'm a woman, we're supposed to develop before you guys." '*Supposed to*' are not the right words, it's more like forced to.

I still wasn't comfortable enough to directly ask what the deal was with everything (Aros, Amana, my job, Bellamy and Kade himself).

'*But apparently I'm comfortable enough to ask about his sexuality...*'

I thought that making things a little weird and less tense would make it easier for me to go around topics and still get an answer. If that fails, then at least Kade would (hopefully) feel more comfortable around me and would want to talk.

It's near the end of my first week at Aros and I still don't know much about Kade. I know people would say that I'm being ridiculous, but I can't help but feel like Kade is keeping his distance from me, Bellamy too. They only approach me when they need to.

'*Is this what working is like? No real interactions?*'

"He's like the brother I've always needed."

'*Needed. Not wanted.*' Noted.

"Damn. I hope I stay here long enough for me to develop that kind of relationship with him. Who knows, he may be sick of having a younger brother and may want a younger-more intelligent sibling...a sister if you will."

Kade tsked. "He's good thanks, you stay where you are with Amana."

"Who said I can't have both?" I teased.

"Alright stingy."

"Don't be jealous, you could be levelled up to be my best friend if you act right." I continued to banter.

"Best friend? What are you five?"

"I take it you don't have any friends?"

"I take it you don't have a life?" He shot back.

The distance between my dropped jaw and my top lip is stopped before it creates a hole big enough for a baguette. I almost swatted at him, but quickly recovered with words I know would piss a lot of boys off. "Ugh, you got me. The plan's actually to marry rich, kill him off, and then live off his hard-earned money."

It's not that I expected the both of us to wink and dramatically high-five each other, but the lack of reaction on his end is embarrassing, for me.

'Why do I feel embarrassed? How is he making me feel embarrassed through his lack of reaction?'

Instead of awkwardly giggling, I breathe out one heavy breath through my nose. "Anyways, we're actually lucky to have someone like them. A lot of people don't, and have to get by, by themselves." I tried to slowly manoeuvre the conversation into something deep. "We might not be attached by blood, but she's there. Amana's my person."

"Yeah, and Bellamy's mine." He looked off into the distance after his eyes flashed a threat. "I genuinely don't know where I'd be without him."

I could tell that there would be an awkward silence if I didn't respond, so I did. "Probably off somewhere being useless and a hassle to someone else."

He scoffed then spoke lower than his usual volume. "Understatement of the year."

'Oh for flips sake.' Of course I said the wrong thing and made things more awkward and confusing. What was he even talking about?

I rotated the top halve of my body away from Kade. My words may have made things more awkward but hopefully this gift would lighten up the mood.

I held onto the lamp I made, then watched Kade who once again took in the environment in the distance.

"Speaking of friendships…" I got his attention and continued to hide the lamp from his view. "I genuinely hope that we become good friends. I thought you were a little shit before…and I still do." I mumbled the last bit. "But I could tell that you're a good nut." I didn't even try to hide how I felt about my choice of words. I held my stretched smile until I finally let out a 'K' sound which extended until Kade reacted.

Kade shut his eyes in disbelief, or maybe disgust, but then let out an airy laugh as if he were trying to hold it all in. "You were doing so well until the '*nut*.'"

"That's what she said!" I couldn't help it, I had to say it to get it out my system and in doing so I made him lively again.

A win-win situation if you ask me.

"Anyways I didn't even get to the best part." I uncovered the desk lamp I made years ago. From his reaction I could tell that he liked the look of the oddly shaped light, but was confused as to why he was getting it. "It's for your desk. I know that you guys stay later than me and like to have minimal lighting so I thought that this would be a good thank you gift."

His facial expression said, *'thank you gift?'*

I took it as a sign to continue. "You know, for the job? I actually like it here. I was scared of working before and was desperate but then you helped me out even when you didn't really know me, so thank you...Seriously."

Kade didn't say anything straight away. He just held the lamp in his hand, sorrow was written all over his face which then quickly became anger?

"Don't grip it like that! It'll break. I made it a long time ago from cheapish material." You couldn't even use a real bulb with it, and it's not a bloody stress ball.

Being pulled out of whatever daze he was in, he thanked me.

"You should really be giving this to Amana."

"I got her a gift too, don't worry. I know what she's done for me."

His eyes went back and forth between mine like he couldn't believe what was going on. It's like I could see him overthink but because I didn't understand, I didn't know what to say.

"Lunch is over." He stated just as I was about to ask if he was okay.

I knew something had happened on his end of this interaction. That much was clear. That much was confirmed with what he had just said. He never cared in the past few days if we were abusing our lunch period. So, what did I do wrong? What am I missing?

Before I could even say anything Kade looked away and was ready to leave. He waited for me to get up but had his eyes and mind elsewhere. It was like the time he walked slow enough for me and Amana to catch up and follow him, but fast enough for him to keep a small distance like he was trying to get away.

I'm still learning about how to communicate and open up, but honestly, the way he's being is kinda rude and confusing.

Learning my lesson—from other circumstances—would be to wait until I was in the right mind to communicate. So that's what I'm going to do, for the both of us. I manually took a deep breath then walked with him to the station. I wanted to show him my annoyance, mostly because it felt like I was constantly getting the short end of the stick, but Kade being able to still have manners and act like a gentleman when he's clearly upset or distracted by something, is enough for me to backtrack a little. And although I'm proud at myself for not being pushy, I'm still confused.

To get past it, I reminded myself that Kade was literally his own person and had his own problems and ways of dealing with them. I also happened to be new in his life so he doesn't really owe me anything. I owed him, big time… annoyingly.

Chapter 4
Medisa
15/10/2021 (Friday)

Although yesterday at work ended weirdly, it didn't stop Kade from making sure I got from point A (work) to point B (Uni). I had time to think about it and honestly screw waiting. It may not be a big deal. I should've just said something yesterday—should've at least asked if everything was okay.

I was distracted all afternoon yesterday, couldn't hear a single word said in class so when I see him today, I'm definitely just going to try and clear the awkward air.

Soon as I entered the campus building, I went straight for the café thinking about how I should approach the situation. As I mentally went back and forth with how to approach him, Kade walked across a few steps in front of me. He had a cup in hand as he walked towards the sugar stand.

He must've not seen me.

I sped up behind him, leaving my own quest of getting some macchiato, to give him a nudge.

"Hey, what you doing here?"

I quickly noticed his eye colour, they were a little different. A shade greener? Or blue? Coloured eyes really do have the privilege of changing hues in different lightings.

Kade looked at me confused as though I was the one out of place.

"Heyyyy." He awkwardly lengthened out the word whilst pulling me in for a hug I couldn't escape.

He smelt different.

"Are you drunk? Why are you hugging me? And what's up with your eyes? They look—"

Cocking his head to one side whilst still being visibly confused, he cut in. "Hungover. And because I want to. Why can't I hug you again?"

'*Is he being serious right now?*'

I leaned away from him.

"You got a trim?" Not the most important thing to address right now but it blurted out once I realised that difference. He must have visited a barber yesterday or in the morning, his hairs glossier and he has more curls than waves.

"Yah. Do you like it?"

"Why are you putting on an accent?" I asked myself if this were something he did when he was 'hungover'. I then decided that too much was going on and we can't move on until I said my speech. "Never mind, listen, I don't know what I did yesterday to upset you, but I'm sorry. If you ever feel like that again or any other emotion I somehow bring up inside you then I hope that one day you'll be comfortable enough to tell me, so that I avoid whatever it is that I do and help you in any other way that I can."

Kade stared and blinked every now and then like he was trying to figure out what was going on. There was a long pause before he murmured '*Medisa?*' as though this whole time he didn't know who he was talking to.

"Ugh." I wanted to shove him and walk away but I fought against it.

"Hey, wifey!" <u>Thank God.</u> Someone actually remembers who I am.

I ended up giving into my desires—shoving past Kade—before walking towards Amana with open arms. "<u>Peace be upon you.</u>"

"<u>And upon you be peace</u>. Who were you just talking to?"

"Kade, he's here for some reason but he's drunk." I turned to point him out but he wasn't there anymore.

'Not my problem. Not my problem. Not my problem.'

I turned back to face her.

"Speaking of Kade. How did you guys meet?" I finally asked after trying to wait for her to tell me herself.

"I was having lunch one day, saw him, then approached him."

"*You* approached him?"

"Yeah. The guy was *staring*."

"Can you blame him?"

"Er, yeah? He was making me uncomfortable."

"Does he like you? Or you him?"

"How the hell did you come up with that?" She seemed to be disgusted, but I couldn't tell if she was acting and trying to swipe it under the rug.

"I don't know. He just gets so weird sometimes and the only consistency I can find is when you're involved, slash mentioned…You're not holding something against him, are you?" I joked, but was also serious.

"Pfft, he owed me."

My eyes turned to slits, going over her face and her words. She's not telling me why he owes her. Unless he's paying her back for not lowering his gaze?

"Maybe getting me a job wasn't enough for him to feel like he's paid his debt? Maybe he wants to do something for you directly?"

"I better think of something *big* then." Her brows flicked up.

"Hey! Don't you know the rumours about him…"

"Nothing about him is *little*." We both spoke in sync, our

deep voices matched as well as our movement as we grabbed onto each other.

"Soooo, do you like him?" Amana said like she were trying to make this a safe place for me to open up.

I hoped she didn't think I had a crush on him.

"Is he bothering you?" She added before I could correct her previous assumption.

"No, no. He's heaven-sent. And bipolar as hell"

"How so?" Her curiosity took over. "Like Ayaan?" Now concern.

"Oh God forbid, no. It's just, one minute he smiles and jokes, next minute he's…he's…he's something?"

"And you think it's 'cause of me?"

I sigh. "I don't know what to think."

"Do you ever though?—Think?"

"Errrr more than you mate."

"Fax." She started.

"No printer." I ended.

It's finally lunch, which meant it was time for me to make ways to Aros. As I tapped out the Uni, I felt an arm wrap over my shoulders.

Kade.

"Are you still hungover? You owe me when you're not, I'm not letting this slide." I pinched his sleeve to give him back his audacity filled arm.

"Where you going?" He ignored everything I said.

"Aros." I looked at him with my confused '*are you dumb face?*'

He continued to follow me out the doors and down the

street to the station. Every time my eyes landed on his, he gave me a cheeky smile.

"*Why* are you following me?"

"*Why* can't I follow you? Aren't we friends?"

I can't tell what Kade I hated more. The sober—mentally not well—one or the hungover one. *If* he even is hungover. He seemed to be more on the drunk side.

Since I ignored his question, he continued. "You can't expect me to drive in the condition I'm in."

Annoyingly he had a point.

We entered the station and tapped in.

This journey was going to be interesting. The first train that arrives, we—I— am getting on. I don't care how packed it is, that train *will* have me as a passenger. I'm not going to be waiting around longer than I need to with Kade like this. Although…if I'm clever about it, I could get some information out of him now.

"If you knew that you were busy today, especially in the morning, why did you drink to get yourself this drunk?" Hopefully that wasn't too many words for him to handle.

"If I tell you the truth, would you do the same when I ask you some questions?"

Dammit.

Why was he still somewhat level-headed? I should've asked something a bit deeper—more personal, God knows that *he* would take the opportunity to do so.

"I will. I promise."

"How do I know you'll be telling the truth?" Despite his serious undertone, he continued to make it feel as though we were about to play a game.

"How do I know that *you'll* be telling the truth?" We shared the same concern.

"I have no reason to lie to that question. Now." He took steps closer to me. "Tell me. Is it fair for me to say that you owe me if I find out you lied?"

"That's fair, but I'm telling you, I *won't* lie."

He let out a single dry laugh then dipped his head a little too low. "I'll see about that."

What's with him? I can't tell if he's a good drunk or not.

The train arrived beside us. It's full but there are spaces here and there. Whilst I had a debate on whether or not to jump onto the train—as now I had the chance to get information out of him—Kade jumped on and dragged me in with him, guiding me to a side where we could stand in front of each other. People around us adjusted to those who continued to come in, then the train doors slid shut. The train jerked forward causing me to lose my balance and before I fell into someone or worse—in between people's legs— Kade grabbed a hold of me with one hand.

"Hold onto my hoodie."

I looked over his oversized open hoodie, then up at his face.

"I'm not saving you next time and I won't offer again."

I didn't even want to stand next to him, let alone touch him, but I really didn't have a choice. There was nothing else to hold onto, I couldn't even space my legs apart to balance myself.

I held onto him but made sure to keep as much as distance as possible in this sardine packed train.

'Astaghfirullah, Astaghfirullah, Astaghfirullah.'

"I didn't drink to get myself drunk. I drank to ease my mind."

I angled my head up at him but he didn't look down. It was almost as if he was purposely avoiding my eyes.

"I have to take care of some family I haven't seen in a long time…it brought back memories." He continued.

Family. Memories being brought back into the light. I could understand that.

"What kind of memories?"

"That's another question Desdemona." He lowered his head so that our eyes met. "You willing to take that risk?"

I clicked my tongue then pouted. "Not sure." I waited a second then spoke before he did. "Was that your question for me? 'Cause, I answered truthfully princess." I smiled a little, feeling clever, but also cringed at the fact I'd called him *'princess.'* He should be calling me princess (I would still cringe).

After realising what had happened, Kade accepted defeat. "Clever girl. You just might be able to work this all out."

'What the hell is he on about?'

I scrunched my brows but stopped after remembering that I could develop wrinkles now.

"Could've used that brain to work out the memories clearly weren't good ones."

'Ouch.'

"My turn. Before you manage to get another answer out of me." He lowered himself so that his mouth was near my ear, then spoke close to a whisper. "What situation were you in that made you *desperate* for a job?" He slowly moved himself back to how he stood before, keeping his eyes locked onto mine. He enjoyed asking that question and reading any reaction it got from me, I could tell from his smug face.

"My family. They don't get along with me—"

"You're going to have to give me more than that. Right now, you sound like you're stealing my story—"

"I'm *not* lying." I faced my side to avoid his eyes and to

make sure that the people around us were occupied. "I got a job because I don't have it in me to sit around waiting for something better to come anymore."

It went quiet, well between us it did. The train continued to make those dreaded noises and passengers still spoke amongst each other.

"Interesting."

"What the hell is so interesting about that?" I tried to hold his gaze until he looked away, but he didn't, and I couldn't stare for much longer. Once I realised he wasn't going to answer I scoffed in disbelief and embarrassment. Regretting even answering him in the first place, I turned my head away, no longer wanting to play whatever game this was.

Another part of me—the stubborn part—wanted to continue, but if that was his starting question than God knows what his others would be.

The rest of the ride I caught him glaring at me here and there in the reflection of the divider we stood next to. What was his problem? And why did he feel the need to make this more awkward than it already is?

A couple stops later, I eyed up some passengers before they got up and worked out that they were planning to leave. Before they even made it out the door, I made it to one of their seats before someone else did. I thought I had left Kade behind but he followed and sat in front of me, making himself comfortable. He could've sat beside me and that would've been way better, but no, he wanted to sit in front. I kept my eyes on him for a few seconds, but the way he stared deep into my soul forced me to look away. Was he planning to keep looking at me like that for the rest of this train ride? Speaking of which, I pulled my phone out to get the time. We still had twenty minutes left on this train.

Great.

Someone continuously tapped my foot and I didn't have it in me to ignore for another second, so I gave it more attention than my phone.

It's Kade.

'Shocker.'

I held a shrug, raised my brows in annoyance and quietly asked, '*What?*'

"How long?" He spoke like an eager child wanting to go home. Does being drunk make you this forgetful? Granted he drove to work and everywhere else, but he still knows the area we work in, right? Why can't he just look at the damn line and work it out?

"Twenty minutes." I enunciated.

He leaned back, continuing to shoot lasers at me with his eyes. Another few seconds and I finally let out my thoughts. "Are you going to keep your eyes on me all day?"

"I'm going to keep my eyes on you for a lot longer than that." He smiled, but there was nothing good attached to it.

"I—"

'How do I even react to that?'

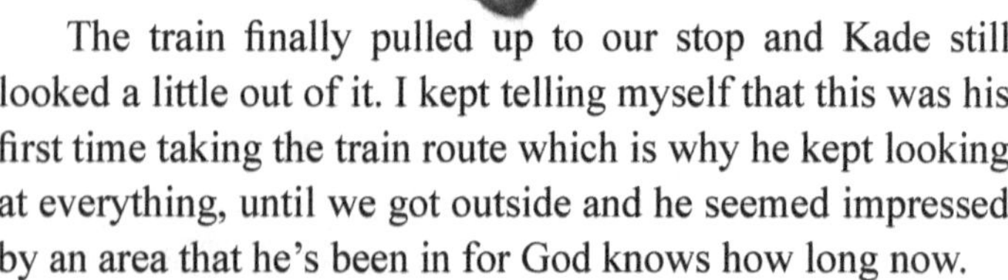

The train finally pulled up to our stop and Kade still looked a little out of it. I kept telling myself that this was his first time taking the train route which is why he kept looking at everything, until we got outside and he seemed impressed by an area that he's been in for God knows how long now.

"Lead the way Desdemona." He extended his arm out whilst slightly bowing his head, motioning for me to take the lead.

I screw faced him and stopped asking myself if he was being serious. '*Desdeona? Desmedona?*' What even is that?

When we got to the entrance (the elevator in the carpark), I unknowingly gave in to my habit where I would step to the side and wait for Kade to open the doors.

I looked to him now. He was doing the same as me.

I really don't enjoy drunk-hungover Kade.

Stepping past him, I uncovered the hidden pin pad and entered my code. I'm surprised I remembered it, but thank God I did because I've been questioning Kade's IQ this whole time, and failing to get the pin right would've definitely humbled me.

Kade beamed on the way up the elevator, it was like I was prematurely experiencing the '*take your kid to work*' day. I ignored him the best I could until he tried taking us to Bellamy's floor.

Smacking his hand away, I tried to bring him back to his senses. "What are you doing? You're drunk—"

"Hungover—"

"You're not in your right mind is what you are—"

"Am I ever though? Why can't we go up?"

"Er, hello? Bellamyy? Your boss is up there."

He let out a breath of disbelief. "My boss?"

The elevator doors opened on our floor.

"Oh my God, I can't be arsed for this. I don't care what kind of relationship you guys have, I'm not letting you go up there like this when he's probably in a meeting or something."

We walked towards the offices as Kade continued to look around, but this time it was like he was making a floor plan in his head.

Quickly going into my office—he followed—I grabbed

a few water bottles then directed Kade into his. Aggressively shoving the bottles into his chest, I told him to sober up.

"My office is a joke."

'You're a joke.'

"Yeah, well you can take that up with Bellamy when you're better." I walked towards my office.

Kade followed behind.

"Actually, I'm going to get going now. Thank you for bringing me here and giving me water—"

I tried to interrupt, but he continued talking before I could even get a syllable out.

"—Don't worry about Bellamy, I'll talk to him later and don't worry about me, I'll call a taxi."

He has water, he has someone to take him from Point A to Point B and said that he'll talk to Bellamy later. He's sorted, he doesn't need me, he's fine. But then why did the words *'do you want me to come with you'* exit my mouth.

"Nah, I'm good." He moved in for a goodbye hug but I dodged it.

"You seriously need to stop forgetting that you can't touch me."

"I will. The next time you see me, I'll be sober and will remember everything." He turned to leave but stopped in his tracks, and as if he had been slapped with a new personality he spoke. "Oh, and Medisa, I'm sorry about how I was to-day—"

'Just today?'

"Can we pretend today didn't happen…please?" His eyes were somehow now doe-eyed.

I sighed, he can't help being this person when he's drunk so I couldn't really blame him. His memories must've been taking a few emotions to the extreme if it got him to pick up a few bottles. I would probably be in the same state if I was allowed to drink.

"Fine. But you owe me lunch then."

He smiled. "Deal."

Chapter 5

Medisa
19/10/2021 (Tuesday)

Today's going to be interesting. I haven't made my mind up on whether or not I wanted Kade to remember what happened on Friday. If he did, it may be awkward considering the questions we asked and the answers we got, but then it may also bring us closer if we spoke about it. If it's not brought up, we could both get away with what happened, him more than me.

If I see him, I'm going to act like nothing happened, save him from embarrassment. However, if he brings it up, I'm letting my mouth run.

Not being able to see him with the quick glance I gave towards his office, I assumed he wasn't in, until I turned to look into mine and he's there looking out the window.

"Our offices aren't that similar for you to mistake mine for yours."

He turned around with a gentle smile. "Hey, I got us the day off. Convinced Bells he doesn't need us today."

My shoulders dropped. "Ugh, seriously, you didn't want to let me know before I left my house."

I could've saved travel money.

"Actually, I've made plans for us and I didn't know if you would come if I told you whilst you were home."

Had to give it to him, that's good thinking on his behalf. If he gave me a choice, I would be stuck on whether or not I should leave my house for his plans.

"Plans?"

"Yep, it's a surprise. But you'll like it." He moved away from the window.

"Do you want to bet on that?"

"Isn't betting haram?" He shot back a bit too quick.

"Oooo look at you doing your research." I dramatically sighed. "I could've made some serious money here."

"C'mon. We haven't got long." Kade laughed through his words.

I really shouldn't be going along with this. Hanging out with Kade during work hours is fine—I think. But making plans for outside of work is a bit sticky. We really shouldn't be left alone with one another outside of work hours, but then again, I really want to know where this is going.

'It's *going* to hell.'

If anything, if things get too out of hand I'll leave, I trusted myself enough to do that. Anyways, wherever his plan was, I hoped it's indoors. It may be a little dry today but I'm still cold. I tried to get some sort of clue from his clothes but he's dressed as his usual stylish self, unlike Friday where he was covered head to toe in normal casual gear, with barely any skin showing. Drunk him obviously has another wardrobe.

He noticed me focussing on his clothes. "Do you like what I'm wearing?"

"I always do." I spoke too casually, but only because there's nothing else to it. He does have a good sense of style and all his clothes are fashionable, even the plain ones. Once, he wore a jacket that was exactly my style, it made him look like some sort of sci-fi -cyberpunk character. I refrained from asking him all morning where he got it from but eventually gave in and asked. He gave the name of the brand—which

I'm sure no one has ever heard of—and told me to check them out because they have a lot of things he thought I would like. When I searched them up, the cheapest item was basically £1000 and that £1000 was a harsh reality slap to the face. I felt like I shouldn't even be in the same room as the damn thing. Till this day I can't tell if he was taking the piss or if he genuinely thought he was doing me a favour…Bloody cow.

"I was just thinking if what I'm wearing is suitable for whatever you got planned."

He held a proud look for a moment as if he didn't expect me to be so intellectual.

"Oh. Yeah, you're good, minus one thing."

I pulled my brows together.

"Your shoes."

"We're *both* wearing trainers." Good thing I wore trainers today and not the usual boots otherwise the obvious point couldn't have been made.

"And that's going to be a problem." He stuck to his shoe argument.

The elevator door opened allowing us into the carpark. As I followed Kade to his car I thought about what would need a different pair of shoes or no shoes at all. Football? Bowling? Yoga? Some other sport?

Kade opened the passenger door for me, making me let out the loudest dramatic gasp.

"You're gonna let me handle your car?" I let out a little giggle too soon whilst reaching for his keys. If I had my license, I wouldn't need to be sarcastic, I would've gotten into the driver's seat one way or another.

He scoffed as he smiled.

"Get in. I'll give you something to handle."

'Damn. He's good.'

"Uh- Astaghfirullah. As-Tagh-firu-llah." I repeated again and again—until I stopped replaying what he said in my head—whilst I held a finger out and tried to hold back a smile. My eyebrows froze in their raised position, annoyingly giving away how I felt.

Thankfully, Kade was someone I was comfortable around. If he wasn't, the innuendoes we threw back and forth would not run. Thinking about it, I should probably stop making or encouraging the innuendoes, but sometimes I genuinely can't help it. I don't think it's too much of an issue anyways, everyone who hears them—Kade and Amana—knows that it's nothing serious…it's only an inappropriate joke that helps lighten up the mood.

I sat inside the car, and by the time I was done inspecting the interior, Kade got in.

"It's about an hour away, so feel free to get yourself comfortable and eat the snacks."

'Ahh that explains the snack shop he currently called a car.'

I twisted the top half of my body towards the back seats. He had all my favourite crisps, sweets and bottled water brand. I wanted to complain and say *'what am I, some sort of child you're trying to distract?'* but picked up prawn cocktail and some cheese & onions instead. As he reversed, I asked if he had any bread and cheese.

"This isn't your local corner sho—"

"Looks like it though. Ohhhh." I curved my hand in between my nose and lips with my thumb on my chin. "Bars-bars. Mic drop."

I was my own roast audience and it was sad, but funny.

Kade laughed abnormally in response, grabbing my attention. There was no indication of him thinking that I was funny, his face held no expression, just dead eyes and sounds that mocked laughter. Whether he wanted to or not, he triggered my high pitch-whistle note laugh. I was fully pissing myself in his car because of his deliverance. He, on the other hand looked shocked and stopped moving the car which added to his dramatic pause. I tried to calm myself down when he turned to face me, but the best I could do was calm myself into giggles.

"That's concerning." After commenting on my laugh and behaviour he put his focus back on moving the car.

I calmed myself down some more. It's been a while since I laughed like that out of the blue. It felt good.

"I only got snacks because we're going to be eating properly later and *no* that is not where we are driving to, that's a separate plan."

I nodded. He's starting to get the gist of my thought process. I liked that. It's useful.

Giving all my attention to the snacks, I got busy mixing the crisp packets. Crushing them until they turned to decent sized crumbs, I wasted no time in scoffing them down.

"Who eats crisps like that?"

"What do you meannn? This is one of the best ways to eat two flavours that go well with one another. Try it." I was about to tunnel them into his mouth using the packet, but that would definitely be me doing too much. "Err." I moved my bottle from its holder and replaced it with the scrunched up crisp packet. "There, try it later when you can." I smiled, proud of that quick solution, then got comfortable. "Has anyone ever told you that you look like a pretty boy?"

"What?"

"I don't mean to sound perverted and I don't know if *'pretty boy'* is an insult, it might be. But what I mean is that you have feminine features, but then you don't, but then you do. I don't know…I don't know if it's your eyes or lips or your skin but yeah…" His eyes are paired with manly but arched brows and his lips are not exactly girly, but they are plump and a nice colour (no smoker lips) and his skin is practically glass.

"That's one way of distracting me whilst I'm driving."

"I could think of another." I had on an expression that read, *'it's not that hard,'* or, *'if you know what I mean,'* then snapped back. "Astaghfirullah. Anyways, you got manly features too. Like the space between your nose and lips is defined—I haven't seen that on a girl."

"I think you're staring at my lips a bit too much."

"Don't act like you don't stare at mine, kohl."

Kade's brows knitted slightly at the name I gave him whilst I tried to move past my jealousy of his thick, dark lashes that gave him that dark eye-line look.

"Anywho, a better way to put it, is that if someone were to ask me to describe how you looked, I would say a lighter skinned Scar in human form…Scar or his son—one of them." I looked to him proud, trying to read his expression to see if he agreed.

"Scar is a pretty boy?"

"Oh my God. I didn't mean pretty boy in a bad way. You *still* look scary and intimidating but—yeah, I give up. We'll come back to this when I have the words to properly articulate myself." I held out my hand as if to physically stop the conversation, then turned to the window.

Kade laughed, not a fake *'let's move on'* laugh, but a real one. It was nice, deep—one of those rich people ones. He also said that he understood and wasn't taking it as an insult, but I already had it set in mind to come back to this conversation when I had the right words.

"Has anyone ever told you that you switch between talking formally and informally? Or that sometimes you rush through your words and may use a word the wrong way, but we still get the gist on what you're trying to say?"

"My apologies. If I had known that pointing out your looks would make you point out my flaws, I would've simply called you a little bitch than compare you to such characters."

Kade pulled over to the side too quick for me to even process what just happened. The most I could do was quickly hold onto the door and my seat as he swerved. His wheels, or brakes, or maybe even a woman on the street, screeched.

"I'm not pointing out your flaws. I'm pointing out what I like about you, you silly girl." His slight serious tone turned into a lighter one towards the end.

"Oh, well that's embarrassing...for me. I'm sorry I called you a bitch, I don't actually think that you're one. I just wanted to hurt you in some way and that word came to mind."

Kade pulled his bottom lip into his mouth with his tongue and raised his brows, as though he had just discovered my first flaw, yet, somehow, found it to be amusing.

"You didn't have to stop driving to tell me that I was wrong by the way."

"I did. You needed to see it on my face that I was telling the truth." His eyes latched onto mine.

Being given no choice, I examined his face. It was more serious now, like he wanted me to believe his words. I, on the other hand, needed no more convincing the second after his eyes burned into mine, I was more focussed on the air becoming thick and awkward. Clearing my throat and trying to distract myself with whatever was going on in front of the car, my mind filled with ways I could subtly open my window before I began to sweat.

Kade got back onto the road. "You've yet to show me a real flaw Medisa."

"Really? I just showed you one and I could name a few if you want?" I joked, but also had the mental list ready.

Kade shook his head. "Get some rest, you being tired will not be a valid excuse later."

A cheeky smile swiftly plastered my face along with the question, *'what we doing later?'* and he, like I wanted him to, read my mind and expression.

"Get. Some. Rest. Medisa." He fails to keep serious when his tone of voice gave away his amusement whilst his lips slowly formed a smirk.

"Just say that you don't want to talk to me."

"Alright. I don't want to talk to you. There."

"Wow."

"Medisa, we're here." Kade tried to wake me up with only his voice, but it wasn't enough, I was drifting back. "Medisa c'mon." He raised his voice while putting up the car sun visor, exposing my closed eyes to some sort of strong light.

"Did you put the visor down while I was sleeping?" I spoke through a yawn.

"Yep. C'mon, ask me any other questions when we're inside. We're a tiny bit late." He was crouched outside the car beside me, my door open. It felt familiar, this scene.

"Cute." I replied with no emotion to the memory of Kade's position.

Still in some sort of sleepy daze I gave myself no choice but to exit the car and follow Kade blindly. It wasn't until we got to the building when I realised where we were. I've been here before, with Amana. This place has an indoor ice rink, an arcade, bowling space and a diner, although I'm pretty sure they don't have a halal option.

Kade guided me through the building and my heart sped up once I realised what was going to happen.

"Jessie! Hey man, I'm sorry that we're a little late. Could you still let us in?"

The male called Jessie walked over to us and matched Kade's height and build. And to show I acknowledged him I smiled as I shyly said '*Hi*'. Since I was still a bit out of it that's all I contributed to the conversation.

Jessie pointed out two pairs of shoes he had on the side ready to go. Anything he said after was mixed in with the noise that came from the rink. Hardly anyone was on, which was shocking until I understood that people were having private lessons.

Hearing Kade thank him pulled me back to their conversation, where I made sure to say my thanks for whatever Jessie had done before he walked away.

As soon as he was at a distance, where I was sure that he wouldn't be able to hear us, I snapped my head to Kade.

"We can't do this, *I* can't do this, I can't skate!" I spoke through loud whispers as if I didn't already check that we could speak freely.

"We can do this, *you* can do this, I can teach you."

"No Kade, you can't touch me remember?" Maybe him not remembering Friday wasn't because he was drunk, but because he has crap memory.

"I know, which is why I'm going to skate besides you and only interfere if it looks like you're going to have a bad fall."

Clearly, he's thought this through.

'Could he not have thought of bowling?'

"I need a penguin." I desperately tried to save myself from the inevitable.

"No, you don't."

'I'm going to kill him.'

"Having a penguin longs out the process and doesn't allow you to push and believe in yourself. You just need to throw yourself out there and trust yourself…and me."

Annoyingly, he's right. Even if I managed to skate decently with the penguin, mentally I would know it's because I'm relying on it and as soon as someone takes the penguin away, I would fall and would have to learn to skate without it anyways.

I grabbed my skates then made way to the bench. "Did you book us a private lesson?"

"No, I got Jessie to agree to let us in without a worker."

"Oh, that's actually on brand for you." I grabbed our trainers then walked over to Jessie. "Thank you for letting us on the rink, I hope it didn't, slash doesn't cause you too much trouble."

"Nah don't worry about it, I should be thanking you for—" His eyes travelled behind me. "For being a fan of skating." He smiled then turned to leave.

'A fan of skating?'

I turned back to see a waiting Kade just as my legs decided now was the right time to shake, and I could only be grateful for their lack of violence.

We head over to the rink where there were about fifteen people skating, some in group lessons and some in one-to-one sessions.

This was probably going to be one of the only times that I

got to be on a rink this empty, I might as well take advantage of it.

"I'm not letting you stick to the edges. You're going to go start off in the middle—"

I opened my mouth to disagree, but I'm cut off before I could speak.

"—I'm not hearing it. I'll take you to the middle myself if you try escaping."

"That's haram."

"God is forgiving."

My facial expression screamed '*dumbfounded.*'

Kade looked around and I was confused what for, the rink and its opened gate was right in front of us.

"Excuse me." He called to a woman who was on the rink. "Hi. Do you think you could take my friend to the middle?"

'*Oh my God this is actually happening.*'

The woman agreed then skated over. Before she made it to us for Kade to hand me over, he lowered himself and spoke in my ear. "Remember to bend your legs and keep them that way."

"Uh—" He might just be better at me with this innuendo thing.

The woman reached out for me. "C'mon Hun, I'll get you there safely."

I shook a little on the way there but she did well to keep me balanced. Soon as I was where Kade wanted me, she left, gracefully skating off into the distance.

I barely squatted with my arms reaching out to nothing, preparing for the fall. Kade the show off skated backwards around me with his arms crossed.

Being too tense and overthinking everything, I thought of ways to be relaxed and less serious.

One good fall should do the trick.

"Are you seriously not going to give me any tips?"

"I only have the one." He was too proud of that one. "Stick to what I said and try to figure it out from there. If in the next five minutes you haven't worked it out, I'll help some more."

I took deep breaths whilst trying to block Kade out. His presence will definitely affect my performance.

"Can you close your eyes or look away or something?"

He shook his head before going back to monitoring me whilst slowly skating around like some sort of shark.

I kept my arms out. If I was going to fall, I needed them to react quick enough to catch myself, or to protect my head. I pushed forward with my right foot, then tried to skate by dragging my feet, but almost instantly failed. By squatting a little lower, I was able to prevent a fall.

Starting again, I pushed myself off, treating myself like a scooter rather than trying to walk on ice. It worked for a few seconds but for some reason my skate would jam into the ice, jerking my whole body forward. I tried again, this time with more of a push and longer glides. My right foot was the one to push off the ice and my left was the chill foot.

"Hey I'm doing it! I'm—" I got a little too excited and shifted my weight to my head, which then forced me to dive into the ice. My whole body pushed itself back in attempts to get into the normal stance, but then I'd set myself up in a worse position as now I fell backwards into the ice, head first.

Everything was happening so fast but so slow at the same time, I didn't even get to close my eyes to brace for impact. On my way down, I was grabbed. I felt a light jab in between my bra cups, my bra was stretched out in front of me then smacked back into position. I now stood like I was when I first got to the middle, only this time, Kade is beside me with his arms out looking just as shocked as me.

"Did you just pull me back up using my bra?" I spoke through out of breath laughs. Not being able to help it, I leaned forward again, everything was so unexpected and funny. Instead of dropping forward or to the ground like I usually did when I laughed, I gently lowered myself into a low squat as I shook with laughter. "When you said that you were going to interfere—I didn't think that you were going to use my bra as a harness." I tried to speak through wheezes, holding onto my heart as if it would help with breathing.

I adjusted my bra.

"I don't know if I should feel violated or not." I continued to crack up, scream-laughter building up before coming out as strangled gasps.

Momentarily—thanks to Kade, I was a string puppet.

"Well sorry for not using the milliseconds I had to sit on the side and think of the best non violating way to save your arse."

He was still in shock. I could tell that he wanted to laugh a little but he wanted to make sure that I was good first. The situation was definitely replaying in his head as it was in mine.

This was exactly what I needed. I felt like whatever just happened was the best ice breaker.

I got back up and almost instantly set off.

"I think I got the gist of it. I just need to put my weight into my non dominant leg whilst pushing with the dominant one, oh, and I shouldn't lean too forward."

I was skating, well, gliding here and there. I couldn't control my direction or breaks just yet so I had to sit to stop, then move to an edge to physically turn my body. Eventually

I got the hang of whatever it was that I was doing.

"Kade look, look! I'm doing it!"

Kade skated backwards in front of me. I couldn't look up at him for too long, but I could hear him praising me and since praise came in by the crumbs in my life, I secretly ate it up.

I *absorbed* it.

After a few laps, we got out to take a break. Kade went to see if the diner sold hot chocolate because the cold had gotten to my throat. The cold mixed with me constantly laughing too hard and raising it, meant that he got what he wanted; a mute Medisa.

He came back quicker than I thought, with a thick padded winter jacket instead of a hot drink.

"Am I supposed to eat that?" I joked.

"They didn't have hot chocolate and I didn't want us to leave without you experiencing something first." He held out the jacket. "Put it on, this will be fun."

'If he stole this jacket surely someone would have approached us for it by now.'

I waited a second or two, but no one came.

"What we doing?"

"Medisa, trust me, you're going to want to do this."

I sighed, then put on the thick jacket. I could smell men's cologne, which made sense, the jacket practically drowned me.

"Can you feel that?"

"Feel what?" I struggled to look at Kade over my shoulder.

"Good, you can't feel me, which means whatever we're about to do isn't going to be haram."

I bleakly sighed. "Me chilling with you right now is haram."

"Well then you definitely need to do this, can't waste this already sinful day without experiencing this."

He motioned for me to follow him back to the rink, and I do, out of curiosity of course. Once we reached the far edge, he made me look towards the wall and have my arms out to mimic the letter 'T'. He positioned himself behind me, ordering me to bend my legs and to not become too loose.

Soon as he made sure that I was okay and secure, we both started to move. I was skating backwards, well Kade was, and he was dragging me along. It felt so freeing, to be able to lean back and smoothly move around knowing that I would not fall.

At some point it just felt like I was fully laying back, putting all my trust in Kade as he took me round the rink again and again.

Was this haram? I couldn't *feel* him touching me, but I *knew* that he was.

'It's haram and I'm an idiot that's taking the piss.'

Maybe I should get him to stop, *or* maybe I should enjoy it while it lasts and promise to never do this again.

Waiting for Kade turned into walking around our floor. I hadn't really had the chance to explore it for myself since I wanted to get on Bellamy's good side and actually work. But I had time now since I didn't need to rush off to uni or home.

The games room is the first place that came to mind. From what I remember, Kade said that he and Bellamy liked to come in here to de-stress and almost ten out of ten times they came up with a solution to whatever problem they had.

The room had a ping pong table, snooker table, air hockey table, a slightly advanced looking basketball hoop game, and one of those arcade punching bag machines that measured your hit. They had other games here and there but these were the games I took interest in.

The door for the room opened, exposing Kade with food containers.

"I thought you left." He sounded relieved as his hand lay on his heart a second before dropping.

"Not till my belly's full." I joked, but thinking about it, I was serious. He practically starved me all day for whatever's in his hands. "Can we sit by the window?"

"Yeahh." He said like '*of course we can.*'

We could've used the tables and chairs in the room, but the sun was setting and it's just nicer to sit on the floor sometimes. The room wasn't directly facing the sun but we could still see it. The colours reflected on the surrounding buildings so we couldn't miss it even if we wanted to.

Kade organised the food and plates as I stayed amazed by the view. I tried to intervene but he refused. He practically demanded that I look away until everything was ready. It's like he had this all planned out, and for it to be perfect, it needed to follow that script.

Before allowing me to look, he got up to turn off the room lights so that they won't turn on even when they've detected movement.

"Okay, you can look now." He sat down, leaving a decent sized gap between us, although it didn't really feel like a gap because it was filled with food.

I took in what he had prepared. We had options. There was roast chicken and rice, which looked and smelt like biriyani. Another silver disposable container had saucy vegetable chicken noodles. Next to that, was smaller containers which held some ketchup, chutney and yoghurt mixed with some onions and cucumber. The drink options were water, smoothies and milkshakes, we didn't really drink fizzy drinks—well, I didn't.

"What the hell?" I looked over the food once more. "Did you make all of this?"

"I made the roast and the noodles but had help with the rice."

"When did you make them? Who told you about the chutney and yoghurt combo? Where did you even keep all this?"

"Sometimes cooking is therapy, so could you please dig in and compliment me, they won't stay warm forever."

"Is Bellamy still here? We should give him some, no?"

Kade sighed, then pulled out his phone like it was a chore. "I'll see if he's still here, but he's not eating till you've tried everything."

I gawked at the food, eating the rice and chicken first would make more sense than the noodles. If I had noodles first, the taste may linger and intervene with the rice, and it would most likely fill me up as well.

"Who the hell helped you make the rice? Do you have an Asian girl I don't know about?" I'd never pictured him with a South Asian girl. I could see him with every race but South Asian.

He let out breaths of laughter through his nose while his whole face reacted. "What century are you living in? We have access to something called the internet you know? Also, Bellamy's not here"

I ate a forkful.

"You need to send me the link 'cause this is one of the best roasts and rice I've ever had, and that's saying something 'cause I've had a lot." I put down my fork and readied my right hand.

Kade smiled so hard his dimple looked as if it would soon be a permanent mark no matter what expression he made, then he finally started to eat. His container mirrored mine.

"You know the best way to eat rice is with your hand and before you say '*that's dirty*' or messy, just try it, trust me. And don't act like you don't eat burger, chips or pizza with those same hands."

"I would never say those things." Kade grabbed and ate the food like he'd done it before and I didn't bother to hide how impressed I was.

"By the way, you didn't say that thing that you say before you eat."

"Yes, I did." I spoke like it were the truth. No doubt came from me.

"No, you didn't."

I had not…

"No, I didn't." I quietly recited what I had skipped and shoved some more food into my mouth, not bothering to look at Kade because I knew that he had the '*I knew it*' look.

We ate a few more handfuls before Kade spoke again. "So, Medisa, let's talk boys."

"Let's not." My fingers fed me another 'spoon'.

"Don't girls like talking about boys? *Obviously* not all the time, but I'm sure it pops up every now and then."

"Only when there's one to talk about."

"Well, *is* there one to talk about?" He drank some water.

"Nope." I popped the 'p'. "You're the only boy in my life." I dramatically extended my arm, pointing at him whilst aggressively biting my bottom lip as my eyes keep to their slit position. I'm sure that made it clear that I'm taking the piss, but just in case, I had to say it to make sure that we were on the same page. "Nah I'm kidding, I'm not interested in anyone. Never have been."

Stuffing some rice and roast into my mouth, I decided to give my belly a little break before the noodles.

"You don't want to get married?"

"Are you interested?" I answered a little too quickly. I'm not uncomfortable with Kade asking, but these types of questions remind me of how boys are now a days, they're nothing like what you would want them to be—the ones available to you anyways— and it just pisses you off and blah blah blah blah blah...it's tiring. I'm not saying I'm the perfect girl, but shit, I am better than the majority of idiots on their high horses.

"No, that would be haram." His body language and tone were as though he was saying *'are you stupid,'* mixed with *'don't be silly.'*

"Oh, *sorryyyy*, Mr. I-do-my-research." I grabbed one of the water bottles Kade had placed closer to me, then carried on to explain myself. "I like the idea of marriage and what-not, but it just feels like I won't get that. I always have something else going on *and* whenever I hear about boys or actually hear a boy talk, it furthers my uninterest—the shit that you guys come out with is ridiculous. It's like there are no real men anymore—and don't even get me started on 'Muslim boys'—especially the ones online—ugh." I picked up some rice.

Is there a word for eating and drinking when frustrated?

"No-no, do go on, I wanna hear what you have to say."

Like that was a cue, we both got more comfortable on our 'food break.' I guess we both knew this conversation could go on for a while.

"Okay, firstly, a lot of them would do the most sinful things, then they want to talk about how hard life is and how they couldn't resist, or-or how humans weren't made to be perfect, but God forbid—God *forbid*, they hear of a girl who's been violated or has slipped up here and there—then all of a sudden, they think God has given them the right to rule and judge. They start to call her names like '*used goods*' and some of them think that it automatically gives them access to her and it's just sick—and then, the same boys who act wilder than animals *somehow* come to some sort of '*religious epiphany*' and would want a girl who is '*untouched*' only to turn her into a baby making machine and would slave her away because apparently that's what God said woman are for—and *no* that's not what He said we're here for by the way—in fact we have so many rights that were given to us before anyone else made a change but that's another conversation in itself." I fluttered my hand to push that conversation to the side whilst simultaneously giving myself a break. "I could go on and on with this topic, but what I'm trying to say is, when a boy sins for fun or is easily swayed by this world, and is clearly still not serious, what makes him, his mum or any girl think that he'll stay loyal to his wife, his family—even himself—when he can't even stay loyal to his religion and fear, slash love God. And this is only the tip of the iceberg of why marriage is off putting these days." I let out and sucked in deep breaths as I forgot to breathe during my little rant.

"Damn. They sound like every other prick, only difference is they use your religion as an excuse for their behaviour—"

"Exactly, exactly! They just give Islam and practicing Muslims a bad rep. Even on things like drinking, some of them—And some girls, would be like '*oh that's just Islam being too strict, we're stopped from doing anything fun,'* like no you idiot, there's a reason why things are haram. God is literally trying to protect us. Honestly, the way they act is another reason why some—mostly girls, I think—want a revert—which by the way is another thing that pisses them off and it's hilarious."

I tried calming myself down as I observed Kade to see if he thought I was crazy, but he looked interested, and understanding. <u>Thank God</u> he was open minded and not one of those religious hating idiots that only want to argue and not conversate, slash learn—something which I hadn't even considered him being.

"Why do some girls prefer reverts to Muslim-borns?"

"*Muslim-borns.*" I chuckled. "Because when a revert sins by… let's just say drinking. You would be more understanding as it's probably a habit that they're still trying to get out of, whereas a Muslim born person has been told from young what to stay away from, so when they do it, there's literally no valid reason, unless of course it's forced down their throat. Also reverts tend to be more knowledgeable, so they could teach you something you don't already know." I tried to quickly come up with another reason because I'm sure there's more. "Oh-oh and if a Muslim can guide someone to the religion, he or she will be granted rewards for every good deed that person does, and then some say that it basically guarantees you a spot in heaven."

"Great. So reverts are golden tickets?"

"*Good* reverts are golden tickets." I lower my eyes from his face to his hands. "And some reverts have tattoos." I mumbled as I scratched the back of my ear.

"What about tattoos?"

Smiling but cringing at the fact he heard and now I have

to explain was probably the hardest part of this conversation so far.

"We believe that our bodies aren't really ours, that our bodies are entrusted to us by God—a gift if you will—to hold our souls-our spiritual beings, so we should look after them, hence why certain food and drinks are haram and why we can't get tattoos or certain piercings or even do stuff before marriage, we'll just be damaging our perfect bodies and inflicting unnecessary pain or confusion." I paused to see if he's following. "That's why if some people are crazy serious about their love for tattoos but also religion, they *may* seek out a revert for them to marry."

Kade replaced the rice with the noodle container as amusement made a shy appearance on his face. "I don't know if I'm scared or admire that sort of dedication. Here try some noodles."

"For real. Anyway, I probably should've asked before I ate the roast, but I'm just going to ask now, just in case. Is this all halal?" The question only slipped my mind because I stupidly assumed that he was used to my dietary requirements.

Kade tuts like he is disappointed in my having to ask. "I would never feed your Gift something haram."

The sound that I allow to escape sounds was like I were trying to summon phlegm. "Shut uppp."

He smiled, and its with his eyes and I loved it, but then it fades. "Can I ask you something about Amana?"

Internally freezing, I almost broke out in sweat. He got me the job because of Amana, and he did all of this today, again, for her—to get in her good books. Which I loved for her, but shit, I misread a lot. Also, what if he asks something and I answer one way, but Amana would have wanted me to answer in another?

"Why do you have such an attachment towards her?"

'Oh oh.. Not what I was thinking...'

"Err, she's my first real friend and she stayed despite me being a little different." And that's a severely watered down version of it.

"What d'you mean?"

"I." I extended until I mentally made sure to be okay with saying more. "Didn't really do much before her, just observe, and maybe feel a 'little' anger or sadness, jealousy, but she opened me up to feel more. Don't get me wrong, I wasn't boring. I just didn't talk as much so where I picked up on things and let it pile until I did something, other people saw outbursts. And then after Amana, I started being a little more external with my thoughts and feelings." Thinking back to it, whether my actions were justified or not, Amana was the only one to confidently stand by me and raise her voice. Everyone else was okay with agreeing in silence and outwardly separating themselves. Maybe not all the time, but enough times for me to distance myself and think—maybe even say—screw you. Even my parents, gosh, my parents, my *siblings*, even seemed to have some sort of vendetta against me, from the moment I developed consciousness... Honestly, I was surprised I didn't turn out to be what they accused me of. But then that's where my gratitude for religion came in. I didn't act on emotions as badly as I could've because I didn't want to go to hell; otherwise, I would've been in some sort of jail or detention centre or something.

I zoned out some more, thinking back to the BS my family put me through while continuing to want a 'normal' child. Ha. Funny.

"My parents and siblings thought I was demented when I was younger, even took me to a therapist at the ripe age of eight—maybe seven—to get the 'psychopath' diagnosed. But I was *way* too aware of the situation, so I put on an act lol." I stuffed the noodles into my mouth realising that I was saying more than I needed to, but quickly forgot the words spoken as the taste of the noodles took over.

This was the first time I had tasted noodles like this, and my oh my had Kade left an impression. It was going to take a lot for someone to top this.

Whilst having a massive chunk of the noodles, I slowly realised how long they were, one part was in my mouth, whilst the rest was still tangled in the container. Kade also decided that this was the right time to watch me eat.

'How embarrassing.'

Panicking, I tried to suck them up and when that didn't work, I chomped down multiple times, severing the links to my mouth.

Kade still watched, part-in-awe, part-confused.

Clearing my throat, refusing to choke in front of him, I thought of something to say before he took the piss. "Speaking of tattoos, what are yours about? Any stories? The smoky one that leaks onto the area near the end of your collarbone kinda looks like three roses."

"I'll tell you the stories another time. Right now I want to know what you think of the food and what progress you've made towards the future you want."

'Crap.'

I hadn't made any progress since the time I told him about my worries and struggles with which route I should take. Kade spoke through all the different options and the best way to go about it that day, and how he would help me with whatever I decided to do, but I thought that he was just being nice and wouldn't bring it up until I did. I guess he was being serious, as serious as I should be if I really wanted my life to work out. This was embarrassing and I *needed* to move the conversation to something else.

"These noodles have set the standards way too high for any other ones. You sir, have trapped yourself with me for the rest of your life, because now, whenever I crave this bad boy, you will be the one that I come to."

'Why was I talking like that? Ewl.'

Kade's obviously happy with my review, but I hadn't said enough to completely distract him to move the conversation away from my future. I needed to come up with something else. "Are you going to tell me what I did to deserve this good day?"

His face changed.

'Bingo.'

He put down his forkful of noodles then moved any container too close to him, away. Something told me I wouldn't want to be eating throughout whatever he had to say, so I did the same. Just thinking about the messiness and awkward crunches was enough for me to do the same thing as him.

He thought about what to say then spoke lower than his usual volume. "How I treated you last week wasn't right. It was out of the blue and I'm sorry. I didn't mean to be an arse but I—"

"You had things going on with your family, I get it—" I never usually cut in when someone's talking, but I did it now because I thought it would be better for him to not be triggered into drinking, again.

"What?" Kade reacted a bit too quickly, his eyes piercing into me.

'Fudge. Fudge. Fudge. I wasn't supposed to bring it up.'

"Er-I I just assumed it was something to do with your

family because when I act out, out of the blue it's usually because of mine."

'*Please for the love of God buy that.*'

I started to sweat a little.

"Oh. Well thank you for giving me some space and for being so understanding."

He bought it, <u>Thank God</u>. I try not to make my relief obvious.

"Don't expect space next time. I was fighting the urge to run up to you, to beat whatever you were holding in, out. Dunno if I could hold myself back next time." I clicked my tongue whilst stretching.

"Do that. Don't hold yourself back next time."

I hoped he knew that I wasn't serious about physically assaulting him.

"You better remember this when that '*next time*' happens. In fact, forget that, there better not even be a next time. I know that we're not close and that we barely know each other, but you can talk to me. I'm not the type to spread it round and I've been told that I'm a good person to talk to."

"You are a good person to talk to. *And* be around."

I jokingly scooted myself away whilst side eyeing him, which made him laugh.

I liked his laugh. It's nice.

'*And smile. And voice. And—*' O-kay, time to get up because my brain was doing too much.

"I can't believe you did all of this to apologise to someone you've known for like a week." Cleaning up any mess made between us and stacking the containers, I glanced around the room squinting. I don't think we realised how dark it had gotten inside the room.

"As disgustingly cliché as this sounds, you're not just

someone Medisa. I could tell from before that you're different." He placed our drinks on the snooker table. If there was anything that I missed, he picked up and cleaned.

"You're starting to sound like every other guy now."

"I'm aware. Makes me feel sick. But I hope you know I'm being serious and have no ill intentions."

"I'm *aware*." I mimicked his tone then walked to the ping pong table, picking up a bat and motioning for him to do the same.

He started the game with a light hit.

"Now that you know the truth behind today, tell me about your future plans, what have you decided or done?"

I 'purposefully' missed the ball as my face gave me away.

"Oh c'monnn. You didn't think that I fell for your little topic change and forgot about it, did you? Good job by the way, *loved* the deliverance. However, I genuinely care and want to help, so, get talking." He picked up another ball then served.

I have to give it to him, he's good. Usually when I change topics it worked, but I guess it won't always with someone like Kade and what's more, I don't know if I liked it or not.

'You like it.'

"You know what? I should probably go catch up with my prayers and then if it's not too late, we'll talk about it." I slowly backed away towards the door knowing damn well we aren't talking about it tonight, then I turned once I knew that I was close to it. I managed to open it but before it was enough for me to get through, Kade slammed it shut and towered over me with his hand resting on the door above my head.

He wasn't too close, but he was closer than usual.

"We're talking about it, *today*."

I mentally pushed myself to face him. He backed away,

giving me some space once he realised I was turning around.

"Truthfully, I don't have anything to say, my mind has been a little occupied lately and it's kinda embarrassing that you're more on this than me." I bit my lip waiting for him to respond, but he just moved back to the door and opened it for me.

I stood confused whilst he held the door open.

"I don't have anything to say, so you're kicking me out?"

"Kicking you out? No. I'm helping you out. Going blank, being busy or holding yourself back while trying to make a big change are all normal. I'm just showing you that it's way easier if you're upfront with me. I'm not going to punish you."

I stopped myself from giggling but couldn't stop myself from talking.

"Punish me?" A cheeky smile is called out and I'm not even sure if my words sounded like a question or a request.

'Astaghfirullah, Astaghfirullah, Astaghfirullah.'

"Go pray." Kade spoke sternly but his face gave him away. I could see that dimple grow from a mile away. He's amused even though he's trying to hide it.

I stayed fixed on his eyes for as long as I could as I walked past, not even trying to hide my smugness.

"Oh, and by the way, before I forget to say it. I loved today. But to avoid continuing being a hypocrite—the whole giving Muslim boys shit for sinning when I'm here chilling and eating with you—we need to keep hanging out, outside of work hours to a minimum, if not stopping completely... unless you're comfortable with my dad or brother being in the room with us."

"Give me their numbers."

"Ugh, could you take this seriously please." A smile tried

to creep onto my face, but I was serious. "The whole reason I'm earning money is to get away and be a better Muslim, not worsen. So this is the last time…okay?" I've actually added a sin by being around Kade. I never used to go out with boys before.

"Okay." His words assured, but his eyes had a hint of something else.

I needed to make sure that this was the last time we chilled together outside of work. Harmless jokes, fun and games are what the devil used to sneak in. Do I really want a crappy life *and* afterlife? No. The answer is, and will always be no. Seeing things through and actually making sure that I stay on the right path however, is another story.

Chapter 6

Medisa

16/12/2021 (Thursday)

It's the last day of the semester and it roughly marked two months since I joined Aros. After the ice-skating day things became less awkward in the office. Every Tuesday since that day, Kade had been taking me to visit the businesses Aros supported. Sometimes we attended meetings in places I may have an interest in, just so that I could have an insight, and honestly, it's been useful. Other times we went to office parties, which honestly, is not at all what I expected. Kade's also been calling me '*Trouble*' like it's my name or something, and occasionally I acted like it bothered me, but really, I kind of liked it.

He'd basically become a male Amana (even more so than before), we hung out almost every work day—during work hours—messing around in the building, helping each other with our assignments and then going out to eat, to either discuss life and the future, or movies, conspiracy theories and anything else that was on our mind that day. He wasn't a replacement for Amana but he was a good stand-in. I rarely saw her since both our schedules were jampacked, but we do make sure to see and talk to each other whenever we could. If anything, being busy and away made seeing each other more exciting and fun, not that we ever needed that kind of boost, Thank God.

Home-life's been different too. There hasn't been much drama since I've started working, there wasn't any *time* for drama. I came home and slept till the next day and most of my cleaning duties had been passed to Ataya. I guess my mum pitied how tired I've become. And it's not like I've completely abandoned them, I still helped around the house on the weekends. *And* they took a cut off my pay.

So far everything was working out well, which I *should* feel good about, but I'm actually starting to feel paranoid. Every time I enjoyed myself, my brain automatically let me know to prepare for the ugly while I'm in the good, and now, after two months of no ugly, I'm kind of scared. How big is this ugly going to be?

On a brighter note, Christmas lights are on in central. Which meant the time where everyone is cheerful and seemed to get along with one another has come. It's dumb that it takes a holiday celebration and a few dropped degrees to achieve this but nevertheless, it is anticipated for and enjoyed.

As I tapped out of Uni to make ways to work, I saw Kade on the chairs at the entrance. He's dressed for the weather with his dark grey beanie and it's grown on me since the first time I saw him cover his hair. He might actually be one of those guys that suited the buzzcut look.

Without a second to think, I ran over so that I could shake his body whilst saying '*boo*', but failed as I tripped and landed on the seat next to him. He raised a brow as he looked down his nose, and before he could cuss me out for the stunt I just pulled, I ran through my words.

"What are you doing here? Is it because I didn't come in the morning? I asked Bellamy if it was okay for me to come in later and he didn't seem to mind. Anyways we're all supposed to meet at the station remember? To go see the lights?" Even when I was trying to cover up what just happened, I took notice of his eyes. "Your eyes are kinda red and the actual colour part is different. Something you wanna talk about?"

"They're contacts." He stood up.

"They look goodddd, but your natural colour is already unique looking <u>May God bless you.</u>"

I didn't buy it.

They looked too real for them to be coloured contact lenses, he probably smoked some weed or something, but then again, he's rich and has access to qualities I haven't experienced and things I haven't even heard of.

"Yeah, I just wanted something different today." He moved towards the revolving door so quickly you would have thought he was disinterested in whatever I had to say.

As we stood waiting for the door to empty, I could feel a weird vibe approaching, *if* it wasn't already with us.

"Shall I call Amana to see if she's free right now—"

"No." He spoke way too quickly for my liking.

There was no hint of humour in that '*no*.'

"I got us time off work today, you're welcome for that, now we have more time to…" He thought of the word. "Chill."

"Bellamy let me have a late start and now he's giving me the day off?"

"Yup." Kade confirmed with his voice a little croakier than usual. Is it the cold or is he in a mood? Or is he in a mood because of the cold? I looked over his layered clothes again and decided that he wasn't made for winter. He wore leather gloves, a hat, an oversized jacket, hoodie and a top underneath. *I'm* not even that prepared today and I get headaches from the cold—I can thank my industrial piercing for that.

I let him know of my worries and how it would be best if we stayed indoors, but he was strong on the '*not wasting time staying indoors, especially on a day off.*'

After bickering back and forth we met in the middle. We're going to spend some time outdoors with the others, but for the majority of the time we will be staying indoors.

It's been a while since we've done something outside of work. I've tried not to spend more time with him than necessary no matter how much I enjoyed his company, but I guess today is somewhat better as we'll be with Amana and Bellamy. Amana wasn't my brother or father but she's as close as it can get. And Bellamy was basically Kade's brother and kept him in check (not that he ever needed to). So basically, instead of chilling with Kade, one on one, we will be free mixing.

'...*Astaghfirullah.*'

Rather than going through the usual route I knew—off by heart by the way—we took a route that Kade knew. We walked through backstreets and alleyways which he claimed was a shortcut to the station and the lights, but it was actually a route to never be found.

After circling dark random streets for about twenty to thirty minutes, I finally had enough of trusting Kade's brain and gave in to the cold, my hunger and frustration.

"I don't care, the next pub or shop we see, we're going inside." I blew into my hands.

Kade raised a brow and looked around, we were surrounded by anything but public buildings.

"We're in *central* London, there's supposed to be a pub on every corner." I continued to blow into my bowl-shaped hands then reached into my pocket for my phone.

Kade stopped walking to watch me pat myself down as though it were a form of entertainment.

"What you looking for De—?" He stopped himself but I still caught the fact that he tried to call me something or by someone else's name.

"My phone."

I continued to search my pockets despite my mind being elsewhere.

"When did you last use it?"

"Forget it. I'll worry about it later, let's just use yours for now." Staying out for longer would probably kill us both off and I'm starting to get hungry. So, crying over something that is no longer in my possession makes no sense especially when it can be replaced.

"I recognise that building in the distance, I'm pretty sure there's a street somewhere here that's lively and has a pub." Kade assured as if he's had a trustworthy map installed in his head.

He led the way and before I knew it, we arrived at the street he spoke about. The pub placed at the corner of the road seemed to be the only thing open with its orangey- yellow lights. As we approached the windows, I focussed on the people inside.

Men.

A group of them looking like a bunch of ruffians.

'Of course, why would they want to get up to see the lights?'

As we entered, I began to feel aware of my surroundings and became self-conscious. I was in a pub that was filled with men. I may not be drinking or touching anything in here but I still felt dirty and somewhat naked.

As if he had sensed me debating on leaving, Kade took me deep inside by pinching the end of my sleeve, leading me to some stools away from the entrance and near a game of darts. He took off his jacket as he made a quick observation of our surroundings, then looked back down to me.

"Take the darts off the board, I'll be back, I've been dying to take a piss." His hands covered his crotch, as though I needed convincing on his motive to leave.

Giggling, I turned to sort our game out. I even threw two practice darts, but before the third left my hand, I felt the presence of someone behind me. The stench of smoke and alcohol engulfed me whole, and before I could turn to face the idiot, he moved to stand in front of me.

As I judged what was in front of me with both concern and disgust, his friends, as if they could see my eye move up and down their bulky mate, all whooped, howled and whistled in the background, cheering him on.

'I hate men.'

The man in my space had a deep cut on his left cheek as if he was clawed by some cat, woman or knife in his youth. He stroked his moustache with a perverted look in his eyes but I was too distracted by his decorated fingers.

He wasn't built of muscle, but he had weight to him, not the fat kind, but the kind where you knew that if he wanted to, he could beat the fu—fudge out of everyone here. His clothes made him look silly, there wasn't anything silly about them, they just made him look stuffed and that thought alone was enough for me to hold a laugh back.

"What you smiling about?"

I am tugged towards him by my waist, triggering my heart to become an organ I was actively aware of.

Leaning back to avoid our faces being too close, I am met with another tangible existence; his arm limiting our distance.

Whilst he moved his face dangerously closer to mine, I failed all attempts made to escape his grip. I could stab him with the dart, but I didn't have it in me. What if I pricked a vital vein or organ, or something? I would have to do time over something I didn't even start. But damn, the urge to do it *is* there and it's stronger than I thought.

His hand made its way down my back and when it got a bit too close to the curve of my arse, I leaned my head away from him as far as I could, then launched it forward hoping it was enough force to hurt or at least surprise him enough to loosen his grip.

My head span after the hit, I couldn't even get my bearings before he made a move on me even if I wanted to.

"Medisa move!"

With my head still pounding, I barely moved out the way when Kade had ripped the man's arm off me. Kade's swing made the man stumble back into chairs, which furthered his decline in stability. After a few failed saves, the chunky man finally accepted his fate to be on the floor.

My heart was still in my throat and Kade's voice was the reason behind its prolonged stay. As attractive as his angry voice was, it was also kind of unsettling. My body was still internally shaking and I couldn't decipher whether it was because I was angry or because I was scared.

The moment my head stopped spinning as much as it did when the headbutt was fresh, I grabbed onto a bottle by its neck and swung for the man's head as he tried to get back up. When he fell back again, some of his friends, as if they had just noticed the scene, got up whilst I was still trying to figure out what my body wanted.

Run? Freeze? Hide? Fight?

I still had one hand applying pressure to my head when Kade had pulled me back and behind him.

"Why didn't you scream for me?" His brows were tense as he slightly raised his voice; partly-confused, slash annoyed, partly-concerned.

I couldn't help but show my own confusion and slight

anger, not that he could see, his attention was on dire matters.

As the men moved their friend out of the way, Kade rushed to put me over the counter.

"Stay. There." He threatened with a shy accent but it's stronger than the last time I heard it.

The poor girls who worked at the bar ran into the back room. I could only pray they had enough sense to call the police and to stay there until they arrived.

Looking back to Kade, I watched in disbelief as he dodged *almost* every punch, kick, chair—anything that was being thrown at him—he hit them all back with tactical movements and snarky comments.

After processing that I was basically not helping and was some sort of damsel, I started to throw whatever I could at the overgrown children, not caring for the price of things.

Two of the men turned their attention to me, making my heart drop and speed up on its way down as one tried to come over the counter.

Before he made his land, I knocked him round the head with a full bottle of something. And it wasn't cheap, I knew that for sure. It was way too heavy and it didn't even break when I hit him with full force.

The second man—who I briefly forgot about— grabbed me from behind. I tried to wriggle out of his grip but it didn't work. He faced me towards the counter, ready to chuck me over, but before he could, I lifted my legs and kangaroo kicked, forcing him to fall back onto the wall.

He dropped me to the ground almost instantly, allowing me to scurry backwards as the first man stormed over to me, understandably more pissed than before. I kept my eyes on him as my hands frantically moved around, looking for something, *anything*, to defend myself with.

There was nothing for me to use and my back had already reached the other end of the bar. When he came close enough, I looked behind him as if someone was there (a last resort). When he gave into his stupid curiosity, I kicked his balls as hard as I could.

As I stood, I grabbed another bottle and swung at his head. His hands went from his balls to his head, allowing me to get another—precautionary—kick in.

Moving past him, I treated whatever I could like a step on a ladder (beer taps, the countertop, etc.) as every single bone in my body was shaking and not allowing me to be as fast as I needed to be.

Kade didn't hide the fact that he was shocked, probably even proud of the mess that I had made, and in that moment of distraction, he allowed himself to be open and took a few bad hits.

My breath hitched.

My mind blanked.

I moved towards him as quickly as I could, wanting to help but also not having any idea how.

As I was about to climb over to get involved, Kade started to *literally* break bones. My body froze at the sound of the first snap. I knew that look on his face. I've seen it before on others. The hard hits he had taken while being distracted had triggered him enough to take this brawl to another level.

The pace at which things were going began to slow down in my eyes as Kade's hits became more brutal. His eyes were set on the bulky man again, so focussed he didn't even realise someone approaching him from behind with a knife.

Being left with no choice and not caring for the consequences, I grabbed a broken bottle then completed my climb over the counter.

A million thoughts ran through my head on why I should and shouldn't do this but before the bottle went in deep, he dropped to the ground, uncovering Kade, who took notice of the shaking bloody weapon in my hand.

Whilst I stood, zoning in and out, I could feel his eyes going over my body countless times as if trying to figure out what to do. Somehow, my daze, my action, had pulled him out of his pissed one.

My mind was racing through this event, my ears continuously heard the quiet ripping of skin, and my fingers held onto the feeling of pushing the glass into skin. Our fault or not, we were going to jail. Every plan I had made for myself, gone. Just like that.

Slowly taking the bottle out from my hand, Kade tried to reassure by saying, '*it's okay, it's okay, you're okay*' as he rubbed the top of my arm.

The man on the floor started to gurgle what I assumed to be his own blood. I was about to give in to temptation and look, but Kade became a wall between us whilst turning me around to look the other way.

The men who could stand pulled out pocket knives, keys, broken bottles, chairs, anything they could get their hands on. And we were nowhere near the doors. So, I stuck my hand out, motioning for Kade to hand me back the broken bottle. I was *not* going to be someone who didn't even attempt to fight…even if I was internally pissing myself.

Kade loosely wrapped his hand around my forearm, letting out an out of breath—incredulous—laugh. "Now-now, Medisa."

Before anyone could make their move, he tightened his grasp and dragged me out the magical back door, where we ran through the streets until we reached the busy ones. We pushed through crowds of people, trying to get away, but I could still hear the men yell in frustration.

Stupidly, we made too many turns and took too many steps into quieter streets. This is where Kade decided that trashing one pub wasn't enough, we *had* to break into another.

The poor owners of this place probably closed early to go enjoy the lights and here Kade is, barricading their doors. I joined in of course, barricading doors happened to be something I've got some experience in.

"What if someone's in here?" I whispered, remembering a family lived on top of one in Eastenders.

Ignoring me, Kade grabbed a hold of my wrist and took me down to the basement, earning himself a few confused and slightly agitated comments before I finally yanked myself out of his grip.

Hissing in pain, Kade lost his balance. And I don't know what came over me—certainly not the strength for this task—but I tried to catch him, only to fall to the ground as well.

Wasting no time, I spotted where he'd gotten hurt and without thinking things through, I lifted his top to get a better view of the wound.

"Easy girl, I haven't got the energy right now." He teased through what sounded like his last breath. I would respond with '*I'm not a horse*' or something, but he's been deeply cut on his side, has multiple multi-coloured bruises—some close to the colour black—and his lip's cut.

'I was late? How was I late?'

Becoming frustrated with how slow I had moved, and because of it I got him hurt, I began to pace, ignoring the headache that chose the best time to return.

Having no phone, I couldn't call anyone and God knows

how eager those men would be to find us, they could go search the area all night if they wanted. Not to mention the mess we left behind. The police are definitely going to get involved, Bellamy might fire me, the University might drop me from the course, I might even have to go to prison for vandalising and breaking and entering.

"Relax, it's just a deep graze."

'Is this boy stupid or is he trying to be funny?'

His wound looked as if it could speak if it wanted to.

Not bothering to put my energy towards having a go at him, I continued to pace the space, getting somewhat faster with each new thought.

Kade pushed himself to stand, automatically calling me to his side.

"You don't just have my blood on you."

My eyes followed his to my hand, and before I saw how deep my own cut was, I shot my gaze elsewhere. My mind didn't need to be aware of that right now, but it was too late, my receptors awoke, shooting me with all types of pain at once.

"For flips sake." Now's not the time for my body to be acting up.

Material ripping made me jump. And when I turned, Kade is busy destroying his top until he had enough of it to act as a bandage.

The act of him grabbing me must've become the new norm because once again, I am pulled towards him. My hand is scanned, I willingly let him do this until he made the suggestion of pouring alcohol onto it. We're not in the wild for us to be using that as a last resource, there has to be a first aid kit somewhere here. That, and I don't want to feel the stinging burn just yet.

After bickering, *again*, I ended up snatching the DIY bandage to put it on myself all whilst screw facing him. The cow literally looked as if he'd been plucked out of a manga, especially right now. His hood loosely being over his beanie, his dirty asymmetric crop top exposing his muscles, blood and bruises splatted all over, plus the devilish look he's been throwing at me—all of it—his whole aura or whatever screamed '*not a real boy.*' As I got to his lower half of his outfit, I smacked my forehead.

"Oh my God! Kade where is your phone?" Before wasting any more time, I sped over and searched him.

Feeling the cool metal or whatever material it was, I thanked God and pulled it out. Once again, I am pacing, only this time with more hope as my fingers struggled with the numbers. Just as I was about to make the call, Kade received a message which I unintentionally read as soon as it came onto the screen.

'I'm waiting for you at our usual place Kas x'

I tried to swipe the message away but it opened the chat instead.

I stopped pacing.

There's a picture of him and a girl in bed above the new message. She's the one who sent and took the picture of him sleeping beside her and her name is *not* Kas. I wasn't supposed to look at the message, the picture, but now that I was, the contents in my stomach swirled. The boy in the picture has black tattoos, not white, slash skin coloured. They were similar if not the same as Kade's, and they wouldn't be a problem—Kade could have made them black—except for the fact that his hair is different and the date and time was literally the other day…where I saw Kade… At work… With white tattoos.

Turning my head to the 'Kade' that was with me, I felt as though my mind was making up changes to his body. It was like I was failing at 'spot the difference'…*If* there was a difference to the boy in front of me and the image I have of Kade in my mind.

He seemed to have known that I'd been exposed to new information, because right after my eyes tried to study him, his persona changed.

Watching him remove his beanie and fluff his hair as his posture began to change was like realising that you're trapped with a male you don't know, alone… Oh wait.

'Idiot.'

His messy hair was long enough for him to tie back and suddenly I put together why he wore the beanie in the first place.

'No, no, carry on complimenting his choice of clothes.'

He no longer stood over in pain, no, he stood upright with his hoodie hanging off one shoulder as he peeled off his gloves, revealing bruised knuckles and scarred-tattooed hands.

I examined his body with more detail as he peeled off fake skin from his arms, neck and abdomen, revealing more tattoos. Other than the additional ones here and there, he definitely had the black version of Kade's tattoos.

"You're not Kade." My close to emotionless realisation was paired with a pounding heart.

The male before me grinned whilst pouring a drink over his wound, as though his reveal wasn't extreme enough.

"No." The hybrid accent was back. "I'm Kassian Koda River. Kade's gorgeous twin brother." He walked towards me, parts of him exposed. "And you Medisa. You are my new friend."

He held my phone between us.

I didn't even have time to think about how he took it off me, I just took it out his hand and saw the cracked screen.

He sucked in air through his teeth. "Sorry about that. Got into a fight at the pub."

Not caring to address him, I switched my phone on, revealing several missed calls and text messages from Amana, Kade and Bellamy.

'What. The. Hell.'

My brain bought pieces I casually dismissed as a mistake or wardrobe malfunction, together. All the little flirts, forgetfulness and digs at religion, his eyes, his slim(er) face, his skin, the hats and his voice being slightly different, his *accent*.

"Oh my God." I pushed my head out towards him to inspect him some more. "Oh my God." I brought my hand to my mouth. "You've been with me multiple times now, haven't you?" I didn't wait for him to respond. "The hair near your nape is shorter than the rest, which means you've had your hair cut to look like Kade's, which means in the past you could've been with me or someone who knows Kade without having to wear a hat or hoodie." I started to feel clever but dumb all at the same time.

As I carried on my little epiphany moment, Kassian stared, all giddy, like a child that's finally being acknowledged and praised.

"Question is, why have you gotten so lazy with it? Why go back to calling me Desmona?—And yes, I picked up on that—Why even call me Desmona in the first place?" I finally shared my disapproval of the name.

He lowered himself so that our faces were somewhat level.

"Because you were never going to get your happy end-ing." Moving back to his normal stance, he breathed in through his teeth like he became uninterested. "I do have to say…I was worried that you were going to be all sizzle and no steak, but I think you've done enough to prove me wrong. You see, I didn't see the hype before, and I had to fight cer-tain urges when I was with you, but you've finally figured it out. Not everything of course, but it's still something so… congratulations." He sneered, slightly bowing his head, then went back to looking down at me with his head pushed back like he ain't already a stupid number of inches above me. "*Desmona*. I like it. It's short and has the same meaning." He spoke to himself.

"I didn't figure it out. You *wanted* me to find out today." I focused on him, brows pulled close, then asked with a low voice as though I were questioning myself. "Why?"

Kassian cocked his head to one side and his eyes fol-lowed the motion like he didn't already have an answer. When he looked back into my eyes, he clucked his tongue. "It's about time you knew, especially when things are going to get exciting."

"What are you talking about?"

He didn't respond, he just held his position, too amused for my liking. I wanted to beat him up, but I also wanted to ask more questions, but I didn't know him. He could snap any minute and I could be dead the next. He wasn't even giv-ing me any sort of clear answer anyways, so I had no choice but to walk away from this.

"I need to find Kade—" I walked around him quicker than I wanted. Part of me did not trust him to be behind me, another part wanted to walk slower, just in case he was will-ing to say more.

"And ask him some questions? Let me ask you this Desmona." He paused long enough for me to stop walking. "What makes you think he'll tell you the truth?"

Chapter 7

Medisa

17/12/2021 (Friday)

"He has a twin brother…with an accent?"

"Yeah."

"He has…a twin brother…with an accent." Amana repeated as less than a question and more of a statement she was trying to convince herself of. Her right leg shook up and down so fast it looked like it was vibrating.

"Yeah." I replied, again. "I thought that he was doing a bit when I first heard it. Almost gave me an ick."

Amana noticed me waiting for her to say something (or laugh) then pulled herself together. "Okay." She cleared her throat. "*So*, he has an evil twin brother with an accent." She spoke as if she was trying to justify Kade's attempt to hide his other half.

"It's Scottish or Irish or something, but it blends with the British accent. Also, he calls me *Desmona*. Do you know what Desmona means Amana?" I waited for her guess but she just shook her head. "It means Unlucky! I Googled it!" My words rushed out. "And before that he called me Des-de-mona or some shit, do you know what *that* means?" I looked to her again and got the same response. "It means ill-fated or unfortunate."

"Well, that's unfortunate."

I let out a dry-not so humoured laugh. "*Ha*, you're not funny."

Amana's smile widened then dropped when she spoke.

"No but seriously, what the hell does that mean? You need to start praying or something, what if he does black magic on you?"

"He's gora. I don't think it would affect me."

"If he can summon a jinn, he can summon a jinn."

"True, but this isn't like that. I don't think his *quarrel* is with me."

'Love the use of updated vocabulary.'

I shake my head. We were drifting away from the main reason of me being here, in her house. "I'm telling you because you need to look out for him. Not be on the hunt for him, obviously, but to know if you're talking to him or to Kade."

"Okay, tell me more." Her leg hadn't stopped vibrating.

"They're twins, but they have their differences, like their eye colours. Kade has these darkish bluey-grey eyes with dark and light brown flecks surrounding his pupil. He also has a light but dark outline stopping the colour from leaking into the whites of his eye. And then Kassian's eyes are more bluey-green but dark bluey green, with yellowy, gold flecks near his pupil…Oh and I think like Kade, he has a dark outline too." As I tried to explain I became disappointed in my inability to describe eyes, or anything in general really, and it showed on both mine and Amana's face.

"I love that." She created one single clap to go with her sarcasm. "Do they have any other colours in the spectrum that you're missing?" Her lashes fluttered.

I whacked her with her own pillow, then proceeded.

"Kassian has curlier hair. Kade has curls too but Kassian's ones are more formed." I looked away to try and visualise the both of them. "To get the real differences—other than the tattoos and eyes—I need them to be next to one another for me to be able to point it out."

'*Duh.*'

"What else do you know?" Amana pushed for more.

"I think his skin colours different. He may be slightly darker than Kade. Oh, and his middle name is Koda and his last is River. How cool does that sound? '*Meet The Rivers*'." I glanced over at Amana who agreed with it being cool, then she added to the cinematic feel of their family name.

"Where are they from?"

"I think that they're mixed, I'm pretty sure that I overheard Kade speak Spanish one time—"

"Medisa, people don't have to be Hispanic to speak Spanish you know, also River or Rivers—whatever it is doesn't sound like it would be from—"

"I know I know, it's weird, but I literally have nothing on them, when I hang out with Kade we don't deep dive into each other's personal lives like that. We hint at certain things but other than that, we just have fun or teach each other new things or talk about the future, or movies…you know?"

I was useless.

There was nothing in my memories that was useful, nothing. Maybe a hint or two as to what they're like, but other than that, nothing.

"Why do you think that he's trying to hide his family?" To be fair, I would hide my family too, but that just makes things worse because that means that he is also related to cows.

Amana sat silently like she was wondering the same thing. "I don't know but I don't think that you should get involved."

Already being intrigued enough to come up with theories, I put her caution to the side. "What if he's hiding *from* his family? Think about it. Kassian made sure that none of us figured out that he was here. He took my phone to prevent me from prematurely finding out—and before when I've been with him, it was random, on days that I now know that Kade had off."

"So, you were with Kade three out of the seven days of the week and then occasionally was with '*Kade*' on a fourth day—and you didn't realise that something was off?" I could tell that she was a little frustrated and thought I was an idiot...I thought the same.

"In my defence I've never been this exhausted in my life and he had really good excuses for his behaviour *and* we didn't hang out all the time." I held my hands up as if to surrender then reminisced the first time I'm sure I met Kassian.

"Do you remember the day when *Kade*." I made bunny ears for his name. "Showed up to Uni out of the blue, drunk? That was Kassian the sly bastard—Do you remember? He must've thought that no one would approach him because he wasn't really trying to draw attention to himself. But then *I* approached him, and lucky for him, he was covered up enough for him to just go with it—And then he made me promise not to bring the situation up again, covering his bloody tracks."

Now that I think about it, how did Kassian know my name that day if that was the first time we met? And why did he choose to see me yesterday? Why not take me out on a day where Kade wouldn't notice that I was missing? What's changed over the past two months?

"I don't remember seeing him drunk but I remember you telling me that he was. You guys took the train?"

"Yeah, that day! I'm sure that was the first time we met." I jumped up a little in my seat then went back to slouching.

"What if *Kade* is the evil one?" Amana's tone was much lower and calmer than mine, a passer-by (a family member of hers) wouldn't think that we were talking about the same thing.

"Wait Kade-Kade or *Kade*-Kade?"

"Kade-Kade you idiot." She laughed like a maniac then rubbed her forehead like this was all stressing her out for longer than it had been.

"I thought you were good friends with him and knew that he was a good person—which is why you got him to give me a job?"

I didn't mean for it to, nor did I expect it, but tension grew in the air. It's annoying when our conversations turned like this, I hated it. It's like walking on eggshells, but instead of eggshells, it's bombs. It only ever got like this with miscommunication, and right now I couldn't figure out who was more in the dark.

"I don't know him *that* well. He could easily be hiding his true self."

"Nice…you basically put me in the den." I joked to ease the tension up a little. I expected her to throw something at me and tell me to shut up, but she just looked like she regretted her decision of getting me a job. "I'm kiddinggg. I'm sure we're blowing this whole thing out of proportion. What's a gora going to do anyways?"

Amana stayed quiet then spoke without humour. "I don't think that we should treat this as a joke, you should stay out of it—quit even—they clearly have money and some power which means they would probably have great influence. Someone like you would be easy to swipe under the rug—no offence."

"None taken. You're right. I didn't sign up to be collateral damage in whatever this is, but we need the money and if I decide to stay for it then I need to know what I'm getting into. And the only way we're going to know the truth is if I ask Kade."

"Or Kassian." Amana whispered so quietly I thought I'd imagined her saying his name. I even stared at her lips a little longer as if she were going to repeat herself. "Swear to God that you'll leave if things get worse. You don't even need to get money from them, I'll work extra hours to make up for the loss until you find another place."

"If it gets too much, I don't think I would have a choice to leave."

'I probably should've kept that to myself...' I thought *after* projecting my thoughts.

Amana looked distressed. I've only ever seen her like this during exam season, or when I've been seriously hurt.

"OR we could just ignore the whole thing and let them find brotherly love again by themselves." I mentally made a Dua for protection against my growing curiosity.

"I know that you're still curious, I am too."

'Ah, she got me.'

"But remember, you're one person, and there's two of them, maybe even more *and* with way more power and influence, so I really do think that you should take your last pay and leave."

I heard what she was saying, I did, but curiosity had already gotten its grip on me. I'm mature enough to admit that I don't just want to stay for the money anymore. But Amana's mind would run on stress and I'm experienced enough to know that it wouldn't stop unless I put this all to rest.

"I'll pray Istikhara then go from there."

"C'mon then." She got up, handing me a towel. "You're

doing Wudu first."

I smiled then made my way to her bathroom. She's not going to let me leave the house until I'd prayed and thought this over and I loved that, for more than one reason.

Praying with her wasn't strange but how quickly she's trying to dismiss and move away from Kade and Kassian was. I thought she would find the situation so cool and movie, slash book-like but her reactions are a little far from it. Understandably so too if I'm honest, but still surprising.

On my way to the bathroom, I thought about my last encounter with Kassian. What was it he said? *'You just might be able to work this all out.'* Maybe he's right, and I don't need to involve Amana as much as I thought. It would just add unnecessary stress onto her already demanding life. I'll just tell her everything after the matter. How likely is it that this thing would be bigger than we thought anyways?

Chapter 8

Medisa

17/12/2021 (Friday)

The weather was nice. Cold with little wind and some sun poking through here and there. The perfect weather to layer up and explore London. I took the longer route to work thinking about how I should tell Kade about Kassian. I'm sure it would do me more good than bad if I just told him what's been going on, but there's still that other side of the coin that I needed to consider. What if it does more bad than good?

I looked to my left to see frost being over a passageway untouched by the sun, people and any sort of animal. The unscathed frost lured me in, I wondered if I could get to the other side without ruining it or if I would try but somehow slip and fall to be ruined *by* it. Knowing my clumsy arse, I would hurt myself and ruin the path for anyone else. Instead of it being cute footsteps to the other side, it would be some footsteps, skid marks and an arse print (and a small one at that). Never minding the consequences of my actions, I walked through anyways, not knowing where it would lead as I still didn't know the area as well as I had hoped. I slipped a little here and there but came out on the other end okay, if being okay meant being a little traumatised by the near falls.

I walked into my office and found the back of someone

who looked a lot like Kade. I tried to read more of his body language but it didn't work, he seemed to be relaxed but also on edge all at the same time. His body was leaning against the desk and his hands gripped onto the edge on either side of him, holding what I assumed was most of his weight.

"Bell, please not now." He sounded exhausted.

"It's not Bellamy, it's me."

He turned to view me as he got up, and I smiled a smile that didn't reach my eyes. As he walked towards me saying my name, I studied him—his body—the way he walked, spoke, his eyes, his knuckles but I couldn't find anything indicating that he was Kassian. Kade must've spotted my eyes dancing because then it looked like he was analysing me for himself.

"What happened? We had plans and you never answered your phone. I asked Amana and at first, she was worried but now it feels like she's avoiding me." He lowered his voice and looked into my eyes and I swear I could see every fleck that made up his.

"What happened to your hand?" Kade's gentle, soothing voice made me feel as though it was something I needed my entire life. I just hadn't realised it until now.

As I switched between which eye of his to look into, I thought about what to do. I couldn't pray at Amana's house because I had started my period and even though we prayed for me to make the right decision, I still felt lost.

Kade's expression went from worrying to a hint of something else, like he knew I was struggling to be out with it. I had to say something but I didn't know how, so I did what I thought was best, I got straight to the point.

"I met Kassian."

I studied his face (again) and took note of his jawline

sharpening, his muscles protruding, his body as a whole becoming stiff as he fixed his worried posture.

Looking down at my hand then back up to my eyes, he gave the impression that he could kill me on spot. Taking a deep breath in, he waited. I knew he was waiting for some sort of explanation but the dominant look he held got more out of me inside than Kassian revealing himself.

"He-he didn't do this."

Kade lowered his head with no look of interest in his eyes. Whilst he inched himself towards me, as though to get a good look into my soul, I slowly backed up and held up my injured right hand with my left.

"This was me. I was trying to defend him—*us*!" I realised I was somehow making it worse so I closed my eyes for a quick second, pursing my lips to try and control my breaths. "I was trying to defend us and I didn't realise the spikey lid was halfway on, so when I hit the guy with it, it cut me."

I didn't think that it was possible, but Kade looked more pissed than before, but by some miracle, he remained calm. Not that this helped, his reaction made my legs feel a lot like noodles and I think I'd rather him shout or something, to make this easier than it is.

"Can you please sit or say something because I'm starting to feel myself shake and struggle to breathe." My hand quivered over my throat and I couldn't tell if my words were coming out shaky or if it just felt like that. I didn't know why my body was panicking, I'm mentally fine.

'Yeah, okay.'

Kade snapped out of whatever he was thinking, took note of my breathing then once again looked to my injury, then eyes. Turning around, as if to leave, he walked towards my desk chair and sat down. Other than the noticeable level that we were now at (him sitting, me standing) nothing else changed. His body remained tense *and* he went back to holding my eyes hostage with his, all whilst having a calm killer look.

'Am I— am I attracted to this?'

Turning to my side so that I didn't really have to face him, I began to pace as I explained what had happened in more detail, making as little eye contact as possible.

During bits of my update, Kade's hand went from holding his face and rubbing his jawline to then creating one giant fist by interlocking his knuckles.

Once I was done talking, Kade sauntered over to me, pushing my breaths to be manually taken slowly.

"Sit down."

For once I did as I was told, I didn't even think about disagreeing.

Once I sat, he turned me—the chair—to the wall, then he walked over to lean against it.

Taking a deep breath as if he didn't want to do this, he spoke. "I am Kade River." He paused for a millisecond. "And I come from a long line of influential people."

The way he straightened himself out as well as let himself go, both looked and sounded like he hadn't said his name in a long time. Also, *'influential'* is just another word for powerful.

"Things were supposed to be different for my brother and I, but things changed. I can't tell you everything, but just know me and Kassian aren't on good terms, we haven't been for years."

I didn't respond, I didn't know how to. I had questions, a lot of them, but I also knew from Kade's reaction to Kassian's name that an old wound that hadn't healed had been picked at.

'Should I even be trusting Kade?

I obviously didn't know anything and if I wanted to get anywhere, I would have to lay most—if not all my cards out on the table and trust that a friend is standing in front of me.

"Honestly…I'm so confused. From this interaction *alone* I have so many questions. And I understand you not wanting to tell me everything, I do, but Kassian said that there's more to come. So, if there's anything that I should know, just tell me now so that I'm prepared." Not liking how desperate I sounded I tried to joke a little. "There's not another one of you is there? A triplet scenario?"

I quickly regretted the attempt after seeing Kade's face.

Kade pushed himself off the wall and took steps towards me, furthering my regret. "Do not trust Kassian. I will find out his reason for being here. You just need to go home and rest. Stay away from work for a week—"

Before I could say anything, he shut it down.

"—I'll cover for you."

He walked me to the elevator then gave way for me to leave. I stepped in, contemplating on whether or not I should speak my mind.

'Screw it.'

"Why would Kassian show up out of the blue to mess with me and you over something that you don't even know about? It doesn't make sense." I asked before the doors shut.

I knew my words implied that Kade's lying to me or hiding more than he needs to, but I didn't care. We couldn't progress if he thought that I was dumb.

Kade aggressively stopped the doors from closing, making me jump out of my skin.

He searched my eyes with such intensity I felt as though

he also had a hidden psychopathic entity sharing his body.

"The River's love games Medisa. If there's money involved, it's good. People involved? Better. Blood, twists and turns? Then it's great. The more the merrier. But it's only seen as a game because we know that we will win. So don't be fooled, the game is rigged." He held a nonchalant expression as his arm held the door open.

When he finally let go, allowing the doors to shut, I could still hear his words like it had been engraved onto my brain.

'Rivers—plural—Kade included.'

Chapter 9

Medisa

17/12/2021 (Friday)

I've had exactly three or four hours to go over what both brothers had said and I still don't know how to outwardly (even internally) react or feel. I mean, I know that some parts of me (the majority) is excited and curious and wants to see where this goes. But the small part was tired and was asking *'can I really be asked for this?'*

Maybe being curious is the normal reaction towards this, but at the same time I feel like it would also be mixed with a little uneasiness, possibly even the feeling of being scared, but I'm not feeling those. It feels a little too early for those emotions.

From what has come to the light so far, I'm actually okay. If being okay meant me thinking of about a thousand possibilities of what's actually going on. The whole situation played in my head again and again, from the first time I met the brothers till the last thing Kade had said today.

During certain recollections I had to remind myself to breathe, but other than that, it's still not clicking that this might actually be more than I could handle. I still felt like staying and finding out more and I just know it's partly because I wanted that thrill, that feeling of being some sort of main character and have things happen around me that's not the same old abusive family story. It sounds stupid and reckless, selfish even, but I'm so bored of my life—minus anything to do with Amana—everything has just been the same repetitive cycle and besides…How bad can a brotherly feud be? It can't be as damaging as anything I've lived through. Anyways, other than my selfish reasons of wanting to see where this goes, I also want to help out a friend. So, if there's anything I could do to help, to at least ease Kade's mind a little, I'm doing it.

As I turned into the wavy road that led to my house, I thought about Kade's control over his emotions. Anyone could tell he was keeping his feelings at bay, and it kind of made me feel normal watching someone else go through that. Fighting for control over anger or sorrow is something I continue to struggle with. It's gotten better for sure but damn, it's not a piece of cake. I'm just grateful I'm not some moping robot anymore (thank you Amana). Someone definitely helped Kade too and it was definitely Bellamy, or on an off chance, he somehow managed to help himself. Either way, Kades been through shit. I hoped so anyways. In the nicest way possible, I really hoped this was over something that was actually deep and not some sort of *'you stole my girl when I was sixteen'* type of thing. Because, One: get a grip and Two:seriously? I might just have to invite them to mines for the weekend to show them some real drama.

It's weird walking down my road at this time after a few months of coming home late. It would be even weirder if I didn't get into some sort of argument today. Being at the house early, means more hours at home, ergo, more chances of triggering certain beings.

As I came closer to the house, I noticed the lack of cars parked up front—minus some van—which meant no one was home to let me in. The closer I got, the more the trimmed bushes were out the way, allowing me to see a man waiting at the door. By the looks of what he was wearing I would say that he was some sort of delivery man. His positioning was statue like, as if company policy was to stay still until some-one opened the door.

Once I passed the knee length wall that marked our drive, I saw the black box he held. It looked like a gift box with its dark beige ribbon and bow.

"Hi."

He turned around.

"You didn't have to wait, our neighbours usually take our parcels for us when we're not here." I approached.

The guy was young and sweating, and it's not even that hot out.

"It's fine miss, I was waiting for you."

"Me? I didn't order anything." As I spoke, he passed the package and waited for me to open it, so I hesitantly did.

The top of the box had loosely put tissue paper and be-neath that was a bunch of shredded packaging paper. What-ever was inside was heavy, and since the wind was whistling, I decided against pulling it out, especially since the packag-ing would make a mess on the drive. Instead of using my eyes to see what it was, I used my hand to get a good feel of the thing. After a few seconds of nothing coming to mind as to what it could be, I pulled my hand out so fast it made the poor boy jump.

"I can't leave until you've read the card."

"What car—"

He held out an envelope whilst my lips were pulled in to form a thin straight line. I was going to ask why he couldn't have just given me the card in the first place, but I kept my mouth shut as the boy looked nervous.

The little envelope was fancy and was sealed with hot wax. The red wax was decorated with a 'R' and intricate patterns surrounding it.

"I've always wanted to send one of these." I showed the boy the detail as if he hadn't been holding on to it for God knows how long.

The boy gave a nervous smile, reminding me that for some reason me not reading the card was basically holding him hostage. An audacious smile grew on my face in return. I kind of liked the idea of that, but now's not the time to force someone to be my friend, there was something weird going on.

'The rings combined can set you free, don't go too far you belong to me. It won't be hard to find you Medisa.'

I laughed but in a *'this is embarrassing'* type of way. "This sounds like something that chocolate man who kills kids would write. Cringey ass—" Before I could finish my well-suited reaction with a bad American accent, the boy walked away as quickly as he could. I tried to go after him but the double front doors inside opened. Before looking to see who it was, and before they opened the front door that would let me in, I tried my best to hide the box under my belongings.

"How comes you're home early?"

Ignoring Ayaan, I picked my things up with the box in the middle, then carried them as if it were a beach ball. A weighted beach ball.

"Hellooo?" Ayaan sang, already getting frustrated.

"I was given a break." As I tried to walk past him, my jacket moved out of place, revealing a part of the box. In an attempt to move it out of his sight, I ended up making my motive clear.

"What's in the box?"

Clearly being sick of my behaviour, he reached for it,

starting a game of tug of war, which he would obviously win. We both had our arms wrapped round its exterior in between the two double front doors.

"Who's it from? Who's it for?" Each question came with a small tug that increased in power.

"Oh, Medisa you got my gift thank God!" Amana's voice is instantly recognised. I wanted to drop to the floor because of the intensity of the relief I felt, but I stayed standing strong. Now that she's here, he wouldn't do anything to me, or the package.

"<u>Peace be upon you</u>."

"<u>And upon you be peace.</u>" Me and Ayaan spoke in unison.

Ayaan went back inside and before anything else happened, I quickly adjusted then guided Amana down the road to the park. It's way past school break so no kids should be in it, making it the perfect place to properly open the box and to update Amana.

"I could kiss you a million times to match the million things you've done for me!"

"Go on then."

I watched to see if she was being serious, ready to pounce if she were—I wasn't going to tap out first.

We shared a look without turning our heads, creepy smiles growing before Amana pushed the conversation forward— I would say this was her tapping out.

"So, what's in the box?" She raised a brow with an attempt at a serious look.

"Wait, you update me first and then when we've reached the jungle gym, I'll update you, then we can open this together, agreed?"

"Agreed."

Amana's been working at this hotel in St. Pancras for a few weeks now and from the sounds of it, she's enjoying it more than any other of her past jobs. When she doesn't work, she dedicates her time to her siblings. Ever since she started earning (it's been years now), they've all been experiencing things me and Amana couldn't at their ages, which is cute to witness, and almost healing.

Seeing them all grow and become wiser was cool, especially since they were slowly taking away chunks of stress that had been on Amana's shoulders. But I had a problem that was growing over time. The relationship between Amana and her siblings was something that had changed. She didn't need to bring it up for me to know, I could see it. I've witnessed it.

Since they were no longer considered to be children and were out of their argumentative stages, Amana's able to talk to them as if they were friends, which made things even easier for her, as who is better to talk and hang out with, than those who have experienced, slash witnessed what you have been through.

Sometimes I got jealous, not of the relationship they have with one another, but the fact that it felt like she was being taken away. When we had been pushing each other to develop proper relationships with our siblings, I didn't mean for her to go as far as replacing me. Now—sometimes— I just wanted her to myself, to be my friend, to go out with me, to share things with me, to talk and laugh and mess around with me (like we used to). To just be *my* sister. Thankfully I'm not demented enough to actually want to take her away from them, even if my access to her felt like it was thinning. In theory I understood that family comes first, I just didn't consider (ignored) that I wasn't actually Amana's family.

Over the past couple of months, I'd decided to not hold onto Amana as much as I did. It's been made easier now since I work too, and it's not like we needed to be glued to each other in order to survive. We just enjoyed each other's company more than anyone else's, and we understood each other, and we always had each other's best interest in mind, and we gave each other enough space to grow and breathe. Basically, I only just realised how attached I actually am to the girl and it scares me, but not as much as the thought of her leaving me does.

Amana says that she wants to run and travel the world, but I know deep down her mind will always be on her family. I also know that if she doesn't choose to leave, her mind would always think of *'what could've been'*. And, I don't want to be someone like her actual sisters, where she feels obligated to help, slash be there for. If she leaves with me, the decision needs to be her own, without influence and I needed to be ready for her to say that she will not be coming.

When it was my turn to talk, I ended up telling Amana everything about the boys even though I mentally decided not to get her involved anymore. I told her every little thing I could remember, including how I was feeling, how the space around me looked, the change in the air, everything. In return she gave me her attentive ear and animated responses.

Once I was done, we sat together in silence with the occasional *'wow, oh my God,'* from Amana and *'I know,'* from me.

"Good thing you told me you got sent home. Imagine if I didn't walk past your house and Ayaan got involved."

"I know. He would've done more than just blow it all out

of proportion, he would've forced me to quit."

"Did anyone say anything about a box?" She ignored my attempt of continuing to make things light-hearted.

I frowned, shook my head, looked at the box again, then let out a frustrated sigh as I aggressively unboxed and dug into the package.

"You made me jump ya bitch."

"It-it it's like a…" I pulled my hand out for the second time, this time slower, my thumb and fingers slowly rubbing against each other. "A hand?" I watched Amana who looked as though she was still trying to process what I had just said. Then, almost like we had timed it, we both began to carefully clear the box of its packaging.

No jump scares this time.

Sitting on either side of the box we stared at its contents.

"What the fu—"

"Don't swear." I reminded.

"What the hell. What the hell. What the hell." Each time Amana repeated herself she got louder, and despite the fact she'd stopped herself from swearing, my brain translated her words to what she had originally wanted.

"Medisa, what the *hell* is that?" She spoke much quieter but with anger, like she was demanding an answer.

"I think it's a skeleton hand. A male one." I took the piss because that's what it obviously was. The structure, slash thickness of the bones were masculine looking. For the tiniest split second, millisecond, or whatever the hell, I thought about how someone would think that my skeleton hands belonged to a small male. I even glanced over to Amana's hands, hers were nice and model like, <u>may God bless her.</u>

After close inspection—literally just bringing it closer to my eyes and rotating it so that I could see under it too—I decided to give my 'professional' opinion.

"It's real."

"<u>Indeed, we belong to God and to Him we shall return.</u>" Amana spoke with an expression that was somewhere in between shock and nonchalant.

"He might not be dead." I watched Amana to see if she agreed, but her face held no hope for the person missing his hand.

"Oh yes, the man woke up one day and decided to send you his *hand*." Amanas sarcastic coping mechanism made an appearance. "Do you know whose it is?"

"Oh yeah, of course I do. Don't you know? It's the new thing now a days to send a piece of yourself to someone." I hit her back with the same tone.

Clearly, we didn't expect this to be in the box and we're obviously trying to handle it the best way we could, especially since it took whatever was going on to the next level. But damn, we're actually taking this pretty well, I'm proud. <u>Thank God</u> we're not the scream type of girls, not that that would've looked suspicious. Two young looking girls in a park with a large gift box and some screams shared between them.

Not suspicious at all.

'Mother-figure Medisa' makes an appearance before Amana is left too long with her thoughts. "I'm kidding about it being real by the way—"

'*I am not.*'

"—It looks so fake—"

'*It does not.*'

"—Whoever made it, obviously tried making it look as real as possible."

'*It's definitely real.*'

Amana's expression calmed down a little, but I couldn't tell if she was buying my lies. So, I went back to scanning the hand. It was attached to some sort of heavy open display thing, as though it were an art piece. The actual bones themselves were clean (minus the designs). Whoever had sent it, cleaned it up and added whatever those marks were, so they obviously were in no rush to get rid of it—*if* of course this was a real human hand. That's my 'expert' opinion anyways.

"My best guess is that it's supposed to be the man from the pub. I recognise the rings." I flicked one of the rings then stopped its rotations prematurely.

"And the engraved designs?"

I looked over the hand once more, there were engravements all over the bones.

"I don't know, they kind of look like some of Kade's tattoos. Smoke, thorn filled stems, random swirls. Could just be a fat coincidence."

'Amana's not that dumb.'

Carefully placing the heavy display back into the box, Amana grabbed as much packaging paper as she could to cover it up. Before she managed to shut the box for what I suspected was supposed to be the last time, I mentioned the note again.

"Ahh beach don't look at me, this is your hand now. I'm not digging in there again."

We both let out light nervous laughs (we breathed out heavily through our noses).

"It's not in the box, it's in my pocket. I read it in front of the postman." I pulled out the slightly bent envelope from my jacket pocket.

"Oh. What does it say?"

Clearing my throat, I read the card out loud for Amana,

despite a loud voice telling me not to. "'*The rings combined can set you free, don't go too far you belong to me. It won't be hard to find you Medisa.'* Some sick cringey ass note—"

"Medisa, I don't think this is something for us to geek out over or make fun of anymore. You need to tell someone—anyone—the police. Someone that would actually help—.'"

"What? No. I don't think it's that simple."

"Medisa this isn't a joke. It's your life! You literally got sent a skeleton hand! A skeleton hand that's dressed in the same rings that the man who assaulted you wore! And if you think I'm going to let you be stubborn, you better think otherwise. I will knock your arse out and fix it myself and you know that I would, and that I wouldn't feel nowhere near bad!" She shouted quietly using her concerned mum, slash older sister-friend voice, so that any passer-by couldn't hear.

It went so quiet you could hear everything in the distance, the kids in school, the noises from houses nearby and the wind starting to whistle again. I thought she would make jokes with me, saying how I got someone rich after me like some movie, but no, she jumped straight to being serious.

"I know where you're coming from, I would be the same if it was you in my position. But Kassian obviously knows where I live, he literally wrote that he can find me if I run." I thought about it and, how did he know? Only Kade knew where I lived and that was because he dropped me home that one time… did we get stalked? "What makes you think that he won't know if I go to the police? The River's like blood remember? Or whatever the hell he said—point is, what if this is a test and if I run or report this, I fail, then the next thing I'm sent is your body—or tongue." I spoke as calmly as I could whilst trying to read Amana. I didn't mean to make it sound serious to the point where her specific life was in danger. It kind of just came out, like I was piecing it together myself as I spoke out loud. "Let me think about this properly, maybe even bring it up to Kade?"

I waited for her response.

"Fine, but promise me—no—swear to *God* that you will leave, take everything that you have and leave. I'll find you another job somewhere else." Amana's eyes glistened more than usual before she blinked back to looking dead serious.

Her eyes caught me off guard. We weren't that kind of emotional. It took a lot for us to react to things emotionally, yet here she was, her eyes glossing up at the thought of me getting hurt.

"I would, but I don't want to come back and find out that you've been calling someone else '*Wifey*,' or any other nick-name that only a best friend, slash trauma partner achieves." I tried to lift the mood even when I was serious behind those words.

When her shoulders dropped and she let out an '*I can't believe you said that in this situation*' type of breathy laugh, I took it as a sign to reassure her.

"I know that it's serious and is stressing you out. But let me find the best way to go about this, and then I swear I'll leave. I have a feeling I only have one chance and if I mess that up, I'm screwed."

Amana ended up excepting defeat, she knew that we would run in circles if she argued some more because if it was the other way round, she would be the same as me.

After a few hours of going down memory lane with the box between us, I ended our day in the park by making Amana swear that she wouldn't come to me anymore. She had to separate herself to not be associated with me. Maybe even talk crap on my name so that it's clear we're now enemies or something. We changed each other's names on our phones and could only physically contact each other when we *really* needed the other, or when we've found a safe way to communicate.

Once Amana left, I walked to the part of the park that's filled with trees and bushes, where no one was around to be a witness to what I was about to do.

I used the lid of the box to dig. I could only get about two-three feet into the ground—I guessed—before getting tired and cold. I placed the once neatly wrapped box into the ground and started to bury it.

It's sad that it has to be buried. It looked cool, but what else could I do? Put it on display for the world to see?

Before leaving, I grabbed some dead sticks and leaves and dropped them on the obvious burial site and surrounding area to cover up the box some more.

"May another bush or tree grow here, Ameen." I made a desperate dua a bit too loud then looked around to see if anyone was passing by.

Making my way back to my family's house, I held the note which was really more of a card, and reread the message again and again, gently gliding my finger over the embossed 'R'.

My mind went back to the hand.

What if the man really was dead and his wife and kids— his mum—his dog or cat, are waiting for him to come back home. I would even feel sorry if he left a bloody fish behind.

"Ugh, for flips sake Medisa. He might be alive."

I conjured up more questions than theories, so much

more that when I arrived at the house I went straight to bed
and tried to sleep off the physical and mental exhaustion.

Chapter 10

Medisa

18/12/2021 (Saturday)

Waking up from what was supposed to be a nap, I could hear my lovely siblings talk about me. It's evident that yet again, they're bothered about something. I could tell that much since I could hear them from bed, when from the sounds of it, they're in the kitchen…downstairs.

"She got some box delivered to her today. I was in the loft showering so I didn't get to the door in time to get it. Amana came and said that it was a gift from her but when Medisa got home, she wasn't holding anything."

"Forget that, you should see her wardrobe, she has things in there I would never be allowed to wear—"

I mentally shut them out, they weren't allowed to add to today. Their conversation was about two different things and didn't make sense together anyway. Unless the topic was, *'What about Medisa has been pissing you off recently?'* Then it would make sense, and I would go downstairs to add to it.

Creating a snow angel in bed in attempts to locate my phone, turned into embodying a submarine's periscope when my leg swiped my phone onto the floor. My hands were used as support as my head slowly scoped the ground with the little light provided through the slits of the slightly opened bedroom door. My phone ended up lighting up at the perfect time, allowing me to see where it was. Grabbing it with my right hand, I used my left to push my body off the floor and back into bed.

'Heh low key I'm fit.'

In the process of hyping myself up, I checked the time.

'00:00'

I cussed myself out for missing some prayers—which I'm actually doing well in keeping on top of—then remembered I started my period today at Amana's. Through squinted eyes I looked around for my water bottle.

"Whatchu looking for?"

I almost jumped out of my skin as my head snapped in the direction of the voice.

Kassian sat on the trunk opposite my bed, against the wall. His right ankle over his left knee and whilst his elbow rested on the raised knee, his hand supported his chin.

I quietly (but quickly) jumped off my bed and charged at him.

"What the hell are you doing here!? You can't be in here! If you're caught, we're literally going to die!" I whispered, trying my best not to raise the volume with the clear anger and confusion I was experiencing. If I could hear my siblings from up here, they would be able to hear us.

"How's the hand?" He spoke too amused for my liking, clearly not caring about the repercussions of him being in my room.

"You need to get out *now*. I'm not joking if they—"

"I'm going to assume you told Kade about me." He continued to ignore me and before any of us could continue, Ataya walked in, flicking the lights on.

My stomach dropped.

Of course she had to come in now. Not only is she a snitch (an exaggerator, a liar, a cow etc.) but her voice is permanently on loudspeaker and there would be no reasoning with her. Ataya reached our shared queen bed and just as she was about to get in, she spots me and Kassian.

Two were frozen, one was entertained.

I unintentionally looked into the mirror behind Ataya—above our bed—and got a glance at myself.

'What the heck is on my face?'

I get a good look at Kassian now, with the lights on. His lips, mouth area in general, had smudged tints of red on them.

My eyes travelled to the body sized mirror besides him.

Our lips and surrounding areas looked the same.

I turned back to Ataya with a certain tightness in my throat. I knew how it looked but it wasn't true. The urge to knock the both of them out to just sit and get some quiet for me to work this all out was strong, but time moved too fast and didn't stop for no one. Before I could do or say anything she ran out the room, snapping me back to reality. No matter how much I wanted to kill Kassian, I didn't turn back to him. I just ran down the stairs after Ataya.

Who ran to Ayaan.

"Medisa was in our room kissing a grown-arse boy in the dark! Look at her face! She's wearing lipstick and everything! It's all over their faces!" She ran through her words before I could get to her or cut in. She didn't need to say all of that either, Ayaan was already triggered by the first sentence.

He pushed past me to get to the room until Ataya casually added, "He's probably not there anymore, if he had a brain he would've left through the window."

I turned to her whilst breathing heavy.

"Shut up Ataya! That's not what happened! We weren't kissing! He—" I stopped myself, I couldn't get Kassian into trouble. He may not be my friend, he may have framed me for something I didn't do, but I needed him, and getting on his bad side was not going to help anyone.

Ayaan came at me fast.

He lowered his head so that his forehead pushed down on mine. The weight forced me back, hurting my neck as I struggled to do something. Pushing my head forward was useless against his strength and pulling back was the same as he was practically stuck to my forehead, following me down as he pushed harder.

"She's lying, none of that happened!" I pushed against his head with as much force as I could. And despite his strength being able to completely demolish mine, he moved back, breathing heavy like he were charging himself up.

"Then why is there lipstick on your face! *Why* does what you look like match what she's saying!" He gave little weighted pushes, not enough to drop me, but enough to make me stumble back.

"You're acting like I couldn't have put it on before I went to sleep!"

It felt like my heart was everywhere but where it was supposed to be. I could even hear the damn thing as my eyes got watery. It wasn't out of sadness, but anger, confusion and embarrassment. Kassian could be hearing all of this.

Ayaan grabbed onto my arms and pulled me in closer. "You. Don't. Wear. Lipstick." He pushed me away, offended, like he couldn't believe that I was making up such lies. And I don't know if I had given up or if I genuinely did lose my footing, but I ended up falling onto the floor after he had let go.

"How dumb can you be?" I didn't shout, I didn't rush through my words. I just spoke. I spoke so that they could both hear and understand.

My brain had already put together that I could lie some more. Ayaan didn't go upstairs to check if there was a boy.

Kassian hadn't come down, so I could only assume that he left.

I could lie and it would be okay.

"What?" Ayaan was pissed, but still managed to let another emotion come through; disbelief, all whilst Ataya stood watch in the same shocked state.

"How *dumb* can you be?" I said louder, almost laughing the words out as I got off the ground, wiping the lipstick stain off with my sleeve. "An interest in something can happen randomly. Why the *hell* would I have to announce that I'm suddenly experimenting with some lipstick?" I kept my eyes on Ayaan then looked to Ataya, who knew that I was lying, she saw Kassian in the room. But before she opened up her mouth again, the whole thing replayed in my head; How quick she was to run down and open her mouth. I felt myself disconnect and before I could stop myself, my mouth ran and said what I was thinking. "You stupid, *stupid* bitch."

And that was what happened to be the straw that broke the camel's back... if it was only ever one or two straws that broke its back each time. Once again Ayaan grabbed onto me and threw me towards the tv room entrance. My back slammed against the open door, then my body—mostly my forearms—hit the ground. I stayed down, taking my time so I could gather enough of myself to prevent my face from showing any weakness.

"He's there look!" Ataya's annoying voice travelled through the house once again.

I raised my head to see Kassian at the doorway and almost instinctively, I grabbed onto his leg, begging him with the gesture to stay out of it, to leave.

He didn't move.

Kassian stayed in place as Ayaan stomped towards us, so

I got up to stand in front, to guard him from these idiots.

Ayaan got too close and was ready to throw whatever he could, and I stood where I was with my eyes closed, bracing for impact. I had timed Ayaan's first move, but instead of feeling it, I felt my body be grabbed and moved away from behind me. My eyes opened at the same time as Kassian got barged into the hallway and onto the storage door under the stairs.

He retaliated by forcing Ayaan back into the tv room where they had more space to fight. I've never seen bulls fight, but if I had to describe this particular clash, angry bulls would be used to help visualise this situation. Ayaan threw heavier punches than Kassian whilst Kassian wasn't even trying to fight properly. His tactic was to childishly taunting Ayaan, which stressed me out even more.

Kassian gave attention to his bloodied fingers after they touched his cut lip. "Can't say that felt as good as her lips. Wait. My mistake. I should've waited for an attack on my dick." His tongue now made an appearance, not just to further taunt Ayaan, but to take his blood back in.

I gasped and almost choked on the air I gulped.

'Why the heck would he say that?'

For a split second, Ayaan looked hurt, genuinely hurt, but then he charged at Kassian with stronger hits as though Kassian's words affected him more than anything he threw.

Kassian now fought like he did back at the pub. Strategically. And with minimal contact. Any hits he did take, he didn't seem to care for, in fact even they seemed planned for.

Eventually Kassian would grow bored and do something about it and as much as I hated my brother, I don't want my mum to be the next person to receive a hand. So, I gathered up some courage and tried to pull Ayaan away.

He pushed me back, then continued to punch Kassian's face as he held him on the ground. Kassian wasn't fighting back anymore, he just coughed up blood or grinned with each hit as if he already had Ayaan's consequence in mind.

Stupidly, but not knowing what else to do, I tried to get in the middle again, triggering my brother some more, and before I could block my face, Ayaan's elbow comes straight for me, knocking me to the cold floorboards once again.

Falling felt long.

Like everything and everyone suddenly decided to move slowly. It was so slow, I felt like I could feel my nerves run round my body like pins and needles.

I caught a glimpse of Kassian's face. He's no longer amused and looking at Ayaan.

He was looking at me.

When my body touched the ground, I felt even more funny. Like I was no longer in control. My eyelids got heavier and whilst I struggled to keep them open, I managed to make out Kassian get up.

Chapter 11

Medisa

18/12/2021 (Saturday)

Waking up in what I assumed was Kassian's car didn't make my heart drop as much as it should've. My head was tilted towards the window but I still made sure to not make any sudden movements. I didn't want him to know I was awake.

The only thing I could see to my right was his hand and a bit of his forearm. He was bloody and his knuckles were slightly cut.

A few seconds after I saw his hand, my brain dropped the memories of what had happened all over me. I instantly sat up and continued to stare at his hand. What kind of damage had to be done for it to look like that?

"Did you—"

"I just knocked him out." He reassured.

'*Thank God*.'

I heavily breathed out.

"After beating the shit out of him." He was proud and collected.

My parents definitely came home and called the police. Beaten son and taken daughter, yeah, that's enough to put them in hospital.

"You don't have to pretend to be asleep to avoid talking to me. I want some quiet and rest as much as you do. We'll talk later on in the day; for now, just try not to move as much."

I didn't have energy to talk to Kassian or think about what was going on, where he was taking me, what had happened and what I was going to do. Everything was happening a little too fast for my liking and I just wanted to rest. If Kassian's car was the only time to do it, then so be it.

I glanced over at him once more. He's a little tense. I would ask him if he's okay then diss him for what he's done, but he's right, we need some peace and quiet after what happened. I turned back to the window and tried to fall asleep with the views and a throbbing head, but sadly my thoughts couldn't be switched off as quickly as I wanted them to.

Chapter 12

Medisa
18/12/2021 (Saturday)

Getting my eyes to open felt like a chore, but as soon as I caught a glimpse of unrecognisable furniture, I got up. Being in a bed that's not mine, a robe that's a little too big, in a room that I don't recognise without my pants, gave me an experience I assumed is what every drug addict, slash alcoholic went through. The numb but throbbing body just topped it all off.

It didn't take long for me to remember that I was in Kassian's car last night and that I actually wasn't imagining things.

He did take me out the house.

My hair was brushed and tucked behind my ear, my face and hands were cleaned and moisturised *and* (to point out again) someone (Kassian?) took my pants off.

The thought of Kassian stripping me, both angered and embarrassed me. Not only was I on early stages of a period (heavy bleeding) but my legs hadn't been waxed for a long time. I know these things shouldn't be my main concerns, but they are. How am I supposed to face him knowing that he's seen these things? How am I supposed to talk to him knowing that he won't be taking me seriously? Anyways, other than those reasons and religion, I'm not that mad or scared (I think). I know I haven't been raped; nothing hurts or is sore, so on that end I'm good.

As I stayed sat up in bed feeling and most likely looking bamboozled and slightly regretful, Kassian walked in.

"Before you give me a headache that could've easily been avoided, let me start off by saying it wasn't me that stripped you. I got a female to do so." He had a hand raised like he was trying to tame me. "You were wearing jeans with dirt on them. Do not look at me as if what I'd done was unreasonable."

"You look like shit." I spat out after not knowing what else to say, perhaps to even move away from the topic of muddy jeans and being stripped.

"So did you, until I had you cleaned up."

Not being able to look at him for any longer, I distracted myself with my surroundings, mentally praying that I wasn't staying in the same room, laying in the same bed that he lays in when he has company.

"Don't worry, that's another suite."

My face must've said it all.

Anyways, with that cleared up, I could move on to more serious questions without feeling weird.

"Why did you make it look like we had a crazy make out session? What happened after I passed out? And where are we right now?" Granted, I could've looked out the window or asked a worker about our location, but as the robe only reached my shins, I mentally voted against it.

"What makes you think we didn't have a session?"

"Kassian, I haven't got time for this shit." My face still buzzed in different areas and I'm also exhausted, mentally and physically. He had some nerve avoiding my questions when it was his fault we both got hurt in the first place.

"Stay here for a few days, rest, eat well, get your energy back. Don't worry about the finances of things, everything will be paid for. My number is on the bedside table, feel free to call if you have energy at night." He spoke with lazy sarcasm as he gathered a few things.

When he headed towards the door, I wanted to get up and stop him but it wasn't an option with my wolverine legs.

"Oh, and Medisa, there are pads in the bathroom." And just like that, he left, closing the door behind him whilst I mentally shot myself three times. Once in each foot (to really make sure that I suffer) and one to the head.

I waited for enough minutes to pass- –until I convinced myself that he wouldn't walk back in—then searched the room for my jeans. After looking everywhere, I was sure that he had them binned, or burnt. Or worse…added to his personal stash. I heard some boys have those.

When I couldn't find my jeans, or any of my clothes really, I approached a window to see if I recognised where he had taken me. I expected to be in a room near the ground, but no, I'm probably on the highest floor in this damn place. The first thing I saw was the *lack of* ground, the second was the view. If I wanted to, I could go to work right now and see Kade.

Was this done purposely on Kassian's behalf?

'*Stay away from work for a week.*' Did Kassian somehow know that was said, and is teasing me to entertain himself? Kade may not have said I was banned, but it felt like it.

I walked to the bedside table where my phone, a piece of paper and a notebook and pen were placed. My phone had died—good, I did not want to open that can of worms just yet—the piece of paper had Kassian's number and the notebook had a note.

'*I'll get you a charger soon. In the meantime, enjoy the views or think of me to pass time.*'

"How about you get me some clothes?" I spoke to the note. "And why is your handwriting neater than mine?"

I opened the bedside table to see what else the room had

to offer. Kassian obviously had enough time on his hands because there were some chocolate chipped cookies in here with four crisp packets and another note.

'*Just in case you don't like what the hotel has to offer.*'

"I haven't even seen what the hotel has to offer." I grabbed the notebook, some biscuits and bottled water, then sat next to the floor to ceiling window.

Readying the notebook and pen to doodle to pass time, I looked over Kassian's message once more before launching myself towards my phone.

Removing the case to reveal the card I received with the hand. I compared the two handwritings and as shocking as the thought were, they were actually different.

But Kassian is the only person other than Kade who knows about what happened at the pub. Amana knows too, but, One: I can't read her handwriting for the life of me and Two: her doing this wouldn't make any sense. The girl could barely catch some sleep with the life she lived and I'm sure that she's somewhat squeamish. The twins on the other hand, are far more capable of doing this…I think. But Kade is another possibility that's not actually going to be considered because he doesn't even know what the man looks like, let alone the exact hand that touched me.

That left Kassian.

I already knew how far he's willing to take things after the lipstick-kidnapping situation, he could've easily changed his handwriting if he really wanted to, or gotten another person to write. Which begged the questions: Is it wise for me to be staying here? Is this another puzzle piece I'm being forced to solve?

I paced the room again and again, replaying scenarios, coming up with theories, questions, and more questions,

I even made some duas, and before I knew it, it was dark. Not that the time or how tired I was mattered. I couldn't stop thinking. I couldn't stop the thoughts, couldn't stop myself from pacing, couldn't even stop myself from rationing the snacks he had left.

Pressing the heel of my hands into my eyes, I tried to get my brain to allow me to fall asleep, but it wouldn't. It kept thinking the same things again and again. One: I didn't actually know who to believe, or side with. Two: this whole thing could be a joke ('game') between brothers and I'm the clown that's getting played (that's not too unbelievable). And three: I should just do what Amana says and leave, take my savings and find a job elsewhere. This is too long and is none of my business (though he did get me kicked out the house, involving me).

My mind's all over the place and I still hadn't gone over what happened at my parent's house. Then there's the case of where I'm going to stay until Uni ends. Going back home, or staying here longer than I needed to, weren't options I wanted to consider. At the moment I just wanted to charge my phone, have a bath and put on some clothes. Maybe even try to find more pieces to this puzzle before leaving.

Where would I go? God knows.

Chapter 13

Medisa

19/12/2021 (Sunday)

A few light knocks woke me up, but not enough to shake the feeling of wanting to go back to sleep. After a few seconds another rhythm of knocks played at the door, repeating until I gave some sign of life.

I did not.

They knocked again.

After accepting whoever it was wouldn't go away, I pushed myself to sit up. There's no way Kassian or room service would request to come in at a dumb time, so I assumed I slept in.

Before I got to the door, a woman on the other side spoke. "Miss Menaal? Are you there? I'm here to deliver your wardrobe."

'My wardrobe?'

I opened the door to see at least five women outside the room, four wheelie clothing racks beside them.

The woman in front invited herself in, explaining how Kassian sorted a *'few'* clothes out for me. A few being enough for the month with at least two outfits a day. And not to be ungrateful, but he didn't take the fact that I couldn't wear certain things into consideration. I don't even think that he took the weather into consideration, so that cut down more than half of what was presented.

"Do you guys provide wardrobes for every guest here?"

'Dumb question even if it is to make conversation.'

"No, of course not. Only special ones." The woman who stood to the side whilst the others dealt with the clothes, spoke. Her face looked familiar, but the reason why wasn't coming to me as quickly as it usually would.

My eyes travelled to the younger girl who gave off good vibes. She mouthed '*the rich ones*' whilst moving her hands as if they held money.

A smile, as well as the heavy breath my nose let out, earned me another look from the one I assumed was in charge.

"You didn't eat yesterday, is there a reason why?"

'*Yeah, your client may be a psychopath playing with everyone in his life, so forgive me if I refuse to eat to avoid being in his debt.*'

"I had the snacks in the room, and then I pretty much slept all day..." This was awkward for no reason. "Do you guys have chocolate chip biscuits and crisps? Oh, and chocolate cake."

The woman had a face on. "I'll have it sent to the room."

"Thank you. I would tip but my phone's dead."

"It's good that you have Kas then, isn't it?"

'*Oh my God it's her.*' I knew she looked familiar.

"Is there something on my face?"

'*No, I just realised I'm being looked after by the guy you sleep with.*'

"No, I just remembered I have someone to call." I meant Amana or Kade, but I hoped to God she thought I meant Kassian. She was being a cow for no reason, but then again, she had her reasons, she was just taking it out on me and not Kassian. So now I'm somewhere between feeling guilt and not actually caring.

Thankfully, the other women in the room had finished moving the chosen clothes onto another rack in the room, so we didn't have to stare at each other's faces for long.

Before they said their long-winded goodbyes, one of the women placed a charger on the bedside table. I wanted to snatch it and run to my phone, but that's rude. So, I *patiently* waited for them to leave.

Once the door was shut with them on the other side, I quietly ran over to the table, and then to my phone. Shoving the plug in, I wasted no time in switching my phone on—something I never do, I always waited until it was fully charged—I looked for messages, calls, anything from Kade, but there was nothing. Only notifications from relatives.

His lack of news is understandable. It's only been a little while since I last saw him, what could either of us have achieved by then?

'Oh, let's see. Receiving a handy care package, holding a funeral for said package, taking a not so useful nap, waking up to the one that's not Kade, getting beaten because of said person, potentially being kidnapped by said person, coming up with more questions than answers, achieving a new wardrobe...Yeah, what could someone achieve in those hours?'

Moving on to the messages from relatives. Apparently, my parents were really worried and thought I was being silly. The whole '*what would people think*' definitely came to play in this situation. Ataya, no doubt, was rinsing the situation as much as she could. She's definitely spreading stories that would only benefit her. I wouldn't be surprised if she's gotten people to pity or praise her. Not that I give a shit about what's said, I would gladly welcome anyone's deeds on my scale. It would probably be the only decent thing anyone of them has ever done for me anyway.

Before dismissing them altogether (at least until this River thing was over), I decided to text my parents. I'd come to the realisation somewhat recently, that I didn't need to pretend I grew up with good parents. I am allowed to admit they're bad parents with good qualities. And it's for those good qualities that I'm sending them a message, letting them know that I'm fine, but won't be returning anytime soon.

Leaving my phone on charge, I paced the room thinking about what my next few steps should be. I'm definitely not going back, but I'm not staying here and living off Kassian's money. Spending my own money is an option, just not a desired one. But if a game really is being played, why can't I take advantage to help myself?

The same rhythmic knocks that played in the afternoon, played again, only this time it was a man with a trolley and not a group of women with clothes.

He came inside to place some food on the table and I tried my best to intervene, to tell him it wasn't necessary, that I could do it myself, but he insisted.

As he walked out the door, I checked the time and it was already half an hour before the sun sets. Quickly grabbing some food, I made way to the balcony to set camp, then made another round inside to get some milk and water. Before I knew it, I was going in and out of sleep with my pillow, surrounded by empty plates, packets and the nights sky.

Something dropped inside.

It took me a second to remember where I was, what I was doing, and that I was supposed to be alone in the room. Whoever was inside opened the balcony door and I mentally thanked God for making my back be to them, I don't think I could fake being asleep with someone in my face.

"Why on earth would she sleep here?"

"Who cares? Let him know she's still here."

After a couple of minutes of them frantically moving around, they finally left.

I pushed myself to get up and casually scan the room as though I'd not heard complete strangers in here a minute ago.

'They're reporting back to Kassian?'

Before wasting another second, I went to barricade the door. I couldn't handle this right now, I'm already slightly paranoid. Dealing with someone watching me isn't something I needed or wanted right now.

I don't understand what they would be reporting back to him anyways, *'yes, she's currently in bed', 'no nothing has changed she's still in bed', 'an update? Oh yeah, she finally moved to the bathroom.'* He should've installed cameras, or even come to check on me himself if he really wanted to know.

Before going back to pacing to think about what I could do, other than eat and look outside, I remembered the new wardrobe I had attained. Having clothes and a fully charged phone, I could explore the Hotel or go out. I didn't need to stay in here.

Chapter 14

Medisa
31/12/2021 (Friday)

It's almost been two weeks since I last saw a familiar face. Kassian hadn't come back since that day, but sometimes it felt like he was around, until I investigated and found it to be my mind playing tricks. Kade had told me to stay away for another week and Amana was busy with work, Uni work and my mum. Apparently, a maid is missed in my household and Amana is constantly asked if she's heard from her yet.

So far, everything's going downhill excruciatingly slow. The wait for the worst of the worst to come was agonising. It's like knowing there's more to come but not knowing when and how. So, you're forced to wait. And you try to prepare or avoid it but, in the end, you know that your efforts will be wasted. No matter what you do, whatever's going to happen *will* happen, so you give up…but not really. Whatever *it* is, it stays at the back of your mind, but sometimes it's all you can think about so you just try to physically do what you can, to keep yourself above the water, 'distract' yourself, whilst your mind mentally prepared for what it knows will eventually come.

I knew I was in this weird mindset so I've been pushing myself to use the hotel gym every day since I first learnt about its existence. There's a swimming pool too which is cool, but it will never see me, someone would have to drag me for that nightmare to come true.

After praying Isha, I waited on the balcony floor with a

blanket wrapped around as my hands covered my ears. I've been here for two weeks, staring at the same view again and again, the only thing changing were the colours in the sky. The view could only entertain for so long but fortunately, today was New Year's Eve, so tonight they'll be different types of colours in the sky—anticipated, slash encouraged pollution—New Year's Eve fireworks.

The new year was going to be different.

I could feel it.

Chapter 15

Medisa
01/01/2022 (Saturday)

Someone outside the room had no patience.

I didn't sleep until two in the morning, so understandably I didn't wake up with the birds as this person clearly wished I had.

They aggressively banged for what seemed like the longest minute of my life. I thought after the first few ignored knocks, they would walk away, but clearly not.

When I finally made my way into the room and to the peephole, strangely enough, no one was outside. But I didn't force myself up this early for no reason, so I opened the door.

There was a box on the floor, almost identical to the one I received at my house. Without taking it inside, I sprinted down the hallway trying to find whoever had placed it at my door.

What was I going to do once I found them? God knows.

Instead of finding someone who looked as though they delivered the box, I found a member of staff.

"Did anyone walk past?" I frantically spoke, too loud and eager.

"I didn't see anyone. I just came out a room." She spoke slow, as if I didn't question her urgently.

"Where are the stairs?"

"Miss, you're on the highest floor—"

"Where are the stairs?!" I hadn't heard the elevator doors open or close, so they definitely took the stairs. Or they're in a room, and I will gladly camp out in the hallway until they come out.

She led me to a door almost identical to the others and I wasted no time opening it.

For a split second I thought I saw a figure about 6 floors below, practically jumping down the steps.

"Hey. *Wait*!"

Apparently '*wait*' meant '*run even faster*.' The person was out of sight and there was no point in running after them. Even if I did take an elevator, assuming the floor that they're hiding on would be stupid and taking it down to the ground floor would also be dumb, the hotel is huge and causing a scene may not be the best thing to do.

"No, she's still here." The maid quietly spoke before I came back into the hallway.

I fought the urge to knock her round the head as I walked past. All I needed was to see a phone or some sort of ear piece to give me the go.

I couldn't see anything—lucky cow—but she wouldn't be talking to herself about my whereabouts.

When I had a few steps in front of her I looked back, my stomach twisted as soon as I saw her do the same.

Something's not right.

I made my way to the room, picked up the box and walked in as though everything was okay. Soon as I shut and locked the door, I waited to see if she would approach the room.

She didn't. Her trolley wheels gave away her direction and it was away from me.

There was a chance that this box was holding a piece of Ayaan, he was the last person to aggressively touch me—or Kassian—assuming there was a trend in these 'gifts.' Would it be an ear? Or finger? Whatever it was, I couldn't let it sit there and wait for someone else to find it before me.

I unravelled the bow, lifted the lid, then finally let out a breath. Whoever sent the box sure knows how to make my heart drop. They didn't fill it to the top with packaging paper like last time, they just placed what they needed me to see. Three white roses attached to the same stem. Underneath was a card. Nothing was written this time, just the embossed 'R'.

I ran over to the bedside table where I had placed my phone. It refused to turn on so I'm left with no choice but to leave blindly.

Kade may not know I'm coming but he better be there.

After arguing with the front desk for thirty minutes, I was finally given access to Bellamy's office. For some reason the elevator to our floors denied my access code. The woman at the front desk had never seen me before and apparently, I'm not on the system so she *also* denied my access.

Another woman on the desk saw that I was distressed-borderline pissed, so she offered to call the floors office. Right after her call, she apologised for the delay and said that someone should be waiting for me at the elevator.

I wasted no time.

I ran to the elevator.

As soon as I had the doors in my sight, Bellamy made an appearance beside them. He must've heard my loud stomps as I ran because he prematurely turned to face me. If this were a normal day I might've been embarrassed.

When I finally reached him, I struggled to hit the brakes on my feet. "I need to talk to Kade."

On the way up, nothing could be heard other than my

heavy breathing. Usually I'd probably be a little self-conscious about it but I was too busy thinking about what to say to both Bellamy and Kade, like for starters, why the hell they thought it was a good idea to take me off the system?

When we reached mine and Kade's floor, I tried to step out but Bellamy held out his hand, stopping me from exiting. Once he got out himself, he pressed the button which led to the floor above. I gave him a *'what the heck? What are you doing?'* look, but he remained unphased as the doors shut. I could swear that before the doors touched, he dropped his serious *'trust me'* face to something that looked like regret. Or sympathy.

I reached into my pocket and grabbed the two cards with the embossed 'R', squeezing them in my hand whilst taking a deep breath.

It's been two weeks. He has to know something.

Soon as the doors opened, I felt as though I came to the wrong floor. The decoration is different to the level below. The whole vibe is a little different, darker.

Instead of being let out into an open space, you are let out into a wide hallway. It's decorated with statues and random artwork and at the end of it, there's an office. I know this because there are glass double front doors that acted as a window into the room. I couldn't see the whole office from where I was, but I could see the desk and the chairs placed in front of it. The desk faced the hallway like Bellamy wanted to stare his guests down as they approached him. Thank God I've never been summoned up here to experience that. I would die.

As I neared the glass doors, I mentally argued on which way they would open. I couldn't be asked dealing with the embarrassment of pushing a pull door with someone inside.

I pulled first, a hidden memory of reading somewhere that all doors must be 'push' doors if you're standing inside of a room, fire safety purposes— I guessed.

Pulling them worked, however, when they shut behind me, I could've sworn it slightly swung inside, making my thoughts leading up to the door a complete waste of time and energy.

No one was inside, so I assumed the boys were downstairs talking about what the best strategy to approach this situation would be.

There's a door to the right of whoever walked in, left if you were Bellamy at the desk. It's not enough to compel me to search whatever that door led to, it would most likely be a toilet anyways as there's nothing else on this floor other than the gallery outside the office. And I doubt Bellamy would make trips downstairs just to use the loo, unless that was the reason he constantly came down and saw Kade, he was using the toilets.

I walked past the desk and to the window, the view downstairs was beautiful, but up here, at this level, its breath-taking.

Grabbing Bellamy's office chair, I sat down and made myself comfortable, using my feet to sway me as I took in the room. To the left there was the 'toilet' and to the right, there's a floor to ceiling bookshelf that covered the whole wall. In between certain books there were statement pieces, miniature 3D artwork. I ran my eyes across them all then stopped on one familiar item.

The lamp I gave Kade.

I got up to take a closer look as if there was a possibility that someplace was selling replicas of my design. The markings and certain imperfections confirmed this indeed was the gift I gave Kade.

Did he gift it to Bellamy? I didn't think people outside of my family re-gifted unwanted gifts.

Somehow, him passing on my gift made it to the top of the list of things that needed to be addressed. I began to pace and pick at my lips. So many things were running through my mind, so many things were much more important than this gift situation, but for some reason it bothered me.

Continuing to pace, I passed the desk a little further than the rounds before, causing me to be hit directly by reflected light. Following the light, I discovered one of the cabinets had not been shut properly, something was jamming it. Without thinking about Bellamy's privacy, but also having no intention to snoop, I opened the drawer to organise it a little, to allow it to shut smoothly. Picking up some files to move them out the way revealed a gold name plate, although calling it a chunky metal bar would be more suited.

'KADEN ARRIO RIVER'

Almost as if he had planned it, Kade walked in from the 'toilet' with wet hair as though he had just come out the shower.

"Medisa?"

I sucked in as much air as I could through my mouth. Bellamy wasn't downstairs discussing matters with Kade, he didn't send me up to allow us to use his space either. He didn't come up because this wasn't even his office in the first place. And judging by Kade's appearance, he didn't know I was here and didn't plan on telling me the truth anytime soon.

With so many questions and things to address running through my head, I didn't know what to say or do. Do I run at him and scream everything? Should I slap him? Should I leave? Should I wait until he said something?

As Kade took steps towards me, I pulled out his name and tossed it across the desk. Keeping my eyes on him, I grabbed a hold of the cards in my pocket and slammed them on the table, attempting to get out my anger and confusion, but it didn't work. I needed to scream, to hit something, to throw something, to *do* something but I just stayed where I was. Kade seemed to know not to say anything. *I* couldn't even think of anything for him to say that wouldn't conjure up some sort of negative reaction from me.

"Are you playing me?" I finally let out.

He looked confused, maybe even hurt, but remained silent.

"Are you and your brother messing with my head for entertainment?" My voice was tired, I was growing bored of this whole thing.

"No. No Medisa I would never do that."

I looked down at the cards, I needed to focus on them, to get the mystery behind them out the way before I dealt with anything that came with the block of gold.

"I got the first card with a note after I spoke to you at the office, a boy delivered it to my house." I used my eyes and an upward nod to single out the card I was talking about.

Kade gave it his attention as I continued to talk.

"It came in a box, a gift box, with a hand, a real, human, skeleton, hand."

If Kade was feeling anything I couldn't see it.

"It's the man who grabbed me at the pub, I recognised the rings. I *know* it's him."

I directed his eyes to the next card. "That came today at the hotel Kassian took me to."

He slightly tensed up, triggering me some more. Out of all the things I said, he reacted to his brother's name. I guess that scratched out the possibility of them playing together.

"It came in an identical box, this time with three white roses, no written message. I thought that it was Kassian sending me notes, but that doesn't make any sense." I spoke to the desk, then looked up to Kade's eyes. "I'm not leaving until you tell me the truth, *all* of it, I don't care how dangerous, upsetting or gory it is, I want the truth or I swear to God I will make your life hell—"

"Okay."

I stopped, then waited for him to continue.

He walked to the chair directly in front of me and the desk, then sat down as though he had come to negotiate. He leaned into the chair and even though his posture was more casual than upright, he still had a powerful look about him, like we were doing this on his terms.

"My name *is* Kade River. I don't go by Kaden anymore. And I have a middle name; Arrio. I just don't really use it, my mum—"

"Oh, but you want to name a whole business after it." I childishly cut in, going off on the fact that the two names were basically two sides of the same coin. It also ties in to the theory of him hiding from his family. 'Aros' is basically him being hidden in plain sight. "Before you continue, as it is fresh in my head, why did you take me off the system?"

"You were never on the system, it was too risky, so we only gave you what you needed to get into the elevator. My pin."

'Too risky? What the hell does that mean?'

Does me not being on the system also mean that any transactions made between us wouldn't have been taxed? Good, I got to have all the money I earned.

"Continue."

"You've already met Kassian, my twin—"

"I have." I continued to act like a child.

"Who you don't know and haven't met is our older brother, Maverick."

"Oh great! There's more." My sarcasm made an appearance.

He paused, thought about his words then continued. "When me and Kassian were eight, our parents died, leaving us with him."

'Oh for flips sake, of course.'

I probably shouldn't have cut in when he was about to say something about his mum…and by older brother I didn't think that he meant someone who was of legal age when they were 8. How old was Maverick when he took on the task of becoming their guardian? How old is he now?

"And Maverick, he er, he- he had problems. We didn't know then what had caused them and we don't know now, but whatever's wrong with him meant that we had to suffer too. If we rebelled and refused to listen to him, he found new ways to make us. And he *always* got what he wanted, one way or another."

Kade stood from his seat to walk over to the window. I couldn't tell if he was reliving his time with Maverick or if he was thinking of the next thing to say.

After a few seconds of looking at his selection of drinks, he turned to face me as if to be out with it. "Maverick owns Baronial Medisa."

It took me a second to remember what that is, and despite not having anything to say, my mouth still parted.

"No one is given the opportunity to join by chance, they're checked then scouted, and if they have the right circumstances, are given a contract." He paused to see if I was following. "Signing the contract means signing your life away. You become a company slave. Whatever they ask of you, you do it. No questions asked."

It doesn't take a genius to put together how that made sense. Maverick owning a company like this aligns with what Kade has said so far. If he liked controlling kids so much, it made sense that power and control leaked into other aspects of his life.

"The higher the level of intensity you are put through, the more money you make. The pay they offered you, that money is given to those who are made to sell themselves."

"How is that even possible? I would've seen it in the contract." I spoke as though I would've read it.

"It's possible. Through loopholes, through threats—blackmails, tracing your signature, edited conversations, fingerprints—there are many ways."

I pulled my hand up to peel my lips then quickly dismissed the action. I probably had one layer of skin left to peel anyway.

"Those cards may not have been directly from Kassian but they may as well be. He stands with Maverick. He would stand anywhere if it were against me." Kade looked into the hallway from where he was standing as if he were lost in thought. "That day at the University, the first time we met. Amana had mentioned how you applied at Baronial." He looked towards me now. "I couldn't help people before, but since I was no longer under Maverick's roof, I wasn't going to sit back and let things play out the way that I know they would. So, I told her that I could get you a job, here, at Aros."

"Okay, but I didn't sign a contract. So what does he want?"

"I left my brothers to live my own life. My guess? They

want me back but not without a few scars."

My brows twitch as I try not to smirk at the thought of Kade actually caring about me.

"No."

"What?"

"I saw the look that just glitched across your face. You won't be a scar, my brothers just *think* that you will be."

"Yeah, you keep telling yourself that. I've been told that I'm magnetic and that people actually feel my lack of presence."

"Yeah 'cause of the lack of headache." He said too naturally as though it had been a lingering thought.

My jaw dropped as I tried not to laugh too heavily.

"I'm joking." He tried to save himself. "You'll be a scar, Medisa." His voice was now low. "I value our friendship and because I do, I've made you a target. Maverick will rinse what he can from you to get to me, it's his idea of fun whilst teaching me a lesson."

I lowered my gaze, still fighting the urge to pick or bite my lips. I didn't know what I expected when I asked for the truth. And truth be told this was a little bigger than I expected. There are still things that need to be spoken about, but this whole new *thing* just raised new questions and is making me forget what I needed to say.

The silence was loud, I couldn't stand it, so I moved to be directly in front of Kade, whose eyes had betrayed his dispassionate face. Once again, we were both in front of the window, almost mirroring that apology night.

"The truth is, I don't know if I could protect you Medisa, but I'd rather go through what Maverick had put me through again than to not try with everything I've got."

I breathed heavy through my nose, holding in an awkward laugh. "Thanks? But I'd rather you not go through that again. Can't have you beating my traumatic life."

His lips lifted a little, finally smiling after what seemed like forever, but it dropped quicker than it formed. My face automatically responded with confusion and before I could talk, or run, he towered over me.

"Now." He tried to close the distance between us.

I wanted to stand my ground but it was either losing my breath or taking some steps back.

I ended up hitting the shelf.

'Typical.'

Fucking annoying is what it is.

'Is it?'

Kade rested both hands a little above my shoulders on the shelf behind. He held me hostage, not physically, but it damn well felt like it with him caving over me, especially as he lowered himself.

His face, too close to mine, held no amusement. And when I tried to look away, he stalked my eyes, tilting his head to give me no choice but to look into his

"Tell me, why did you go to a hotel with Kassian?"

Chapter 16

Medisa

01/01/2022 (Saturday)

Though I escaped his non-physical-physical cage, it took me two seconds to recover from what he had said. Any longer than that and he would've caught on. God knows what he would've caught onto, but the prolonged pause would definitely toot his horn.

In attempts to move on, I tried to clear up the actual reason on why I went to a hotel with Kassian. All jokes aside, I knew that he still wanted to know.

"We got into some trouble at my house. Long story short he made it look like me and him were up to no good—*physically*—then we got caught together…alone, resulting in a physical fight. I lost consciousness then Kassian somehow got me out and gave me a place to stay. I don't know the details of what he did when I got knocked out but yeah…I basically can't go back. Not right now anyways." I probably could've worded that better.

"Knocked out?"

"If it makes you feel any better, it wasn't Kassian that done it, it was my brother."

"It doesn't."

"Hmm?"

"It doesn't make me feel better. Why would it?"

'Why do I suddenly feel embarrassed or awkward?'

"I'd much rather it was Kassian so that I could beat the shit out of him myself and let you watch. But 'cause it's your brother I'm guessing you wouldn't want that."

"I wouldn't want you to do that even if it was Kassian…I think." Knowing how spontaneous I am and how oddly I reacted to things, I genuinely do not know if I would protect Kassian or if I would let anger consume me. So, a point to me for being truthful.

"What is it with you and Kassian?" He asked out of curiosity, obviously frustrated at the fact that he couldn't seem to figure it out.

Clearly staying at the hotel was a big no-no and I should've come to Kade sooner. I'll remember this lesson the next time someone breaks into my room and has his way.

"I don't know. I don't want to say that I feel sorry for him, but I do. There's something he's hiding and if we could help him with whatever it is, he might join us in whatever we're going to do about Maverick."

Kade's face was like he felt sorry for me because of how deluded I was.

"There is some sort of good in him." In attempts to explain my plan, I somehow made myself seem more naïve than I actually am. "He let me stay at an expensive hotel for two weeks when he could've left me at the house."

"*Two weeks?* He's the reason you had to leave in the first place." He wasn't shy to show his frustration.

"Oh yeah, I forgot to mention when it all went down. And I was planning on leaving anyways, he just sped up the process."

He scoffed as though he couldn't believe what I was saying. "Do you always give people a chance?"

"Always."

"Not everyone has good in them."

"I know. But sometimes I like to know why they are the

way they are before I pass judgement."

Kade's eyes thoroughly search my face, my eyes, as if to fact-check my words. When he came to, he walked past me and told me to follow him into the 'toilet.'

And the 'toilet' was indeed not a toilet.

It was a kitchen, big enough for an island despite it being smaller than the office. The floor, island worktop and wall worktops were all charcoal matt marble, these were complimented with burnt orange stools and grey cabinets. I thought we were going to stop here to eat but no, he carried on walking through, glancing back to make sure I followed.

I had taken my shoes off and held them in my hand—a habit I suppose—and when he saw, I was told to wait a second. A minute later he came back into the kitchen with a pair of slippers. <u>Thank God</u> they were his size, I think I would be disgusted if he gave me a pair that actually fit.

Moving away from the kitchen, we walked into the tv room which followed the same colour scheme with the added material of wood. There were three doors here. One for the kitchen, one for the bathroom and another for the bedroom, which I came to see also had access to the bathroom. All doors minus the bathroom door were left open, allowing me to see into the rooms. We didn't go into the bedroom, but I could see it followed the same cosy look and was bigger than the kitchen and tv room, if not the same size.

"What d'you think?"

"I like it, it's not too crowded, not too empty. I just find it a little weird how you liv—"

"Great. This is where you will be staying from now on."

'Come again?'

"Make a list of everything you need, I'm not hearing any excuses, especially after you stayed at a hotel at my brothers expense."

"Technically, I didn't willingly go in. He carried me while I slept or whatever you call it when you're too exhausted to move."

I admit, I knew what I was doing when I said that, and Kade's face was…*something* after that revelation.

"But this is cool. I love it. I would willingly stay here. Yep. Love. It." I gave one single clap to make it more convincing but to also add to my sarcasm.

Kade faked his stretched smile—I was ready to run—then demanded for a list to be made today.

"Has a dog been in here?" I attempted to get his mind off buying me things.

"No, why?" He stopped in his tracks

"I don't think I could pray here if a dog's been inside. I would probably need to clean it or something." I don't actually know how the dog and prayer thing worked. "My mum said dogs were stained by the devil—" Something like that. "—so they shouldn't be kept in the house." I never really cared to look into it because I was more of a cat girl.

"Oh. Noted."

"I would probably still need to, just in case another type of bitch's been in here." Once again, I became my own roast audience, until I saw his reaction as I failed to hide a grin. Needless to say, it didn't take long for me to say that I was kidding.

Making myself as comfortable as a guest could be on a sofa that's not theirs, I admired the interior. Just as I was about to suggest we watch something, or perhaps even talk about what else was on my mind, Kade came and stood by the door.

"By the way, the bedroom is yours now too. I'll be on

the sofa or downstairs if being outside your room makes you uncomfortable. I'll have the keys to the main door, but tomorrow I'm going to put a lock on the inside of each door to make you feel more comfortable. You get to choose who comes in whilst you're here."

"Oh no, it's okay really. I'll stay downstairs." I got ready to stand but notice Kade about to hold out his hands, basically telling me to sit back down. "I sat down because I thought we were going to chill here for a bit." I explained.

"I actually have to go somewhere, so get comfortable."

"Okay, cool. I might steal a pillow and take a nap." I spread my arms and fingers out beside me, feeling the material.

"If you're asleep on the sofa when I get back, I'll carry you to the bed."

"Oh my days Kade. The sofa is *fine*, seriously."

"Don't force me to sin Medisa."

'*Sin. What an attractive word.*'

There was no point in bickering, he wouldn't hear me out anyways. I just needed to make sure that I woke up before he got back, I had to.

'*But do you really want to?*'

Chapter 17

Medisa
02/01/2022 (Sunday)

Even though my eyes were closed and I was in a dream a few seconds ago, I could feel Kades presence. If my senses were correct, he was right in front of my face.

All of a sudden, I started to feel a little insecure and tried to mentally calm myself down before I triggered sweat. Sweating wouldn't even help me in this situation. It would grow, forming a wet moustache and little droplets on my nose. Yeah, that's definitely a sight Kade's dying to see.

"I thought I told you not to make me sin?" He whispered softly, dangerously close against my skin. And if my body didn't want to sweat before, it definitely did now.

Being the pro actor that I am, I scrunched my brows, slash eyes, then forced them open as though I were just waking up. Kade was crouched down on the floor close to where my head rested, his head tilted, following my movements as I sat up.

"We'll take turns, one day me, one day you." I yawned.

"This isn't up for debate Medisa. Let me look after you properly." He continued to speak with a low, soft voice, as if there was someone else sleeping in the room.

I didn't know how to respond. The idea sounds nice, but I didn't want it if it meant I was taking away his comfortability. But he wouldn't listen to reason so I'm going to have to think of something else.

Lazily searching for the remote around my seat, I tried

my best to not engage in eye contact. I failed when he stood in place, waiting for me to stop pretending I don't notice him.

Kade's eyes subtly gave away how he continued to not believe just how annoying I was. "You are living *here*, and I'm going to get comfortable downstairs."

"Do you wanna watch a movie?" This was the best thing my brain could think of to get him to move away from the topic.

"This late? Are you sure you can stay up for it?"

Looking around through squinted eyes, once again yawning, I wondered where the hell the clock was. "What time is it?"

"2 AM."

Soon as he said the time, I instantly regretted the movie suggestion. We hadn't even thought of something to put on and I'm already backing out, especially since movies nowadays are two hours minimum.

I'm exhausted. I didn't know where the feeling came from, but it was there, and it was heavy. Annoyingly, my true feelings about the suggestion and time showed, earning a light smirk from Kade.

"How about we talk? The first one to shut their eyes for longer than five seconds has to go sleep on the bed."

Annoyingly, he may win this.

'*Smartarse.*'

Without saying a word, I shot up towards the bathroom. If I had a chance at beating him, it would be through doing Wudu with cold water. Eating would be an option too if my body didn't force me to fall asleep as soon as I got full.

Whatever drowsiness the water cleansed me off, came back with each step I took back towards the sofa. We would need some good stories to tell, otherwise I'm dozing off sooner than I thought.

As I sat on the sofa, pulling my feet towards my body for some sort of comfort and warmth, I had my eyes on Kade. No offence to him but he looked like he could do with some rest himself, whether or not he was actually feeling it however, wasn't clear.

"Before I forget." I spoke through long slow blinks, trying to hold in another yawn. "When I slept at the hotel, two or three people came in to check up on me at night. And I don't think that they were the usual girls."

"Would you be able to recognise their voices?"

I shake my head.

"For a while I thought I was having one of those realistic dreams, but then after certain events and one or two things being moved, I thought otherwise. And I don't think that they were there on Kassian's behalf. The workers that I know have a direct link with Kassian, checked up on me during the day. Whoever those people were, they came at night when I was asleep and left once they saw me."

Kade took in what I said. It's one of the things I liked about him. When I needed him to listen, he did, and I've never had to tell him to just let me rant.

'Maybe he zoned in and out at the right times?'

"Truth? Or do you want me to lie to a degree?"

"Truth, obviously."

"They're girls who work at Baronial, and you're right, they don't work in Kassian's favour. Which means Maverick has another plan for us that Kassian might not know of, or agree with."

"Yeahhhh. I figured as much. You know that you don't have to lie to me?" I very quickly go back to the 'truth or lie' question. "Or keep things from me by not telling me everything? I can handle it. I'm not a glass doll and I'm actually really level-headed. So, from now on I want truths... please."

I flipping *hated* it when people lied to me. Or kept things from me. It genuinely makes no sense as I considered myself to be someone who's understandable and very much the devil's advocate... though I may not be able to say that after I've been lied to, or kept to the side.

"I know, I know. What I don't know is if your level-headedness is bottled insanity."

"Ah, to-may-toe to-mah-toe." I waved off then moved on to the next thing I wanted to say. "How does Baronial work? How does it make sense that they have a 'slave contract' but are also expected to live normally around those that know them?"

Positioning myself so that I'm curled up and leaning my side into the back of the sofa, I waited for a response. Thank God his sofa isn't them nasty leather ones, it would've made getting myself warm a little harder.

Kade got up and went to his room as I continued to adjust. Sadly, my top wasn't long or baggy enough for me to take it over my knees as I brought them as close to my chest as possible.

He came back out sooner than I expected and passed me a nude-brown fluffy blanket, then got back into his seat.

"You have this weird habit of walking away with the intention of coming back with something useful, but because you don't let a girl know that you're coming back, it makes her think that she's said something wrong and that you're done with the conversation."

Kade looked like this was the first time he was hearing of his odd behaviour.

"Sorry, I'll work on it." He extended his arm out onto the back of the sofa as if someone was sitting next to him. "Does a boy have to talk like this now?"

I threw a pillow—which he caught—then got the conversation back to what I wanted to talk about. "Tell me more about Baronial." I could feel myself falling asleep and was sure this topic would keep me awake. "How does it work?" I yawned out the words.

Kade got up once again, this time putting a finger up as if to say '*One sec*,' then moved into the kitchen. After taking his damn time opening and closing a few drawers, he came back with some chocolate chip cookies and milk.

Either he knew what he was about to say was going to be long and interesting, or he knew how to put me to sleep.

He got back into his seat for the second time.

"Like Aros, Baronial has different sectors, it just swaps the people around. It would be obvious if people's lives changed or if people went missing. So, they are given a 'faux' job—where people with close relations would see them—and they are given the job at Baronial, their *real* job." He used his hands to keep me interested and well informed on the different types of jobs. Left was for the faux job. Right was for Baronial.

I kept my mouth shut and my thoughts to myself. It'd be inappropriate for me to think or say that I thought it was cool and actually quite a clever system. These are people's lives that we're talking about, almost was mine, it's not a game.

I really needed to get that into my head.

"Baronial has rich clients, the type of money that would drive people crazy for, and delirious with. Since we give those clients what they want—Males/Females for pleasure, sport, or any other sick thing that they could think of, or even something as normal as a server—they provide 'faux' jobs for said workers. And since the workers are under Maverick, he uses them to get information on his clients for his own sick uses."

The way Baronial operates reminded me of things that you would hear and see in movies. It's shocking that it's an actual thing but more so because it's something that's happening so close to me, and not in other countries or certain areas.

'So much for people coming over for a safer environment.'

"Each worker is granted a wish."

My face questioned him.

"Sounds childish, I know. But whatever is written for their wish must be seen through and cannot be changed or ignored. For some, a wish is a certain amount of holiday time or something they think is beneficial. Some others use it on their friends or family." Kade checked if I was following, then continued. "For example, Baronial wouldn't be allowed to approach friends or family, or Baronial would have to pay their friends and family a certain amount—to pay off debts, medical bills or just straight set them up for life. However, a person cannot choose to save both friend and family. They can only choose one group."

"Another one of your brother's games?"

He nodded slowly, half lost in thought, half with his attention on me.

"It's sick, but not that sick. Only a bad or fake friend would hate on the decision of someone trying to save their family instead of them—assuming that they are aware of it. And besides, the Baronial person doesn't even have to save anyone, they could've wished for something for themselves, so they can't even be called selfish in the first place."

To think, if I had ignored Kades offer and went through with things, I would've been in the same position as these people for the rest of my life. Would the normal reaction be to feel mad, lucky, or scared? Whatever the hell I'm supposed to be feeling I'm sure it's not supposed to be curiosity. It's like my mind refused to see this as my reality, it heard the word '*game*' and went with it. And what's weirder is that I'm aware that I'm supposed to be feeling something, but I'm not. I'd much rather be 100% delusional than be confused and curious all the time. Why isn't my mind exploding at the fact that the literal man who runs this whole operation is after me to get at his brother? He's known to have done things under a contract but now he's after me regardless if I have one or not, and he has contacts—clients—who would be willing to give up someone they don't know for a few extra pleasantries. I won't be able to walk down a road without thinking if I had walked past a client or employee.

Extreme paranoia-obsession is another thing that I could expect to come anytime soon, if not now.

I focussed on Kade. How could someone who was brought up by Maverick turn out to be the complete opposite?

"How many people did you get to sign the contract?" I'm not stupid. He hadn't specifically said he worked in his older brother's company, but he doesn't have to. One: he said he ran away from his brothers. Two: it's his older brother and Three: he said '*we*' when talking about what Baronial does.

"I can't remember, I was practically a slave myself." His face held regret but also a '*I did what I had to do*' expression.

I understood what he meant, I did, but it didn't stop my mouth from running. "I would have never brought people on knowing what they would go through."

"I said and thought the same, but I had Kassian. Maverick

deemed him the weaker one then quickly found out I would fight for him. So, whenever I didn't do what I was told, sometimes Kassian was the one who suffered the consequences."

The room fell silent.

I didn't instantly rush to his side to let him know that I didn't blame him. I waited and thought it over. He put people through hell—they're probably still in it—to save one person.

"You did what you had to do. I get that. If someone threatened me with Amana, I would do whatever they wanted regardless of what it was. I shouldn't have spoken so impulsively, I'm sorry."

Kade let out a light smile. "If you're really sorry, you'll sleep on the bed."

"And just like that, I take my words back."

Kade grabbed onto his heart as if he were experiencing pain, then he fell back, still holding onto the phantom arrow I shot.

I chuckled as I scrunched and threw the blanket at him. "I'll sleep on the bed, *if* you consider—and when I mean consider I mean that you're going to do it—bringing Kassian onto our side, okay?"

He leaned back onto his elbows allowing for the top of his body to be a little upright, then sighed. "Medisa. Love. It's not just up to us. He needs to want to be on our side."

'Don't act like that 'love' didn't do something to you.'

"How hard can it be to convince him?" I said with a little too much hope, giving us too much credit. But if we could get him to see that Maverick's being dodgy on the side, then maybe it'll be easier than expected.

"I don't know. You should go sleep on it." He threw the blanket over himself as he turned away to 'sleep,' ignoring anything else I had to say.

If there was something to throw at him, I would, but since there wasn't and arguing was pointless, I gave in and moved to the bedroom.

As soon as I stepped into the room, I could've sworn I heard Kade say goodnight.

Chapter 18

Medisa

02/01/2022 (Sunday)

Waking up in a non-Muslims home was something I never thought I would experience. Waking up for Fajr, was another story.

If Kade was still on the sofa, it meant that we currently shared the bathroom, and that's okay. But trying not to wake him up an hour before sunrise was something else. Turning the doorknob and locking doors as quietly as possible was a mission, and trying to quietly wash myself was another. On top of all of those, I didn't want to use any of his towels, so I went back to the room to manually dry myself (aggressively swinging my legs off the bed to air dry my feet a little faster).

And as much as I hated having to go through his wardrobe, it needed to be done. I know from Kade's previous outfits that he owns at least five hoodies. And if I wanted to pray, I needed one of them. The problem was, his hoodies were expensive, so the action of pulling its strings to tighten the hood around my face, hurt more than anything I had done to my own clothes.

After praying I couldn't fall asleep.

My actions (praying) and my actions (staying with Kade) contradicted. An idiot is what I was, for not helping myself whilst living at the house and an idiot is what I continue to be as I allowed myself to be here. But then again, we're not sleeping in the same room, and he did offer to sleep elsewhere whilst I stayed here.

I quietly paced the room to tire myself out, but that just led to thoughts of my family consuming my mind. It's weird how almost two weeks away from them felt like months, but it also felt like it was just the other day that I had left them. It also felt like I somehow erased years of pain, but I know that's just my brain going back into that weird phase where I forgive them for what's happened.

To retaliate I thought of Ayaan fighting Kassian and how embarrassing that was, or how Ataya didn't even give me a chance to explain. Or any other time when they both decided to tag team. Basically, I thought of anything and everything that wouldn't let the stupid soft part of my brain win, which was funny because I was fighting to keep myself with people who literally got me in some sort of life-threatening situation than go back to my so-called family.

And then that led onto the thoughts of the River's.

Even though I've been told the scale of what's going on and what may happen, I still didn't seem to care. If a literal hand being sent to me wasn't enough for me to understand the weight of everything, I don't think anything will. And that's what the scary thought was (scary for other people because I didn't seem to feel that as well).

I felt like the explanation for my lack of 'care,' would be, that in the back of my mind, I know that I've managed to go through years of what people have put me through, so surely, I could get through this.

Whatever *this* was.

'bish guess what' I texted the only person that I knew would be awake at this time.

'What did you do?'

I got back into Kade's bed and sent her a quick video, front camera first, then I showed the rest of the room.

Caption: 'Kade's room'.

'NO WAY NO WAYYYY'

I giggled as I wrapped the thick sheets over my head like a headscarf, going back to laying down.

'YOU HOE IS HE NEXT TO YOU? WHAT DID YOU DO? WHAT DID YOU DO? DID HE DO YOU?'

I started to die. Literally die.

The best and strongest laughter is the ones you have to hold in, or keep quiet, and this was one of those times. I rocked back and forth to try and contain myself. Might've even knocked the heel of my hand against my legs a few times.

'I DIDN'T DO ANYTHING'

'DON'T LIE'

'IM NOT'

'HOW BIG IS IT????'

'HWRFIWRHGI AMANA'

'ASTAGFURILLAH IM JUST MAKING SURE—TESTING YOU...probably got a small dic anyways'

'Bruh'

'Wait where is he? And where are you?'

'He lives ABOVE our offices... you know that floor that I never went on HE LIVES THERE oh oh AND hes the CEO of AROS'

'No bloody way'

'I swear'

'Where is he right now?'

'Hes sleeping on the sofa just outside and im waiting for him to wake up so that I can eat something'

'girl hes waiting for you to leave LOOOOL'

There's no word to describe the way I silently laughed other than the word 'vibrate'.

'Hey man I don't even want to be here.. this is his bloods fault.'

'Yeah don't lie to me future mrs River'

'Allow it' Theres no chance of that happening, yet I still had a stupid smile on my face.

'You should turn the heating down during the night and watch him freeze from HIS bed'

'Omds im going to do that.. just for one night though' I silently giggled.

'Go get some food you pussy'

'No man we slept late'

'Why, what did you do?'

I could practically hear and see the way she said that.

'Ill tell you in person'

'Okay stop being a chicken and get something to eat'

'What if I wake him up?'

'No ones telling you to go bang on some pans... GOOOO and send pictures of the food you eat so that I know you're eating'

'Ayt cool'

I mentally prepared myself to go back into the bathroom. It's been some time since sunrise anyways and he's someone that works, so he should be used to waking up early.

When I finally managed to quietly open the door, I quickly noticed a note stuck on the mirror above the sink. '*Your toothbrush along with some towels and any other things you may need are in the cabinet to the right.*'

"Cute."

To my surprise, when I opened the cabinet doors, I found everything I needed and more. All organised as though the whole cabinet was mine. Maybe I only knew dumb males? I found it hard to believe that Kade's male brain came up with this, slash was this useful.

He had scented nappy bags for me to place used pads in, an electric tooth brush with all its different types of heads, different sized towels and a basket with all types of creams and scrubs. Hate to say it, but I'm impressed. Even before when I came to do wudu, I saw the bidet, but that was less surprising because he genuinely doesn't give off a dirty vibe. If we were strictly talking about hygiene.

Once I was done in the bathroom, I made my way to the kitchen passing through the tv room. Kade wasn't on the sofa which wasn't that surprising until I made it to an empty kitchen. Before I could think about what time he left, I noticed another note on the fridge.

'Everything is yours so don't hesitate to eat something. There's bread, cake, biscuits and some halal meat too if you feel like cooking. If not, just order something with MY card or wait for me, I'll cook something up.'

His card was placed on the side.

'There's a notepad on the island, use it to write the list of things that you want and need (I better see a list by the end of today). Also, Bellamy is going to come back here with me (little heads up to mentally prepare yourself)
—Kade'

After grabbing some cake and milk, I sat at the island facing the window. With his note on one side and the notebook and pencil on the other, I thought of what I could write. I wasn't going to treat this list as his shopping list, I was going to treat it as a bucket list. I knew what he meant when he said a list of things, and I knew that he knew that I knew. But I don't think that there's anything else I could ask for that he hasn't already provided.

I managed to write a few things before I heard the key in

the door. I thought I had enough time to run out the room but I didn't. They would've saw the back of me as I ran through the tv room door. The cake was also my downfall, I couldn't leave my plate out (they would know that I'm awake) so taking it with me was the only option.

As soon as the door handle moved, I panicked and threw myself to the floor, out of sight thanks to the island. They continued their conversation whilst dealing with what I'm assuming were plastic bags.

I waited a few minutes for them to leave, the need to pee growing.

The plan was to simply crawl around the island if I heard them come closer, but they randomly stopped talking, stopped moving, hell they probably even stopped breathing. I tried to wait it out, but I couldn't take it anymore. So, I slowly raised my head to look over the countertop. Both of them were sat on the stools, looking as though they were waiting for me to finally get up.

With brows raised on each of their faces along with amusement, they watched me stand.

"Hi." I spoke with a smile like I wasn't just on the floor.

"I saw you drop as soon as I opened the door." Kade's dimple was more than enough to let me know how much he enjoyed this situation.

Bellamy pulled out a box from a bag as me and Kade went back and forth on my motive to hide. I said I dropped some cake on the floor and he thought otherwise.

"Medisa." Bellamy cut in. Hearing him say my name was weird, but in a good way, like we were finally friends. He handed over two boxes over the counter then continued to talk. "Both of them are yours. The camera is because you displayed some sort of interest in it to Kade, and this one."

He pointed at the phone. "Is to give you a break from anyone with any connection to your old phone. Only have people on here that you truly need."

"Like me and Bellamy."

'And Amana and Kassian.'

I nodded to show that I understood.

Bellamy stood and approached me. "Let me reintroduce myself. I'm Bellamy Hayes." He put a hand over his heart instead of asking for mine. "I'm Kade's…" He thought of the right word to use. "Partner."

Instantly whipping my head to Kade, I spoke before I thought. "Knew you were gay."

We both childishly snickered until I realised Bellamy had no idea what we were laughing about. "I'm kidding, it's a joke from before when I was trying to figure out why you were so lenient with him."

I don't think Bellamy knew how to react. But when I saw how he looked between us, I guessed it was along the lines of, *'great, now there's two.'*

Chapter 19

Medisa

03/01/2022 (Monday)

So much for not hanging out with each other outside of work hours. Kade's taken me to do some shopping. I told him that I could do it all online, I just needed five to ten good recyclable outfits, but he said no.

No explanation. Just '*No.*'

We started off at the normal shops, you know, where things were 'decently' priced, but with every shop he took me to, the prices of things became a touch more ridiculous. Kade also had a habit of cutting in whenever I picked up something '*cheaply made*'. Apparently, he knew a place that offered similar or better designs with better materials. What he didn't seem to grasp was that I got the better price.

I'd been trying to avoid anything short sleeved or skin tight, or even something that exposed far too much, but I have a horrible shopping habit of buying clothes for when I have my own place. As for the clothing I needed for the public's eye, they're much more difficult to choose. It needed more brain power because I needed to think about how I would layer it since almost every bloody thing is skin tight or exposing something.

Every now and then, I would compliment a dress or two and 'slick' Kade would approach the exact item then follow me a second after. I didn't understand why, but I had a feeling he was up to something.

'*And I purposely ignored it.*'

The next place was one of my choosing. I wasn't expecting much from it, but as soon as we went in, I saw loads of things with potential, and this was just one of the floors.

As I went through the hangers, trying to find my size for this cute top, Kade was doing the same right behind me for its matching joggers.

"Are ¾ tops okay?"

"Not unless I wear a long-sleeved shirt underneath or something on top. Something on top is better though."

The sound of hangers being moved stop and I could just sense a follow up question.

"Is clothing the only thing you're changing about yourself?" He's now two steps to my side, and I couldn't have him staring at my side profile for long so, I moved on.

"Err no. I need to be stricter on prayer and stop swearing, listening to music—which I've already cut back on—and er, oh and free mixing which is exactly what I'm doing right now." I gave him a proud-sarcastic, slash attitude-infused wide smile, then moved into another section of the shop; lingerie. "If I catch you staring at a picture, I get to flick your forehead." I hold my finger out to him like someone who's lecturing.

Kade was about to argue but gave up.

Looking to the floor he continued our conversation. "Do you think that it's a bit much? I mean, difficult?" He corrected himself.

"No." I spoke plainly. "Difficult yes, but not too much. But it's only difficult 'cause pretty much every sin has been normalised." I reach for the pieces in the back. "So it's a good thing I've never been one to stick to the norm." I shrugged. "I'm not saying that I'm going to transform into the perfect Muslim, but I am going to try." I hand Kade a bunch of sets, adding to the pile of clothes that's already in his arms.

We walked over to the counter and gently dumped the pile of clothes onto the last few piles we made.

"Cash or card?"

"Card please." I smiled as both my hands held onto my card.

"Okay, that'll be £6945.74, just slot your card in here and enter your pin please." She pointed out the card machine whilst I momentarily froze.

'Did I even have that much in my account?' That's all my savings gone.

But I couldn't back out now, that's embarrassing.

Just as I moved to put my card into the machine, Kade flung it back. He'd done it so quickly I felt as though something else had taken it from me. I was even stunned for a few seconds as the cashier and Kade acted as though my card hadn't disappeared. When my card continued to patter in the background, I turned like there was no tomorrow to retrieve it. When I got back—out of breath—Kade was already picking up bags.

"Can we have the receipt please?" I asked with a plan in mind. If Kade wanted to pay for things, fine, I'm going to make his pockets hurt. I'm just also going to be collecting receipts so that I can return things later. "Okay, lets go to the stores that you have in mind now."

When we finally got back, the bedroom floor and walk in wardrobe was filled with bags and boxes. Not just from the things we had physically gone in to buy, but from the online shopping Kade had done from my wish lists. So, not only did I have everything from my shopping list, I had more, way more. Including the things I had touched and left in store. Kade must've had someone follow us and purchase them when we left or something. And the only thing, the *only* thing, that made me feel good about all this was the fact that I kept all the receipts.

"Medisa?" Kade called from what sounded like the kitchen.

Dinner must be ready.

I walked in as he finished off plating our food with a smile that gave away *something*...? I didn't know what it was, but I did find out when I went to wash my hands in the sink and found burnt paper. Strips of them, either turned to ash or blackened enough for them to not be accepted.

I gasped as I tried to pick them up. "You didn't."

Kade hissed as though he'd burnt himself. "I did."

Chapter 20

Medisa

05/01/2022 (Wednesday)

"What is it?" Kade asked as though he were saying '*out with it.*'

"I-er…I…"

"Yeah?" He dabbed his paintbrush multiple times on the canvas.

"I have a question."

"O-kay?"

"It's erm—it's personal?"

"Personal to who?"

"Personal to you."

"Oh." He stopped painting altogether.

"Yeahhh." I breathed out.

"About Kassian?"

I shook my head. "About your parents."

He took his time reacting, though I would say his slight pause and the way his eyes took their time looking into each of my eyes was enough.

"I…" I tried not to say '*erm.*' "Forget it—" I made an attempt to erase.

"What d'you want to know?"

'*All this build-up for me to not have a question ready.*'

Great.

"What do you remember about them?" I asked before I broke out in sweat under the pressure of his eyes.

Kade's brows twitched before he looked down at the

paint between us to summon what I thought would play on his mind every day; the memory of his parents.

"Not much." He bit the inside of his mouth. "I can't remember what they look like, and the warmth—the phantom pressure I felt from my mums touch disappeared a long time ago."

I stopped blinking.

Stopped moving.

Might've even stopped breathing and I couldn't stop analysing him for the life of me.

"She liked to paint, and to play on some instrument I don't have the luxury of remembering. And she loved us. I might not remember her smile or her laugh, but I know that."

My smile was light, and I tried my best to not make it look pitiful. I didn't want to question why he didn't have pictures of her because that would lead to upsetting reasons, perhaps even bad memories. He doesn't remember her face, and I do not need to push to know why.

"What was her name?"

"Karmen Kiliç River." He smiled when he said her name, but it slowly dropped once it was out his mouth.

"And your dad?"

"Maelon River. I can't recollect much about my dad but I know that he loved her. And he was good to us."

I wanted to ask the question that's been on my mind so bad, but it's none of my business. If he hadn't told me yet, it's because he doesn't want to.

"Errr?" I tried to come up with a lighter question, faintly scrunching my face.

Kade turned as though he were breaking the fourth wall, then gestured *'yeah?'*

"What did you mean by *'made up of almost every coun-*

"Seriously? That was months ago."

It's too late for me to calculate how many nights I had stayed at Aros for, but I knew that it was one too many for me to be behaving like this. It's stupid for me to have this…anxiety? I needed water, so I should be able to get some water. Why did I have to be scared? I know Kade, it's not like I am awkward around him, and it's not like I stomp, so why can't I just do the simple task of filling up my bottle?

'Screw it.'

I will have a filled water bottle in the next 5 minutes.

I slowly opened the bedroom door and peaked through as my body pushed itself through the large-enough-gap I made. Any wider than that and I bet the door hinges would've squeaked (they've never squeaked prior to this).

Kade was sleeping on the sofa and the room still had on its accent lighting, making it easier for me to cross over to the kitchen. Out of nowhere he took an aggressive deep breath behind me and I almost died one step away from the kitchen.

My heart beats went back to normal after a few seconds when I'd turned around to see if that odd breath was him waking up and being startled by me, but it wasn't. He was still sleeping, but the lighting in this room does allow me to see that he's breathing faster than he was when I had first walked in.

"Kade?" I'd quietly called out as I took some steps towards him. I think there's a rule against waking a sleepwalker up but I didn't know if that same rule applies here. "Kade?"

Now his breath was becoming a little more intense and it

just occurred to me that I may not be the right person for this. I am not well equipped for this particular job. What should I do? It was like an asthma attack or something, but his eyes are closed and he's started to look a little dewy.

My hand jammed towards him and then back again.

'Screw it.'

Putting my hand on his arm, I gave him a little shake. "Kade?" I said a little more urgently, desperately needing him to wake up. When that didn't work, I upped the intensity of the shake and before I knew it, his arm swung loose and came straight for my nose, knocking me back from my kneed position.

"Ow." I quickly gripped onto my face with both hands, feeling pins and needles, a weird amount of pressure and un-invited tears.

This guy just hit me in his sleep and it was up there on the pain scale. I couldn't imagine the intensity of his strength when he meant it.

Kade woke up and was beside me straight after my pain was vocalised. His hand hovered over my face, unsure if he should add to the suffocation I was inducing on myself.

"What are you doing awake?" He asked.

'Bruh.'

Despite not being able to move on from the fact that he hit me in his sleep, it's laughable really, I replied. "I was thirsty. Are you okay? I think you were having a nightmare." I spoke through my hands with a voice that gave away just how much I was squeezing my nose. "Do you want me to keep the door open so that I can—"

"No, no it's okay. Don't do that. I'm okay. How are you? Are you bleeding?" He looked like a liar, but I shouldn't push too hard. I should also probably stay away from the sarcastic

'I'm good! How are you?'

"No, it just felt like a weird amount of pressure. I'm okay now."

"You sure?"

"Yeah." I moved my hands away to prove it (I did not feel okay).

"I'm sorry for hitting you." He took responsibility whilst also trying to seem as though nothing was wrong with him.

"It's okay. Don't worry. I'm going back to bed unless you want me to stay awake?" I half expected him to lash out on me for making him out to be someone who's 'weak' or scared, but he just flashed a smile.

"Nah." Kade spoke as he grabbed my bottle and stood up. "I'll fill this up for you then go back to having sweet dreams." He smiled with his teeth now, the fakest smile I've seen from him yet.

He was definitely having a nightmare. And from how startled he was, I'm guessing they are new? Or I was the thing that startled him and he doesn't want to talk about it with me (fair). But then, no offence to him and I also don't want to sound ungrateful, but why choose to then sleep right outside the room I'm in?

Hopefully this doesn't make him awkward around me tomorrow, and the day after that, and the day after that, and the day after that, until eventually we spoke about it.

'I'm such an idiot.' I texted Amana as soon as I'd got back to bed, then googled *'how to deal with someone whose dreams affect the way they breathe?'*

Chapter 21

Medisa

07/01/2022 (Friday)

Time in Kade's care has been completely different. No more strange packages, no more strangers spying on me, no more feeling left out. Kade and Bellamy—mostly Kade—busied my days with whatever they could think of and honestly, I kind of liked it—no, I *enjoyed* it. For the first time in forever my mind was on a break. I could be in another room and not hear someone speak ill of me. I could rest, I could eat whenever, I could talk about whatever, watch whatever and most importantly, I could *breathe*.

Like Amana, Kade became someone I couldn't imagine having a future without. I've spent so much time with him that we might as well be siblings or something. Not that I know what having a proper sibling is supposed to be like, but I suppose it's something like what the three of us have, *if* sisters called each other 'wifey' and a brother was someone like Kade.

Just when I got used to spending my days with Kade and maybe even Bellamy, Aros decided now was the best time to have some sort of emergency. And with the boys gone, I am left alone with another side of my mind. And that side decided that today would be the day I got some fresh air and maybe possibly even meet Kade's *favourite* brother Kassian.

The idea of leaving for a bit doesn't sound too bad. It's not like anything we would like to avoid would definitely happen today.

'Said no one ever.'

Ideally, my plans should have been done early morning to avoid any sort of trouble because what bad guy wakes up early morning?

'What bad guy sleeps?'

But instead, I took my time getting ready, even decided to do one of those cute girly loosely pinned back hairstyles. Today would be the first time in ages that I got to walk around my area. It's kind of exciting, and looking good would add dramatic points to the feeling of feeling good. So, I guess in a way I could say that taking my time was worth it, until I actually looked at the time—15:30—and debated on if I should still leave.

Still having a few hours to kill before they got back, and already being ready for this, I pushed myself to leave.

I got this.

Sunset approaching doesn't matter. This little excursion won't kill anyone, and if worse comes to worst, I could just call one of them.

I'd done about a lap around the park before deciding to leave. It'd gotten really dark and the park started to fill with old school rejects with herbal endeavours, and I refused to be seen (alone) and approached.

Walking down the curvy road that outlined part of the schools land, I remembered how scary it was sometimes to be walking home from school, hours after it had finished. You would've thought they would have proper street lights on a school and park road, but no, they didn't, the lights were about as dim as the worst students.

Even though there are houses on the other side of this wide road, and sometimes afterschool clubs still running, the road itself was not only dark, but also quiet and felt as if it muted all sounds. I used to think that I could shout for help and no one would bat an eyelid, not because they didn't care, but because they simply couldn't hear.

A van started up as I walked past, snapping me back to reality. If it wasn't for my baggy clothes, I'm sure the driver would've saw me try to jump out of my skin.

Amana hadn't answered my calls before, which left Kassian to be the person to get my mind of its body walking alone in the dark.

Whilst I struggled to find which pocket I had put my phone in, I stepped out onto the road to get to the outer part of its bend, closer to the houses. And just as I have a feel of my rectangular friend, the van pulled up and opened its doors right in front of me.

Being able to process what was going on wasn't even a thing. I did try to resist, but with bare minimum effort. Even in a situation like this, I couldn't risk looking like an idiot and embarrassing myself, which was ironic because not fighting enough was also being an idiot.

They tried to tie my arms back but I kept moving them in all sorts of directions to avoid theirs, giving them no choice but to tie them in front of me. <u>Thank God</u>, it's a win if you ask me. There would be almost no hope for me if my hands were tied behind my back.

'Ignoring the 'being taken to a second location' fact.'

Though I basically made their job much easier by not fighting as hard, I still earned a slap across my face. And the bloody thing held weight, which off course called for waterworks.

I rapidly blinked.

As if hitting me were a trigger, I no longer felt as scared. The bastard hit me for no reason, earning himself confused-pissed death stares and more struggle, as now I was willing to make whatever this was, harder.

They all wore masks that barely exposed their eye area. And I couldn't recognise their eyes, I would say it's the lighting but it's not, I genuinely did not know who these people were. Before I could rush through my memories of any time I might've unintentionally pissed off a group of men, or encountered a group of perverts—level difficulty: hard—one of them removed his mask just to spit on my face. And no, not a normal spit, just like the slap, the spit held weight.

Moving my head to the side in disgust, I wiped his thick slimy creation off with my sleeve.

'I'm going to be sick.'

Before I could say anything, another man grabbed a hold of my hair and yanked my head back. Any more power and I'm sure I would've died on spot from a broken neck or something.

"You're going to regret what you did to us you bitch." He was too close to my face for my liking and with the last word, he threw my head away. His words were filled with such anger, even the way he'd delivered his words—through his teeth—were as though he were about to explode from the emotions he held…

'Men.'

Continuing to be visually confused didn't help the situation at all. The four men's chest's heaved, their shoulders and chest moved up and down with every breath as if getting me into the van was hard work (what I told myself because the alternative would be that they all held the same amount of anger, if not more, which meant that I was definitely screwed).

"The men from the pub?" My eyes switched between the group. "I don't know what you're talking about—"

A different man this time stepped forward and slapped me, forcing my head and body to move in the direction of the swing.

'It was a half lie.'

"You killed Pete."

More tears pile up as I got back on my knees, trying to steady myself on the floor of a moving van.

"Screw. You." If I could spit like the man before I would, but since I knew that I couldn't, I saved myself from the embarrassment. The wonderful sensation of pins and needles stayed on my face, reminding me of the size of his hand in case I had forgotten. Dizziness was now also making an appearance and I quickly prayed nausea was not next. "I don't know what you guys are talking about, I don't know a *Pete*." Frustration may have come out with his name. I don't even know why I felt the need to say that, of course I didn't know any of them on a name-to-name basis.

One of them, the one who hadn't done anything but zip tie my hands together—and too tight at that—slowly crouched down in front of me. The way he acted was enough for me to believe he was the leader of this particular group.

He removed his mask, then his unexposed sheep followed.

'I'm so screwed.'

"You don't remember Pete?" He frowned. "What about Will?"

It took everything in me to not answer back with an attitude. Were these men okay in the head? Am I missing something? Since when were we all introduced to each other?

My heavy breathing was put on hold as he grabbed me by my clothes to a stand, forcing my back against the vans wall. Before the situation escalated some more, the van came to a stop.

Seconds later a few knocks are heard.

The 'leader' in the van who I named Dick, held my face by my chin a lot harder than needs be, then invaded my personal space once again.

"Don't think you've escaped your fate." He ended his sentence with a lick up the side of my face. And as disgusted as I was by his fat tongue, I chuckled, causing him and those behind to lose part of their anger to confusion.

"You just licked off whatever remained of his." I signalled with my eyes and an upward nod to the other man. "Spit."

When Dick turned to face me again, I couldn't help but hold an expression that visibly showed suppressed laughter.

'Idiot.'

He released his grip from my face, then out of nowhere smashed my head into the side of the van. Before I fell to the floor, he grabbed onto me. Getting one solid kick to my gut, I flew back and with my luck, which was no luck at all, the van doors opened at the same time. So no, I did not have a short fall and landing, no, my back fell on the ground outside, stealing air from my lungs.

My legs were practically out, which basically called for more pain as they had to drag me to where they wanted.

I fought to stay awake. If this was how they treated me while I was conscious, I didn't even want to think about what they would do to me if I was unconscious.

Dumping me in the centre of a construction site, they regrouped with others as if they hadn't abducted me.

There were a few uncovered areas I could run to, but my body felt stiff. Not to mention, they only needed one good runner amongst them to get me.

Dick and his original flock began toying with me, playing about with how they lurked. Some were doing the most, acting out their intentions like bloody weirdos. Others had this look in their eyes like they couldn't wait to put me through pain. The last of them looked as though they were okay with being an audience. Once I scouted the group and any extra, I kept my eyes on Dick. Yes, I was scared. Yes, I was sweating despite the weather being cold. But I didn't care. I wanted to do something to this man, starting with wiping that fucking smirk off his face.

I stood up. My muscles pleaded for some sort of massage or stretch, but I did not show it. I didn't know what I was going to do, but I figured standing up was a better position than being on the floor.

These men thought I killed someone. Pete? I don't remember doing that, I only remember one guy getting the worst of it and that was someone Kassian dealt with. I'm guessing that was Will? Are they blaming me for that?

Would it be stupid for me to quickly get Siri to call someone? My hands are bound with the zip-tie pinching into my skin, sawing its way to my bones, but my lips are free.

"How did you know where I was?" I moved myself accordingly. When someone took a step towards me, I took one back, when one of them took a step to my side, I took a step to the other. Maybe I could stall until someone checked my location?

Dick slowly shook his head. "Your phone. Which one of your hundred pockets is it in?"

"It must've dropped when you guys grabbed me."

He scoffed. "No. No it didn't, we checked."

One of them jolted towards me, grabbing me before I could take a step away. My arms, waist, legs are checked until finally he found my phone. And I don't know why, I really don't, but I latched onto it. A stupid mistake really because he faced me with such hatred, delivering a clean elbow to my lips. And I swear, I felt and heard it rip, and despite me moving my attention towards trying to stop it from bleeding, or the pain spreading, he somehow got me on the ground, booting me, again and again.

"Alright stop you dumbass. We need her to unlock the phone." Dick pushed him away then squatted besides me. "I understand if you need a minute to catch your breath, but that's all you're getting."

'I might actually die tonight.'

There's no way I was surviving this. Even if Kade does see my location, it would take him forty minutes to get here.

"Alright minute's up."

I said nothing.

If I was going to die, there's no way I would willingly give them what they want. I wouldn't even give them what they wanted if I was guaranteed life.

"Your pin?"

"You're wasting your time." I finally spoke. "My friends have taste."

Dick almost looked impressed, humoured even, until he stuck the side of my head into the ground, twisting it as though there was a hole for my head to squeeze into. Pressure built. My skin burnt. The ground was like dirt, sand and cement, and it did not feel like a good exfoliator. I tried to pry his hand away, but it didn't work and that's when I pinched and scratched.

Pulling me to my feet by the zip-tie, he moved the burns from my face back to my wrists.

"Cut away her layers." He spoke to his sheep, and they did as they were told. They cut through my jacket and hoodie before dragging me to a rusty chair.

I was in pain.

There's no simpler way of putting it. I'm running out of energy when I need more. Especially since they mixed some things in a bucket a few steps in front of me. Despite the number of breaths I took, my heartbeat dramatically increased at the thought of that being cement. They were going to drown me in cement.

One of them walked over with the bucket and all I could do was mentally prepare. This was going to happen, the least I could do was take a deep breath to give myself a fighting chance.

When the substance poured onto me, I quickly felt how cold and runny it was, and not just that, but it had salt mixed into it. Every single cut, bruise, scratch, everywhere that had an opening stung as the water rushed down my body and seeped into my wounds.

"Tie her hands back."

Whilst I tried to scrunch up from the pain, folding my body over onto my legs, stomping the ground and hitting my own thighs, wanting to scream but not being able to, they cut my wrists loose and tied them back with another zip-tie.

"Oh for fucks sake."

"What?"

"She has the face detection password."

I never liked the idea of the face detection lockscreen, but since this phone was a clean slate and there was nothing valuable on it, I used it.

Now Dick stood in front of me, waiting for me to lift my head. When I didn't, he fought me. This pull and push game resulted in my neck muscle being pulled, allowing him to win.

The phone didn't recognise me.

"Hold on." Dick wiped away my hair and rubbed over where blood had dried, bringing about more stings. "Ahhh there she is."

The phone unlocked.

Chapter 22

Medisa
07/01/2022 (Friday)

I don't know who did it, but one of them cows knocked me out. I was still clothed, <u>thank God</u>, and was still on the chair, so nothing happened, but shit, I still got a heart attack the moment I woke up and saw Kade in front of me, and Kassian in the back.

They were together.

They were, with me and these men, together.

Everything was a blur after that. Kade had picked me up and walked out, leaving Kassian inside. I thought we were going to leave him all together but then Kade locked me in the car and went back in. A minute or two later, Kassian rushed out and got into the driver's seat, then *we* left Kade.

Kassian drove in the opposite direction of the city. I didn't know where he planned on taking us this time, but I didn't care. I needed him to turn back and get Kade but he ignored me.

I tried moving to the front of the car, ignoring the sore feeling all over, but winced as soon as a new sharp pain came from my leg. I knew the majority of my body was bruised, but the pain I just experienced felt as if my leg was on fire or was being drained of blood. So, I sat back down and went back to nagging him, hitting the back of his seat whenever I could.

When Kassian finally noticed me as if this whole time he was in his head, he pulled up to the side of the abandoned looking high road, then got out the car. My eyes followed him as he was visibly not so jolly, then he opened the back door a bit too aggressive for my liking.

Scurrying back to lean on the opposite door in attempts to move away didn't stop him from doing what he wanted.

My legs were grabbed.

I was dragged.

My body gets folded over his shoulder.

A few cars go by, but not one beeped or stopped as Kassian popped open the boot with me on his shoulder.

"No *wait*, I won't say anything anymore! Don't put me in there I'm claustrophobic!" I desperately tried to change his mind whilst gripping onto his clothes.

Kassian froze.

A few seconds later and I am put on my feet.

"You're hurt." He used four fingers, a flat vertical hand, and an attitude to point me out. "I can't tend to your wounds in the back of the car, so you'll sit comfortably in the boot *with* the hood up as I take a look at what they did to you."

'Oh.'

I do as he says, thinking that he would examine my face first, but no, his eyes shot straight to my leg where my jeans gave away a serious looking injury.

"Don't even think about it."

"What?" He smirked, sounding oblivious.

"You're not allowed to see my legs and I can't—"

He ripped into my jeans using the cut made at the site, exposing parts of my thigh.

I'm mentally relieved for waxing the other day.

"Sorry, you were saying?" His *'no shits given'* made clear.

I quickly threw my hands over the exposed skin.

Kassian's retaliation was removing and holding them down to my sides, leaning his face far too close to mine.

"We haven't got time for this act. You're bleeding all over the place. What kind of man would I be to let that continue?"

I opened my mouth to speak but he cuts me off.

"Ah-ah I haven't got the energy for this, as you can see, I'm hurt too. Now, *sit quietly*, before I find something to restrain you, clean you up, then leave you in the boot."

Taking a step back, he examined my thigh. The cut wasn't deep enough for it to be deadly, but it was spewing out blood like I've got an infinite supply. Giving it attention was probably my biggest mistake so far. It's like all my receptors woke up at once.

Kassian slid a large first aid box next to me.

"I always said that I would have a first aid kit with some blankets and food in my car." I made conversation.

"Don't think that you both share great minds, I brought this on the way here knowing that someone would need it."

Placing a small towel under my thigh, he pulled out some water, pouring it all over the cut, cleaning off any blood on and around, hopefully getting rid of anything that would cause an infection. Using some sort of cotton material, he pressed down on the open wound with a little too much pressure.

"Now for the fun bit."

My face dropped as Kassian pulled out some sort of antiseptic solution, and once again, I tried to cover the cut on my thigh, this time hovering my dirty hands over it.

"Hold onto something, it'll be over quick. Just breathe in when I say."

I gripped onto the top of my injured thigh. "Do it."

"Take a deep breath and hold it."

Soon as I did as I was instructed, he generously poured the liquid, taking breaks in between. I applied as much pressure as I could to the top of my thigh whilst leaning into the other. *'It'll be over quick'* is added to the list of lies Kassian has said.

Once whatever that process was, was done, he bandaged me up and done me the favour of covering up my exposed thigh.

"Your turn." I hopped off the boot then circled him, pointing at where he should sit.

Surprisingly, he didn't argue, in fact, he didn't even try to engage in any sort of conversation. Truth be told, I wanted to be annoyed and blow off some steam, but I needed to be clever on how I went about this. It's not every day a girl gets kidnapped then gets to spend time with Kassian River. So, I started off by saying something that would definitely have his attention.

"It was Maverick you know." I spoke as I cleaned his cut brow.

Any sort of unseriousness left him as he stared me down. He didn't say anything but I could tell that he was stunned, maybe even annoyed. It was like his eyes were saying *'careful.'*

But since I started, I may as well finish.

"He knew enough about the pub incident to send me gifts and any other sort of message, like how he has eyes on me. I even got a message at the hotel which is why I left. And today…How did they know where I was? How did they know to call you?"

Kassian dropped his stern look for a second as if he was actually contemplating what I was saying.

"Your current revenge plan is making you blind. *'An eye*

for an eye would make the whole world blind.'"

"Did you just quote Gandhi?"

"Did I? Ew. Anyways, what I was trying to get at was that you don't see Maverick doing you over because you're so distracted by wanting revenge on Kade."

His face went back to being scary serious as I searched for some sort of answer from his eyes. Then, he stood, grabbing the antiseptic cream out of my hands. If this was a good time to stop, I ignored the message. Kassian had to hear me, we needed him on our side.

"They wanted to kill you back there and if you think otherwise, you're dumber than I thought!—*Sit back down* I'm cleaning you—" I grabbed the cream back as he shockingly did as he was told. "I don't know why you're siding with him—I don't even know why you have a problem with me! But you have to realise, Maverick is not your friend in this."

This was supposed to be a gentle approach but I'm practically pleading, *forcing* him to listen.

Kassian continued to be mute so I just carried on aiding his face, applying a little more pressure than needs be. Looking at some of the cuts and bruises he had attained, I sighed and tried one last attempt before I dropped it all together.

"I wanted to be close to my siblings so bad when I was younger, but they constantly took me for an idiot and abused me whenever they felt like it. And there was *never* a good reason for it. And since I knew what they were like, I stopped being a beg. I didn't need their attention, or praise." I hoped he got what I was trying to say. "Later on in life, I met my best friend, and she was everything that I wanted in a friend, everything that I *needed* from my family. And even when the abuse continued, it didn't sting as much 'cause I knew that I had one person in my corner. One person who would be with me no matter what, who saw and actually respected me." I cocked my head to the side to catch Kassian's gaze, his eyes were glossy. "Maverick isn't in your corner Kassian, but you'll find someone who is. Me and Kade are—"

He aggressively scoffed. "Kade?" He stood up once again. "Kade—He—"

His phone began to ring near the first aid kit.

Kassian scoffed again, this time as if he couldn't believe it. "Speak of the Devil." He answered the phone before I moved to prevent him from getting to it, heard what he needed to, then hung up.

"Let's go get him."

I stood my ground like a child about to throw a tantrum. "No. Tell me what happened! Tell me what he did that was so bad that you're taking it out on me." I stood back as he packed whatever was in the boot, worried that he would chuck me in. "What did he do? What did I do?" I spoke with my hands, arms, body as I followed him to the front of the car. "I know what you do at Baronial with people you don't know, but you've spent time with me and you're still okay with what could happen? How much of a shitty person are you pretending to be? How far are you willing to take this?" I thought of the time at my house, at the pub, right now. "I know that you have a heart, you're just pretending that you don't." I searched his eyes, his face for something, anything but he gave nothing I could understand. Nothing I said seemed to be working, I needed to hit a sensitive spot.

'But not too hard.'

"How big of a heartbreak was it that you're letting it blind you from the truth!" I followed him as he walked away. "Maverick doesn't care about you! He wouldn't—"

Kassian aggressively opened the passenger door then

turned to me so fast I almost fell back.

"Get in the car Medisa or I'll put you in the boot."

He's angry? Hurt? Whatever he felt he tried his best to contain it, but I knew better. Whatever it was that Kade had done, better have been worth it because I don't think that there's anything else that I could say or do that would get Kassian to help us.

'Or tell me something I don't know.'

Childishly, I sat in the back instead of the passenger seat. If I couldn't get us to stay outside and talk this out, he couldn't get me to sit where he wanted.

Kassian slammed the passenger door shut.

We made our way to Kade silently. I had more to say but there was no point. How could I bring sense to a boy who spent his life doing what he does to survive? I looked out the window to try and focus on something, to take my mind off and to control my breathing. But no matter what unrelated scenario or topic I came up with, nothing could distract me from what happened, what is happening and what could happen. The more thoughts I produced the drowsier I became, and just like that my thoughts became the author of my dream.

Chapter 23

Medisa

08/01/2022 (Saturday)

When I used to fall asleep in the car as a child, sometimes I woke up as my dad pulled into our road or drive. It was like my body was alert at all times and knew that we had reached our final destination, 'home.'

It seems now my body has already claimed Kade's accommodation to be the new final destination. Soon as the car was parked, my eyes began to open and since I sensed where we were, it wasn't that shocking to the system when it was confirmed.

What *was* surprising was Kassian's presence.

Kade opened my door. "I know what you're going to say but I'm still going to offer."

I was still in the process of waking up so I had no idea what he meant.

"Would you like me to carry you upstairs?" He glanced at my thigh.

"It's okay. It's not that bad and we have the elevator so I'll be alright. Thank you though."

He stepped to the side, and I knew his eyes would be on me so I tried to walk normally. It wasn't that hard, but I still felt pain, and this intense soreness here and there. <u>Thank God</u>, he owned the parking spaces near the elevator so I didn't have to take too many painful steps.

As expected, the way up was awkward. Kade and Kassian made a few remarks in another language, but that was about it. I was just a spectator waiting for this damn metal box to take me to my new bed.

Once the doors opened, we unintentionally cat walked down the hallway. I'm sure it's all in my mind and in reality, we all looked like shit and had some sort of flaw in our walk, but still, the atmosphere was there.

As beaten as we all were, quite literally, except maybe Kade, we all chose the kitchen to be our rest point. I suppose getting some rest wasn't the only thing on our minds.

Kade almost automatically busied himself with cooking, triggering Kassian to begin his wandering with little interferences here and there.

Standing out the way and looking in, it looked as if this was their home, their daily routine, and I was the one that was out of place.

'You *are* out of place.'

Kade walked straight into the tv room after saying, '*I'll be right back,*' leaving me with Kassian. Kassian noticed him walking away then sabotaged the dish by adding a few things.

"I can feel your eyes on me you know." He watched me through our reflection in the window as he stirred the pot.

I didn't know what to say—no, I knew what I wanted to say, I just didn't know how to word it or what to say first.

"I'm sorry."

'Good start.'

"I shouldn't have said what I said, the way that I said it."

'Wordy.'

"It was kinda selfish but believe it or not, I kinda like you."

'Too much?'

He turned around amused, brow raised.

"Not like that. I mean as a strong acquaintance or something. Anyways, I was angry and physically hurt too, so the fact that you were, slash are being blind to what is clearly happening, pissed me off a little."

Kade walked back in before Kassian could say anything, joggers and shirt in hand.

Kassian (purposely?) kept his eyes on me for a little longer allowing his brother to see that something was going on, then he went back to stirring.

Taking the clothes off Kade, I thanked him quieter than I'd intended, then grabbed some tape and a plastic bag. After locking both bathroom doors, I got comfortable in front of the mirror. I looked like shit, but also somehow good? The cuts and bruises looked like they wouldn't leave behind any marks when fully healed, so I had no reason to be too upset.

I taped the bag over my thigh, got into the tub, then quickly scrubbed myself, and I mean *quickly*. I did not care for washing properly, I needed to get back out there to witness their interaction. This must be the first time in ages that they were around each other and I was missing out on it.

Once I dried myself and removed the plastic bag, I got busy with my body and clothes. My ribs and abdomen held bruises about the size of two mean fists, and the side of my face was red. Parts of my cheek even had that scratched, sandpapered skin look. I actually looked and felt pretty badarse if I ignored the part where I didn't actually fight back.

After weirdly admiring my look (again), I slipped into the joggers and top Kade had passed. Carefully unlocking and opening the door, I tried to hear any of the conversation the two might be having, but there was nothing, I couldn't even hear any utensils being moved or drawers being opened.

Coming back into the kitchen was weirder than being with them in the elevator. They're both silent, passing each other and me looks, like I didn't have eyes of my own.

Walking back over to my seat, I noticed more of Kade's appearance. He had a blood-stained towel chucked over his shoulder after he'd wiped his face, neck, hair and hands. My brain obviously didn't register *how* much blood he had on him before now.

"So, which one of you is going to tell me what I missed?" Kade spoke like a responsible friend, adult and brother.

Not being the best thing to do, but still doing it, my eyes moved over to Kassian. We didn't exactly finish our conversation.

"You first brother dearest, we all know that's not your blood on you. What did me and sweet Medisa miss?"

Kassian clearly didn't want to talk about the high road situation, and Kade shrugged the question off as though none of us knew that this evening was Maverick's doing.

Before going back to making a side dish, Kassian smirked at Kade's answer as though he had expected him to reply in that way.

And once again, I sat speechless as the twins moved around the kitchen and made food together. One minute they stood against each other and the next they randomly mentally agreed to be civil and cook us all a meal.

No one (minus me) wants to talk about the construction site—fair enough, but we needed to talk about where Kassian now stood. I just didn't know how to bring it up without looking like a bitch for bringing it up out of nowhere.

'But it's not out of nowhere, I was literally kidnapped.'

They bickered, bringing me out of my head. It was mostly Kassian saying that Kade wasn't making the food the right way, and then adding his own spices and cheese to the chicken pasta.

By the end of it, both boys took out bowls for themselves and one for me, leaving me with the choice of choosing whose bowl I would eat from. Both stood waiting for me to choose. I, however, giggled, and hesitated. I kind of liked them together. Of course, I knew choosing a bowl, in a way, is choosing a side in this petty thing they got going. So, I got up to get my own bowl which was instantly shut down as I was ordered to stay sat.

Thankfully I didn't have the luxury of choosing whose bowl was at the bottom as they were given to me placed with one on top of the other.

All of us were comfortable at different places in the kitchen with large bowls of saucy chicken pasta and garlic bread. Kassian was sitting on the countertop next to the stove, I was on the stool and Kade leaned on the island. We basically had a comfortable view of each other.

I tried to concentrate on literally anything else, but I couldn't get my mind off the conversation, or rather the pleading, to get Kassian to understand that Maverick is not someone that he should be siding with. It must've gotten through to him, that's why he's here, right? Even if he was pissed, I apologised, but did that even make a difference? Did I make things worse? He's Kassian, but not the same as he was before, the jokes and taunts are still there, but with different underlying emotions.

I couldn't take the silence mixed with forks attacking plates anymore, so I mentally prepped to speak.

"The right way or not, it still tastes the same." Kade beat me to it.

"I won't argue with you on that." Kassian spoke lowly.

I wanted to be a part of what they're talking about. I wanted to know who originally made the pasta, what the right way was and how they taught themselves to make it, but sitting back and taking in their reactions, reading their bodies, I decided to sit this one out.

"Our parents used to make this every now and then—" Kade must've read my mind because he cleared up my curiosities even though I was okay with being left a little in the dark, if it meant that they got along. "—we would beg them too and then—"

"Then we begged Maverick to, or to at least tell us how to make it." Kassian cut in to finish the sentence when Kade had slightly paused.

Without moving my head, I looked over to Kade, whose knuckles turned white around the fork as Kassian continued.

"You should see, or at least hear about the conditions he gave us for it—"

"Enough." Kade got up to put his bowl away. "She doesn't need to know all that."

"I'd beg to differ, if I'm going to be on your side, I should have a say and I say…" He looked at me instead of Kade. "She needs to know as much as she can to be able to defend herself."

I couldn't see his face clearly, but I knew that Kade was throwing him a *'on our side?'* look, hell, even I was.

"Don't all jump with excitement." Kassian leaned over the stove to get more pasta. "I'm no idiot, I knew that he specifically wanted me there today, not caring about the outcome. And I would've been blind or in denial rather than come to my senses. It would've taken me ages to accept it without Medisa. She just helped speed up the process." He shrugged his shoulders before throwing a wink my way.

"I'm not buying it." Kade spoke.

"Suit yourself."

He did switch up a bit too fast for my liking too. It's weird. Loathing Kade to the point where you are willing to hurt innocent people, to then joining Kade? I don't know, seems a bit off. Kade obviously felt it too, but we needed Kassian to make things easier.

"Kade." I didn't continue until he turned to face me. "Just give him one chance."

I felt like an idiot for asking. Kade is hesitant or against Kassian because he knows him. I don't.

He placed himself so that he's able to look between Kassian and me with ease.

"What about your revenge? Am I supposed to buy that you've dropped it?"

"No." Kassian spoke casually. "Because I haven't dropped it. I'm simply postponing it."

They shared looks between each other until Kade let out a heavy breath.

"Leave whatever happened in the past in the past, Medisa doesn't need to know everything. Other than that, I agree." He turned his head to face me. "Medisa, we'll teach you whatever we can as soon as we can." He looked back to Kassian. "And you, if you're still playing games—"

"I'm not. But we will be. With Maverick. I'll be your insider." Kassian looked so ready for this new chapter, like he had ideas for days.

"He would find out and plan something malicious for us." Kade tried to test him, see if this was what he truly wanted.

"For me, you mean. In his sick head, I'm the one that would be betraying him in this scenario, and I'm ready to risk it if it gives us a chance." He paused for his brother's approval.

Meanwhile, I go over what's been said, and what I know

about Maverick so far, and he just sounds like a living head-ache. The *only* reason I would want to meet him at the moment, is to feed my curiosity about how the twins may look when they're older.

"If this is going to work, you need to leave now. Talk to him in person, convince him that his little test failed in making you turn away from him—"

"Okay, but if any of that really works, how would we communicate, Maverick made it seem like he knew about every step that I took. How would you guys train me if he watches all of us?" I cut in. I'd been way too quiet.

"Leave that to me sweet Medisa. Leave that to me." Kassian smiled, showing off his dimples.

'How did I not clock he has two and Kade has one? Did Kassian not smile around me before?'

"Speaking of training and communication, do I have to learn the languages you guys were speaking too?"

I hoped so.

"We haven't got *that* much time." Kassian chimed, triggering Kade's death stare.

"And there's no point. Maverick understands every language we speak." Kade said what Kassian should've.

"We're just accustomed to speaking to one another in those languages when there's a third-party present."

'Third-party being me.'

"Like those who work for Maverick." Kade adds after my thought is formed.

"But he could just hire someone who also understands you?"

"Yes well, he won't. At least he didn't when we all lived together. He wanted us to try him, not to teach us to grow some, but so that he had the opportunity to demonstrate what happens when we do."

"He sounds like a prick." I genuinely felt some type of way towards Maverick despite not yet meeting him.

"Aren't we all?" Kassian's eyes stayed on Kade. Postponed revenge and its anticipation sparkled in them.

"Alright, get out, we'll discuss the details later. We need to rest and you need to do some acting, which I have no faith in." Kade signalled for me to follow him into the tv room.

"No faith? I fooled Medisa for days pretending to be you."

I snapped my head back to Kassian, scrunching my eyebrows, he did *not* need to bring that up.

"I didn't know that he was, slash is a twin, but Maverick does." I defended myself.

"Fair." Kassian continued to smile but directed it towards Kade. Kade flipped him off as he waited for me to be by his side.

And just like that, we had a little team. Did I trust it? Not completely. Did I like it? 100%

Chapter 24

Medisa
09/01/2022 (Sunday)

Yesterday's events felt like one of those necessary (but unnecessary) circumstances that needed to happen in order for us to have Kassian on our side. I'm sure Kade would've been enough, but having Kassian would make things easier, having an active insider and all. Also, if I'm going to get back to my original plan of being able to provide for myself, I needed to see whatever this was through. It's not like this is all completely in my hands, it's not like I could ignore this all and continue living life—No—I'm practically given no choice given the circumstances, so technically I'm not willingly sinning, or rather, I'm not happily doing all this (staying with Kassian, staying with Kade, training with the two of them etc.) I needed to do these things in order to survive, otherwise it's practically suicide, which is a major sin. So, on the sin scale, I felt like I was good.

Turning over onto my injured leg, I winced, then groaned. The quicker my leg stopped hurting, the quicker we could all train, and the more time we would all spend together which would eventually lead to Kade and Kassian fixing whatever happened between them.

Dangling my legs off the bed, I was about to pull my joggers down to get a good look at the cut when the devil himself knocked on the bedroom door.

"It's not locked, you can come in."

Kade walked in with my water bottle in hand, filled and

diluted with chlorophyll. After handing it over to me, he went back to stand in the doorway, leaning on its frame.

"How you feeling? I called for my doctor to get you checked. I would do it myself but I googled and it said something along the lines of needing to be a doctor, or it needing to be an emergency or something."

He's cute for trying I'll give him that.

"Thank you, although I'm pretty sure your doctor brother got me covered."

"As dumb as he is, he's actually good when it comes to stuff like that. We all are."

My face hid no confusion. "What, does every River have a failed medical degree?"

"Something like that."

My face dropped. There's no way he's being serious. How would they even be able to learn all of that information? Where did he even get the time to learn all of it? Especially if they had the lives I've drawn in my head based off their little comments.

"What does that even mean?"

"It means that if we wanted the degree, we would have it. We don't know *everything* that there is to know, but we do know en—"

"Yeah-yeah I got it. You guys aren't just all looks." I held my hand up as if to wave him off.

"No. Definitely not." He held a proud look allowing for a small appearance from his dimple.

"What's your favourite module in this '*degree*'?" If Kassian's is for example, healing, medicine, treating open wounds, I wondered what Kade's would be.

"Anatomy." He answered almost straight away.

"What do you like about it?" Somehow, I am not surprised. It's the right amount of complexity and beauty, ergo, perfect for Kade.

"The colours, the layers, the intricacies…" He thought about what else to say. "I like drawing or painting or even sculpting parts of the body."

If I had known about his creative skills and interest earlier, and I mean way earlier, I think I would've liked him quicker than I'd come to like him in the path that's played out.

I've only ever seen Kade paint once. And that should've been enough for me to know about his liking towards being creative, but no, instead I was distracted and wanted to know about his family tree and what not.

I mentally shook my head.

If I had allowed myself to come away from the drama, after witnessing his knowledge on colours (painting in general really) I would've known more about him. I could've allowed him to be himself and geek out instead of constantly entertaining me.

"After graduation, or after this is over, can I see your drawings and sculptures?"

He froze.

"Yeah." He whispered whilst almost eagerly nodding. "Of course."

I smiled, then felt some sort of tension or awkwardness lurk in.

"Anywaysss." I quickly came up with something to say. "When do we have to go see him?"

"Hmm? Oh no you're not going anywhere, he's coming here."

Kade rests against the doorframe, hesitant to leave but also hesitant to say something. His brow slightly raised, questioning as though he knew that I wanted to conversate about yesterday's antics.

"Can we talk about what happened yesterday?" I made sure to say it in a way where I'm not pressing the matter, even though I really, *really* wanted to talk about it.

"We can. I didn't want to make you uncomfortable by saying something first, or too early."

'So *he does want to talk about it.*'

"No, I want to, I just don't know how to go about it."

"Okay." He pushed himself off the doorway and into the room. "That's okay, just say it how it is in your mind and I'll listen."

'*And I'll listen.*' Felt good hearing that.

Those words were all I needed for me to tell him everything. From the moment I got ready to go for a walk, up until what happened on the highway. I also mentioned how I thought I was going to die, but then was like nah. It didn't matter how harsh they were being, I would survive, but only to be put through something worse (a pattern I noticed). I also apologised several times and called myself an idiot for getting myself in that position (which then made him and Kassian do what they did). I rushed through some of my words, probably didn't even make sense on a few sentences, but I got everything out and I could tell that Kade was taking it all in, word for word, he listened, he didn't interrupt, he didn't zone out.

"Can I come sit at the end of the bed?"

"Yeah." I nodded as I patted the covers, calling him over.

He sat down and turned to face me. "I'm sorry you felt so cooped up in here that you felt the need to sneak off to do something normal whilst I was away. We'll go out more often now I promise, *together*, if that's what you want, or you could go with Bellamy instead." He joked and I snorted.

"The men yesterday were weak enough for Maverick to manipulate, anything that they had done to you was because of him, not because of a phantom fault they forced on you. You're strong Medisa, look at everything you've been through, how you handle things. Most people would freeze or scream, but you think logically. And I need you to think logically right now, on this silk bed I *deeply* miss, and see that you didn't put us in danger, Maverick did. You were in a bad situation and by the end of the day you made it better, by still having some fight in you and forcing Kassian to see the truth. As for getting yourself out of these types of situations, we'll teach you, *I'll* teach you and then you won't need us, you'll be more of a badass."

"With a fat ass." I tried to add on a joke with a bad American accent, obviously not grown enough to hack the seriousness between us yet.

Kade faked clearing his throat. "Yeah er… We'll work on that too."

My mouth dropped open wide enough to catch something. Before he tried to take his words back—which I'm sure he didn't plan on doing—I whacked him with his own pillow.

He was right about everything, but I needed more— not from anyone else, but from myself. I needed to be able to handle my thoughts, and be able to disregard a lot of them, especially the whole *'since things never work out for me, I may as well give in and have fun.'* Which is probably the dumbest—but tempting—thought so far. I told Kade about these thoughts because I didn't want him to continue to think I've got a mind made of steel, when it's been breaking down from the start (birth), I just got a good curtain to hide it.

"I understand you. You make perfect sense to me, so don't feel odd. I don't want to say that your thoughts are normal or natural because I don't want to invalidate them, but I do want to let you know that it is something that you'll be able to get through. I know because I did and I continue to. And if you ever get to a place where you can't pull yourself out the dark, you don't need to worry for too long because you have people like Amana and me to pull you out." He was serious and somewhat tense but all of that goes in the quick second he added Kassian to my small list of heroes.

The conversation was coming to an end so I quickly asked what had been on my mind and would stay on my mind if I hadn't brought it up. "What happened to you yesterday?"

I could've had a different approach but I didn't know how else to put it.

Kade didn't say anything, or maybe I just didn't give him enough time to respond.

"You had no open wounds but you had blood on you. What happened?" I had a picture in my head of what he'd done, but it wasn't vivid enough. I wanted to know the details. It's like I craved them. Like I needed to know what he was like when he's not with me.

Without the obvious mask.

Kade's eyes transformed, like I had awoken another side of him.

"I think you know what happened." Suddenly, his voice was hypnotic. It was low, seducing, almost eerie as it masked his matter-of-fact undertone, and his eyes matched it. They were wild but calm, all at the same time, like he was some sort of psychopath. Knowing that he could easily play a happier version of himself and could switch it off, scared me (a little) but for some reason I wanted to stay with *this* side of him. "You act as if you're unaware of things, like you're the ditsy-witty friend, but I know you. And you're more than that, more than you yourself could possibly imagine." He continued with his amused predatory gaze as he swirled his finger into the side of the mattress, like he were keeping himself put and stable. "And you know that yesterday, we had a problem. So I fixed it."

Not being able to pull my eyes away from him, I took in his expression again and again, realising I didn't actually know what to say.

"Alright c'mon then." Cheery Kade came back, all that was missing was a single clap. "Let's get you to the office, he'll be here soon." He practically shot up to stand. His tone of voice closer to his happier self rather than the low threatening-borderline-seducing tone he just had.

"What?" All of a sudden, I remembered why he came into the room in the first place. "This early? What if I was still sleeping?"

"Then I would wrap and drag you by the covers to the office… no skin-ship."

"Nice. Sounds like a plan." I grabbed the covers, hiding myself under as I got comfortable, but they were pulled off as quick as I had chucked them on.

"Training starts today."

'What?'

"Today's lesson is self-discipline." He took the bedsheets and pillows into the tv room, compelling me to follow. "They've arrived downstairs. I'm going to go get them. Get your arse to the office." He quickly left, leaving no time for me to argue.

After a quick rinse and face wash, I made my way into the office and swayed on its chair whilst looking out. Today felt like a good day, the weather was good, we got things out the way in the morning, and now I'm about to be examined, allowing us to know when physical training can start.

I heard the elevator door open, but I couldn't decide if I should turn my chair to let them know that *I* know that they are here. But watching them walk down to approach me is way too awkward for my liking so maybe I should stay 'oblivious' to the fact that they are making their way to the office. Before I could come to a decision, Kade opened the office door and called for me.

I turned around to a man and a woman.

"Hello, I'm Charlie." He put his hand over his heart instead of holding it out to shake mine. Kade must've given him the heads up. "Would you prefer us to call you Miss Menaal or Medisa?"

"Medisa please."

Both man and woman smiled. They weren't old but they were older than us, if I had to guess I would say thirty-to-forty and extremely fit, the both of them. I didn't know where to look so I just looked at Kade, <u>thank God</u> he decided to stay in the room. Logically thinking, he obviously stayed to make sure that everything goes well but, illogically—emotionally—thinking, he also stayed because he remembered how hospitals, doctors, needles etc. freaked me out a bit.

The woman checked my eyes as Charlie prepared things on the side. After the questions and examinations, they said I had no broken bones (though we did have a scare with my ribs), but I did have a mild concussion (I needed to be scanned, just in case). Also any public injuries would heal nicely.

If the two of them held concern, they did well in hiding it. No questions were asked, no worried expressions, they just did what they were called for. In movies, when doctors see these types of marks and bruises, they become concerned and get the police involved, but seeing as they came here and seem to be a bit more on the secretive side, I'm going to assume they're a different type of private than the usual private doctors.

'Because I know what normal private doctors act like.'

Charlie told me to sit on the desk for him to have a better view of my thigh, then turned around, giving me time to pull my joggers down. Ava—the woman—gave me a few towels and sheets to sit on and to cover exposed parts that didn't need to be seen.

When Charlie turned back around, he got to it straight away, carefully cutting the bandages Kassian neatly put on, uncovering butterfly stitches and the cut that was surrounded by a nasty looking bruise.

"You guys did a good job with what you had, but this needs some stitches."

My sweat glands woke up.

I don't do needles.

I tried to hide the fact that I couldn't breathe and even laughed at the 'suggestion' of stitching the cut. But from the looks of things, Kade had told them about my fear of needles and I half expected them to whip out belts to tie me down.

Everyone did their best to try and get my mind of what Charlie was about to do to me. Ava asked me questions, which didn't really get my mind of the needle that would be constantly going in and out of me, but I appreciated it. Kade done what he does best and switched up the conversation to something frisky, which then of course turned into something sexual.

Charlie and Ava laughed as they spoke about their experiences with partners and the types of injuries they had gotten during the deed. I let myself get distracted and laughed at all their stories—all but Kade, who when I asked, '*what's the worst injury you got or gave,*' he said, '*I've never unintentionally physically hurt a girl and intentionally would be another story.*'

I didn't even look in his direction when the question came out my mouth. It was like I was curious enough to ask, but not enough to listen. All I know is, as soon as he answered, it was like my leg knew that it was being stitched up.

When they were done, Kade offered for them to stay, to eat and drink but they refused and got going. I had to go in to their facility at some point and was advised to stay away from any physical activities for about two weeks to be safe. If I prematurely began doing things and my injuries got worse, I would have to be brought in so that I can be monitored or something.

I don't know what kind of private doctors they were but, something felt unorthodox.

'*Was it the way they'd arrived and left? Or was it the way they didn't bat an eye towards the injuries?*' I slowly batted my eyelashes as the sarcasm stayed in my head and not expressed to Kade.

Chapter 25

Medisa

24/01/2022 (Monday)

This past week or so, I contemplated how I should be around Kassian. He's 'on our side' but I needed to stop being so naïve and polite with him. I'm going to try to be more like Kade (strict) until we trusted him.

I threw my wig, mask and glasses onto the one table set up in this place, tensing up at the sound. The impact was louder than I thought and made Kade turn around as though we had been caught.

'Noise activates his 'fight. Noted.'

I held my shrugged position as I quietly apologised.

Moving around, I lifted my head up to the high ceilings. You could see the skeleton of this thing and some parts of the roof were damaged enough to allow for slow water drops to enter, creating growing puddles on the floor. The lighting was decent, we came at a time too early for the sun and on a day where I doubt it would show throughout the day, but it was okay, okay enough for me to see the other end of the room.

Even with Kassian's little training touch ups, this place was something out of a game. I didn't think abandoned, 'untouched' places like this existed in London. Buildings like this just seemed like an American or post-apocalyptic thing.

"I knew you'd be here early." Kassian leaned on the doorway we entered from, switching his eyes between me and his brother. He approached us all smug. "How'd you like it?"

"How d'you know that Maverick won't find us?" I asked.

"I don't." He failed to reassure.

"We've taken all the precautions we can, so we should be good for a while." Kade fixed what doubt Kassian failed to diminish.

"Care to fill me in on said precautions." I questioned Kassian.

"You both left Aros through doors every other person that's not you, uses." Kassian explained as Kade undressed, revealing his training clothes beneath his disguise. "You wore a wig, glasses etc. You took a vehicle that's not too showy in someone else's name—"

"I know what *we've* done. What precautions did *you* take?"

"This building's been under my name for a while now, so it won't look suspicious when I come here every now and then, since I *have* been coming here. And I've been giving Maverick little bits of information about you to keep him happy and away from what's actually going on."

"What kind of information?"

"Information that seem like they could be beneficial and lead to something, but in the end are nothing."

I began to undress to reveal my own training clothes. "Yes. But like what?"

Kassian opened up a small briefcase on the table.

"Does it matter? It won't affect anyone."

"If it don't matter, why can't you just tell me? Let me be the judge of how valuable it is." My annoyance came through and before I got too close to Kassian, Kade stood in the way.

"Your university timetable, those on your course, the journeys you make while at Uni or after, your life at school etc." He filled in the gaps that Kassian refused to.

"Are you kidding me? How is any of that not beneficial?"

I looked to Kassian who approached with a pair of knives. "Next time you need to give information, ask me, I'll think of better, *safer* things to tell him."

"Safer for who?" Kassian lowered his head, almost threatening. "Do you think he won't see past the information you'll magically come up with?"

Clearly, Kassian still had his head up his arse. Clearly, this team thing is just them making decisions and filling me in when they felt like it, and *clearly* the only way that I'm going to have some sort of release is through this bloody training.

"Give me a knife." I already knew that we were going to start off with skills that mostly needed the top half of my body. The stitches on my leg had healed, but just in case my leg needed more time, we're going to start off with knife skills.

Kade leaned against the table as Kassian gave me a weapon.

"Kassian is going to be teaching you today. The knives are blunt and close in on themselves, so that you are protected from being sliced or stabbed."

"But not bruised." Kassian chimed in as he demonstrated the knife going in on itself.

"At the end of the day, you can fight Kassian as though it were real, this is of course, *after* we've taught you a few things." As he spoke, he continuously threw a real knife in the air, allowing it to rotate, then catching it as it got close to his hand.

"I thought that you were good with knives and… everything else?" I asked Kade.

"I am." He reassured. "But then what use would Kassian be? We need to make him feel like he's doing something useful."

Kassian rolled his eyes, pairing it with a *'I'll show you'* smile as he held a knife upside down between his fist. He was going to take out whatever emotions Kade's words conjured up out onto me.

"You ready Desmona?"

"Cue the training sequence." I boredly rotated my finger as though I were playing with film.

Both Kade and Kassian were amused and worried, almost like they had no faith in me. Then Kade approached swinging, completely switching his mood to something more serious as Kassian stepped to the side, monitoring us.

I *somehow* just about managed to miss Kades shot. "What the heck, I thought Kassian's teaching me?"

Kade came at me again. "You need to learn to expect the unexpected. We're not just going to lay everything out for you."

I didn't dodge in time and with my brain lagging, I am grabbed and held in place. He could slice my throat or stab me in the gut one too many times, but he doesn't.

Whilst I heavily breathed in his arms, he stayed still like this were just another day. After a few seconds he let me go, then Kassian spoke about where I went wrong and what I did good in those few seconds of Kade's attack. After verbally giving me feedback, he showed me what I should have done and all the ways I could've disarmed or killed him.

Training got a little more interesting. Scary, but exciting. Kassian somehow became the 'nice' laid back—but not really—one and Kade became the 'strict' harsh one. I didn't know what I expected, but it wasn't this, not so soon in the lessons anyways.

In the evening, I had prepared to lie my way out of knife training. I wanted to move on to another type of skill, or have an extended break since this was just the first day and I was tired as hell.

Constantly having my hair tugged, my legs being pushed in, or straight up being swiped, being put in some sort of arm-lock or head-lock, was exhausting. Not to mention the runs I was being forced on. The only breaks given outside of my uni schedule were, lunch breaks, toilet breaks (I may have lied once or twice) and prayer times, that's it.

There was no mercy for my lack of stamina.

Kade had somehow planned for my excuses (new request), because when I approached him, he had been setting up some new toys. Instead of knives and ink, it was guns and silencers.

He loaded a gun then slid it over to me, despite me being right next to him. "Pick it up."

I had on a big dumb smile, trying to get him to break out of his emotionless gaze, but he didn't budge.

Being strict really suits him, *I'm* almost scared.

We moved into another room where different types of targets had been placed. Some were hung from the ceiling, some were on the ground, some were slightly hidden and the rest were straight up exposed targets.

"You have two minutes to shoot the bulls-eye on every single target."

"That's not enough time."

"Tough luck. Time doesn't work its way around you."

It didn't take long for me to learn the basics. The first

week of training was hardcore. They didn't hold back. Even though the knives were blunt and went in on themselves, they still hurt. Sometimes we (me) would get too carried away and we would go home with some bruises.

When me and Kade were alone back at Aros, he didn't go back to being how he was before Kassian got involved. He remained in his personal trainer mode, just a (slightly) watered down version of it.

I told him, '*I like learning how to fight and defend myself, but I won't be a pro in a few weeks,*' hoping for him to ease up on the lessons and discipline, but no. He just said, '*that's not the point. The point is to make you get used to dealing with someone bigger than you. Get you used to doing more than barricading or jumping in the middle and freezing.*' And that's when I realised, he went and spoke to Kassian about that night in my house.

Each day was the same as the first. Like Kade said, they weren't just planning on training my body, they were trying to train my mind too. They swapped after each round, one gave nowhere near his all whilst the other monitored and gave pointers, then vice versa. After the intense sessions, they gave one to one lesson's and incorporated sneak attacks.

As the days went by, I could feel them getting faster and stronger. Either this was because I was improving, or because they wanted me to experience different intensities… I liked the first assumption more.

At the start of the second week, they thought it would be best to get things going a little quicker with new skills. They threw knives, kicks, punches and whatever else at me, slower than those things would happen in real life but fast enough for me to improve my reaction time. If I didn't react in time to a punch, they would pause, allowing me to see their fist and its target, which would usually be my face. If I were too slow for a kick, they would drop me to the floor and whenever I got too tired to use my fists or was put in a position where my fists could do no damage, I was told to think about putting my legs, fingers and elbows to use. It's funny how one forgets they have other limbs in moments of panic. But also, I wasn't completely useless and I didn't want them to think that. Where they had the skill to stop before inflicting maximum damage, I did not. I couldn't squash their eyes, try to pull an arm or leg out of its socket, or even bite a chunk of their flesh. So I voiced that, and them being them, found a way around it. If I had the opportunity to plunge my thumbs into their sockets, I would have to tap their cheeks. If I could bite, I would have to say *'bite'*, or if I was comfortable enough, I could lightly use my teeth (Kade's suggestion), or kiss the area (Kassian's suggestion). And if I wanted to try and pull bones from sockets, I would have to hold them in that position for more than five seconds, then they would count it as me detaching their limbs (Kassian laughed and said it was impossible for me to do that to a person).

As for the way they treated each other, if I didn't know they were brothers (ignoring the fact that they looked the same) I would say they got a little 'enemies to lovers' thing going. When they had those moments, I sat back, not only because I was exhausted but because I knew, in a weird way, they needed this, and whether they wanted to admit it or not, they needed each other and I didn't mind being used as an excuse for them to spend time with each other.

Chapter 26

Medisa
06/02/2022 (Sunday)

Kade wore a vest today. One of those ones they wore in movies. I mean they wear them in real life too, but I rarely see it. Anyways, he is wearing a bullet proof vest and I'm a little worried he has one for me too. I've seen the items we have for today and I did *not* see paintball guns.

"Do you see these red dots?" He prepped my gun.

I looked over his dotted vest.

"You have to shoot every single one of them. There's five in total and you only have eight bullets."

"Fake bullets?"

"Would I wear this for fake bullets?" He basically called me dumb.

"This is stupid." The temperature in the room rises. "I could accidently shoot your head, or arm, or leg." Not to mention, Kassian was not with us today, so what should I do when I shoot said arm, leg or head?

Kade did not entertain me, he just placed the gun in my hand. "You've been shooting every day. Now you need a realistic target."

"I'm not shooting you."

He took an agitated breath. "You will."

Despite my words and want to not do this, he walked over to his starting position. And instead of being a normal human being (giving me a countdown to at least prepare to have a heart attack) he ran.

No, he *sprinted* towards me.

I froze, shook, jumped, all in one place as my organs moved before my limbs as Kade came straight for me. He pulled out a knife which I prayed wasn't as authentic as the bullets and fought me. I, of course was knocked straight on my arse with Kade on top of me. My arm strength was nowhere near his, so the knife's tip slowly made its way down to my eye.

Kade's face had no sign of struggle, not one sign. My strength's child's play to him. I'm no real threat, or test. I can't even count as training for him.

He teased with the knife, allowing it to be pushed away, then he brought it closer than before, and I had nowhere near the right amount of strength to push it away. He wasn't even using both his hands, he used one, the other kept his balance besides my head.

My arms quickly became sore and numb all at the same time, so after fighting and getting nowhere, I let go.

Kade allowed the knife to touch my skin. Not penetrate it, no, just touch, and that's when I felt the cold, sharp metal.

Too exhausted to move and complain, I lay flat on the floor whilst Kade half-straddled, half-hovered over me.

"I'm not even a proper threat to you and you still froze. Do you think a stranger is going to give you a chance? *No.*" He stood up. "So pick yourself up and shoot me. All five markings or close to—"

"Kade what if I accidently shoot your arm, or legs, or head." I spoke, my worry now more intense than before.

"I trust you enough to not shoot my head."

"I think you trust me a bit too much mate."

"*Medisa.*" He warned.

"I'm being serious." I almost whined.

He took a deep breath then uncovered a small shield. "I have this."

"You didn't have that before."

"You weren't going to shoot before."

"Wow."

"Just make the right shots and trust that I can handle it. Later on—God forbid it—when someone is coming at you, you have to trust that they will kill you and know that you have no choice. Give them a mercy killing."

"A mercy killing?" I tried to raise one brow.

"Yeah, that's what it would be unless I get there first and provide otherwise."

Bold of him to assume I will be parting from him after he just expressed how someone could approach me with a knife or gun… or even their fists.

"Ooooo big man." I took the piss out of his seemingly serious words. "You're well 'ard."

'At least he's no longer orchestrating his words and slapping on a faux personality.'

Chapter 27

Medisa
07/02/2022 (Monday)

I made my way to the chapel by myself today. I left after Fajr, as the sun was coming up and somehow made it to the building with ease; I didn't get lost or approached by a stranger who wanted to test my new skills. <u>Thank God.</u>

Kade and Kassian's 'burner' cars weren't parked at their usual place, so I assumed I got here before them.

Trying to avoid the horrible screech the door made every time it was opened and closed, I lowered my head into my shoulder and used my spare hand to block the other ear. Unsurprisingly, the room was empty, but before my body fully stepped inside, my head is covered with some sort of bag and my arms are pulled behind.

Instead of feeling zip ties, I felt metal. I've never been put in handcuffs before, but that didn't mean I hadn't thought about it, and let me tell you, these felt completely different to what I had imagined.

All of a sudden, I was made aware of my hair and the bag touching my neck, making me feel a hundred times more uncomfortable as I couldn't do anything about it. Logical thinking told me that this was a test, but it was also telling me to not be too sure. I wanted to somehow pause time to think about the best way to go about this, but alas, I'm but a girl.

Getting shoved into the room was probably one of the most agitating things about this whole situation. Not only could I not see who shoved me, but I couldn't do anything about it with my hands tied back. Even if I did use my legs, how would I know where to kick? I would just look like an idiot…no thanks.

A stool is dragged across the floor, that much I could hear. Whoever's behind this attack is light on their feet, could be a girl, but then again Kassian and Kade are supposed to be pros at this sort of thing, also Ataya's a girl, but she's loud as anything.

I'm aggressively pushed down onto the stool, then the bag is snatched off my head.

Kade is stood directly in front of me with no expression. He walked over to the lone table, pulled out his phone and angled it up so that I could see his screen. He had a timer ready.

"Would be nice if you escaped today." He pressed the 'start' button.

"How the hell do you expect me to get out these cuffs with no key, pin, stick—"

"Tik-tok." He dismissed my obvious confusion.

I looked around but before I could spot anything useful Kassian quietly barged in. He walked straight for me like I had done something stupid, then got me up from the stool.

"Whatever kinky lesson this is can wait till later, someone was followed." Kassian quietly spoke as he ushered me and Kade into the small connecting room.

Even if I wanted to turn around, I couldn't. Kassian forced me into the wardrobe looking thing, then followed behind. Kade got in too, but he stood in front of me.

Never in my life did I think I would be sandwiched in between two Rivers.

My arms began to hurt and as soon as I tried to adjust, I accidently rubbed them up against Kassian.

"Easy girl, there's no time for that now." He whispered.

I quickly moved myself forward, allowing for there to be a little space between us. The wardrobe doors were fully shut, but they still had a small gap between them, allowing for some light to enter.

The chapels squeaky door opened and at least two people had walked in, the floorboards gave that much away. Before they entered the room we hid in, Kassian gently yanked me back into him with his hand over my mouth. I could practically feel his expression, and seeing Kade's jaw tense was all the confirmation I needed. Kassian thought he was slick and, in some ways, I agreed, but that didn't stop me from digging my heel into his toe. I only stopped twisting my heel when he tapped out (on my body instead of the floor) and released his 'grip' from my face.

Soon as the coast was clear, Kassian was forced out. He was the last to enter the building so it made sense if they'd assume that he was in here. If he kept hiding, they would know there's something up, something that he was trying to hide from them.

As he distanced himself from us, I turned myself around so that my back was to Kade, praying that he would have the sense to get me out of the cuffs.

"Care to tell me why you're following, fellas?" Kassian spoke in the background whilst Kade uncuffed me.

"Boss wanted to check where you've been running off to these days."

The stool is dragged, then someone who I could only assume was Kassian began to create a rhythm with his fingers on the table.

"What? Can't a boy let off some steam in peace?"

That's a good response, it made sense. The chapels decorated to look a little like a gym, a gym designed for no more than two-to-three people.

"You wouldn't mind us joining you today, would you?"

"Not at all."

My knees began to feel the weight of my upper body, so I moved to get comfortable, making things worse. The wood below my feet creaked as I moved. Kade instantly grabbed a hold of me, stopping us both from breathing. I had the task of keeping my weight at where it was. If I put more weight down, the wood would speak. If I lifted my foot up it would sing. I had to stay exactly where I was, which was in a position more uncomfortable than the last.

"Anyone we should know about?" The man spoke as if he could see through Kassian's lies.

"It's an old building you git. Why would I bring your sister here when I have access to the best suites in London?"

My breath hitched as my hand flew to where Kade held me. I gripped onto him as if he hadn't heard what Kassian had said. And instead of gripping me back (like Amana would) he exhaled as though he regretted sending his brother out.

The man who had been insulted—I think it's him—walked towards the room we were in. His footsteps were getting closer and closer. I couldn't tell if Kassian's insults shocked me more, or if the fact that the man hadn't done anything in response did. He chose to ignore and walk towards where the noise came from, he had to be someone who was used to Kassian's mouth, it's the only explanation.

Before he came inside, Kassian—I assumed—began to punch the punching bag. The chain it was attached to needed to be oiled and the bag itself made some noise, enough noise for Kade to position me opposite him and away from the light the gap let in.

I was sure he would give himself up if it got to it, but

that wouldn't make any sense. Any one of us being exposed would lead to the same conclusion; Kassian being disloyal.

"If Maverick wants to see me more often, he should've told me on one of our little dates. In fact, let me call him now while you search the place. Hopefully he doesn't get annoyed when I find another place to run off to, since you guys weren't exactly discreet in finding out what I'm up to in this one."

The man walked away from the room, giving me permission to breathe out.

"Put the phone down Kassian, we're leaving."

The chapel's annoying door was opened, but before it closed, the man made another comment. "Tell your girl I like her perfume, it's… all over this place."

'Shit.'

Kade got out first, then opened the door on my side. He hovered a finger over my mouth about a hand away, stopping me from expressing whatever the hell was going through my mind.

We heard a car drive off, but I was still told to stay quiet.

"You can come out now." Kassian spoke after a few minutes, and as we walked out the room, he continued. "They're gone, I saw them out. They both got into a car and drove off. And I doubt they will be coming back anytime soon."

"He knows. They know. Which means Maverick basically knows." I ignored his words.

"They don't know that it's you. It could be any girl."

"But *I'm* the girl that you're supposed to be tricking, it would make more sense if it were me. Why would you bring a sneaky link here when they obviously know that you would take them to a hotel?"

"Medisa." Kade spoke with a tone he hadn't used since the start of this training arc. "We're okay. We'll stay here until I know the coast is clear, then we'll train back at Aros. Kassian will continue to come here to stick to his story and then maybe we'll be nice enough to let him join us at Aros."

My bloody nose had to become immune to the smell of my perfume. If I had known it was strong, I would've stopped spraying after the first two pumps.

"So, what? We're gonna camp here for a bit?"

"Precisely." Kassian confirmed as he sat back onto the stool.

I looked to Kade to see if he backed Kassian's words.

"Only for a little bit." He placed the cuffs on the table.

"Aw, we're done with them so soon?" Kassian turned his instigating head towards me. "Let me know if the taste in there wasn't enough, will you?"

Anyone could spot that he was trying to wind Kade up. Kade was smart enough to know that, but why did his demeaner change? Why did he pinch his nose as if he were wiping it? And why did he tell Kassian to stand up?

"Kade—" I tried to intervene. We didn't have time for this. I looked between them knowing I couldn't really stop this.

"Don't worry sweet Medisa, just sit that pretty arse down somewhere."

Before I could take a step forward to do or say something, Kade spoke, "Get comfortable Medisa, let us show you how things could play out."

He kept his demonic eyes on Kassian and I took it as a sign to get comfortable against the wall.

Kade was obviously tired, or at least on his way to be. Not physically, but mentally. I might not know a lot of things but I could definitely spot a person that's mentally tired. Whatever he's planning to do, whatever he's planning to fix, he wanted to fix it today, right now. It's just disguised as a lesson for me.

Both of them charged up their punches before attacking one another. Kade made the first two hits, both landed. He backed away a little as he opened up his arms to his side as though he were asking for a hug.

"Use this opportunity because we haven't got time for this bullshit. Using Medisa to piss me off will no longer be ignored."

Kassian came at him, but Kade dodged then kneed him, holding him in place.

"*C'mon* Kassian. What was that?" Kade mocked. "Hit me like the man you want everyone to believe you are." He hissed into Kassian's ear.

His words were a low blow, but they touched all the right places, because after that Kassian fought hard. He didn't hold back. And whether he saw it or not, cared for it or not, Kade *did* hold back. He let Kassian beat him, he let him get out whatever rage he held, all whilst smiling. I didn't know if the grins were because he was trying to further piss him off, or because finally, his little brother was letting it all out.

At some point, when the blood and grunts became too much, I pushed myself to intervene. My deep breath alerted Kassian of my presence before my hand did. When he whipped his head in my direction, I jumped, calling him out of his head in time for him to see his bloody creation.

Kassian knelt.

He slouched over as his hands hypnotised him.

Kade sat up, ignoring his new wounds by giving his attention to his brother.

My eyes went back and forth between them before I decided to leave them alone.

I needed the fresh air anyways.

Chapter 28

Medisa

07/02/2022 (Monday)

"Change of plans. We're not training today."

My eyes jumped to a very confused Kassian whilst Kade gathered some of our things.

"What are we doing instead?"

"Right now? We're going back to Aros." Kade threw Kassian's car keys at his chest.

This was strange.

We almost got caught, they got into a fight, then we all sat in silence for a bit and now Kade—the anti-risktaker—wanted us all to leave and go to Aros. Did we know why? No, no we did not. Did I further question and say that it wasn't a smart idea after what just happened? Yes, yes I did. Did Kade care for what I had said? No, not really.

Once we got to Kade's office, me and Kassian awkwardly stood waiting for Kade to reveal what was going on in his mind. Kade rearranged a few things on his bookshelf, then turned around to face us, now ready to give his presentation.

"I wanted to keep this a secret, especially from someone like Kassian—"

Kassian boredly put his middle finger up.

"But I figured we all need this." Kade continued.

'Where was he going with this?'

"Anyways, we all get to choose one thing to do today, one thing that we all have to experience together. And my thing is…"

'Just go with the flow Medisa.'

He opened up a part of the shelf, revealing a whole section of his floor which had been hidden to everyone but him. He stood to the side, inviting me and Kassian in. We didn't exactly jump up and down with excitement, probably because of the shock from the size of this place, but we did show some sort of amusement. This 'room' was basically the size of his accommodation, but looked way bigger since there wasn't actually any walls.

"I know that you got issues, but a rage room? Seriously?" Kassian spoke as if he wasn't impressed.

"Part time gym, part time rage room…I had Bellamy add some things for us to break."

By '*some things*' he meant a lot of things, a lot meaning the room looked like a breakable scrapyard.

Before exploring what we could break, I quickly noticed what had been prepared for us in terms of safety and weaponry. Set to the side there were helmets, thick clothing, bats, golf clubs, sticks, metal poles…pretty much anything that could be used to break things.

Kade had these LED lights placed here and there, basically setting the tone for whatever would go down in this room. It's like the lights allowed us to bring out another side of ourselves without being scared or embarrassed.

Picking up a bat to get to it, I am blocked by Kade's body as he held out a jumpsuit and helmet.

Quickly putting on the uniform, I looked to Kade since I obviously needed his approval before running off. This is when he'd done the strangest thing…He pulled me closer via the helmet and looked me over, making sure that it was on properly and for the weirdest reasons, I had butterflies.

Me and Kassian started things off. At first it started as watching each other take turns in 'politely' breaking things, but then, at some point, we all went mental. We smashed everything and anything until there was nothing else to break.

Once Kade switched the lights back and we walked out, we came out a little different. It was like we all made a mental agreement of '*what happens in the rage room, stays in the rage room,*' as our lighting and surroundings changed.

We all (me…maybe Kassian) huffed and puffed our way to the games room.

Kassian was the winner of the punching bag game. Kade was not that far behind and I, I was only third because I didn't want to further upset them.

Somehow, time had passed a lot quicker than any one of us had anticipated. Realising the other two things we had to do was going to run into the night, we all rushed our showers—I went first so that I could pray whilst they washed— and got out the doors to head to our next plan.

Kassian's group experience choice was a place that served as a bar-restaurant-club-dance hall and today they had pretty much all age groups inside, no limit despite it being quite late.

It's strange seeing people here like this on a Monday. The majority of people were dressed up in costumes and looked as though they had no care in the world, as long as they were having fun.

I was with my people—*if* these people also had the need to make sure everyone around them felt involved and was enjoying themselves.

Out of the three of us it seemed like Kassian was the

only comfortable one. Me and Kade sat on the side near the dancefloor, immediately—purposely?—forgetting that this was supposed to be a group experience.

Whilst Kassian went to go get us some drinks (a shot of macchiato for me) I distracted myself with those on the dance floor. This place had a live band with all sorts of instruments, as well as a DJ. I thought they would take turns but at some point, I could swear they were complimenting each other's sounds.

Soon as the drinks hit the table, Kassian handed me a rented dress to wear over my clothes, he placed a cowboy hat on Kade, then wasted no time downing his glass so that he could head to the dance floor. Just as all hopes had been raised, he turned around to face me and Kade.

Kassian held out his hand, dropping my heart-lungs-gut-everything inside me.

"I-er-I can't dance." This place was already like a scene from Footloose mixed with that one scene from Titanic. It looked so choreographed and natural at the same time. I couldn't possibly join. I would ruin the flow. I didn't even know the specific routine that everyone seemed to know.

"Course you can."

"No, Kassian really, I can't—" I couldn't even finish my sentence because a cute little boy put his hand on mine and called (lightly tugged) me to the floor.

Kassian didn't seem to mind losing a partner, as long as I was up and participating. We moved to one side, Kassian busy knowing the moves, and me and Charlie (the young boy) readying ourselves to join.

"You're going to have to teach me, I don't know this dance." I tried gaining some sort of sympathy from the boy, and now, since a child was with me, I didn't mind if I looked silly.

"Copy me, I know the moves."

And he did. Despite his age, he seemed to grasp the art of teaching, complimenting and acknowledging emotions.

Glancing over to Kade, I quickly took in the biggest smile on his face as he cheered with our camera in hand.

Almost as soon as I got the hang of the dance Charlie had shown, the song switched to something else, getting the people on the floor hyped and ready for another routine.

Just as I was about to disappear, Kassian cut in and steered me away. "This one's easy, trust me."

My insides started to act up again. I'm not a bad dancer, I just felt like eyes were on me, making me feel a little uneasy. An older woman seemed to notice and decided to take me under her groups wing. Soon after being temporarily adopted, I felt okay again. The music got a little louder, a little livelier and just like that, everyone was dancing together.

I got a quick look at Kassian, he was dancing away with Charlie and a few other kids, looking happy as ever. I turned to try and find Kade, but I couldn't see him.

Another song played, starting a new routine where we would rotate and switch partners at this one part of the dance. This routine was fun, a lot of turns and synchronised claps. At some point Kassian was my partner. There wasn't much touching involved thank God, it was more like being in each other's bubbles.

"Yes Medisa! See you *can* dance!"

I tried not to shrivel up from this sudden hype man.

My partner switched from children to women, but as another switch came about, or rather, mid switch, I quickly realised my next partner would be a man. And as kind hearted as he looked, I couldn't dance with him.

Trying to smoothly switch out quickly went wrong as I bumped into someone else.

I didn't fall on the floor like I thought I was, I was caught by someone behind me as if we were doing a trust fall exercise. The man who was supposed to be my new partner quickly came to my side and asked if I were okay, bless him.

"Yeah sorry, I just got a little dizzy." I awkwardly smiled, appearing half as embarrassed as I felt.

Lucky for me he was nice and made me feel a little normal before joining the crowd again.

Soon as he got back into dancing as though nothing had happened, I realised the person who had caught me was still there. They were probably waiting for me to turn around so they could cuss me out.

Slowly turning towards them, I readied another apology.

"You can take a break you know?" Kade lowered his head to mine as though he were trying to read my eyes.

"I'm okay, I just didn't want to dance with a man."

"Oh, so Kassian doesn't count as a man?" He failed to hide his amusement.

"Ahhh, no." I joked, then found Kassian surrounded by all types of people, dancing and laughing away. And that's when I remembered Kade hadn't been joining in on our group activity. So I whacked his arm and before he could say anything, I spoke first, "You're supposed to dance too, you cow. You're dancing to the next song."

"I didn't want to scare the kids."

After a second of being visually confused, I clocked he was talking about his face. It had been marked up from the fight him and Kassian had in the morning. I probably—definitely—would've been scared of him as a child.

"Oh please, you look fine. And besides Charlie wasn't

scared of you—that's the boy who you got to approach me. And yes, I did realise you had influenced him."

He continued to stare at me but I couldn't tell what he was thinking. Before I could say anything, the music changed and not wanting to force Kade to dance, I decided to go back to the table.

I didn't make it to the table.

Just like before, like a scene from a movie, everyone was up, cheering and dancing, blocking my path to my seat. I somehow got another child partner, but this time was surrounded by people I was comfortable with.

Kade was dancing too, someone had passed him their child, which then turned into a bunch of them wanting a go as he threw them in the air or twirled them.

Soon as he put a kid down, a girl approached him. And by '*approached*' I mean she threw herself at him, touching him, snaking up him, having her hands make their way up and down his body.

I couldn't stand the site of it even if she was good.

He had some sort of poker face on, but one that wasn't amused—I told myself.

Politely grabbing her hands to peel them off his chest, he spun her around so that she could find someone else to dance with.

Before I knew it, I was smirking and before he saw me watching, I quickly made my way to our table. This time actually making it to my seat.

Kade joined after a few seconds, and a few after that, so did Kassian with the biggest plastered smile.

"Let's go to the back rooms." His chest moved in and out faster than usual, I could only compare his behaviour to an excited child in need of a break.

"What's there?" I asked.

"You'll see."

"No, no, Medisa's turn's next."

"Oh come on. It's right there and besides you took us to two places."

My eyes smoothly went from Kassian to Kade. Kassian was right. Kade took us to his rage room and the games room. He knew this, I knew this, and Kassian who knew that he won, knew this.

"Great!" Kassian stood up. "Follow me."

Chapter 29

Medisa
07/02/2022 (Monday)

He took us to a karaoke room.

At first it was just me and Kassian messing about, but then we decided to do solos and Kassian did not shy away from being the first to perform.

"Oh, okayyyy. I see you, Shre—

"Medisa I swear if you call me that green ogre *one* more time."

I snickered. "D'you get it? 'Cause he—"

"We *know why* you're calling me Shre—! *Stop laughing you're not funny—*"

"O-kayy." Kade took the mic off him.

Barely taking his time choosing a song, he put on 'Shower' and when he started to sing, I couldn't stop being so tense.

My wide smile was cemented and so was Kassian's. His voice wasn't bad, it was good, it's just that after seeing him be so serious and strict these past two weeks, I didn't know how to take this. I was cringing, but was also like '*hey, I kinda like this.*'

He pointed at us with fingers that were usually put together when people imitated a gun. When he sang the part about being lit up, something July, he looked at me, but he damn well ain't singing about me.

Not after his unhinged lessons.

When he got to the part where me and Kassian could join in, we joined *in*, we la-da-deed the heck out of it and then cheered and whooped when Kade couldn't go on.

It was my turn now and like the two of them, I too chose to have the original song in the background. It adds to the performance.

As the song played, I cleared my throat with the biggest smile on my face because I was so ready. I hadn't listened to, or sung this in a *long* time. Kassian had a similar look on too, like he was surprised I chose the song and couldn't wait to see Kade's reaction to it.

I played with the autotune as the first verse started without me, then quickly rushed in saying the line about tattoos and girls being turned on, wiping my free hand over my arm like I had tattoos myself. Kade raised his brow, and Kassian's expression was almost as if he was saying '*okayyyy.*'

"Is we fucking when we—" As soon as the words came out my mouth, Kade got up to stop me from continuing. And I did everything in my power to not let him take the microphone off me.

The lyrics got more and more…sinful. But the atmosphere and how fun it was, took over and I couldn't help but carry on. There were a few times where Kade almost got me, but then Kassian got involved. And thankfully, I got back in time to say the best bit (my favourite part).

Kassian hyped me up, so I'm blaming him for my behaviour. Kade stood there as I jumped around, his head slightly tilted, but he wasn't fooling anyone. I know there's a part of him that enjoyed how we were behaving.

Being stingy as hell, I decided I wanted another go. And despite Kade's monitoring and '*no's*' I searched for another with the same vibe, but before I could voluntarily choose one, the door bursts open, making me jump and start a song.

Kassian who had just lit his cigarette, looked up, at first

worried, then annoyed. Kade had instantly turned around to who it was, then started to throw hands. And I, I stood part discombobulated, part unbothered, microphone in hand. And as the both of them fought with three large men who had the decency to shut the door, *'na, na, come on'* blasted on in the background.

"Here Medisa, hold this." Kassian passed his lit cigarette.

Now, I stood dumbfounded with a cigarette in hand. Music blasting in the back.

Having absolutely no reason to get involved, I kicked one of the men's balls from behind, which got me his attention. Taking steps back like there was no tomorrow, I managed to dodge his first attack, and his second—only because his balls were still in pain—but by the time his third attempt came around, I was too gassed to avoid it, and he had somehow gained his strength.

Falling onto the table against the wall, probably hurt more than his backhand did. It was like it hit all my funny bones.

The man held me in place and was about to stab me, but Kade—despite busy being pressed up against the same wall—grabbed a hold of my top (like he'd done at ice skating) and dragged me a little to the side, just about making me miss the knife. Because of this, the guy got the knife stuck in the table and out of the two of us, I was able to process what had happened, quicker. So, I had the upper hand and I used it to not only hit him with the microphone, but to grab one of the speakers to smash it into the side of his head. By then, Kade and Kassian were both done with their assigned men, and the song had finished.

All three men were tied down with God knows what (the twins did that whilst I went and made sure no one heard what had happened). And now, only one was conscious.

"What did you expect was going to happen? Your plan, at best, is banal."

'Banal? What the heck does banal mean?'

I missed a little of what was said as I nodded my head agreeing with words I hadn't heard before.

"Yes, do tell us you weren't expecting to win here? What was the plan here anyway? To distract? To hurt? Or to kill?" Kassian joined the conversation.

The man didn't say anything.

"How fatuous." Kade took Kassian's cigarette and for a second, I thought he was going to put it out on the man's face, but he just flicked it at him.

A part of me became disappointed from anticipating something that will not come to pass. Another part is grateful.

"Yeahh, you silly fatuous cow." I added, and honestly, I just wanted to join in, but I didn't sound as insulting as the twins.

"Medisa." Kassian called me as though he were about to tell me something, but stopped in his tracks. Unlucky for him, I'm observant, and I saw that he'd looked to Kade before stopping.

So I looked to his brother. "What?"

His eyes travelled over my face as his tongue took in his bottom lip, then I saw as he mentally thought 'screw it'.

"'*Silly*' is basically the definition of fatuous."

I took turns looking into each of his eyeballs. "Oh…" 'Embarrassed' wasn't enough to describe how I felt. "I don't understand how you guys didn't go to a normal school, didn't have a normal childhood, spent most of your lives doing

Maverick's bidding—" I gave each point a finger as I listed. "—and yet you have a better vocabulary than me."

The man held back a laugh, earning our attention.

Kade turned back to me, losing the venom in his look. "Why don't you get yourself a drink and think about what your two things are?"

"Okay." Usually, I would try to stay, but something told me that in order for us to progress, I would need to leave. That, and it's about time I got to flood Amana's screen with voice recordings with the latest update.

'And any behaviour that would lead to jail-time should be avoided.'

The best time to explore and walk around Central London was at night when no one else was around. If there were people around, they were cool, they weren't the 'loud for no reason-start a fight for no reason' type of people. They were basically on the same level as you. They just wanted to roam the streets of London, without the noise and company of thousands of strangers.

We walked around Buckingham Palace, Oxford Street and the edge of the River Thames, taking pictures and videos whilst running around freely, talking about life and random facts like dolphins swimming in the Thames.

After a quick pit stop—buying several meals—we made our way to Southbank Skate. I'd only been twice before. Once with my course group and once with Amana. And now I got to sit down and relax here with two more friends.

We stayed at one end of the park, sitting at the top of a slope with our meals surrounding us.

"What would you say is the weirdest thing about you?" Kassian randomly asked when things got comfortably quiet.

"Where do I begin?" I blew air out from my mouth as a hundred things went through my mind. "Oh, oh, sometimes when I sleep. I wake up and move around or engage in conversations and then I'll fall asleep and not remember any of it, or if I do it's like a blur. And I only know that I do that because Amana told me." None of them said anything to this reveal so I think of something else to say. "And not to make things depressing or anything, but I realised that I have conversations in my head as if someone else were with me. Like I would pretend that I'm being interviewed about my life or that I'm in some sort of therapy session *or* that I have a friend that's constantly with me. And I would narrate—or we would discuss my life and do deep dives into things and make jokes and they would say comforting things, or call me out on certain things and blah blah blah… I don't know. I think I do it to comfort myself. To make it seem like someone's listening and understands why I am, the way that I am…Oh and sometimes I view things that are happening in real time as though they are already in the past. I think that I do that so it's easier for me to move on. But don't worry, I'm working on that one." I raise my hand as though they were physically worrying and I had to tame them.

We all had our backs to the ground and looked up to the concrete ceiling as though we were star gazing. No words were said after I outed some of my weirdest traits…

'I should jump into the Thames.'

"What about you guys?" I turned my head to each twin, then back up to the concrete roof.

"I do something similar." Kassian finally joined the conversation *he* started. "Except I imagine how life would look if our parents hadn't died. Or when I do something or meet someone new, I would think about how my parents would react. If they would be proud, or guide me a certain way." Kassian spoke softly and I could swear on my life that Kades breath hitched a little after he heard '*parents.*'

"I don't think that's weird." I kept my eyes on Kassian. "I think that's normal. Someone *not* having those thoughts might be a little weird."

Kassian smiled, raising his arm above my head as I lowered it into my shoulders. I don't know why I thought he was stretching and was about to put his arm around me, when he just wanted to fluff up the top of my head.

"You're actually alright Medisa. Not at all what I expected and a little too good to be true." He paused whilst I revelled in his words. "And I'm sorry for what I've done to you. You don't deserve this." He searched my eyes as my facial expressions went from a big-headed '*thank you, thank you very much*' to a '*oh crap he's being sincere.*'

He found something else to look at that wasn't in my direction. I don't know if it's because he felt shame, or because of the fact I hadn't said anything, but after he looked away, I forced myself to talk even if I hadn't gathered my thoughts.

"I never blamed you."

He looked back to me like he wanted to make sure I was telling the truth.

"But if it makes you feel any better, I accept your apology." I added.

Kassian's eyes became glossy and it was getting a little too emotional for me, so I ruined it all by opening my mouth, again.

"You're a cow for what you did at my house though. That shade of lipstick was not made for me."

He let out a laugh that sounded like he were holding his breath, and I joined in once I realised that I had not in fact ruined the conversation.

"Why don't you just talk to me and Kade instead of talking to yourself?" He moved the conversation back to my weird thing.

'Probably because he couldn't get past how bizarre it is.'

"You guys wouldn't follow the script."

"Script?"

"Yeah, the script in my head. You guys wouldn't follow it."

Kassian's laugh was like he were trying to bring up phlegm. "A lot of people want to meet and talk to us, and here you are, with the ability to abuse your power over us, choosing to talk to our characters in your head. And I would just like to say that we are way too advance for you to assume our responses."

He's right, they could be way too unpredictable at times.

"I do speak to you guys about what's in my head for like 70-80% of the times."

"What's a conversation that's in the 30-20%?"

I thought about it for a few seconds as if this was going to be the only time for me to have certain conversations. I couldn't make it be too obvious on what I was trying to figure out. It needed to be childish but with potential for them to give an insight without me being too direct.

"If you guys could meet and be with your younger selves for a small period of time, what would you say or do?"

Kassian sucked in air through his mouth then blew it out as a failed whistle. "I'm gonna need some time to think on that one. Brother? Care to answer while I think, before Medisa goes back to having conversations in her head."

I turned my head to face Kade, anticipating his answer.

"I would tell him to spill the drink." Kade's tone—despite his words coming out as if he were hypnotised—was one of urgency and regret. His expression was as if he were lost in thought, but somehow also saw red.

Before I could match words with my clueless face, Kassian gave his answer. "I would advise young Kassian to take Kade to where he goes to when he escapes. It would make things better."

I smiled. "How so?"

Kassian glanced over to Kade, then back to me. "He would've been exposed to parts of my life he should've seen, and it would've changed how things played out."

'I guess this means more healing has been done on Kassian's end.'

Kassian dry sniffed. "What would you do?"

I positioned my head so that I was facing the ceiling, then took a deep breath. "I would hold her."

'Should I say more?'

"Unfortunate things started to happen to me when I was young, and I remember a lot of it. I also remember feeling alone and wanting someone to comfort me. So, I would hold her, and wait for her to sleep, then I'll be there, in the exact same position when she awoke."

'My public vocabulary is improving. hehe.'

"And I'll struggle to not tell her who her chosen family would be. But I'll definitely tell her that she does have someone eventually."

"Three someone's." Kassian spoke as he held up three fingers whilst simultaneously making an 'o-k.'

"Hmm?"

"You have Amana, Kassian and me." Kade added whilst

turning to face me to make sure that I knew it.

A smile crept on my face, which then turned into me scrunching my nose and covering it as I took everything in.

I loved this.

"That reminds me." I turned the top halve of my body towards Kassian. "You haven't met her yet. Amana."

He was taken aback.

"I think you guys would get along and not that I'm encouraging you to look at her, but she's gorgeous. Like, supernaturally pretty…*ethereally* pretty." I tried to think of other words but my vocabulary hasn't improved that much.

My eyes travelled back to Kassian's face to see if he's paying attention.

"You've gone red." My smile grew as my finger pointed him out. "If this is how you're reacting to my *words* about her, I don't even want to know how you'll react when you actually meet her." I leaned away from him and looked his body up and down. "Maybe I shouldn't introduce you guys."

"Shut up." His face became a deeper red.

'Andddd there's the Kassian I know.'

Chapter 30

Medisa
11/02/2022 (Friday)

The first day Kassian hadn't contacted us, we assumed it was because of the fact we literally spent the day and night wide awake and on our feet. So, if he was having a rest day, it made sense. But then he hadn't replied or come the second day, which then turned into the third.

It's now been three days since we've last heard or seen Kassian. After the first hour of not hearing anything back—I assumed he slept in—Kade had sent cleaners to the chapel. They scrubbed the gym of our prints and anything that we left behind, then Kade convinced a bunch of kids to use the chapel to hang out, smoke or what have you.

Any lessons I needed to learn were eventually put on hold. Neither of us could help but have our minds on Kassian (Kade wasn't exactly vocal about it but I could tell).

If Kassian was taken by Maverick, there was nothing but our new friendship that kept him from giving information or do something crazy to satisfy Maverick. And the only information valuable enough is my friendship with Amana. Kassian could tell Maverick about our meeting points and how Amana knew everything. She could be taken and used to lure me out.

I could warn her beforehand, just in case. It might give her a heart attack, but a warning is better than something popping up out of the blue… ignoring how the warning would be out of the blue.

As soon as Kade deemed Kassian missing, he took my phone away. Something about '*extra precautions*' and to prevent me from trying to leave and play the hero. And now, with a few days of disappearance and Kade being gone for hours, I decided being a sitting duck wasn't an option. So, I got myself ready to leave, whether it was a smart move or not, I had to do something, even if it meant exposing myself to keep eyes off Amana.

Kade can't get mad at me. If I had my phone, I could've got her number and used someone else's phone to call her, but no, he took my phone and I don't memorise numbers.

Leaving the building enough times allowed me to be somewhat confident in leaving on my own. I made my way through and out the building the way the other employees would. But in the rush I was in, I didn't wear a disguise. I just prayed the attention was elsewhere, like on Kassian, or on Kade, where ever he was—only because they would know how to handle this all.

Just as I was about to be close enough for the doorman to let me out, someone called out to me.

A man.

I stopped walking as he approached.

I've never seen him before. Not in person, not in pictures, nothing. Quickly going over my thoughts and memories once more, I confirmed I had not seen or met this man before.

My hand gripped onto the bag I carried. The bag that had what Amana would need to escape if she chose to.

Hitting him over the head to make a scene was an option. It would make it harder for him to do anything to me. And if anything were to happen to me, people would know where to start looking.

"I'm your driver and bodyguard." He had a nice smile. Welcoming, friendly, but when he reached out for my hand or bag, I held it closer to me.

"I don't have one of those."

"The last time you went off like this, you got yourself and others in trouble."

'And now I'm leaving knowing that it could happen again.'

"Kade just wants to make sure that you have security this time round."

"Yeah? Then where is he?" I tried not to sound rude but failed. We hadn't met before so he didn't need this from me, but given what I've been through which he obviously knew about, I'd say I had a right to be a little suspicious.

"He's trying to track his brother down, or at least get some sort of grip on what's going on. And don't worry, you'll barely know I'm there." He spoke as though he knew my destination.

"And where is that?"

"Wherever you wanna go."

'Wanna, not want to.'

I observed him for a few more seconds then gave in. I didn't have time to waste. I'll just be a little more alert and if he does try something, I get to test if training has actually helped.

He took me to a car parked up on the road, which made me wonder if I had two drivers. One in the parking lot and one here? And they couldn't have made it any more obvious with this damn vehicle. It's some sort of black SUV, but de-signer?

Planned before we got to the car, I reached for the back

door. If he pulled a stunt, I'd have the upper hand in the back. I could have him in some sort of grip or make an easy run for it if I needed to.

As he shut my door and walked to his, I searched my bag to make sure I had everything Amana would need in case things went to shit.

I forgot her new I.D.

The car door was now a wall I bumped into. It hadn't budged from me trying to get it open, and I knew that Kade had that child-lock feature on his car, but a car like this wouldn't have that.

Why would it?

As I freed a shoelace and wrapped it between my fingers and palm on each hand, I leaned my body and head towards the middled seat so that I could properly see my supposed bodyguard.

"Hey, does this car have child lock or something? What if we get into an accident and I need to get out?" My mind jumped from scenario to scenario. One: this guy and Kassian going missing is all a test. Two: this guy really is someone who works for Kade. Three: he works for Maverick.

Not bothering to turn around, he lazily looked through the centre mirror then back to whatever he was looking at before.

'I would say that's enough for me to come to a fair judgment.' I shoved my arms over his head rest and yanked my elbows back, trapping him with my bootlace. His body flapped about until he made use of his arms, trying to grab onto me, but that only made things worse. Despite the lace feeling as though they were rubbing past my skin, I dipped and pushed myself back with the help of my legs against the back of his seat. My intentions weren't to kill him, but to knock out, or injure

whilst I ran away.

Before I could say something to calm him down before letting go and legging it, almost all car doors opened, allowing for these giant men to get in. The passenger seat was now taken and someone tried to get in through my door.

Freeing my hands from the burns of the lace, I kicked at the man beside me.

"Let's get this over with." The new passenger boorishly spoke over my kicks and grunts.

Getting nowhere with the man at my door, I backed up until my head hit the other side. The two front passengers couldn't have cared less for the drama happening in the back. From what my peripheral vision could see, both of them kept their eyes on the road and to those around.

Failing to open the door I pushed my body up against—forgetting that it wouldn't open to those inside—I wasted no time in elbowing the window like I had superhuman strength.

Taking quick turns from the window to trying to kick the man who was now crawling inside, I also fought against the thought of my actions being useless. Someone had to hear the noise that I was creating. And someone did, the door opened and before I could rejoice, I realised it was another man trying to get in.

'What? Was he in the toilet or something?'

I lunged towards the boot, my thinking being that I did not want to be trapped between these men. As I struggled to get over the seats, the new man wasted no time in grabbing my legs. I kicked and persevered, not even bothering to look at any one of their faces.

I tried to look for the thing they say could open up boots from the inside, but my panicked eyes couldn't find it. Not knowing what else to do, I went back to hitting the glass, praying for someone to find it suspicious. Then the car started to move, so I knew I was gaining some sort of unwanted attention.

Just as I was about to kick out a light, or window, or whatever the hell, my body is dragged back by my hair. And before I could do anything, my head is slammed against the side of the car, suspending all movements.

"What the fuck! We were fucking told not to hurt her!" A part of the car is hit multiple times with a heavy frustrated palm.

I grabbed onto my head in foetal position, trying to stop it from hurting as much as it did. Feeling liquid on my hand, I knew not to pull it away. My ear was bleeding, he'd hit my industrial piercing and it was causing too much pain for me to get back into action.

The men continued to speak in the background and when I tried to look around, my head spun. I couldn't tell if I was going to pass out, or be sick, or both.

All undesirable options.

They gently pulled me over the lowered middle seat. I couldn't physically fight, all my attention was on the pain or the 'spinning room' feeling.

My hair is gently moved away from my face and is replaced with a cloth. I tried to get rid of their hand but nothing worked. The more I put up a fight the more pain it caused my head.

Trying to hold my breath with what little oxygen I had consumed before the attack, I eventually gave in. What was I going to do if I managed to stay awake anyways?

My mind woke up before my body.

It didn't matter what I tried, my eyes refused to open, my body refused to move and my brain kept taking me in and out of dreams or pure darkness.

"She can't do that it's haram."

'Kassian?'

"Oh, look at you expanding your vocab."

'Kade?'

"I didn't expect you to allow this to happen."

I wanted to talk, to look them both in the eyes and see what was going on but my brain still felt a little drugged. Did I really get taken again? Or was that a failed lesson? And what the hell was Kassian talking about?

"You're acting like pawns have a choice dear brother."

I know that it's Kade talking, I *know* it. But at the same time, I'm not registering it. Trying to make sense of the situation did the opposite. I continued to come in and out of what I assumed was a drug-induced sleep, being pulled between different 'realities.'

I've heard people talk about shifting before. I didn't think it was true, but since so many people insisted they magically teleported themselves to another world, I gave them the benefit of the doubt. Of course it could also be possible that all of them were mentally ill, but right now, with my body, mind and soul being in a room I've never been in before, I'm sure that somehow, I've shifted.

The feeling of being in another realm died out as soon as I felt pain gather at the side of my head. And my stomach... It's like I hadn't eaten for days.

The kidnapping was real.

Someone had dressed me whilst I was knocked out. While the outfit isn't completely modest, it is better than what it could've been. They'd dressed me in some sort of choker dress. It was nice. The choker exposed my collarbones and was made out of gold designs that ran down to the side of my arms to form cold shoulders. My would-be bare arms and shoulders were covered in some sort of glittery/embellished mesh material. It looked uncomfortable and itchy, but it was okay. It felt and looked premium.

I didn't need to get up to get a good look at myself, the bed had a mirror installed on its roof, so I couldn't avoid seeing the whole dress even if I wanted to. Someone done my makeup, not adding too much to change me, but to enhance what I had. My eyes had liner and mascara, my under eyes brightened and my cheeks defined and blushed. My hair was straightened which added to the look, but honestly pissed me off. I've kept my hair away from heat for a long time, only for someone to decide that they needed to burn once again.

There was a sudden need to touch my industrial piercing, but I stopped as soon as I felt some sort of tightness around my elbow. The feeling was familiar but not missed. Someone stuck a needle in me, took or gave God knows what, then tightly taped cotton to stop me from bleeding. And as violating as that is, it had already been done and I am not someone with a time machine, but I am someone who's grateful for it happening whilst I was unconscious.

I wanted to say how bored I was of the whole '*get knocked out and get a makeover*,' thing but honestly it had its ups. If, of course, I didn't register the whole 'life and death' situation going on. Which I didn't, but I did somewhat acknowledge it.

The room itself was grand. It didn't have that boring

modern look that everyone and their dad went for now a days. It had that old money look. The bed wasn't even a normal size, and it had four posts with sheer curtains to barely hide what goes on inside.

Moving a part of the curtain to one side, I quietly placed my feet on the ground. Whoever's holding me here might not know I'm awake—going by the assumption that this room has no cameras—so that gives me the opportunity to somehow find another way to escape that *isn't* the obvious door.

Before making a move in any direction, I stripped the mattress of its cover and draped it around me, covering basically everything. I don't care if they stripped me out of what I was wearing to put me in this, I am not consciously allowing them to see how good I looked… even if a part of me wanted them to.

The only light source in this room was coming from the fireplace which honestly felt like the biggest fire hazard. I suppose if one was rich enough to afford a room in what I assumed was a house that mirrored it, they wouldn't care for silly little nuisances like fires.

As I approached the flames, a woman walked in and the sight of me startled her silly—made me jump a little too—but she quickly recovered. There was a metal tray in her hands and once she came to, she held it out to me. We awkwardly stared at each other until I hesitantly moved my hand towards the folded piece of paper.

'Make your way to the Garden Hall. I've been anticipating this meeting for a while Medisa. Try not to make me wait.'

My eyes moved back up to the woman. "Garden Hall?"

Curtsying (I think that's what that was) she made her way to the bed. I didn't understand why, until she grabbed a pair of heels which had been placed as though they were slippers.

"Oh crap I didn't see those. You don't need to pick them up because I won't be wearing them." I moved towards the bed, hands waving. Already feeling weak was a disadvantage, but stripping the mattress genuinely felt as though it sucked what little energy I had left, so no, I would not be putting myself through the experience of walking in those things.

She was offended, or somewhere between annoyed and curious.

"I won't even be able to walk three steps in those." I let out a light laugh to make the situation feel a little less serious.

My efforts were ignored.

Despite me saying I was truly okay with walking barefooted, she held onto the heels as she guided me to where ever the hall was. I did say I could carry them—since they obviously *needed* to be seen—but she moved them away from my hands and continued walking like she couldn't wait to get rid of me.

I didn't want her to think I saw her as someone who was 'less than,' or think that I was a cow. So, I caught up to her and tried to make eye contact as she guided me through the large decorated hallways.

"I'm Medisa by the way. Weird circumstances, but it's nice to meet you." I tried to give a friendly smile to match what I had said, and although she did give a quick smile back, her eyes said something else. "You don't have to take me all the way, you could just tell me where it is and I'll try to find it myself."

"Trying isn't enough." She half-snapped. "You need to be there on time. He already knows that you're awake."

That caught me off guard.

"You think that you're helping me with this act, but

you're not. You're going to get me in trouble. So please, let me drop you off. And don't do anything stupid. You're already disobeying his wishes by looking the way you do."

That also caught me off guard.

I sucked in some air, debating on whether or not I should say something, but decided leave it at a nod.

As we made our way down a large spiral staircase, I finally gave attention to the lack of workers (there wasn't anyone else besides her) and how the manor was candlelit. I wanted to ask so many things, but instead, did my version of biting down on one's tongue. I peeled away at the skin on my lips, trapping lipstick and 'dead' skin under my nails.

If I didn't dislike the guy, I would feed him compliments all day every day. As someone who admires interiors, I'm already being won over—if I ignored how he treated his younger brothers, strangers around the world and what was that last one, oh yes, kidnapping me.

At some point we made it to two large doors.

"You'll need to walk in there alone, Miss Menaal."

I outwardly cringed. "Please. Call me Medisa."

Ignoring me, she whispered '*be careful*' before dismissing herself.

Taking in as much air as I could, I let it all out as I pushed the heavy doors. Taking in the new view, I quickly realised why they called it the Garden Hall.

The high arched roof was covered in all sorts of plants—vines and wisteria are what I could recognise at first glance—and cute lights with a grand chandelier at its centre. I didn't get to take in the detail of this rich hall as my eyes landed on a table too small for this room—and quite literally being some sort of large tree—and the twins.

Both stood and looked in awe as though they were still

processing things. I held Kade's gaze, then looked at Kassian. All of us were dressed like we were celebrating something.

Awkwardly marching towards the tree-table—trying not to get distracted by the beauty of the hall—I recalled why and how I got here in the first place. Barely extending my arm, I pointed at Kassian. "Where were *you*?"

He didn't look beat up, so he wasn't put through it.

Scrunching my brows, I realised I should be asking Kade the same question, so my finger moved towards him. "Where were you?"

Before he could talk, the large doors on the other end opened. No one walked in, but I could sense they were about to—*he* was about to.

"Medisa, please don't do anything rash. I'll explain everything later, I promise."

Two groups of waiters walked in, lining themselves on either side of the hall with their backs to the vases and plant covered walls.

My heart upped its pace.

A shirtless man walked in after. His lack of clothing exposed his scarred skin and not to take away from the boys, but this man had the scariest, battle wound looking, healed lacerations ever. They weren't intended to look like pretty designs—though they were—they looked like his hobby was to put himself into sticky situations, just so that he could fight his way out.

Moving back up his body, I had enough time to take in his long black *wet* hair. He tried to dry or at least dampen his dripping hair with a white towel, not caring for the watered-down red stains he made. And his eyes, his eyes were on Kade.

"Move away from her Kaden, she won't run away."

'Won't or can't?'

Maverick was already sat at the head of the table by the time a troubled Kade took his seat opposite Kassian.

Their older brother leaned back onto his chairs arm, placing his chin between his thumb and folded middle finger as his index pressed against his cheek. And he had *no* shame in staring deep into my soul.

Was this it? His big reveal? We've been preparing for weeks and this was it? Him walking in as nonchalant as he did? It's very anticlimactic compared to what I had in my head.

'I say as I want to cower from his gaze.'

Nothing was being said, but my mind was loud. I couldn't help but take in his presence and looks. I was already thinking of what I would report back to Amana. *'Holy shit, the man is fine. FINE. The twins are wow but this man is wow-er, to the point where someone could maybe briefly forget what he does for a living.'*

Not only was he tall, but he had muscles, bigger than the boys, and on top of that, his long hair was wet, and he has facial hair that actually suits him. I've never been one for facial hair, but there's something about that pirate—though his is borderline Viking—look that always gets me. And I *have* to bring up that necklace he's wearing. It just—chefs kiss—adds to his look.

I had no idea if someone's said something because my mind keeps coming up with ways to compliment him. Annoyed by my own thoughts, I reminded myself of how this man was a prick. Stupidly good-looking, yes, but still a prick.

A maid, or waiter, or whatever the hell this person's occupation was, came close to Maverick, taking away his stained wet towel and replacing it with a flowy white pirate looking shirt.

'Ugh. Just add to the look why don't you.'

My eyes stayed on the towel the man took away.

"It's blood." Maverick spoke, casually and to the point. "Do take a seat, I don't want your legs to give out from what I'm about to say."

"Is it worse than sending me a hand?" I spoke without thinking. My tone was more bored than entertained.

He let out a short chuckle then turned to Kassian. "I see what you mean…I like her." His ravenous expression was tinted with *something* when he gave Kade a look.

'What was that?'

"Such candour."

A game was being played in here too, how foolish of me to think that this was going to be a normal gathering. I needed to keep my sarcasm and witty comments to myself before I triggered the freak into doing something unhinged.

Whilst I got my thoughts together, Maverick signalled to who I'm guessing is the head of the waiters, slash maids—a butler?—who then clapped, telling those with the food to come in.

Maverick played with his steak knife, twisting it into the table. "I'm not going to ask you again Medisa."

I gave him a *'who do you think you are?'* look, getting a smirk and *'K'* sound out of him as if he liked where this was going, but also couldn't believe it.

"You're not a child—"

"I am." I said too quickly. "So imagine how embarrassing it is for you to be that old and still act like one." Honestly, God knows if that made sense, but I felt so high on some sort of adrenaline—or drugs— that it all kind of just spilled out.

"Olivia, approach the table."

'Where was this going?'

Through scrunched brows I found Olivia. Some of the workers made who he was calling obvious.

Olivia, the woman who walked with me here, hesitantly stepped forward.

"Wait-wait! I'll sit. I'm gonna sit." I quickly pulled a chair out then aggressively sat down, but Maverick couldn't give a shit.

He tutted as his hand reached out towards her.

"Don't be scared, don't worry. Nothing's going to happen to you, come here." He spoke to Olivia like a lover as he gently pulled her towards him, but I could sense he had something evil planned. And from the way everyone held themselves, they felt it too.

"Maverick don't do this." I tried to keep myself calm but I could hear the urgency in my own voice. "I'm sitting down!"

"Close your eyes for me Olivia." He ignored me as he gave her a devilish smile. I could only see his side profile but my brain made his face whole just fine, it's like I were Olivia.

She whimpered.

I could tell she was trying to hold it in, but I heard it.

He softly kissed her hand before placing it on the table.

I couldn't sit and watch, so I pounced up, scraping my chair on the floor, almost causing it to fall. I went past Kade, who stood to stop me, but I curved him to get to Maverick as quick as possible.

"I get it, *I get it*, just let go off her *please*." I raised my voice as I got closer to Maverick.

"Do you?" Maverick raised his arm, his elbow still on the table. Then without remorse, he slammed his knife down into her hand all whilst looking at me, pure gratification across his face.

I stopped moving, not because of the knife in his hand, but because of her screeches and the pure psychotic look on his face. He picked the knife out her hand then slammed it down again, not one ounce of remorse on his face as some of her blood splattered over him as he kept his eyes on me. After repeating the stabbing action, he finally stopped, leaving the steak knife in her hand.

Olivia's screams pierced through the hall. Everyone lined up against the walls tried their best to stay and look neutral, whilst I kept my hands over my ears as her cries attacked and echoed as though they were coming from inside my head.

Blood pooled where her hand was stuck as she continued to cry out, purely from the pain. She hadn't even seen what he'd done to her yet.

"Ugh." Maverick grew tired of Olivia's cries, and instead of freeing and dismissing her, he pulled out the knife with ease, wiping it clean on her sleeve. Her hand stayed on the table, her arm shaking, waiting for him to allow her to leave. Maverick forced her head up, lovingly shushing her till she quietened. His blood decorated hand moved from her chin to her cheek, holding her in place whilst simultaneously caressing her with his thumb.

"If you don't shut the fuck up in the next five seconds, you'll no longer have the means to produce your own." The knife was held low, too low and he wasn't shy to poke her a little.

Olivia tried to catch her breath as she forced herself to stifle her cry, her gasps. Her breaths came in quick two's or three's, like she were both suffocating and trying to self-comfort.

"Do you hear me?" He whispered as if he cared for her

feelings.

I tried to move closer to help her, but Kade held onto me. I hadn't even realised he came up beside me and for some reason, him stopping me pissed me off.

"Someone take her away and clean this up."

Olivia's cries quietened down, but she was still struggling to breathe. I know what that felt like, crying so hard you couldn't breathe, constantly gasping for air. I hated it like I was the one being put through it.

"You fucking pig! I sat down! You saw me sit down! You didn't need to do that!" With each point made, I tried to get closer to him, but Kade continued to hold me back.

"Oh, but I did. I did. How else was I going to get you to know to obey me. It's evident sending you a hand wasn't enough to show you how serious I am, how *genuine* this all is."

I didn't realise before, but I was breathing heavy and had some sort of lump in my throat. It's anger. The type of anger that up until this moment, only my siblings could summon.

"Obey you? This isn't even my fight. I don't even know why I'm here! As far as I'm concerned, you're just fucking bored and need to get a grip!" I pushed to get closer to Maverick, my chest heaving in and out as though the air had gotten thicker.

Kade went from holding me to also blocking my path.

"Get *off* me!" I tried to pull my arm out of his grip, to shoo him away, but he didn't budge.

"Trust me on this." He urged.

"Trust you?" Maverick laughed. "Are you sure she should do that?"

Even when Kade spoke low, close to a whisper, Maverick heard.

"Leave her out of this." Kade turned to him.

"Sit *down* and let Medisa say what she wants." Maverick's voice switched from someone who enjoyed this night, to someone who dared you to piss him off.

Kade stayed stood in between us, holding me by him.

"No?" Maverick raised a brow. "Did I just stab a girl's hand for fun?"

'That's it.'

Kade's grip loosened and in that quick second, I freed myself. Grabbing whatever I could—a drink—I got close and threw it all over Maverick.

He took it all in, in fact he enjoyed it too much. Then, as if he'd teleported, he stood towering over me. I heard Kade move forward, but Maverick moved faster and held his knife to my side.

"Ah-ah be a good boy and go back to your seat. We all want Medisa to spend at least one good night here…don't we?" He lowered his head, turning it to the side my industrial piercing should be.

Feeling his lips gently brush over my ear, got more of a reaction out of me than his knife being pushed up against my side.

"I did tell them to be gentle." Softly speaking into my ear, he angled my face up to his with the blood-stained hand. Looking over where my industrial piercing should be, he continued. "I want you to know that they paid for that mistake with their lives."

Instantly forgetting he held a knife to me, I disgustedly tried to move out of his grip as I wiped his touch. "Is that supposed to make me feel better?"

"There's nothing wrong with it if you do. But what I want you and everyone else to take away from that is…" He looked to the boys. "If I could easily kill men I've known for years, what makes you think I give a shit about what I do to you?"

As his hair continued to drip, my mind travelled back. Breaking eye contact with Maverick to look to the man behind, the man who still held onto the stained towel, I pieced together what he was doing before this get-together.

Maverick followed my eyes then smiled, long dimples on each side. "Clever girl."

After releasing me from his grip and tapping my head, he turned to go back to his seat.

I scoffed, which could have been taken as a panicked breath. "Why do they follow you if they know that you have no loyalties towards them, that you'll—"

"It's cute that you think they have a choice in the matter." He helped his thirst with some wine then stood in front of me. "Have you boys not told your new friend what we do? What we *like* to do?" He shoved his face as close as it could get to mine.

"Speak for yourself." I spoke to him like I didn't just witness the monstrosity he'd done to Olivia for my 'mistake.'

His eyes flickered between mine, and I didn't know if this was his way of reading me or if he was starting to lose some control. His jaw moved as though he were grinding his teeth, but that quickly stopped when a grin appeared.

"What was that you called me earlier? A pig?"

There were about three things Maverick could force me to do that came to mind almost straight away.

None of them were good.

Maverick dragged me to the first chair after his, pulled it out then pushed it in as I was forcefully sat down.

'What a *fucking gentleman.*'

Kade and Kassian got up and moved closer to my seat.

As they were about to pull on the chairs next to me, Maverick spoke. "Boys, if I wanted us to be seated this close, I would've seated us at a fucking picnic table."

His words were calm but his face held no amusement.

They both stayed where they were.

"Oh, okay." Maverick tugged my head back and held the knife to my throat until they got up, which happened quickly after he literally cut into me. I almost grabbed onto the blade to push it away but had to firm it for the sake of not giving him any satisfaction.

After everyone was seated the way he wanted, Maverick made two plates, one for him, one for me. My eyes tried to follow what he was plating, but when he noticed, he told me to place my eyes elsewhere before he fed them to the twins. Even with the threat, I tried to keep my angered eyes on him, until I felt Kade's burning into the side of my head, then, I moved my sight away from Maverick and down to my hands below the table.

As soon as I heard a plate be placed in front of me, I immediately looked at it like I was excited and not dreading it. This was one of those times where I wished I wasn't right. The bastard filled my plate with pig and didn't even try to make it look appetising.

"I'm not eating that."

"And why not?" He stared, slow blinking as if he's cute or something.

"You *know* why." It's why he filled my plate with it.

"Ah yes. I do remember Kassian telling me about how strict you are with certain things."

I briefly looked over to Kassian who looked towards the plate, my eyes and then in front of him to Kade. That's when I spotted the tray of roasted potatoes to my right. I reached over to see if I could get the tip of my fingers to touch it, but before they got close, Maverick spoke. This time his voice was a little deeper and had more threat. Like Kassian, he had an accent, but his one was stronger and could be heard in more words than his.

"You touch that tray and I'll assume you no longer need your fingers."

I folded my fingers, then pulled my hand back. This was getting repetitive and if I felt that, I didn't want to know how fed-up Maverick was feeling.

"Perhaps you need a drink to accompany the meat." He spoke like he cared.

And I would like to say he poured some blackcurrant or something, but it was obviously some sort of alcohol. My best bet? Wine.

"Listen, Maverick."

The way he turned his attention towards me, made me think I shouldn't have started my sentence like that.

"I get it. You want me to know that you get whatever you want, I get it. So can we please stop whatever this is and talk about what we were supposed to before I disobeyed you."

'*Disobeyed.*' I hated saying that, if I didn't want to sit, then fair enough. I did get knocked out and taken—in fact, how long was I out for? What day was it right now?

Maverick laughed, it started out small, but then it grew louder and when he suddenly stopped and dropped his smile, my stomach sank a little.

"Drink." He handed me the glass then raised his. "Let's all drink to Medisa finally getting it."

My heartbeat felt heavy, like I could feel each time it had expanded.

He was taking things too far.

'Olivia's hand wasn't far enough?'

"She's not drinking or eating any of that." Kade finally spoke.

Maverick sucked in air through his teeth. "We can't be disrespectful to the cook or the pig that died for this. It would be a waste. Wouldn't it, Medisa? And isn't being wasteful a sin?"

I sat in place, I didn't turn to look at him whilst he spoke, I didn't look at Kade as he protested. I looked at my plate and felt sick by the sight and smell of it. Never in my life did I think pig or pork, or whatever the hell, was appealing. I didn't care how many people around me complimented it, it's disgusting.

"Honestly Medisa, after all I've done for you. The least you could do is finish your plate."

'Did I hear that correctly?'

"All that you've done for me? What the hell have you done for me?"

"Dealing with a dead body is not easy you know? There's the clean-up, the disposal, the—"

"What body?" I hadn't killed anyone. I know it. Right? There's no way.

'Unless...'

"The body of the man you murdered of course." Maverick's eyes slid to Kassian as his chin dug into his neck. All that was missing from his body language was his thumb pointing at me, and the words '*this girl.*'

Now my eyes were on Kassian.

Kassian whose internal battle could be seen despite no changes being made to his expression. Kade was looking at him too, except with him, I couldn't tell if he were pushing for Kassian to speak, or to keep his mouth shut.

It got to a point where Kassian didn't need to say any-thing, the prolonged pause was enough. I obviously had done something which killed someone. However, my mind is not on the person or their family, it's on my own punishment. My sympathy is towards myself rather than the person. I'm more worried, more scared, of the consequence than what I had done and how it would affect others. I didn't want to go to jail. That wasn't my plan. Then there's the part of me that continued to not take anything seriously. It won't believe it until I saw some evidence, which meant I shouldn't waste energy on this.

Maverick sighed once he realised I wasn't making a move for the drink or plate.

"Let's make this fun for us all." He placed a hand on my shoulder. "The longer Medisa refuses to eat, the more I'll fill her in on what you boys have clearly missed out. If any of you would like me to stop, Medisa must drink the whole cup."

I noticed the twins exchange a few looks before turning their eyes to me.

'They better not be thinking to force it down me.'

Starting from his end, to then going down Kassian's side of the table, Maverick decided it would be best to walk around. It was like watching duck-duck-goose or musical chairs, without the music.

"Let's start with family."

We all simultaneously took a deep breath in, then kept our eyes on Maverick, who moved around somewhat care-free. He stopped walking once he was directly opposite me, then he leant over the back of the chair.

"What tradition so deeply engraved in our history, in our bloodline, so *sacred* to our name, did Kaden break?"

The hall was quiet.

And as much as I wanted to know more, I didn't want it this way. This felt like I was stealing their secrets. Was this a test in itself? If I knew more about them, did it seal my fate? Did it add more chains to my body or a gun to my head?

"C'mon boys, this one's easy. In fact, there are at least two things." Maverick balanced his weight on the chair's back legs. Once he realised no one was going to answer him, he stared at Kassian.

"He cut his hair—"

'Oh my days, is it really that deep?'

"—Abandoning our signature look, our tradition, our rule." Kassian watched Kade, who didn't bother to look back at him. "Cutting one's hair shorter than their ear is a good way to outwardly show no longer being a part of the family, or in his case, going against the family."

My mind went back to when I first met the boys, specifically Kassian. He didn't just go and get a normal haircut, he did something that broke a tradition, a rule, all in order for him to get revenge.

Maverick made it to the other end of the table then chuckled. "This one's good." He rubbed his chin. "What did Kaden do that Kassian got the blame for?"

Kassian's confused eyes waited for an answer as he wondered what his brother did. Kade just looked pissed and on edge. And I, I still hadn't processed the last piece of information, so I just looked between the three of them confused as I manually breathed.

"Okay, fine I'll help." Maverick made his way back to me. He leaned over the chair beside me and I didn't need to look at him to know that he was trying to get my attention. "Kaden can be… territorial. Not just over his space, but over people too."

I kept my eyes forward, trying my best to not give any sort of reaction. On the inside, I was trying to work out what the hell Kade did that relates to me, that Kassian somehow got the blame for.

Maverick moved to the other side of me.

"He craves some sort of release. He tries to bottle himself up because his saint side—it's small, but it's there—doesn't always agree, and when that happens and a trigger is also present, he blacks out to stop himself from feeling guilt. Though I'm not quite sure if that part's true… The blacking out? We all know you enjoy it." Maverick placed his hand on my shoulder again. "All but Medisa." His thumb gently stroked me, angering me a little. I couldn't tell if it was the comforting act, or the fact that he was touching me, but I felt so irritated and *uncomfortable*.

'Also, am I supposed to skip past the trigger part? Do I trigger Kade?'

"Medisa, would you like to see the state of the men at the construction site after Kaden had left them?" He snapped his fingers, resulting in one of the workers moving around. "Good thing I put them through what I did. They would've never been able to handle themselves as well as they do now without me. I basically made them, gave them their person-alities." He was too proud, and all I could think about is how he reminded me of my siblings.

Before I could hold a meeting with my thoughts, I picked up a knife and went for him. The position I was in made the deliverance of the strike a little awkward but nevertheless, I made contact. Some of the workers gasped, Kade stood—I heard his chair scrape the floor—and Maverick aggressively pulled me to a stand by my hair, angling my head up to him, forcing me to tip toe, whilst he lowered his to mine. Yes, I made contact, but he stopped it from going in too deep. I don't even think I got an inch of the knife in, more like a centimetre before he gripped onto my wrist and forced the knife to face me instead. We both breathed heavy whilst bits of blood and the drink from his hair dropped onto me.

Maverick swatted something away from us. I didn't know what was going on because my concentration was on the pain from my head and feet, and his angered eyes which did not leave mine.

He huffed, but paired with his latest smile it was like he was pleased, or honoured even.

"Young missy you are close to tap dancing on my last nerve." Once again, his knife is held to my throat, but this time it was angled up as if he would stab instead of slice, which honestly made me feel a little better.

"Not much patience for an old man." My chest heaved in and out whilst my mouth refused to zip-it.

"You take one more step and I'll kill her now." His irate tone comes out of nowhere as he addressed Kade—making me jump—as my mind thought, '*As opposed to later?*'

My eyes were fixated on Maverick's as I tried to process whatever the hell just happened. The pain from my scalp and toes muted me as I tried my best to keep balanced, and Maverick almost became expressionless as he continued to force me to face him.

"Dismissed."

The moment the workers began to move, Maverick threw me over his shoulder and began to walk away. I did try to hold my body up to see what was going on, but between the crowd of workers and Maverick getting to the doors, I didn't see much. But I knew no matter what the boys felt, they wouldn't dare to walk in the direction Maverick was going.

Maverick didn't bother to tell me to stop moving. He just altered his hand placement or grip, stealing a gasp here and there when I tried to wiggle my way out of the position. I even tried to kick his balls—he saved them—but I wasn't bold enough to do some serious damage to his back. Seconds after, I gave up. I could hurt him enough for him to drop me—wishful thinking—but then what? He would just get pissed off some more and do God knows what.

Maverick locking the door to the room that was obviously our final destination, was the gunshot that made my heart race. I was no longer on a somewhat tame journey (plopped on his shoulder), I was where he wanted me to be, which meant that I now had to face whatever he was going to do to me. I want to say that now was the time I fought him, made whatever he was doing difficult, but the truth is, I didn't. I was just trying to steady my breaths so that I was able to think straight.

The room had a huge ensuite where Maverick forcefully sat me down outside of the shower space—the shower space being larger than the bathroom at my parent's house. And before I could do anything, he handcuffed me to the towel railing then searched for hair pins or anything I could use to get myself out. I didn't know what kind of mastermind he thought I was, but there was no way I could get myself out with *both* of my hands tied about a head above me.

He lowered himself to be around the same level as me. His low '*hmmm*' was like purrs from a lion, and paired with the slow tilt to view me, he looked more of a predator in here than he did at the table.

"What are you thinking right now?" Maverick asked. "Does this feel real? Are you all here? Or are you stuck back at Garden Hall?"

Satisfied with no answer (shockingly), he began to strip. Not that there was much to it, his shirt was already half undone.

Whilst I *tried* to busy my mind, he showered in front of me, not caring if he had a spectator. And it wasn't my intention to, I was just making sure that he wasn't looking at me as I tried to get up, but I saw it. I saw it for a millisecond and almost had a heart attack. I looked away as soon as I saw it, but it still flashed in my head and I couldn't even cover my face with my hands. My brain then decided now was the right time to remind me of the relationship between Maverick and Kade. They shared genes, which meant that they have *certain* things in common.

'Now's not the time.'

Steam filled the room because he hadn't bothered sectioning off his shower. Eventually, it became humid, and my dress began to feel uncomfortable as my hair started to frizz and curl.

My wrists and arms started to hurt.

He could've at least given me cushioned, slash feathered cuffs. I'm not that under a rock for me to not know of their existence.

Tugging at the cuffs, thinking if I pulled them hard enough it would break the rail to which it was attached, I almost detached my wrists—exaggeration?

I couldn't tell if he heard me pulling on the rail, or if he was done with his shower, but he came out and wrapped the lower half of his body with a towel. After cleaning and covering the small cut I gave him, he carried a footstool over from God knows where, then sat in front of me with his legs apart.

Pulling myself up so that I sat up straight, I brought my legs closer to me instead of leaving them in between his. Maverick let me do all this as he stared in silence. And despite his eyes being like Kade's, it was as though he had no whites, no colours, just big black spheres, showing me his sinister mind.

I'd been blessed to have only been scared over insignificant matters—knocking on a classroom door, entering a room late, having control over my own life—in the past. I knew this now. Because for a moment, for a tiny moment, I allowed fear to replace my anger when I looked into Maverick's sadistic eyes.

"I'm glad you're a part of this, you've made things more fun. But in your next life, could you girls learn to stay out of things?" He cocked his head a little to the side.

"Muslims don't believe in reincarnation you prick." I don't know what possessed me, but I tried to kick him.

I failed of course.

He'd caught my ankle then refused to let it go. My face dropped whatever expression it held as his grew a twisted smile. I made a mistake and we both knew it.

"You're really risking this one life of yours then, aren't you?" He held my leg in the air and made no hesitation to softly kiss the area above my ankle. He knew he was getting under my skin, the eye contact and smile confirmed it.

Trying to pull my leg away from him only strengthened his grip. It was like someone was tightening a clamp around my ankle, but I refused to show that I was in any sort of pain.

Without thinking, I tried to kick him off, which only worsened the situation.

With both my ankles in his possession, he pulled me closer to him. And as my wrists were still hung above me, only the bottom of my body moved towards him.

Even though I was dressed in something covering, I still felt embarrassed by the position in which I was forced. Thankfully, the skin that was in contact with the cuffs felt as if they were ripping, so my mind had something else to think of.

The air started to feel thick and for some reason only I seemed to be affected by it. Maverick stayed calm and collected, even after my attempted kicks.

To release some of the tension on my wrists, I tried to pull myself up so that I was against the wall, but Maverick pulled me back to him, inflicting even more pain.

I tried again, but this time he held me in place.

"See even now, after all I've done, you're still trying to fight back. You still *want* to disobey me."

Even with my lungs feeling as though they were no longer taking in oxygen, just hot thick air, I still managed a sarcastic gasp. "Whatever will we do?"

His lips flashed a smirk before he leant down and stole what little oxygen was around me. "I knew that you had some fight in you. I saw it when you 'accidently' killed that man in my pub, and I saw it again around the neck of the man I'd sent to fetch you. I'm seeing it now. And I just want you to know, that fight…it's made things much more entertaining, but—"

"I guess I should pack it in then?" I had no desire to let him continue, not when the lack of oxygen was becoming concerning.

I tried not to make my need for air obvious. It's like those times I've fought to hold in those loud, strong, crunchy coughs in class.

Maverick allowed himself one syllable of a chuckle. "You're feeling it already, aren't you? The air becoming thick, your lungs wanting more. Guess you aren't much of a swimmer?"

The poker face I had started to slip at the mere association of water. There's no way he knew about my fear of water, Kassian hadn't even been told.

After gently placing my ankles down, Maverick made his way to the door. "I'll come back when you're a little quieter. Judging by your breaths, I'm going to take a quick guess and say that's soon."

Moments like this made me want to thank my past for giving me the ability to not 'overreact' in situations like this. I'm pretty proud of my ability to be able to look around for something that would help without exhausting too much energy. But then things started to move a little slow and inhaling no longer worked. Once my gasps for air became quick and loud enough, my mind and body started to freak out.

'Is he sucking all the oxygen out from the room?'

Before I gave up entirely, pretty much accepting that this was how I died, the door opened. I wanted it to be Kade, for him to somehow have found the room that I was in, but it wasn't.

As soon as my arms dropped down, freeing me from one ache only to bring about another, I was ready to pass out.

My eyes constantly opened and closed. I had no idea how long each interval was, and I had no interest in trying to keep them open.

I was done. I was sick of it all.

My hair stuck to exposed skin, the dress I wore developed attachment issues, and my lungs felt as though weights were being pressed onto them. At some point I felt tugging from multiple sets of hands and I heard uncoherent voices, I think.

I don't really know.

After a few minutes, I managed to—barely—open my eyes. Despite my vision being hazy, I could make out some sort of old-fashioned office with two, maybe four men in front of me. When I looked to my side, I saw Kade, sitting right next to me.

He smiled then reached over for my hand.

'That's weird. He's never done that.'

"It's almost done now." He placed a soft kiss on top of my hand.

My clouded vision became more intense even though conversations were still being had. I would push to question this all, but this was how dreams worked; random and never making sense.

Out of nowhere a pen and clipboard are taken away from me as my vision worsened. Certain things came in and out of focus and my mind became a little more aware of how limp my body actually was.

A small crowd began to clap and congratulate as Kade lifted me into his arms. He carried me out the room, away from everyone else.

'I didn't recognise anyone. Where's Amana? Kassian?'

"You must be thirsty, drink this."

A cup is brought to my lips and angled so that the liquid is poured into my mouth.

'Water?'

I ended up drinking it all, hoping it would clear my mind or wake me up—kind of like using a toilet in a dream would—but my lids got heavy again.

Chapter 31

Medisa
14/02/2022 (Monday)

As soon as I woke up, I felt the need to vomit. Usually I tried to hold it in, but I had no choice but to let it out into the bedside table. After two, maybe three rounds of vomit, I stayed over the drawer until I emptied myself out, backing away after I only produced spit.

Finally having the chance to use all my senses, I notice movement in the background. Someone took steps towards me, and embarrassed for not spotting them sooner, I kept my gaze lowered and faced away.

"Drink some of this."

Maverick.

I'd almost forgotten we'd met.

"You drugged me."

"Only a little."

I continued to scowl, observing the drink in his hands.

"It's a little concoction to help you get back to normal." He took a big sip then angled it towards me, waiting for me to take it. "Although 'normal' isn't the word I would use to describe you."

It took a few seconds for me to finally give in and drink whatever the hell it was. I was hungry, thirsty and tired, and I needed the little energy it would provide.

As I chugged down the concoction, Maverick continued to talk like he wasn't the current villain in my life.

"Do you know what word I would use to describe you?"

I stopped drinking then lazily spoke. "Bitch?"

My heart jumped at my delivery as it could be interpreted as me calling him one, but amusement ran across his face, pulling the corners of his lips up.

He sucked air through his teeth. "Maybe you should use today to explore the grounds."

'Does he have a twin too or something? Why is he behaving like this?'

He walked towards the door, then spoke before completely disappearing. "Oh, and Medisa. It would be stupid to run."

'Nope. It's still him.'

"Oh gee, a whole day to explore."

I stayed in bed, in no rush to leave the room right after him. *"Do you know what word I would use to describe you?"* I mocked.

Alarming how I hadn't spent three full hours with Maverick and yet I'm already tired of him. Kade and Kassian spent years with this guy and somehow turned out to be okay…I think. But I'm already triggered and want to do something about it. That being said, I needed to be smart. I didn't know Maverick as well as everyone else, so actually listening to people's advice would be nice. It could keep me and others out of trouble. Using what I know about Kade and Kassian's habits and triggers would be another smart way of figuring Maverick out. They could have picked things up from him without realising.

Just as I was about to pace the room, a woman stood at the door with a jug in hand. Not giving her the opportunity to put it down, I took it from her. She then tried to (quickly) dismiss herself, but I told her to wait. When she listened, it took me a second to realise it was because she had no choice.

"How's Olivia?"

Before staring too deeply into my eyes, she looked away as though it helped her from saying what she actually wanted to say.

"She's okay."

'Her hand was stabbed, how well do you expect her to be?'

"She doesn't want to see you right now."

'She blames you for what happened—as she should—and never wants to see you.'

"I'll let her know that you've asked about her, but please do stay away."

'I'll let her know about the nerve you had to ask about her.'

"She told us you were different, but please don't pay attention to us. If he sees any sort of connection between you and someone, he'll make them suffer the consequences of your mistakes."

My brain stopped translating her words.

"I really am sorry for what I did. I didn't know I swear. I won't give anyone attention in the future. I just... I was trying to be nice. But I get it now."

The woman went on her way. I didn't ask for her name or tell her to call me by mine. If I were to keep them somewhat safe, I wasn't allowed to do that anymore.

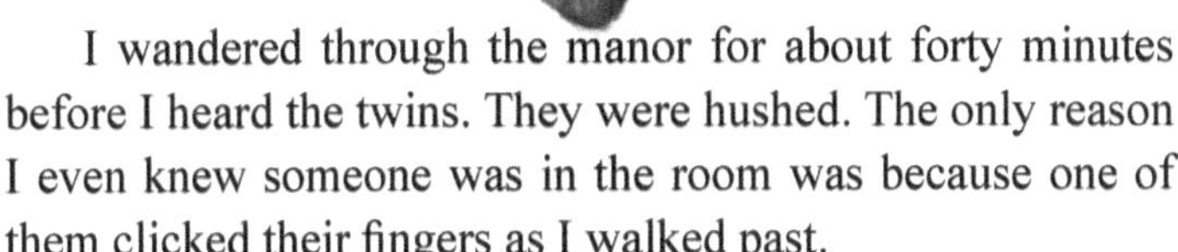

I wandered through the manor for about forty minutes before I heard the twins. They were hushed. The only reason I even knew someone was in the room was because one of them clicked their fingers as I walked past.

Before I opened the room door, I listened in. Rude—yes, but if I learnt anything from before it's that these two kept information from me *'for the greater good.'*

"Do you not understand!" Kassian whispered loudly. "This isn't like before! He's not casting her to the side like he's done before. You fucked up and you know it."

'*Like before,*' explained why Maverick had said '*you girls.*'

I opened the door too quickly and too soon in the conversation to face the both of them. Kade leant on some sort of fancy drawer with its fancy oval mirror and Kassian looked as if he was pacing the room lecturing his brother.

"Alright, that's the second time I've heard him say something like that. Kade what did you do?"

As Kade walked over to shut the door, Kassian continued to speak. "Yes, do tell her brother, do tell us what your plan was."

Kade raised his hand to Kassian, signalling for him to stop as though he were going too far. When Kassian was silenced, Kade sat me down on the fancy stool that matched its drawer, then leant against the window sill, against the light.

"I made a deal with Maverick."

I turned towards Kassian whose body language gave his disagreement away.

"He wants us to be a family—"

'Us?'

"—But he sees you as an obstacle preventing him from achieving that—"

'*Oh thank God. He didn't mean me.*'

"—Now obviously I wasn't going to let him '*take care of you,*' and we don't want to be back. Not unless he's dead or close to it. So…" The Kade that existed in the early days of Aros spoke, not the one who trained me. "To get what everyone wanted, *including* your safety, we… *I*, suggested marriage."

It felt like someone had hit the 'pause' then 'play' button on my Dunya's avatar. My mind was stuck between so many words, thoughts, memories and plans of escape.

"Marriage?" I chuckled wryly. My eyes travelled to Kassian for some sort of validation, but once I saw that he was serious, they jumped back to Kade. "*Marriage*?" I said a little more shocked. "Who?" I could feel my face expressing how I thought. I obviously knew I would be one participant, but I needed confirmation and none of them said anything. "Kade. *Who* is getting married?"

I got up, but before I reached Kade, another voice cut into the conversation.

"A marriage between me and you of course." Maverick leaned on the doorway.

I held my breath. I didn't care for marriage, not on the outside anyways. It was always something that I desired but not enough for me to seek out. If it happened it happened. I could always make my own money, buy my own house and adopt kids, I didn't need a man. But now, hearing the word, and being associated with it, my heart dropped.

"That wasn't the deal." Kade stepped in between me and his brother. His older, bigger, brother.

"No, but I like the way it would go. What's yours would become mine. You all would be taught a lesson and, in a couple of years, when we have kids running around, I'll get to teach them some lessons too." He addressed Kade.

'Yours? Kids? What?'

Maverick pushed his body off the door frame, his eyes on me. Kade stayed guarding me whilst I stood still, still in disbelief as they went back and forth.

'I can't marry him. Not him. Please God not him.'

"She leaves *now* and we'll stay here. We won't leave

again.”

Maverick sucked air through his teeth. “I’m afraid I can’t let her do that.” A smirk formed, which then grew into a smile. “C’mon Medisa, has it not come back to you yet?”

For two, maybe three seconds I stood confused. My narrowed eyes focussing on Maverick as I tried to understand what he was saying. A second or two later and I quietly gasped at the realisation.

Without thinking about what I was doing, I grabbed onto Kades sleeve, pulling his attention towards me.

“It’s too late.” Kassian said as he slowly sat up straight, piecing things together himself.

“He’s already done it.” My words provided no comfort.

“What?” Kade whipped his head to Maverick.

“12 am. You missed it. They all thought it was true love once I told them about her terminal illness and how we wanted to marry before she passed.”

Really? That was enough for no one to question a drugged girl signing papers?

“The process was too quick for me to have even bothered with the invitations. But don’t worry, you’ve already met my wife.”

Kade launched himself at Maverick, landing his first punch, though it did not look like Maverick even attempted to dodge. Kassian shot up out his seat as if that were a signal he missed and pulled Kade back.

“One’s enough! Think about this!” Whilst he had succeeded in pulling Kade away, he hadn’t in trying to keep it that way. Kassian ended up becoming a victim, taking an elbow to his face, allowing for Kade to be free of his grip.

Kade got a few more punches on Maverick. With each hit he gave, the bigger the eyes and smile got on his brother’s face.

At some point Kassian went from trying to be neutral, to being against Kade. Whenever Kade got rid of Kassian, even if it was only for a split second, he went after Maverick. It was pure chaos watching them go back and forth, and their older brother was loving it.

After a few minutes, Maverick straightened himself out as if he wore a suit, then headed towards the hallway whilst Kassian had Kade distracted.

"C'mon wifey, we have duties to each other now."

'*Wifey*.' Maverick was not the type to say that. Kade: yes, Kassian: yes, Maverick: No.

He knew about what me and Amana called each other. It's not a coincidence. This had to be some sort of threat or warning or something. But what did I do instead of being a good obeying wife?

I ran.

Chapter 32

Medisa

14/02/2022 (Monday)

As much as I thought adrenaline would be on my side, it was not. The shaking—something we tried to train and control—was back and was most definitely not in my control. I knew that he was following me, he made that clear when he called out to me and laughed.

When I had run down multiple hallways, large rooms and down some stairs, I thought that I had lost him, but when I stopped to catch my breath, I heard his whistle. His tune wasn't jolly, it was haunting, like he knew where I was going and couldn't wait for the hunt to end. As some parts of this place were a little empty, his whistle would be all around, making his location impossible to figure out. It was like he surrounded me, and whenever I managed to hide to catch my breath, I noticed how he strode. He didn't run in attempts to get me like I was used to. He walked in a specific direction and was calm, something which somehow scared me even more.

Every time I ran past a worker, I cussed myself out for not being careful. They were obviously making this much more difficult.

Eventually, I got back to the Garden Hall. It was empty now. No workers, no food or plates, nothing. I could hide in between the plants, but there's something so obvious about me choosing to hide here, so I went against the idea.

Choosing another doorway in the Garden Hall, I was let

out into an actual garden, which was just a bunch of land going as far as the eye can see…That's what I thought anyways, it's dark so I couldn't really trust my eyes.

The 'garden' had huge vases and plants I quickly hid behind before someone saw me. The vases were about eight feet tall but I still felt the need to crouch a little to get a good view of the other side of them.

Scoping the grounds to see where I should run to next was more intense than actually running away. It was like I had a time limit and had to make a quick decision before I got caught.

I went through my options.

The horse stables was an automatic no. I didn't know how to ride a horse and even if I did, they could kick up a fuss about a stranger approaching them. I may as well start being loud now if I even thought about taking a step towards the stables.

The pools are definitely not an option either. Not only is it lit by dim lights, but if Maverick finds me there, he could decide to throw me in for fun. Then I would drown and die, or he would somehow save me, realise I'm scared of water, then use that knowledge against me for the rest of my life.

The hedges were another dumb option. I didn't know where it led to, I couldn't see if people were on the other side and it was quite a bit away. The only advantage was that it was the darkest place.

Soon as I thought that the coast was clear, I ran towards the hedges, making a dumb option, even dumber. They weren't just two overgrown hedges, sectioning off a place. They were two overgrown hedges marking the start of some sort of maze. Every other corner had a dim light on, every *other* corner had some sort of marble statue, which at this point served to be a jump scare.

It was colder in here, and every turn I made sent more chills down my spine because my stupid brain kept thinking that a statue was someone finding me.

A branch snapped somewhere, but I was too in my own head to even realise what direction it had come from. I stopped moving to not give away my own position then heard another snap. I looked to the floor to see where I could step because if they were getting closer, I needed to get away. But there weren't any branches or leaves on the path. Someone was snapping branches for fun. They were teasing, trying to scare me and God forbid I ever admit it, but it was working. I had this sudden urge to pee, giving me flashbacks to when I used to play hide and seek.

Another stick is snapped.

They're somewhere behind me.

I started to run, giving up my position almost instantly because as soon as I ran, they started to run too. The feeling of giving up and letting myself be found increased and as I fought those thoughts, the lights went out.

I stopped running, moving, breathing, everything and anything I could control, I stopped.

Rationing my breaths proved to be harder than I thought, especially since my heart was pounding and the urge to pee had increased.

It had been quiet for way too long. I needed to move away from where the last snap happened. So, putting my back towards the direction I needed to go, I faced what would've been behind me, quietly edging myself backwards.

My eyes hadn't adjusted to the dark yet, so gently brushing my hands against the hedges was what kept me somewhat grounded. I was supposed to back up until my back touched a hedge, but it had instead touched something much harder.

I froze.

'It's a statue. They're at every other corner in this damn maze.'

I stood still to get more of a feel, until it started to breathe, then almost instantly, without processing, I tried to sprint. Before I even landed the first step away, huge arms latched themselves around me, and like before, I am thrown over a shoulder.

"That was fun. We should do that again."

Maverick.

Why did it not occur to me that he most likely grew up in these damn hedges?

The dim lights turned back on as I kicked, slapped and tried to push myself off him.

Nothing worked and I grew tired.

Whilst Maverick strolled along his property and past some workers who didn't bat an eye to obvious kidnapping, I continued to fight or grip onto anything that would slow him down, but nothing made a dent in the progress of trying to be free of his grip.

Eventually, somehow, we made it to what I guessed was his room. Normal people had walk in wardrobes, Maverick? Maverick had a torture chamber connected.

"I made this for you."

He threw me off his shoulder and into his arms out in front of him, dragging me to some sort of chair. It was like some sort of child's high chair, but for someone my size, and it was drilled into the ground.

I fought, kicked and shouted at him to *'get off me'* but he continued to do what he wanted.

For someone who I thought enjoyed the chase, the hunt, the anything related to some sort of torture, he held no emotion. In fact, just catching a glimpse of his non-existent expression almost scared me enough to do what he wanted me to.

"This marriage doesn't count, you're—you're not even a Muslim—this wasn't even an Islamic wedding, you're delusional if you think—" I struggled with my words just as I struggled to get out of his grip.

"No, *you're* delusional if you think that I give a shit." Making sure that he looked me in the eyes as he spoke, he momentarily paused any action of mine that led to some sort of escape. Letting out a dry chuckle, he continued, "You can't pick and choose what you want to practice love. Did you not stay with Kaden and Kassian for weeks on end? Did you not hang around them before the drama? You don't even cover your hair, and isn't that the most outward way to show that you're a practicing Muslim?"

Gagging me with his words, I was left with no choice but to communicate how I was feeling with my hands. Before I could give him a proper hit, he caught my attack, moving me a little closer towards the chair that was specifically made for me.

"Here's the real kicker—"

I continued to struggle against his grip.

"—If you did practice your faith tenaciously, I would've left you alone."

He now stood behind me with his hands over and around me, holding my arms against my chest. Picking me up, he made my legs float, but gave me the opportunity to kick things away from us and keep us away from things, as if it would make him change his mind. But it just resulted in him lifting me a little higher and shoving me down onto the chair.

He strapped my legs in first, too tight for my liking. Stupidly, I bent down to fight him at my ankles, trying to undo what he'd done, but he interlocked his fingers with mine, stood, then held my wrists above my head.

I looked up to someone who now showed he was enjoying this a bit too much.

"We're in a legal marriage sweetheart, get used to it." Slowly stroking my arm, his tongue pulled in his upturned lip.

His touch was soft.

It was bloody annoying.

I tried to pull away but he had developed another grip. With one hand he held my wrists up and with the other he gently stroked my face.

"Get ready for either the best or worst nights of your life. It all depends on you of course." His grip loosened a little giving my hands a gateway to escape.

Yanking my arms down and out of his grip, I managed to grab a trolley with metal items. Not caring for what I'd grabbed, I swung at him.

"Come near me and I *swear to God*, I'll knock you out!"

Maverick laughed, then mocked a surrender, but as soon as I lowered myself to free my legs, he kicked my hand harder than he needed to.

The pointy metal object was now across the floor and my right hand—my dominant hand—felt like it had been crushed. Almost instantly, my body arched over itself as I grabbed onto my hand and squeezed, as though that were a proven method of stopping the pain.

Maverick—refusing to allow me to help the pain— pushed my body into the chairs back support, then spoke whilst aggressively strapping my left wrist in place with some sort of leather belt.

"You are quite *literally* my plaything." He tightened the strap. "I chose you, and you're perfect. You tie us all together."

I 'hid' my right wrist behind my back as if it would make a difference. But it didn't even delay. He pulled on my arm to bring it forward and succeeded, but I bent my body over and pulled to really fight him tying me down.

"I could've easily killed you long before you developed a relationship with Kade." He forcefully pulled my arm out onto the arm of the chair, almost mocking how I addressed his brother whilst simultaneously making a point.

Aggressively wiggling my arms to try and loosen the straps didn't work, they didn't budge, they just did more damage to my dry arms.

"Me and Kade are just friend's you *idiot*." I was panting now, almost struggling to breathe as sweat droplets formed.

"Maybe. But if I find you guys so much as breathe too close to one another I would—"

"I'm a bloody Muslim you *cow*." I moved my arms around in frustration, allowing the straps to heat my skin.

"You're my wife now." He walked around me then out of my peripheral vision.

A tap was turned on.

Automatically, my mind went to him waterboarding me. I wouldn't survive that, the thought of it alone was triggering hyperventilation.

Maverick rushed over with a container and cloth, which he put down as soon as he came into my view.

"Hey-hey-hey, what's wrong? You're okay." He soothingly whispered as he stroked my hair away from my face.

'Was this some sort of trick? Good cop bad cop type of thing?'

Studying my face, the tap, then my face again, his words

purred out of him. "You're scared of water." His eyes glistened, like he was thinking of new ways to scare me into obeying him. "Whatever you think I'm going to do, I'm not going to do it. Unless of course you thought of this." He dabbed the wet towel on my still buzzing hand.

It felt good but I didn't shy away from having a confused '*what the fuck?*' face.

"Like I said, you're my wife now. I would never strike you, but on this one occasion I did have to disarm you through a little violence."

I couldn't believe what I was hearing.

"You don't hit females but you're okay with stabbing them?"

"Is Olivia my wife?"

'*Unbelievable.*'

I scowled at him.

"Is Olivia my wife?" He stopped soothing my hand, waiting for a response.

"No…she's not."

"Who is my wife?" Maverick did not let me look away. He tilted his head to follow where my eyes tried to escape to.

I searched his eyes and thought of how he wanted me to say it. How if I didn't, he could easily snap my neck, and how before I met a River, I always said how I would and could never pretend to love someone in order for me to escape.

'*I guess it's never too late to be humbled.*'

"I'm your wife." My words came out heavy and defeated.

He used his thumb to stroke my face as his fingers gently held it in place.

I moved my head away. This was too intimate for my liking. I didn't even like the man, and I don't care what he says or wants me to believe, I am not his wife.

"Does slicing my throat not come under striking me?"

He observed my neck. "'*Slicing*' is a bit much. That's a papercut compared to what you gave me."

"You cut me first."

He took a deep breath, a '*sick of it*' mixed with a '*you're right*' expression plastered on his face. "How would you like me to make it up to you?"

I dry chuckled. "You could go up to the highest floor and drop from its window."

Now he actually laughed.

And his face resembled an older Kade which forced a softer look out of me.

"I'll keep that in mind." He moved to fill a cup with water then came back to feed me.

If I wasn't still scared of being waterboarded, especially in this position, I would've declined, but since I was tied down, I chose to be compliant. I did try my best not to look up at him as I drank, to not give him some sort of satisfaction, but something in me knew, no matter what I did, he would be satisfied either way.

"I am not a cruel man Medisa. What I did to Olivia, she deserved. She tried to have a child of mine."

He did not need to explain himself, and yet, he did.

"Well if you didn't keep people on edge all the time, they wouldn't feel the need to get themselves pregnant to protect themselves. Do you know how cruel you have to be for a woman to be willing to put herself through *childbirth*—to birth *your* child?"

"Careful."

"Or what?" I pushed it. I knew I was pushing it and yet I said those words and tried to move my hands.

He moved towards the door.

Maverick was finally leaving me and I couldn't stand the hours he planned to leave me in this chair for.

"Am I even your first wife or is she buried on the grounds somewhere?" I tried to make him come back, to give me a chance to get out.

He stopped walking and a couple seconds go before his response, "She's under the ground somewhere."

It wasn't the answer I had hoped for but I did ask for it. Where would be a smart place to bury her? At the end of the maze? In the maze? Under the pool?

"I'm joking. I am quite humorous." Somehow, he had teleported in front of me again, but this time he was seated. He straddled a chair whilst resting his arms on its back, almost childlike.

"Yes, you're killing me already." I responded sarcastically with no emotion in my quick-witted response.

"Not quite." Maverick studied my face with dilated pupils and a faint smile—eerie as fuck—before launching off his chair to head towards the sink, this time with the plastic tub.

'He's *definitely going to waterboard your arse now.*'

I cussed myself out for not letting this end sooner and for bringing up anything death related.

He came back and began to wipe my face.

I must've looked really sweaty or dirty, or maybe he was trying to cool me down for what he does or says next.

"To properly answer your question. Yes, you are my first wife." He stopped wiping my face, placing the tub and towel to the side. "Since we don't know my limit with wives let's not push it too far, huh?"

"It's my first time *being* a wife."

Maverick chuckled then continued to cool me down.

"And I'm not having sex with you." I put my foot down.

Once again, he stopped in his tracks, only this time he cocked his head slightly to the side. "And I'm not a rapist, but like I said, you're my wife, eventually it's going to happen."

Putting the things away, he made his way towards the door again.

Did he mean willingly-willingly or willingly-I will lose the strength to fight what he makes seem like the inevitable.

"Oh, and Medisa, this old man with little patience wishes you a Happy Valentine's."

Chapter 33

Medisa
14/02/2022 (Monday)

If someone approached me a few months ago and told me that one day I would be kidnapped by my mates brother, married to said brother and then locked in some sort of torture room *whilst* he had sex in the room next door—so loud I could visualise everything—I would've laughed at them, asked if he was fit, then told them that I wished something like that would happen. Then I would've been on my merry way, knowing that it wouldn't, and that realistically, scenarios like that only sounded good in my head.

I didn't know how many hours had gone by, but with nothing to keep me distracted—minus the moans which I tried to ignore—my belly was nonstop rumbling. If today truly was Valentine's Day, then the last time I ate was about three days ago, and even that wasn't a proper meal.

Despite Maverick being *busy*, I tried to call out for him, but soon realised it was pointless. He either ignored me, or couldn't hear me. And to make things worse, there was no headrest on the damn high chair, or any cushions. So, on top of the hunger and all that came with it, my arse, my head, neck, spine, arms and legs all ached. I needed to get out of this chair or knock myself out to fast-forward to a time where I am out of it. If someone wanted to drug me right now, I would welcome it, in fact, I *invited* it. At least I would wake up in new clothes and somewhere much more comfortable.

Things are thrown and smashed in the other room.

'Did he move on to murdering the poor girl or something?'

I tried to move my mind away from the hunger and vocals coming from the other room, so I thought about something worse. By this country's laws, I am Maverick's wife—allegedly. Despite not really caring for a husband, I did not save myself all these years for him to come and be the first person I get with.

It's not happening.

It can't.

I let my head drop so that my chin touched my collarbone. My eyes blinked slowly waiting for my brain to allow my body to pass out whilst the moans and pleas continued on in the back. I wondered if the woman was a worker, or someone he knew from the outside.

Could she help me? Does she know he's married?

I woke up, my eyes still closed.

Large hands lifted me from the chair, then scooped my legs to pick me up like a bride. My head rested on their chest as they took me out the room, the temperature and smell drastically changing.

I so badly wanted it to be Kade, but I knew that it was Maverick. From what I could feel and remember, he wore his shirt like he did at the dinner, buttons undone. Was he really carrying me out right after he did the deed? Disgusting.

"Medisa try to open your eyes. I'm going to help you."

Mentally giving him a dirty look—he was way past helping me—I am put down on some sort of cushiony bench against a wall.

A damp towel is dabbed onto my forehead.

330

"I'm going to need you to sit up now."

And just like that, with only the sentence as something to prepare, I am almost instantly sat up. A straw is put into my mouth, and that's when I opened my eyes. I may be desperate, but I'm still picky about what I consume.

"It's water with a bit of sea moss."

I studied it a little before taking a continuous sip. He's right, it was water and sea moss, and for once I didn't mind the sea taste of it.

Whilst I drank, I looked around the room to see where he'd taken me this time.

A kitchen? It was in between industrial and homey.

"It's where the workers cook for me." Maverick stood by the stove, adding something to a pot.

'He's cooking?'

After stirring the pot, Maverick came and sat beside me with a new drink and a plate of fruit he'd cut.

I wanted to be stubborn, I did, but I could literally feel acid piss forming inside me, so I ate and drank whilst he watched. I had to. If I were to do something about this kidnapping-marriage situation, I needed to be healthy. I needed to be full.

"Did you know that you're borderline diabetic?"

His words stopped me from chewing on an apple slice.

"I had you examined the day you arrived. Your genes aren't exactly ideal, but I've made you an exception."

"What does that mean?" My mind went back to when I first woke up here. I *knew* he took my blood.

"It means, sweet wife, that I'm willing to allow your blood to mix with ours."

I didn't say anything because I had no idea what to say.

"As for everything else, I've either sorted you out or

will."

"Sorted me out?"

"Not only are you borderline diabetic, you were also drastically low in almost all vitamins and minerals needed for someone to be healthy. So, I put you on drips and gave you the amount you needed for every necessity you lacked. You're welcome."

As Maverick moved to the stove again, this time picking up the small pot, I pulled up my sleeve to see the mark the needle had left behind.

"I'm not eating whatever that is if there's meat or alcohol in it."

Maverick raised his brow. "Baby you don't have a choice in the matter."

He *had* to call me '*baby*,' and now I *had* to convince myself I didn't like it.

After grabbing a thick cooling rack and a spoon, he walked back over to the table.

"It's vegetable soup, so you can stop looking at me like that now." Sitting beside me, he clipped my hair back then readied a spoon, blowing over it to cool it. He fed himself first. "There's no way you wouldn't love this. It's perfect."

The next spoon was mine. I tried to fight for it, but he wasn't having it.

"All this energy wasted, and for what?"

"It's degrading."

"Others would say it's loving, adorable even."

I tried for the spoon again, but he moved it away.

"You'll eat from my hand or you won't eat at all."

I hated it. Somehow, he's made it seem even more degrading, and with no escape and basically no choice, I contemplated it.

"Do you not want the strength to fight me? To have some sort of revenge?"

"You're so jarring."

A smile grew on his face as I took a deep breath to ready myself for the humiliation I was about to go through. After that, there was no struggling for the spoon. He fed me, wiped my lips when some soup had dropped, and stroked invisible hair away from my face.

"Are you using the 'good cop bad cop' strategy on me?"

"No, I'm using the *'I'll be nice until you piss me off'* strategy." He fed me a spoon.

I let out a short dry chuckle. "I thought I had pissed you off?"

"So far, everything you've done is amusing." He gave me another spoon then paused before filling another. "But I'm warning you, amusement can quickly turn into boredom. And you haven't even touched the tip of the iceberg of the things that I could do to you."

We held each other's gaze for a few seconds before I broke it off.

I got up to leave but am held back by my forearm. If I hadn't known it was Maverick next to me, his light touch would've fooled me into thinking it was someone else.

"If Kaden so much as touches you, or you him, I won't hold myself back on your punishment. I meant what I said about watching your proximity."

"But you're allowed to sleep with other women?" I questioned like I was offended and not as if I was pointing out how dumb this was. It also made it seem like the possibility of something happening between me and Kade was there—it wasn't.

"Would you rather I sleep with you?"

I yanked my arm out of his feather grip then walked away, holding onto where he had grabbed me.

"Prick."

Chapter 34

I roamed the manor, trying to find at least one of the twins. It was getting late and I had to sleep somewhere, and I refused it to be away from familiar eyes, or on Maverick's bed. I tried to find the room where I last saw them, but it was no use. This place was a maze and asking a worker wasn't an option.

Eventually, I let myself into a random room. There was a balcony attached and it looked out onto the part of the garden that had the pools and courts.

"Medisa?"

I thought I was hearing things, but they called out again when I came back out onto the balcony, then something light was thrown at me from an angle.

Kassian stood at a win-door above me, to the right.

"I was trying to find you guys, but I gave up. I'll come up to you now."

"No-no." Kassian waved a hand. "Don't worry we'll come to you. Stay right there."

'*We'll.*' He was with Kade.

Kade who had Maverick's eyes. The same shape, colour, everything. I know it because I stared into Kade's these past few months and then I was forced to look into Maverick's. They both had eye patterns and colours I've never seen before, so it's kind of hard to forget. And describe.

As for behaviour, slash personality—if Maverick had

any good qualities—it was shared between the twins. But what I wanted to know was what they shared in the bad ones, barring kidnapping and forcing oneself into another's life.

There was so much to talk about. Like, what the hell happened to the two of them pre me being taken and after the dinner. It also wouldn't kill them to tell me about what this marriage now meant for us. And I wanted to tell them about the chase in the maze, the torture room and Maverick saying '*Wifey.*'

There're a few knocks at the door, but it was way too soon for Kassian to be here. So, I slowly approached the door, wary about what part of the floor I should step on before it squeaked my position away.

Light knocks are made again.

"Medisa, it's me." Kassian whispered.

I moved the chair from under the handle, unlocked the door's built-in lock, and as if I wasn't just happy over the fact I found them, I grabbed his shirt, pulled him in, then pushed him up against the wall.

He obviously let this happen but was also taken aback.

"*What* did you tell him about Amana?" I tried to ask nicely.

"What?" Either he was still taken aback by how random this was, or Kassian genuinely didn't know what I was talking about.

"Amana. You *know* who I'm talking about. She's my friend. What did you tell him about her?"

"I haven't told him about a girl called Amana. I don't even remember that name being on the list of people on your course." He defended himself in a way that was supposed to calm me down, and not in a '*you don't know what you're talking about, you're being stupid,*' way.

Removing my hands, I took a step or two back.

"She's not on my course. And if you didn't tell him, how does he know?"

"How does he know what?" Kade spoke as he entered the room with a few bags.

"He said Wifey. It's something me and Amana would say to each other sometimes. It can't be a coincidence. He knows and you guys need to get her to safety…please."

Kade slowly took his bottom lip in with his tongue as he processed what I'd just said. Then they both exchanged looks as they moved deeper into the room.

"*Hellooo*? Did you guys hear what I said? We need to get Amana away." I slightly raised my voice as I grew annoyed at the lack of answer or solution.

"Leave this whole Amana thing to us. We don't know if he's made a strong link between the two of you yet. He could be testing the waters, testing how close you actually are, before he makes a move. If we go after her and he finds out, he'll make it his life's mission to get her. So, we'll keep an eye on things from a distance." Kassian finally spoke up. "Also, I told him that you have a habit of caring too much about strangers, like they're your friend or something. So do with that what you will."

'Trust them Medisa. They know what they're talking about.'

Kade emptied the bags on the table that filled the gap between three sofas.

"We have things that we know to be true to discuss, and you need to eat as much as you can because I don't know how long it'll be until you can have halal meat again."

Kassian was already comfortable on the vintage lounge looking sofa, whilst Kade waited for me to sit so that he could too.

So I did.

We each sat on our own vintage lounge sofa in the room that slowly became dark. Not risking turning the lights on, or sitting on the balcony as someone could see and prematurely stop this meeting, we lit a small fire.

"Are you allowed to come and go as you please?" I stuffed my mouth with some food.

Kade shook his head. "We don't have that privilege anymore."

"He snuck out to get you some food." Kassian cut in.

Had I missed something? Kade wasn't going to tell me that added detail which would've worked in his favour, but Kassian—who when I first met him, hated Kade—made sure to tell me.

Strange. Cute wingman, but strange.

"I knew it'd been a long time since you last ate some proper food, and I wasn't going to sit around and watch you slowly wither away."

As I was about to lift some weight off his shoulders and tell him about Maverick feeding me, his choice of words triggered a thought that took up more importance. '*Slowly wither away.*' Those words implied this were it for us. As if we're going to stay and do what Maverick commands us to do.

"When are we leaving?" My eyes switched between them. "You do have a plan, right? To leave?" I spoke with casual hope and little worry as I adjusted in my seat.

'*Their faces say otherwise.*'

Kade came and sat on my sofa.

"Medisa, Love." He spoke with a certain gentleness I'm still not used to. "That's what we need to talk about."

His eyes moved to Kassian.

Kassian's eyes almost read, '*oh you want me to tell her?*'

"While he was away trying to find you some meat, I'd done some research."

I stopped eating, I needed to properly hear whatever was about to be said.

"We think you have less than three months to live."

'o-kay.'

I had a lot of things in my mind as to what he was about to say but that was not one of them. If I had a drink in my hand, I would spill it. If it was in my mouth, I would choke on it, and if I had a reset button to have this conversation from the top, I would press it.

Kade jumped in, his face giving away his regret for allowing Kassian to be the deliverer of the information.

"What he was meant to start with, was that the marriage is legit. You are married to Maverick—"

I'm going to be honest. I did *not* think that was fake.

"But after three months as the 'Heads' partner you will have a say and piece in everything, making you a threat to everything that he, and everyone before him has done to give us our reputation and fortune. So, we think after three months he'll either file for a divorce—"

"Or kill you—or have you killed." Kassian cut in with his theories.

I stayed silent, not being able to tell if I was processing the information correctly. I understood what they were saying and it made a lot of sense. But on the outside, I wasn't reacting. I sat silently, thinking, thinking about what I could do with the money and assets they have, the life I would lead, but also thinking about the threats that came with it and how I didn't want that much responsibility.

"That's why he said that I'm terminally ill, to make my death less suspicious."

Just one look at the boys and I knew that they had already made that connection. What if the drips he had me on were actually small doses of something deadly?

"I won't let him do that, I swear it, you won't get hurt, you won't be murdered."

Kassian picked up one of my crisp packets. "Should I tell her the next part, or are you?"

'Oh, <u>Thank God</u> there's more.'

I thought they were going to dump that on me and say *'that's it.'* I slowly turned my head from Kassian to Kade, waiting for him to go on.

"We're going to stay here for eleven weeks—"

Eleven weeks doesn't sound too bad. What is that anyway? How many weeks are in a month? Four? How many fours in eleven? Two.

"—Up until then, we're going to do as Maverick says, but when there's an opening, we're going to make a run for it and keep you hidden until you have access to everything. Then if you want, you can free a lot of people, including yourself."

They planned for roughly three months of basically being under Maverick's thumb, but what they refused to tell me (probably for my benefit) was that we would be hunted by Maverick for a little longer than that. Realistically, if we go through with this, Maverick would put all his efforts into finding us and making our lives hell until he grew bored and wanted me dead. It wouldn't just be *'wait three months and maybe 1 week of sorting things out'*, it would be *'wait three-to-six intense months—if not years of constantly looking over your shoulder.'* All because we decided to run away before he kills me. And what pissed me off the most was that I didn't even ask for any of this. I didn't ask for the River name and what came with it. Getting to your brother through doing things to me—his friend, I could understand (somewhat), but forcing marriage onto me, knowing what that would come with, and then acting like it's my fault or unreasonable to try and prevent death is pure madness.

'That's a River for you.'

Unless that's what he wants? He wants me to bring about my own death so that he can say that it was our own faults... He'd gaslight them and in the end have them under his roof without me, like before. Like he wants.

One side of me didn't care. She didn't mind following Maverick's rules because she wants to be pampered and left alone. But the other side of me, the one that takes the wheel sometimes, she wanted to push Maverick's limits, purely to piss him off for thinking that everything will go his way.

Picking up the plate to finish off whatever's left, I went over my thoughts again, this time a little more rational then emotional. Was Maverick a cow? Yes. Did I want to stay under his roof for three months? No. Did I want possible paranoia, slash murder and a bunch of responsibility to be dropped onto me? No. But will I go through it all, on the small chance of being able to free God knows how many people from their contracts? Absolutely.

"Three more months." Said like it was a walk in the park.

"Three more months." Kade repeated after me. "I'll be with you through it all. I promise."

"Me too. You won't be alone." Kassian tossed the empty crisp packet—the one Kade got for me—in the middle, as he pulled his feet up to get comfortable.

"After all this, I want a raise." I stretched as I attempted to loosen Kade up a little. I'm not stupid, I've noticed how he's been a little off since our last encounter.

"After all this, you won't need a raise." He spoke with

humour back in his words as he moved towards the door, where Kassian joined him.

They whispered amongst each other until Kassian's shoulders dropped. A second later and he leaves the room. When Kade turned to face me, I did not care for the fact that he saw me be nosey, in fact, I was about to ask him what was going on, until he told me to follow him.

"Woah."

We were in a 'small' ballroom.

It was dimly lit, giving a cosy vibe, and whilst I was busy admiring the randomly layered balconies that poked into the hall, Kassian rushed in with an instrument in hand.

I turned to Kade, confused, only to see him stood by, waiting for me.

"You wanted to experience a ball, a masquerade ball, so I thought giving you a taste would help you look forward to the one I will throw you one day."

Kassian began to play the most enchanting tune, something out of a fairytale, and Kade, he took it as a sign to bow as he held his hand out.

And I almost took it.

When he sensed my internal battle, he spoke again. "It's okay. Just hover."

I did as I was instructed.

Kade's hand hovered over my waist and hand as mine hovered over his arm and hand. We must've looked like a bunch of lunatics, but it brought out my laugh and though I felt awkward, I eventually didn't want it to stop.

Kade led the dance (obviously) and I followed. There

were times he instructed before a move happened so that we were in sync. '*Twist*', '*hop*', '*extend your arm out*', '*twirl*'. To him the directions made sense, but to me, it was fun guess-work. Eventually he didn't need to tell me what to do, and we danced around the hall as Kassian played.

"Medisa?"

"Yeah?" He took some time gathering his words, or maybe he was deciding if he wanted to go through with what he wanted to say. "You are…" His eyes flickered between mine. "Comely."

"*Comely*? You think I'm funny?" This was a weird time for him to be saying this. I knew that he thought I was funny, I've made him laugh plenty of times.

"Yes." Kade giggled out the word. "You are funny, and comely, and you are beguiling." He becomes more serious with his words though his face still presented his crow's feet.

'Beguiling? I'm sure I've heard that somewhere before… where did I hear that? And he said 'funny' and 'comely' separately… which means comely does not mean funny…'

"You're complimenting me?"

"I am."

"Why?" He must've felt bad about the whole '*this girl might actually die because I know her*' thing.

"Wanted to say it out loud for once." His voice was low, like he was both confident and regretful in his decision in telling me.

"How long have you been holding it in for?" I tried not to be too dramatic with my delivery and gave more of a curious tone than '*damn.*'

"Not long."

"Sureeeee."

"Okay." He rolls his eyes. "Longer than I've let on."

I chuckled, ignoring the weird buzzing feeling and alarm bells. "Alright, pass me a dictionary and give me a day, I'll give you some compliments."

"You just want to look up what '*comely*' and '*beguiling*' means."

"No." I say in a way that's obvious that that was one of the things I would do.

"Comely is—"

"No don't tell me. Finding out what it means gives me something to do in this place. Like a little manhunt, but for some definitions."

"Right." He nodded his head as his face said '*I won't make a joke*.' "I could teach you to ride?—a horse—I could teach you to ride a horse."

If I didn't know any better—I did not—I would say he made himself flustered. And if I were someone who jumped to conclusions—not enough for it to be noted—I would say he remembers that being on my list of things.

I lightly gasped. "Yes-Yes. Please let's do that. I've always wanted to ride a horse."

I almost touched him in excitement as we danced.

"Okay. We'll have your first lesson tomorrow." He got me to twirl. "I hope your ready Medisa Menaal."

"I hope you're a good teacher Kaden." I realised only after I had said it, that I had called him by a name he said he doesn't go by anymore, so I almost froze, not wanting to annoy him.

"Don't worry." He's almost cocky with his words. "I'm catered to you."

Kassian approached the end of his composition as Kade told me to lean back, as he leaned in.

The air got thick quick and the dim lights did not help

the mood.

Well, it did.

But it's wrong.

As Kade's eyes were solid in their position on my face, my eyes ran all over his. It wasn't until we were as low as I could go, that I took in his eyes and lips as he took in mine.

Was he about to kiss me?

Did I want him to kiss me?

My heart made its presence known as I questioned it, not exactly ready for an answer but also, not exactly needing one.

Maverick was right. This loophole-fine line we had created—I had created, shouldn't exist. And though some would argue that it's not too late, I am still too stubborn and am stuck in the middle.

Before things are too prolonged, I am tripped and I— of course—forced my lids shut as soon as I felt the 'fall' feeling. When I did open them, both me and Kade were on the floor.

Somehow, he'd made it so that he took the fall damage. He even protected my head, though he did not need to as I was the one to fall on top off him.

Scrambling to get off Kade before I got used to his arms wrapped around me, I noticed Kassian all too smug of the stunt he pulled.

"You guys just *summon* tears to my eyes." Kassian pretended to wipe tears with the most impassive face.

Kade's chest heavily moved in and out, his cheeks red, so I quickly moved my eyes to Kassian as though I hadn't noticed.

'And not to hide my own.'

"Kassian, I didn't know that you're musically talented." I said anything to get away from anyone mentioning the fall.

"Yeah, I had to pick up a talent to distract our grandparents with."

"Kade, do you know how to play?" I tried including him because something felt weird.

"Yeahhh, of course he does. Whilst I played for them, he was in another room using his fingers and instrument on an interactive audience."

I didn't know how to react, but my eyes did flicker between the two of them and I did smile because I felt even weirder than before.

I could've done without that piece of information.

"I'm kidding, I'm kidding." Kassian tried to save himself and his brother. "Kade practices art-art not the musical form of it. He spent a lot of hours in his studio."

I turned to Kade, praying my face was back to normal. "Is your work still here?"

He nodded. His chest going back to its usual up-and-down pattern.

"Can you show me your studio one day?"

He nodded some more. "Of course."

After coming back to the room, we all flung off our shoes and got comfortable on each of our own fancy sofas.

I positioned myself so that I was able to face the both of them. I couldn't believe we were going to be living life like this for the next three months, but at the same time, if it was going to be anything like the last hour, I prayed they were three long months.

I shook my head at my thoughts.

"What do you think happened to Maverick? For him to be the way he is?" I spoke out of the blue. "It's a thought that's been growing for a while now, I just haven't been able to give it any attention because of how fast things have been going. But now we have three months and he's been playing this weird grey character and I'd have to remind myself of what he's done."

"You'll drive yourself mental trying to figure it out." Kade adjusted himself. "We came to a conclusion to save ourselves from the torment…"

I wait for him to uncover something new.

"He doesn't need a tragic story to explain why he is this way, because he's always been this way."

"Yeah but—"

"Don't try to find reasons to justify his actions, Medisa." Kade warned like he were two comments away from being riled up.

"I'm not. I'm not trying to redeem him, I swear." I don't even think I bought the words that came out my mouth, even if I did sound like I meant it. I won't forgive or excuse his behaviour, but if there is a reason for it, it does take away a little off him…in a way, doesn't it?

'Oh bloody hell. It's too early for Stockholm syndrome, isn't it?'

"Medisa." Kassian called, getting mine and Kade's attention as he sat up. "There are going to be times where you think Maverick is good… *Don't* trust that side of him. I made the mistake of telling him that you have a certain soft spot or weakness towards good but broken people."

I remembered Kassian saying this before.

"What happened to Olivia may not have had a big impact on you because you didn't know her. You didn't spend time with her. But you've spent time with me. So hopefully what I'm about to tell you will help you remember what he's like whenever he puts on an act."

I could tell Kade was uncomfortable and somehow knew what Kassian was about to say, but he allowed him to continue, to say his piece.

"Kassian, you don't have to tell me anything, especially if this is to make up for telling Maverick things about me." I sat up, saying words I mean but also not minding if he did decide to tell me more.

"No. No, I want to tell you."

I nodded, mentally preparing myself for whatever he was about to say whilst barely managing to say 'okay.'

"Maverick taught us a lot, he did. We know several languages, how to defend ourselves, how to cook and clean, how to handle our businesses, people, many things, the list can go on. Something else he did for us, is give unique goals or wishes. For example, for a time, mine was wanting clear skin, or skin that didn't itch or hurt when it was touched. Do you know why Maverick was responsible for that wish?"

Slightly pulling my brows together, I lowered my gaze to his body then quickly looked up into his eyes before I made him uncomfortable.

"Because he used my body as his canvas."

Whilst Kassian looked strong saying the words, Kade momentarily shut his eyes.

"Not with the usual tools of course. With needles, blades, knifes—anything that would make a mark. He scratched away at my skin creating these *beautiful* patterns, again and again. Redoing them if they disappeared... At first it was my hands and arms, but then it moved to my neck, back and abdomen."

Kassian thought about his next words.

"He made Kade watch. As punishment. None of us were allowed to move whilst he did it and Kade wasn't allowed to close his eyes. If he did, Maverick would cut or scratch a little deeper or come up with something else to torture him with."

For the split second that I had looked at Kade, I couldn't understand the expression he held.

"Eventually, with the number of times he etched onto me. My skin started to remember. To scar and lift a little from where he had touched. It started off pink, or a deep red, then it turned to lighter shades, or white."

'*White.*' Not meaning to, my eyes dashed to the parts of Kades skin that were showing. He had designs all where Kassian had mentioned. Being confused and trying to put everything together in my head, Kassian realised and answered some questions for me.

"I had a fear of needles, knifes and such, until eventually Kade got me off my ass and taught me how to handle one. To literally fight it away. And then there was a day he came to me, acting hurt and like he needed help undressing." Kassian began to shake his head and chuckle. "I should've seen it coming, he'd been covering for months. Anyway, when I helped remove this idiot's jacket and top, I saw he had gotten each and every scar I had, tattooed onto himself. Somehow, he had it memorised down to the smallest one."

Kassian spoke about Kade like he was his hero. His eye's glistened and I loved seeing the joy on his face talking about what Kade had done for him. Joining in with Kassian's smile, I glanced over at Kade, who had some sort of bittersweet expression, like he too was watching the scene of the big reveal.

"Soon after that and a speech or two from Kade, I wanted to own them, so, I got them tattooed. I darkened the colours, turned them all black so they're more visible and in doing so, I got rid of what was left of my fear whilst also rubbing it in that pigs face."

Unknowingly looking at Kassian with pure admiration and somehow getting my mind of everything else, I waited for the right time to respond.

"Anyway, the point of stepping onto this little memory lane, is to prove to you that Maverick does not care. If he could do that and so much worse to his kid brothers, he could and would do anything to you without losing sleep. So don't be fooled by any act of kindness, be wary of it."

"Be *offended* by it." Kade spoke like he was already angered by Maverick's behaviour. "Because it just means he's trying to screw you over."

The room becomes quiet.

I had so many things to say but I continued to sit and admire the both of them whilst simultaneously wanting to torture Maverick.

"Well shit. I thought I would at least get some tears." Kassian laughed.

I joined in as Kade grinned.

"I just wanna hug and *squeeze* you." I admitted as my hands surrounded an invisible ball. "Maverick is an idiot for treating you guys the way that he did, he's missing out on two of the most beautiful, amazing, somewhat funny—" Both their smiles grew to the point where I could see their teeth. Kade's smile dropped into a polite one as if a thought had come to his mind, but I still continued to finish what I wanted to say. "—People that I'm so happy that I've met and become friends with. I genuinely trust you guys with my life."

Kassian put on a face as if he were about to cry (he even fake sniffed a couple times) then held out his arms, resulting in me copying his expression and doing the same. Not one of us got up, but we did stay in place and air hugged each other.

"Ugh, can we get some rest now." Kade summoned a

teenage attitude whilst me and Kassian continued to air hug each other. Eventually we both gave up at the same time and laid back down.

"Kade?"

He hummed in response.

"Thank you for going out of your way to get me food." I laid on my back, then called out to the unexpected friend. "Kassian?"

"What?" He snapped.

"Tell me a bedtime story." I joked, but honestly, I really didn't mind a story right now.

"I don't feel *that* bad for you."

I giggled as quietly as I could.

Though I constantly thought about what the right reaction would be to things, sometimes I did love that I didn't process or react the way a 'normal' person would. If I did, I don't think I would be able to experience funny little moments like this in the dark. I would probably still be hooked on the fact that Maverick practically force fed me.

"Medisa?" Kade called out.

I hummed back, mirroring his response from before.

"Shabba Khair."

I said it back, turning to lay on my right side whilst having no control over my prolonged smile. And just as I thought we had the perfect end to the night, Kassian opened his mouth. "What the *fuck* does that mean?"

Chapter 35

Medisa

16/02/2022 (Wednesday)

My face and hair are stroked, making me adjust until I realised my head was no longer resting on a cushion, it was resting on a lap.

I shot up, giving attention to each sofa. Kade was gone. Kassian was gone. I looked back to who I was resting on, and there Maverick was, smiling as if my sudden shock and realisation amused him.

"I've arranged for you to be dressed. I would stay and lend a hand, but I've got something special planned and it needs to be seen through."

'Great, I'm going to be dressed again. Hopefully it's not something too showy.'

As though he'd read my mind, Maverick continued. "Kassian had informed me of your modest dress sense and believe it or not, I like it, but—"

Of course he had a *'but.'*

"—If I catch you disrespecting me, I will peel off the layers, the sleeves, the materials covering you, so that your new wardrobe would expose parts of you only your husband should see."

"Where are they?" I ignored his threat.

"Careful. I might count that as disrespect."

I couldn't tell if he was joking or not.

Keeping my eyes on his, I was somewhere between wanting to say something stupid, and thinking about what he might have done to them. How did he even get them to leave so quietly and what did he have planned for me?

"Breakfast options are laid out in the Garden Hall. It's quite late for it, but I guess the benefit of being married to me is that you can have it made whenever you want." He got up and stood in front of me, angling my head up to him by my chin. "After you're done, you'll be taken to get dressed for the day. If I hear anything about you making the staff's job difficult, I'll deal with you myself. Do you hear me?"

I didn't speak, my gaze was forcefully held as I tried my best—but failed—not to scowl. I couldn't even shake his grip away.

"Nod, if you hear me." Maverick demanded with some sort of threatening-seductive tone that furthered my annoyance and hatred towards him.

I fought against the nod and spoke instead. "I hear you."

Seeing a twisted smile appear on his face almost made me regret going against nodding. And if he actually held the twins somewhere, I shouldn't provoke him to do something to them.

"Good. I'll pick you up when it's time."

Soon as he left the room, I tried to spot any signs of struggle—there wasn't—he obviously came in here with more than himself to extract the boys from the room. How tired was I that I didn't wake up? Were the boys drugged before they woke? Was *I* drugged?

I picked up the rubbish from the night before then made my way to the Garden Hall. It wasn't that hard to find, if I could find a way outside, I could follow the perimeter until I got to the Hall.

Just like Maverick had said, breakfast options had been out on a table larger than the one from our first dinner. I got myself some drinks—Mango, tropical and water—then made my way around to fill my plate.

I picked up some waffles, some crepe-pancakes, some melted chocolate and some fruit. Even with my selection, there was still quite a bit left, I didn't even make a dent in what was put out.

I searched for staff.

There was a group cutting some hedges and cleaning up what I'm guessing were the other parts of the garden.

"Hey, could you guys come here please?"

They looked at me, then to each other, hesitant to listen and honestly with what I accidently put Olivia through, rightfully so. I know that I said I would ignore them and pretend they weren't there to avoid situations like that, but I couldn't let the food go to waste. I heard bakeries and other fresh food shops force their employees to bin what hadn't been sold, so just in case Maverick had the same rule, I called them into the Hall.

As they slowly making their way over to me, I scanned the room thinking about calling some more.

"Wait here for a second." I signalled with a finger whilst walking in the opposite direction from which they had come.

Calling the first few groups I saw inside, I took them back to the Hall and wasn't surprised to see some of the group from the gardens no longer with us.

Those who remained continued to be confused.

I cleared my throat.

"Hi, I'm Medisa and apparently I'm Maverick's wife." I let out a scoffed awkward laugh, then cleared my throat after seeing their faces in this grasshopper environment.

'Tough crowd.'

"I know that some of you probably don't like me, but I

swear I never meant any harm, I never knew how far things would go and I'm sorry that the consequence for my stubbornness was to punish one of you." I looked around to see some confused, some upset, some angered and some still wanting to hear me out. "Anyways, an apology wasn't the point for this gathering." I spoke a little lower. "I don't know what you guys do with the food that I don't—*we* don't eat." I corrected myself assuming they don't see me as one person, but as someone who is now with the Rivers. "But on the chance that it's thrown out and gone to waste, I want to share it with you."

Some of them turned to each other, either not believing what they're hearing or waiting for someone to make the first move.

"Please take what you want, I swear I won't tell anyone and he won't know if we all keep this a secret."

No one moved.

"Please?" I needed at least a handful to eat most of what was already out.

Once I realised it was pointless, I dismissed them by going back to my plate and drinks, avoiding eye contact and forcing food down my throat. A few seconds later I heard people leave, but also heard some approach the table. They grabbed smaller plates and filled them with as much as they could.

When I smiled at them, they smiled back and I wanted to talk to them, I really did, but I didn't want to put them in danger, or get to know them enough to care when, slash if they got punished. But again, I lost a battle with logical thinking and walked over to a group of them. I couldn't not talk to them when they were right there…that's awkward.

"I understand if you don't want me to talk to you or vice

versa, but please do tell me if talking is even an option."

An elderly woman who I immediately linked to my mum, took a step forward and put her hand on mine. "It's an option…and a risk that I'm willing to take." She smiled then attempted to pull out a seat before I stopped her and pulled one out for her first.

She was tan, not like the boys, but like Maverick, or maybe even a little darker. She also had an accent, except hers, if I had to guess, was from Mexico or something. Her smile, made me smile and although I'm not too familiar with it, she gave off motherly love.

'Trying to bond with people who you know are seen as disposable is a mistake.'

She put some more food onto my plate before finishing plating hers.

"I have a daughter a little older than you." She grabbed eggs to put over her bagel. "I'm here in her place because she deserves to live and I've already achieved what I wanted in life." She tried to grab a jug, but I beat her to it. Then I filled her cup to the brim whilst she continued to talk. "I don't care what the punishment is for doing more than we need to for you, even if it's death, I will thank you for freeing me."

My face dropped its polite smile to which she noticed before placing her hand over mine.

"You need someone to talk to, you come to me, you hear me? You come to old Abigail."

"Thank you."

Satisfied with my response, Abigail went back to eating.

I didn't have it in me to move on from the topic or leave it as that, so I continued. "I swear I'll do what I can to better everyone's situation. I'm going to find a way to protect you and a way to release all of you from your contracts."

Abigail gulped down some orange juice then stopped munching, holding her food in her cheek. "Lady, I'm trying to eat. We can talk business right after this."

Taken aback, I laughed. Maybe my time here wouldn't be so bad?

I looked around at those who ate, they had plates full of food, combinations I would love to try and combinations I would avoid.

As soon as my eyes made their way back to Abigail, the main entrance to the Hall swung open. My heart dropped but it was just a group following the man who I'm sure is the butler or something of the sort. Everyone but me stood, lowering their gaze, regretting their decisions. Quickly scouting their reactions and the reactions of those who just entered, I got up and sped walked over to the obvious leader in the room.

"Don't bring this up to Maverick." I held a finger out. "Something as little as this isn't even worth mentioning. And it's not their fault for abandoning their duties. I used my *'lady of the house'* title to get what I wanted and what I wanted was people to share breakfast with. So please, don't bring this up."

The man I've never been introduced to—which was strange—kept his eyes on me for exactly three seconds before looking around to everyone else. If I wasn't so close or desperate for a response, I wouldn't have noticed his lips slightly upturned and his head slowly nodding.

"You are all to resume your duties in exactly five minutes." His voice was loud and demanding, but more *'please listen to me for your own sake,'* rather than *'I better not catch you still eating in the next five minutes, otherwise I will be a snake and make sure that you're all punished.'*

I let out a breath as my shoulders dropped.

"Thank you. I'm Medisa by the way." I introduced myself knowing that this information had to be known, but, I wanted him and I to have some sort of good introductory—ignoring what happened at dinner and how I just approached him.

"Miss Menaal."

Despite being out of school, I won't be getting away from being called that anytime soon.

"I understand and appreciate what you are doing for those below you."

I scrunched my brows, not being fond of the words '*below you.*'

"But you must stop. Nothing is ever really hidden, remember that and it will do you well."

Something was dropped in the background, grabbing both of our attentions. When I looked back at him, I made sure I was the one who spoke.

"Look, man who hasn't been, slash isn't introducing himself to me. None of you guys are below me. I may not have signed a contract but I'm still stuck in the same prison. I understand things may be taken out on you— '*the workers,*' so I'll try to stop but I can't walk around as if I'm above you all. Also, I feel like I need to make up for Olivia and for sleeping in a place that they cook, clean and God knows what else in…you know?"

He waited three seconds before he responded. I'm guessing he wanted to make sure that I was done, but in those three seconds I started to slightly regret how much I had said or how I went about saying it. I didn't actually know this man. I didn't know if this '*letting the workers eat for a few more minutes,*' was a one-off thing or a '*I'm a good man,*' thing. And if he is 'the butler,' wouldn't he be in constant contact with Maverick? Did I screw up?

"Charles. I am Charles Brown, the major-domo."

'Is that like a butler orrr…?'

"And I promise you Medisa, no one wishes they were in your position, they all understand, most think the same as you, *'stuck in the same prison.'* So you don't need to do these things because they would do more damage than good. Wanting a friend is natural, but calling fifteen workers away from their duties is noticeable. One needs to be enough. I will find—"

"Abigail-Abigail!" Realising I cut him off, I calmed down and cleared my throat. "Sorry. Please can Abigail be that one friend."

He looked a little sad that I specifically picked her out, but he still accepted my selection. "I'll arrange for your time together."

I smiled and thanked him. "Mr Brown, can I also come to you?"

"No."

'O-kay. I did not expect that and now I'm embarrassed and feel like opening up a window...on the highest floor.'

"I'll come to you. I can't guarantee the number of times you will see me, but I will make sure it happens. Can't have you throwing parties when you grow bored."

I let out a little huff after realising that he was trying to be funny. "Oh, thank God you joke. I thought I would have to be somewhat *'proper English and mature'* around you."

He raised a brow, obviously the way I articulated myself was new to him, but I'm sure he understood.

"Abigail, would you please escort miss Menaal to her room and would the rest of you begin to clear up."

Abigail elegantly rushed over, and when we caught each other's gaze, we both produced smiles that reached our eyes.

As we walked away all giddy, I mentioned how Charles—Mr Brown, was nicer than I thought.

"Better nice than distort. He's been here since before the boys were born. Lord knows what he's seen and knows."

I went quiet for a little, processing what she had said. '*Before the boys were born.*' Does that include Maverick? What does Charles know? And how do I make him a friend?

Chapter 36

Medisa

16/02/2022 (Wednesday)

We stood outside the room that was apparently mine.

"Strange."

I turned my head to Abigail who obviously knew more than I thought. She was old, yes, and I assumed because of it and her casual vibe that she'd been here for a long time, but I didn't consider how long, or what she'd picked up along the way.

"This is Maverick River's room," Abigail added.

I looked back to the door and thought *'of course it is,'* why would he make such a big move as marriage only to have his wife sleep in another room?

"How many rooms does he have?" I mentally recall my bespoke chair, the room next door and Maverick and his partner.

"When you own a place, all the rooms in it are yours."

I gave a polite smile whilst contemplating leaving. Before I made the choice, a group of female staff headed our way with a machine on wheels in between, splitting them in two.

Abigail stayed until she was dismissed, apparently, she wasn't needed and I would be properly taken care of without her help. I didn't argue for her to stay, I couldn't risk someone bringing it to Maverick's attention.

Maverick's room was filled with colours I've always wanted to paint a room with. He even had a wall with a limewash plaster look, and like the other rooms, this room had arches, pillars and roof rafters that went perfectly with the colours of this room. His balcony was bigger than the one I was on last night, and it had its own arches with plants lining them. I wouldn't say it to him, but I loved his room and everything in it.

"Miss Menaal, we're ready for you." A woman came and guided me into the bathroom.

The bathroom was completely different from the room's colours. Deep tones of blue with certain types of grey, and the largest tub I've ever seen. It was too large for me, so large that I'm sure that if I sat in there with it filled, I risked drowning. It was however, enough space for someone to comfortably join me.

The thought caused mixed reactions. '*Someone*' meaning my husband made me smirk, '*Husband*' being Maverick made me sick…I think.

'*He just looks like an older Kade.*'

"We're going to leave then come back in when you're ready. Please take off your clothes and lay on this with a towel covering your bits."

Turning away from the tub, I noticed they had set up one of those wax-massage chair-bench things. My arms weren't scarily hairy, but the thought of Maverick seeing them and thinking that it was so bad, he needed to arrange for laser hair removal, I considered death.

"Could I shower and exfoliate first…I can't remember the last time I washed."

They side-eyed each other then checked the time, making it clear that they were unsure.

"I'll be quick I promise." I tried to persuade but really, I didn't care on what they would eventually agree with. I *was* going to have a shower before this.

"Okay, but be quick." She searched her apron. "Take this. Don't worry about not getting it all, we'll deal with that."

I took the razor from her hands—the last time I used one, I was eleven—then pulled my lips in, giving them the awkward '*I don't really know you but I'm going to smile to show you I'm nice,*' smile.

Once they left, I explored some more. I knew I had limited time for this shower, but I was hesitant in stripping in the man who allowed people to sign their life away's—the devil if you will—bathroom.

Grabbing the largest towel I could find, I loosely wrapped it around me. I got rid of my tights and knickers first—making sure to hide my knickers in the folds of the tights—then moved up to my dress, which was harder to remove with the towel covering me.

I made my way over to the shower part of the bathroom and kept the towel on, there was no way I was risking a camera being here or not. I refused to give Maverick the satisfaction of being the first male—first person—seeing me naked. So, I turned on the water a bit too close to boiling and had a shower with the towel on, moving it around when I needed to scrub another side of me.

I was told to sit and wait to be collected, so that's exactly what I had done…minus the sitting part. The laser session was over quicker than expected but that was because I stupidly thought it would be one woman doing it. There were actually three women lasering me. Two on my legs, one on my arm and then at the end one woman gave me the option of what kind of vagina hair I wanted.

I went for Hollywood. I loved being 100% hair free and the best part was, I never felt a thing. I know that others say that it's the worst pain ever, but I honestly enjoyed it… that's what I would say if Maverick scheduled a wax session, but no, this was a laser from hell.

My hair and makeup were done too…again. It was requested by the man of the house for my hair to be straightened, so that is what they did. It wasn't straightened so that it was so sleeky it outlined the top of my head, it was straightened with a certain bounce, volume. When it came to makeup, I was adamant on having no lipstick and eyeshadow. Heavy layered looks annoyingly didn't suit me, but it's okay because I still got to have contour, liner, mascara and some blush. I just know by the end of it they were sick of me constantly interfering and wiping off what I didn't like. It's obvious their talents were with heavy looks, but I wanted the light natural but somewhat obvious contoured look.

If Amana were here, she would get it done perfectly the first-time round, she was attentive and talented like that. She's able to see what beauty you naturally have and does things to enhance it. She didn't hide the face you had, which is what it felt like these women were doing.

The clothes Maverick had picked out today were a little better than what I had worn at dinner, in terms of western modesty. It was a tight black corset maxi dress, sleeveless, paired with an extravagant, puffy, cropped, bolero jacket and gloves. The shoe choice were heels—of course—but they weren't too high—Thank God—and they weren't the type of heel that asked girls to balance on a stick.

All in all, the outfit and I looked great, and I hated myself for thinking it and feeling good. Especially since—for some reason—I wanted people—Kade, Maverick—to see how attractive I was and it pissed me off some more. Who were they that one side of me wanted them to see? Nobody special.

Just as I watched myself in the mirror, slowly lowering my hands down my sides, Maverick walked in, all ready to go to whatever it was we've gotten dressed for.

"I was going to tell them to style your hair up, but I figured I'll be doing that later." He walked towards me, buttoning up his sleeve.

"How old are you?" I asked, insultingly.

"Thirty-three." A smile creeped onto his face.

Thirty-three.

He's thirty-three. Kade's twenty-three.

Ten years.

There are ten years between him and the twins. Something happened to their parents when they were eight, which means Maverick was eighteen. An eighteen-year-old took over whatever empire came with the River name and two boys. That eighteen-year-old also happened to be a complete psychopath.

"Let me see Kade and Kassian before we go." I purposely said '*let me*' and not '*I want to*'.

He tutted, carefully moving the smallest layer of my hair back with the longer pieces, behind my shoulders. "Silly girl, you've yet to willingly do something for me before I do something for you."

"I didn't realise this relationship was transactional."

"Don't tell me you've fallen for me already?"

"God forbid." I spat too quickly as a smirk made an appearance on his face.

I not so eagerly put my hand under his held-out arm and over his bicep. We walked slower than usual, unless this was how normal people walked. I wouldn't know because I always rushed, always speed walked or took larger steps, all which I now learnt are quite difficult to do in this particular dress.

We made it to the front of the house with no slip ups on my end—Thank God—but I was teased and tested a few times.

A car pulled up as we came down the entrance stairs and I unconsciously held onto Maverick a little more as I waddled down the stone steps. When he finally released me to go open the passenger door, I tried not to look at him for too long as I took careful steps towards the car.

The second Maverick sat down and pushed his seatbelt over and behind him, he launched his car down the private road. I couldn't move as freely as I wanted or be comfortable because this man wanted to give me a free rollercoaster experience.

Eventually, the scenes changed from the road being surrounding by clear, somewhat levelled land, to being surrounded by huge, chunky trees.

"When we get there, I want you close to me, don't even think about getting away. People don't know that you're my wife and I don't plan on releasing that information anytime soon. Which means, as soon as you are out of my sight, these people will not hesitate to do to you the things I have not yet indulged in. Do you understand? *No one* will help you, even if you pleaded."

Somehow, the intensity of the speed we were travelling increased, and I am pushed further into my seat where I quickly nodded.

"Good, because we're here."

It was dark and we drove for a few acres, but I'm sure

we're still on land he owned.

There was some sort of large, old-looking structure, out in the middle of nowhere being eaten by the trees, vines and other plants. I could only describe it to look like a stone gazebo…with walls.

Two men stood outside its entrance and Maverick didn't even acknowledge them, he just walked straight in with me half a step behind.

This place was a doorway to a grotto.

An unworldly, underground grotto that we continued to go deep into. There was music playing somewhere. It was loud, entertaining, and was mixed with muffled cheers, roars and screams here and there. I didn't ask what was going on because I had a strong feeling I was going to find out whether I liked it or not.

Maverick held a door open for me.

The room was like some sort of VIP cinema. The few seats in here gradually got higher and all walls were made of stone, minus the wall the seats faced. Instead of being a screen that played movies, it was glass in a large arch. Glass that allowed you to view some sort of dirt arena.

Surrounding the dirt 'ring' were more archways, all connected to dark rooms. If I counted correctly, there were ten big rooms altogether including ours. All rooms were about half a level above the ring, and each had a window in its archway. A window that not only showed the ring, but also the fifteen-to-twenty-five slimmer archways above us if you stood up close. It was one big underground arena, all on Mavericks land.

I couldn't see into the other rooms which meant all the windows were two-way mirrors. I turned back to Maverick who sat in his front row seat, smiling as his head rested on his hand.

"Take a seat, it's going to start soon."

I made my way to him as I tried to use context clues to figure out where this was going. As I sat with one leg over the other, I unconsciously began to vigorously shake my right foot.

A microphone is tapped a few times, then the lights in the room are dimmed like a movie was about to begin. I stopped wiggling my foot as soon as two people were pushed up into the ring. The tv screens in the room provided a closer shot and since you couldn't hear the music in here, the sounds of their feet on the floor were crisp. Like someone was down their providing fight club ASMR.

Light brown curls, tall lean figure, no tattoos. I know that man. He was beaten and starved but he wore the same clothes.

I faced Maverick who already had his possessed looking eyes on me.

Leaning forward, almost falling off the edge of the seat, I tried to think back to what had happened. I'm sure he said he killed them?

The man against my so-called bodyguard fought hard, and I can safely say that it's not a good watch; watching someone desperately fight for their life.

"Is this to the death?" I spoke too eager to hear the answer and when he didn't reply fast enough—although I'm not sure much time had passed—I asked again. "Maverick! Is this to the death?"

A drink is poured for him as he continued to ignore my question.

Fists, elbows, knees and dirt from the ground were all used against each other. My 'security' was barely winning until he took of his belt and choked the other man.

I didn't say a word.

I had no reaction other than peeling away at the layers of my lips. I took in the man's look before he was knocked out or had passed away, something I hadn't been sure of until fake security man snapped his neck.

The tip of someone's fingers stroked my back, automatically making me sit up straight and turn back to Maverick.

"You okay?" He pulled me towards him so that I could rest in his arm—I had no choice. "That was just a warm up, the real fun starts now."

The microphone is tapped again, then 'security man' is taken out of the ten-sided ring. A tablet is handed to Maverick, he didn't let me see too much, but from what I did manage to catch, it was a bunch of male pictures with numbers lined up next to them. Large numbers next to the pound sign.

When the tablet was given back, the microphone was tapped again, and this time at least twenty-to-twenty-five people were shoved into the ring.

"Now we all know that we've gathered here today for some money and entertainment. But what you don't know is that we have an old champion back. Will he keep his streak? Or will one of your men ruin him?" Someone spoke into the microphone like this were some sort of horse race.

'...You've never been to a horse race.'

A singular beep goes off and just like that, everyone in the ring goes crazy. They had weapons this time. From what I could make out, two had metal poles, two had wooden bats and two had a knife. The rest of them had to use their bodies or steal a weapon. I would say that I wanted to look away but I couldn't, my eyes refused to. The thing that made it somewhat difficult to watch, was the screams, the '*help's*', the '*let me out's*' and the '*I'm sorry's.*'

On one side a man's eyes were being squashed in, on another an arm is bent or twisted the wrong way. Blood squirted pretty much everywhere and when it finally got to a smaller group of people, one stuck out like a sore thumb. He didn't look clean like he usually did. He looked like a predator, blood all over him and not the faint kind, the '*I just stuck my hands in your guts*' kind.

Standing up from my seat, I walked over to the glass as though I were being charmed.

The once clean friend is hit at the back of his head, forcing him to his knees as he grabbed onto where pain gathered.

Maverick came to where I was as I held onto the glass like I could squeeze through. "I may deny myself the privilege to touch you, but there are other ways to inflict pain and gain pleasure."

He's not a small man—Maverick, he's a bloody giant, and yet he managed to make it feel like he were speaking into my neck.

I turned and tried to shove him, failing immediately as he stood tall, not even a little off balance. "He's your brother!"

Maverick held his hand up to the men who moved closer at my sudden outburst. "Which means that he should be able to survive this."

He stayed by me, right next to the two-way mirror and made proud, encouraging noises and remarks, pointing out whenever Kade had done something beastly.

When it got to the last five people, I recognised two of them; Kade and security man.

All of them were out of breath and had space between them. Without taking my eyes of Kade I demanded for the fight to stop.

"You have your final five! You could use them to start the

next game off!"

Maverick shook his head, giving me a disingenuous apologetic smile as if there were nothing that he could do.

Knowing that the match wouldn't be stopped, I started to throw things at the glass. What was that going to do? God knows, but in the moment, I needed to do something to let my frustration out. The pointy heeled shoes wouldn't allow me to throw good kicks, so I used my hands and the side of my fists as I stupidly tried to break the glass. Maybe it would distract his opponents?

Just as I was about to use my elbows again, I am grabbed and pulled away from the glass. The last thing I saw was four people left in the ring.

As I'm dragged down a tunnel, I didn't bother to conceal my heavy breaths. My mind ran through options. I could tell Maverick I would be the wife he wanted if he saved Kade, regardless of what his image of a wife was.

'Selling yourself like that wouldn't make sense. Kade made it to the top three, he can definitely make it to be the last man standing.'

I couldn't risk it. I won't risk it.

"Stop the match and I swear I'll do whatever you want!"

Maverick still gripped and held my arm in the air, as if I would run off. I tried to plant my feet in the ground, make it harder for him to take me away until eventually, he turned to face me.

"I *swear* it." I searched his eyes to see if I could notice a change, and there was, his eyes were darker, and he went back to dragging me until we reached a door.

Soon as the room came into view, I quickly noticed so did the match, except this time there was no glass in between. We were half a level below the dirt-ring, so we didn't have the view of the whole arena, just what the strip allowed me to see.

Joyous Kade stood behind a man who no longer put up a fight. The man already looked like he was close to death on his knees, as though a little push to the ground would suffice. Especially with all the gurgling, weeping. But Kade, who *saw* the state of the man, held the top of his head with one hand and with the other, gripped his jaw, his fingers in his mouth.

Once I realised what he'd intended to do, I ran towards him, even if I felt a little sick and my own jaw tightening.

"Ka—" A hand flew over my mouth, an arm snaked around my waist and I was swung away. My eyes had instinctively shut and when they opened, I saw the aftermath of Kades brutal move.

He had done it as my voice cut off, so even if he did hear me, there was no point in him stopping, he would've been halfway done with his tug and the man would've been in more pain.

As my eyes switched between Kade and the man's body dangling in his arms—his loose ripped-into jaw swinging, his blood gushing—Kade frantically looked around as though he were hearing things, until his eyes finally found me.

I had that weird heart dropping feeling, momentarily forgetting I was his friend and not his next victim.

Whilst my eyes stung from the way I held them wide open, Kade looked as if he had snapped out of some sort of daze and was coming to realise what he'd done. Maverick still had his hand over my mouth whilst leaning himself over my body, holding me in place. I hadn't even realised that I'd slumped in his grip, so I tried to stand up straight, instead of at the curved right angle he held me at.

He shushed me until I stopped trying to talk, then spoke

into my ear. "We're going to go out there and congratulate our winner, do you hear me? It'll do you well to not make a scene."

I stopped moving, not because I agreed with what he wanted me to do, but because I didn't know if that's what I wanted. Going out there, being surrounded by bodies and a live audience I couldn't see, all to congratulate Kade, who I knew could fight and stand his ground, but not to that extent.

Maverick took me not struggling as a sign to release my body, allowing me to straighten up as he held out his elbow once again.

A small section of the stage lowered for us to be taken up—a completely different entrance from the players.

As we both walked towards the middle, I tried to keep my eyes off Kade for multiple reasons but I had already taken in his look. Black compression, blood up his arms, messy, slash slightly wet hair and a '*little*' blood and sweat on his face.

I knew it.

I *knew* it!

I bloody knew it.

Ever since I met Kade, I've always felt like there was something I was missing, something that was purposely held back to keep me in the dark. And now I know. I mean, I'm not dumb. It was hinted at a few times, but shit, now I knew why he didn't want it to get out; he was brutal.

Kade's eyes on me would've made me walk like an idiot, but luckily for me, I had his brother offer his fake support. I must've looked like a right bimbo next to Maverick. All dressed up by his side, holding onto him as we were surrounded by bodies and his rich clientele.

Maverick gently let go of me to say some words about the

match, something about the winner's streak. He held Kade's arm up in the air as he congratulated him and just as he was about to drop it, someone started to cough.

Someone woke up, someone was alive.

And I got to them before Maverick did.

It was security guy. I rolled his body so that he was on his side instead of his belly. He looked like crap and I wondered if it was Kade who made him look this way, but then thought otherwise as security guy (ignoring the bruises, cuts and blood) looked better than anyone Kade had been up against. He choked up blood and I tried to do what I could to make him comfortable, not caring about the scene I was creating in front of the live audience (mostly because I had forgotten about them as soon as I heard him cough).

Ignoring the audience in the smaller arches, I lowered my head so that it reached his ear. Whispering, or at least trying to make it seem as if that was what I was doing, I checked his pulse. "You're making a scene, stop struggling and you might just live."

'Ugh... I sound like Maverick.'

Surprisingly, he did as he was told. He didn't look like he was in the condition to do so, but he did, unless he had actually passed out, or away.

I slowly got up, gently placing his head on the ground before turning to Maverick, shaking my head to say that he had passed.

Holding out his arm, a gentle gesture calling me back to his side, Maverick announced security guys death. But I knew, I knew from the look of his eyes that he knew I lied to him, and he enjoyed it. If I didn't know any better, I would say that me and security guy were lucky.

But I did know better, so I knew we were screwed.

Chapter 37

Medisa

17/02/2022 (Thursday)

Although I was dressed in black, I was sure people could see the patches of blood I attained from helping security guy. I mean, I could definitely *feel* it.

Kade kept his distance and was taken elsewhere and I was too caught up in my own thoughts to have realised I was being led outside.

Maverick held me by my waist as he spoke to multiple groups of people on their way out. Some were accompanied by their wives, current girlfriend, plaything, scandal etc. Maverick tried to fill me in whenever he could, or I worked it out myself simply by observing how they spoke and touched one another. I wondered if they made their own assumptions about me and Maverick, or if they were too up their own arses to have even realised that I was not willingly by his side. That or, they thought I was a Baronial girl.

I wasn't too outwardly awkward or uncomfortable, I had on the smiles and let out small laughs. I put on the best act I could when we had eyes on us because I knew that I was already in deep shit for the stunts I had pulled inside.

Each group (each room) came out two minutes after the last, I'm guessing to hide identities and avoid mixing. Maverick's men were the ones who brought them out their rooms and to their cars. When they stopped for small talk, I couldn't relate to anyone and the conversations were on topics that were more offensive than interesting. If I wasn't distracted by what I had seen and done, I would most likely be responding with the *'most outrageous comments, views and opinions'*—how some of them described something that's classed as controversial to them, because it outed their lack of humanity—rather than smiles and light nods.

At some point a man was giving me the eyes, it was as if he could see me naked and honestly, with how tight this dress was, there wasn't much to leave to people's shitty imaginations. I couldn't help but squeeze onto Maverick's arm whenever I felt uncomfortable, it was the only way I could release what I was feeling without using words. And as big of a cow Maverick was, he did steer the attention of those perverted men away, in a way that was subtle and not 'rude' or 'insulting'. He knew how to handle the situation without offending anyone (though I would feel much better if more was done).

I excused myself and not because I wanted to find out about the victor, but because all of a sudden, the dress felt too tight and the heels somehow shrunk. And because I did this in front of Maverick's guests, he called for someone to drive me back, instead of disciplining me then and there.

Back at the Manor, I'm taken to his room. It didn't take a second for me to shut the door, find some of his casual comfy clothes, then speed walk into the bathroom, locking myself in. After tying my hair up and out the way—can't ruin freshly straightened hair—I struggled to quickly strip out of the dress and heels.

Wasting no time under the shower, I washed off any blood that had soaked through to my skin. Once I knew I was clean, I dried myself off and slipped into the giant's clothes (a black top and grey jogging bottoms).

I speed walked over to the rooms door and just as I was about to turn its handle, someone on the other side had beaten me to it.

"It seems I've missed the real show." Maverick took a step in whilst I took one to the side, out of his way. "You seem to be a little too comfortable here." He walked over to his rooms personal bar to pour himself a drink. "Shall I list why I think so?"

"No need."

'Saving security man by lying in front of a crowd, calling out to Kade even though I am not his wife, not sitting down when I'm told, barely cooperating other times, being 'too nice' to the workers and giving them breaks from duties... What else am I missing?'

He chuckled then drank where he stood (something I would never do). Once he was done with his drink, he poured more into the glass and I took it as a sign to leave. A drunk Maverick was probably much worse than a sober one.

"I take it you don't care for Nicholas anymore?"

I dropped my head.

I was *so* close to leaving. Just one step away from being outside the room and being able to make a run for it, but he had to open his fat mouth.

"The man that was in charge of capturing you, he can be nurtured back to health." Maverick continued. "*Or* you could take those steps away from me and I'll neglect his health."

I closed the door on myself.

Even if he helped kidnap me, I won't be the reason why he dies.

"There's a good girl. Now come here, there are a few things we need to go over."

I moved to and sat on the sofa instead of where he stood, clearly pushing mine and Nicholas's luck. Maverick's eye twitched, but he quickly 'recovered' from his emotions when he picked up and opened a bottle before coming over to the sofa.

"Drink." He held the bottle in his hand out.

"No." I shook my head, scrunching my brows as if to say *'are you dumb?'*

Maverick dipped his head to be closer to mine, then spoke as though he wanted to prevent a third party—that did not exist in this room—from hearing him. "You will drink, or you'll be the one doing unimaginable things to Nicholas when he has fully recovered."

I looked to the bottle then back to his calm burning eyes. Waiting for the poor guy to fully recover just to brutally kill him off, was a bit much.

'Grudges must run in the family.'

"Don't test me, Medisa."

I took the bottle from his hands then hesitated bringing it up to my lips. All those times of never giving in to peer pressure and the normalised western ways just for me to give in now. But surely saving a life by sinning is better than being a reason a life is taken away?

'But is he worth the risk? Worth finally giving in to a sip?'

I brought the bottle to my lips but didn't lift it up to allow the drink to pour into my mouth. Whilst I debated and hated on the position I was in, Maverick pushed the bottle to be at an angle for the drink to fall into my mouth. And just like someone who was starved of water, I chugged it down because I knew after one normal sip, I wasn't going to bring it to my mouth again. I only stopped gulping when I needed to gasp for air.

Coughing whilst searching for air and hoping for water, I caught a glimpse of Maverick's expression.

"Finish the bottle."

"No. I've had enough." I held the drink away from me

and up towards him, facing away to clear my throat.

"Enough will be when you've finished the bottle. Get to it before I flip a coin on which twin would be added to the consequence."

I felt a little lightheaded, not too much, but enough for it to be alarming. It was clearly going to grow in strength over time and soon I would be knocked out or be doing things I wouldn't remember.

"They're your brothers. If something were to happen to you, they would be the ones to carry on the name." Since he was one for tradition, hopefully this would distract and send us down another path that didn't involve drinking.

"I too have a dick between my legs Medisa. What makes you think I won't spread my seed before I go?"

My stomach, heart—something internal—dropped. Was that his plan for tonight? Stupidly, I hadn't even considered Maverick mixing something in this.

"Now drink up before I give you something never-ending from the tap."

"I'm *tired* of these threats."

"Oh? Would you rather I just do what I warn you about?" He pushed the drink into my chest.

'Get waterboarded or drink? Both have consequences.'

"Waterboard me." I called for a bluff that didn't exist.

Maverick beamed with pleasure, his brows raised in surprise and pending satisfaction. "Do not say I am a man who does not give his wife what she wants."

My heart pounded against my chest, pleading for Maverick to notice that it did not want no part in this.

"Well, c'mon then." He pulled me to a stand. "We've got plenty of bottles to go through and a chair that's already missing you."

'...He's not going to use water.'

Chapter 38

Medisa
17/02/2022 (Thursday)

The movies weren't lying when they said your head felt as if someone had knocked it in. I couldn't even give it all my attention because my stomach started to act up as soon as I woke up. Drinking on an empty stomach obviously wasn't the best idea, but at least I could say that it wasn't planned (on my behalf anyways).

Being in the room I slept in the night before brought me comfort, but before I could feel good about it, I had the need to vomit and there was nowhere for me to go. This room was basically a place for you to store and try on clothes with a bunch of sofas for people to sit and give their opinion.

As soon as I shot up, Kade, who I didn't even realise was next to me, sleeping on the floor with half his body on my sofa, woke up, somehow knowing what my current crisis was.

"The fireplace." He rushed out his words, pointing in its direction.

I barely made it there in time and once it came out it didn't stop. I managed to get out the drink and parts of break-fast, then the constant gagging for more only produced and let out thick saliva. Kade handed me some tissues and water, which he thankfully moved away to get, missing the attrac-tive sounds that came with vomiting as well as the initial en-chanting smell.

I leaned against the wall directly next to the fireplace,

pressing my hand onto one side of my head. I couldn't believe some people did this to themselves for fun.

Kade moved around me like I were a glass doll on the verge of breaking down, then finally sat on the ground in front of me, leaving some space between us.

We sat quietly until I couldn't take it anymore, we had to address the elephant in the room, well, at least the elephant in my room. The elephant in *his* room was probably something to do with me vomiting.

"I don't see you as some sort of monster. *If* that's what you think." I stopped to gather my next words. "Don't get me wrong, I don't really know why you did that to that man, and it definitely showed me another side of you. One I had suspected but not to that extent, but I just can't see you as someone to hate, or blame. I don't think I ever will, so stop putting on a mask every time you're around me. Own it, and introduce me to your sides, your thoughts, your actions, so that I don't have to see you through Maverick's twisted lens. Because then, yeah, a part of me might actually hate you, or be wary of you. So, I'm just telling you now."

Kade's expression was like he'd made the worst decision of his life and it'd only just occurred to him that his actions have repercussions. He must've also been thinking about how his mask was practically translucent, wasting both of our times and his energy, as I basically already knew.

"Kovu used to scratch me all the time when he was a kitten." Since we're talking about his sides, I might as well say what else was on my mind, even if it was a little out of the blue.

Kade didn't hesitate to show sudden confusion, but I ignored and continued because what I'm saying would make sense in the end.

"A lot of them healed as white lines and are taking forever to disappear, allowing me to see them but also make out how old they are. The cut on my thigh that was looked at by *your* doctors, is basically the same. The only differences are that its slightly raised and wouldn't fade as much, if at all."

His face let me know that he was trying to understand where I was going with this.

Before I said the next part, I took a deep breath, making sure to look him in the eyes. "I know what you did for Kassian and I know that you don't plan on telling him. I've seen your skin up close Kade. You took his punishments for him, covered for months then slapped on some tattoos to try and cover it up." Unless of course his skin had a reaction to the ink, then this was embarrassing. Also, Kassian's patterns are something he was forced to look at for God knows how long, so I don't understand how he hadn't clocked what Kade had done…unless he did? Or he hadn't realised because Kade's body was able to heal the parts that were constantly showing, thus leaving behind the tattooed pattern.

Kade's eyes glistened as he clenched and unclenched his jaw a few times. I could see the weight it had on him and instead of allowing for some of that weight to be taken off, he refused to admit what he'd done. It was like he thought he didn't deserve no praise, no admiration.

"You have a noble heart Kade. So just do me a favour and remember that. Don't be one of those people who don't allow themselves to be loved or forgiven… because they're annoying and—"

"Thank you."

I stopped talking, I was rambling anyways.

"Thank you, Medisa. For not telling Kassian."

I pulled my brows together for a quick second. There was

something in his '*Thank you*' that made me feel sad and angry, it's like he's not getting it. Like he wasn't understanding that he could never be the bad guy because he's either forced to do something, or his own actions have good intentions behind them, regardless of how he goes about executing it. But I've spent enough time with him and Kassian to know that I never knew the bigger picture, so I politely smiled back instead of trying to drill him with my perspective.

"I've been thinking…"

'How should I word this?'

"What Maverick said about you craving some sort of release…" I studied him for some sort of permission to continue. "I don't think it's the blood that calls you back. It's the lack of control. I think you're conditioned to think that you beating, or killing someone would make everything else around you okay. If you won, Maverick didn't punish you or Kassian, he would feed you, he would let you guys out and experience what you guys thought was freedom. And now when things fall apart, you think that violent acts is what would help keep things controlled, including your own emotions."

He didn't say anything, but he did bloody stare.

"Thank you for coming to my lecture." I pulled my lips in, suddenly feeling sheepish.

"I agree." Kade spoke after too long. "But I also just enjoy harming people—only the ones that deserve it."

I guessed that explained the psychotic grin as he teared a man's jaw from his head.

"O-kayyy." I chuckled out the word. "That's cool. That's-that's…admirable?"

Kade's crow feet and dimple smile came out, then he slowly lowered them into his neutral-ish face.

Pulling my knees to my chest, hugging them as my head rested on top, I watched as Kade pulled up one of his knees whilst his other leg stretched out enough for it to be a few steps away from my sock covered toes.

We both sat, admiring each other's looks for too long, probably even going over the things we just said.

The silence was comforting and I wanted more of it, but the headache came back, forcing my hand to be pressed up against its side again.

"What did I do?" I didn't need a mirror to tell me that I was no longer wearing Maverick's clothes. I also didn't need another pair of eyes to tell me that I happened to be wearing clothes Kade wore in the ring.

"Nothing. You were just feeling a little hot so I gave you my shirt…and jogging bottoms"

"What happened to the ones I was wearing?"

"Your vomit is over their ashes." He was proud.

My head turned from the fireplace to him, then back again. It took me a second to register, but we still let out low energy laughs in the end.

Even with the dry blood, bruises and small cut on his lip and cheekbone, he looked beautiful. His dimple could still be seen and his eyes actually smiled with him as he laughed. And his laugh, the stingy cow let it out for too little. I needed to hear more of it because as deep as it was, it was soothing.

"Did I stop you from cleaning yourself up last night—or er… early morning?" I realised I didn't actually know what time things went down or what the current time was. Also, he clothed me in clothes that now held dry blood, so he obviously hadn't gotten round to cleaning himself.

Joy stopped reaching his eyes.

"No, I actually had no plans to get cleaned up. I er…I

was distracted."

He'd just come out from fighting multiple men and I basically said that his priority was to get cleaned up. Of course something else was on his mind, the boy went through it.

"I thought I'd lost you after what I'd done and I didn't—still don't know where Kassian has been taken." Kade elaborated.

"We'll find Kassian today, don't worry, I'm sure he's still here—"

'That could mean there's a chance he's dead.'

"—On the grounds." Now I tried to elaborate. "Not dead."

'I hate myself.'

He fed me more of his chuckle—despite most of it being heavy breaths through his nose—as he slowly nodded, looking around as though he were thinking of how to word his thoughts.

"What you saw me do in the ring. What I did to that man, you might have to see me be like that again." He watched me as if to look for some sort of approval, or anything that indicated the opposite.

"You do what you have to do to survive and protect, I get it." I stopped leaning against the wall. "Just don't hide things from me. I hate that. So, if there's anything that you're keeping from me, tell me now." There are many things that I suffer from, trust issues being one of them.

"Perhaps I could shed some light on some things?" Maverick walked in with some cards.

"Perhaps not." I knew what he was trying to do and I'd rather hear everything from Kade and Kassian.

As he got closer, he examined Kade's clothes, then mine. He stopped shortening the distance between us when he slapped down printed pictures on the floor next to me. The date, 16/12/2021 was in the corner.

I couldn't even properly recall the details of yesterday, how the hell was I supposed to know what that date was significant for?

The centre of the picture was a man who looked like he was in the ring yesterday, except his cuts were much deeper and his bruises much darker, as if fists weren't the only things with which he was beaten with. If I was supposed to recognise this man, I couldn't. There was nothing about him I could pick up on, not his clothes, not his size, not his face, nothing until the next picture revealed his hand. Every part of him was covered in injuries except for this one hand, the one hand that was lowkey slipping away from my mind until this picture revived what it'd looked like. There was someone crouching in front of the injured man, his back was to the camera and he had his arm raised with a hammer. Looking closely at the picture, the man with the hammer also had other tools.

I gave the two images to Kade, who I could tell wanted to see what I was being exposed to.

The third image had another date, 17/12/2021, and the pub man looked significantly worse. He also happened to be getting his hand sawed off. From the other images I couldn't tell if he was awake, but from this one, with his mouth open, I knew that he was.

"Medisa, maybe you shouldn't be looking at this right now." Kade's soft words were laced with desperation. A thought of him snatching the pictures flashed across my mind, that's how strong his undertone was.

I didn't bother holding the third image out to Kade, I kind of just let it fall to the floor for him to get if he wanted. The fourth image revealed who the tormentor was, and honestly, I knew. I knew from the shape of him, the tattoos that made an appearance here and there, and from the build of him, I knew that it was Kade.

We both stood up. I needed to breathe and wanted to pace and Kade stood because—from the looks of it—he wanted to follow to catch me in case I were to lose balance.

Had I been naïve this whole time?

From what I could remember, Kade was dismissed as a suspect as he had no time to do what he did to that man, but then these images showed otherwise. And I've seen what Kade can do, so I can't dismiss thoughts of him gifting me the hand of the man who'd groped me.

Were they all just bored and in need of some entertainment—driving someone into insanity? Was Kade the first one to change his mind, triggering his brothers?

No.

That didn't make sense.

Maybe Kade had some sort of split personality? That's a possibility given his harsh upbringing. And I have experienced polar opposite behaviours from him. But I also knew that Maverick liked to twist things to get into your head. These pictures could've been altered to frame Kade.

It could even be Kassian.

'His face says otherwise.'

"Kade…" I thought my decision through. "We're going to talk about this later." My head involuntarily shook, needing him to give me some sort of reassurance. "Maverick." I turned my head towards him, gathering the anger I felt from this confusion to address him. "Give up. I won't believe your words, your side, your anything. You can try as much as you want, but I won't see them differently."

"Even when boundaries are crossed?" Maverick questioned but did not wait a second for an answer. "Kade took advantage of you last night." He spits the wildest accusation in a way I could not dismiss. It wasn't sarcastic-concern or even bitter.

My face dropped as I turned to Kade for some sort of... *something*, that denied what Maverick had said. But he looked caught off guard and as though he couldn't believe what Maverick was trying to pull.

Which makes sense.

The Kade in my head was a protector and has a good heart, I just confirmed what he'd done for Kassian. The same man wouldn't indulge in something that's against someone's will. He wouldn't, but he told me himself that he has before, for Baronial, and to survive. I couldn't remember last night after being forced to drink. I couldn't remember meeting Kade, or how I even got into his clothes. But he wouldn't do that, he's not like that, he wouldn't give in even if he had those urges. But he was acting strange when I woke up. But that was because he thought I saw him differently after what I'd witnessed, he said so himself. He would never touch me like that, he doesn't even have those thoughts towards me. But he is a boy, and I should know better than to trust one.

My body started to act up as I went back and forth with my thoughts. I tried to force my brain to remember what had happened, but nothing came to mind. And a headache, light cramps and my thighs pulsing was not helping the side of me that was with Kade.

"You motherfuc—" After witnessing me try to make sense of things, probably even look as though I believed Maverick, Kade moved towards him but stopped as soon as I cut in, holding my hands out to each of them.

"He didn't assault me." I said the words but wasn't 100% sure if I believed them.

I hated myself for that.

"Oh, so my wife *willingly* engaged."

Kade jerked his body towards Maverick as if to start a fight, but I quickly stood in the way—again, facing Kade, pre-clinched as if it was guaranteed that he would hit me.

Realising I hadn't been hit, I gradually opened my crinkled eyes and kept them on Kade, my back to Maverick.

"We *didn't* sleep together." My words came out as though I were trying to confirm with Kade, whilst also trying to convince myself and Maverick.

"Explain how you got to be in his clothes."

It was one thing after another with Maverick and I was not in the right place to be handling any of it. I wanted to eat and lay down whilst someone massaged me.

When I twisted my neck to Maverick, I caught a glimpse of the fireplace. "I vomited over yours and needed a change of clothes." I spoke like a professional, sure of the fact, and with no hint of a lie. "And who swaps clothes after engaging in any sexual activity anyways? I would've been way too tired to even think of doing that."

'Shit.'

I made it seem like I was speaking from experience.

Maverick searched my eyes, his annoyance wasn't well hidden but he kept to himself, until I messed up. Then his expression changed and he spoke to Kade. "Whatever relationship you two have, ends now."

I moved forward to speak, but he snapped at me before I could say anything.

"*Now!*"

I jumped at his sudden rage. My headache and other

pains disappearing almost instantly.

"If I see you so much as breathe the same air as Kade, I'll break you." He looked over me, to Kade. "You want her to stay as she is, a breath of fresh air? Then you better treat my words as a law you *will* follow."

With the way he was behaving, I should've kept my mouth shut, but my thoughts practically poured out. "No. No, I don't care about what you *think* we've done because *nothing* happened. We don't deserve this."

Maverick huffed a laugh before calling in a worker. A small woman walked in with a phone in her hands, ready to pass it to him until he ordered her to show it to me.

It was a picture and I'd internally groaned at the fact that there was more to see. But when I took a closer look, it was me—well, the back of me. I was straddling Kade, leaning back onto my arms that held onto his manspreaded knees. We were on the sofa that Kade had slept on the night before. I could only see one hand of his in this picture and it was gripping my thigh. From a person who wasn't in the room—which basically includes me—you would assume I was getting something out of this close interaction, even if I was wearing jogging bottoms.

"*Lying* to your husband." Maverick spoke through his teeth as he gripped onto my arm.

Kade gripped onto my other, not allowing Maverick to take me away, but his hold on me loosened quickly after.

Even if I knew what moves to pull to get out of Maverick's grip and out the room, I couldn't. His alcohol still had its effects on me, and his strength and determination to get me to where he wanted, overpowered anything I had to get away.

"Stay back or I'll make you watch me go the whole way!" Maverick lashed out when Kade moved in our direction.

Going back and forth from being numb to actually feeling something—fear, embarrassment, shock, even anger— Maverick forced me over his knee. His forearm held the top half of my back down to prevent me from getting up. I tried freeing myself, tried hurting his legs, but nothing made a dent on the amount of pressure he pushed down onto me. My heart pounded and I'm sure that he took pleasure in feeling it, making it all ten times more humiliating.

As he was about to rip off my jogging bottoms Kade intervened. "If you do this!"

I knew he caught Maverick's attention because there was no aggressive pull to strip me of my bottoms.

"Don't do this." Kade's words came out more hopeless than angry. "I'll do what you want, just please, don't do this to her."

I tried to get up again, tried to intervene with words, but failed as I'm pushed down with more force. Even with my head spinning and a lump in my throat, I tried again. "Kade don't—"

"Hush now wifey, Kade is talking."

'*Wifey*.' He said it again.

He's using Amana against me, but I can't *not* do anything. Kade's my friend too.

Getting too caught up with what I was going to do, who I was going to save, I didn't intervene with the rest of their short conversation.

Suddenly, I am released and pulled to my feet. I heard something along the lines of us never being allowed to be next to each other unless Maverick was with us. Which basically meant that from now on, we would never have meaningful conversations or be able to update each other in any progressions.

I speed walked over to Kade before Maverick could stop me. I could see it in his eyes before I even got to stand in front of him, that the Kade I wanted wasn't there.

"Kade, don't do this. Let him do whatever he wants to me, I can handle it. I'm strong remember? I'll handle it. Please, just don't do this."

Kassian's still missing. Amana's on some sort of watchlist. I can't leave or talk to anyone. I won't know if anyone's safe. My time will be spent alone or with Maverick. I'll become unhinged. Or I'll completely lose who I am, walking around aimlessly like some sort of living dead.

Maverick laughed in the background as I stood directly in front of Kade, trying to get him to look at me, trying to get him to listen to me, but he refused to and I couldn't read him.

"You promised."

Kade's natural face was one that looked angry, outing him as someone who was on the verge of murdering everyone in his way. This expression that he held now was similar, but it felt aimed towards me, like I disgusted him.

Dropping my head as my eyes became a little moist, I didn't have to turn to know that Maverick was grinning. I could practically feel that shit and it just added to the rage I needed to release.

I refused to pent this anger up.

I refused to.

Turning around as quickly as I could, I charged at him and just as I held my arm up to swing forward, I am held back. It obviously wasn't the pesky woman who grabbed me, it was Kade, but it was still shocking to see.

The bastard could've let me get one hit in.

As soon as Kade let go I put all my energy into pushing him away from me. He'd done me the decency of stumbling back a little as though I had enough power to move him, and that just pissed me off some more.

Storming out the room, I took a quick look back before the door was shut, as though I might have the opportunity to try to pounce on Maverick again.

Maverick manspreaded over the couch I slept on the first night in there. Kade stayed standing where he was, not bothering to look in my direction or give any hint of a plan. And I walked away like a mug, still having anger and a sense of urgency in me.

Chapter 39

Medisa
17/02/2022 (Thursday)

Using the rest of the day to get my energy up by forcing down what I could, convincing myself that this was all a part of Kade's plan, *whilst* trying to find Kassian, was basically a waste of time, as I barely succeeded in any one of those things.

It was dark and I needed a place to sleep. I could feel my lids getting heavy, but I refused to sleep without someone I trusted. Abigail was nowhere to be found and I didn't bother to ask around for her for obvious reasons. So, I ended up leaving, walking towards where the death match was held.

I barely made it away from the Manor before Maverick drifted a car in front of me, blocking my way whilst also making me jump.

He got out the car, slammed his door shut, making his emotions clear, but it didn't deter me from my mission.

"Where you going?" He spoke as if he wanted to join and not as though he were angered by my attempt to leave. He even touched my left arm, trying to grab and stop me, but I turned and swung at him.

It landed.

I punched him.

He had lowered himself to grab my arm and make it so our eyes were somewhat level, but got himself a punch instead.

It wasn't exactly planned, it definitely wasn't expected, it kind of hurt, and now, looking at him, I realised I may have made a mistake. He had a cut on his lip, but there's no way I did that.

Since a mistake was already made, I punched again and again as he straightened his posture. I then grew bored (and my knuckles hurt) so I moved on to using my legs. Just as my kick was about to land, he grabbed onto my leg, prematurely ending the move and snapping me out of whatever I was in.

"Not the goods." He dropped my leg. "You ready for bed, or is there some more that you'd like to do?"

I knew there was no point, that there would be no difference in the way he stood, but I still made the decision to put as much as force as I could into a push.

He didn't budge.

"Is that it?"

I didn't move, I just breathed heavy through my nose and when that wasn't enough, my mouth. I continued to scowl at him, my hatred refusing to simmer down. Unfortunately I couldn't bring myself to act as the loving wife to get him when he least expected it. That probably would've been more effective and satisfying.

Lowering his head to do or say God knows what—something I would never know because I decided to give a full swing bitch-slap.

"*Where's* Kassian?" I continued to breathe through my mouth, quick breaths, not calm slow ones.

Maverick kept his head to the side, acting more dramatic than when I'd punched him.

"Where is he?" I took a step towards him, urgently needing an answer. I raised my hand again, not exactly knowing what I was going to deliver next, or if I even had the energy to.

Before a decision was made, Maverick grabbed onto my wrist. "He's alive and well. You'll see him tomorrow, maybe even the day after."

When he realised I wasn't going to do anything else, he took me back.

When we reached his bedroom, he changed in front of me and expected me to do the same.

What a joke.

"I'm not sleeping in here." I put my foot down.

"At least change into your nightgown."

I pulled a confused look for a quick second then dropped it before he realised. He wasn't forcing me to stay? There had to be a catch.

Deciding to go through my gown selection instead of being forced to view them, I regretted the decision. All of them were beautiful, but I would never give Maverick the satisfaction of wearing one for him.

"I'm not wearing any of these."

"There are longer ones in the back."

"I'm not wearing any of those either." I pushed my luck.

Sighing, he walked over to his side of the wardrobe again, opening its door and fishing for God knows what. When he was done, he walked over and gave me a full black set. Black jogging bottoms and a black sweatshirt.

"We won't get any sleep if you continue to stand there and look at me like that."

Ignoring his words—mainly because I am stubborn enough to stay where I am and ruin both of our sleep—I walked into his bathroom and changed.

On my way out, I slightly opened the door to see if I could make out where he was, but I couldn't spot or hear him.

Tip toeing out, then around the room, I carefully unlocked the door, trying to make as little sound as possible. As I took a step into the hallway, I looked around the bedroom, still trying to find and avoid him.

Someone gave an attention seeking cough.

'Kade.'

Goosebumps rode all over as I slowly turned to view Maverick, who was leaning against the wall that faced his bedroom door. Before giving him a chance to speak, I made a run for it.

Of course it didn't take long for him to snatch me right up and carry me back to the bedroom, but I still tried and that's progression.

Forcing me in bed, locking me in place as he spooned me, he spoke with a tone closer to ones I recognised. "I could fight you every day, but just so you know, at the end of it, it will be like this. So save your energy Wife, before I put it to use on something worth my time."

I stopped trying to fight his arms. "So when you said that you weren't a rapist, what you were forgetting to add was the word 'yet'?"

"Precisely." He adjusted his hands on my body, making the 'skin' he touched tingle.

There was no point in trying to fight this one out, I already knew that I was locked in place. My twig arms won't develop some sort of superpower to get out of this.

"I can feel your heart, wife."

"It's because you've pissed me off…" I refused to call him 'husband.' "Prick."

"Darling, if we're going to be giving each other nicknames, I think Rick would be just fine."

"I don't care. I don't like you."

"Would you like me to make you feel better?"

"Knowing you're going to hell is enough comfort."

"Such candour." Admiration laced his words.

As I felt his chest move in and out, all I could think about, on top of the mountain of things that we had to deal with, were the words '*God forgive me.*'

Chapter 40

It's been weeks since Maverick and Kade struck that dumbass deal. ~~Let's start there~~. Never mind, I don't actually have the energy to write down my thoughts about it (also I only have this one A4 page). Anyways, this bright idea of writing down what I'm feeling/what I'm going through, to then prioritise and plan what I should be doing, came from Mr Charles Brown himself.

Maverick hasn't really been interacting with me. My guess is, he really is going to kill me off, so there would be no point in wasting his time or energy. But if that's the case, why is he being stingy with the desserts and all things sugary? Why is he treating me with all these beauty treatments?

Another thing he's been doing is purposely talking about what Kades been up to when I'm in the room. Oh, and the bloody giant keeps finding me at night, it's disgusting and his persistency is getting ridiculous now. (let's not even get into me secretly enjoying it and having to fight Stockholm syndrome) I have to keep saying 'Astaghfirullah' until I fall asleep. Also, he has <u>willing</u> women sleeping with him since I ~~can't~~ won't... so why can't they just stay the night?? Every now and then, I take the piss and hide in a closet or something, or even under a bed etc...he still finds me. This one time I even laid myself out like a gingerbread man so that I took up most of the space, but he dealt with it (another thing I won't be going into) Other than that, I've been staying away/trying my best to listen to him since so much is in his control.

Moving onto my 'alone' time. I work out, and my thighs and butt have actually been growing. I can't actually do anything else because I don't know the correct forms and I don't want to mess my muscles up. So I just run, cycle and work on my legs/butt. When I'm not working out, I pray or walk around the estate. I don't always have the option to pray the ~~obligortory~~ obligatory prayers (on time) but when I do, I pray for Amana, Kade, Kassian, Charles and Abigail and the other workers and for my family (Maverick might even get a shoutout) I ask for guidance/forgiveness—God knows we need it.

~~Speaking of~~ I've seen Kassian a few times now. He seems to have the most 'freedom' out of the three of us. He owns some sort of club and managed to take me over once (took me to Kades studio too), which conveniently happened after the night I told Abigail of how bored I was of everything. (I refused to try new things—like horse-riding— because I wanted to experience it with them or Amana... not by myself)

Kassian's club is definitely something. He had a great selection of music, an amazing interior (kinda reminds me of that one cartoon atlantis movie) with pink-purple-blue-red LED lights and his seats were way too comfortable. He needs to replace them for harder ones because there's no way that people get up to dance (a lot of them actually do, I'm just lazy and not trying to add another sin). The change in scenery and Kassian being able to make me laugh and get my mind off everything really did help. Up until that point I was just telling myself to hang in there until the 3 months were up, and then if nothing happens (on our side) then I should begin to internally panic. Any premature reactions would be a waste of time and energy.

After the club, everything started to feel okay, until I saw Kade. I had been forced to attend his fights whenever there was a big one but I never really saw him outside of them. The few times I did, it was only for two seconds because if I stared at him, I would stop being so 'obeying' and patient and would just walk up to him.

Oh and his hairs growing (he looks fit-er).

Kade's 'act' never dropped, even when he was alone. When he stood, walked and spoke, he did it like he owned everything and everyone. I've overheard several people say that he scares them more than Maverick does, which just makes me think about what he could be doing/has done. (side-note: they all keep their heads down here. Even when being addressed, they keep their eye-contact to a minimal) I'm worried that he's forgotten our plan, or even forgotten something as little as a genuine smile.

He said I'm 'beguiling' (charming, or enchanting in a way that captivates or fascinates) and 'comely' (nice to look at.. attractive) and yet... THAT ISN'T BLOODY ENOUGH FOR HIM TO SNEAK A LOOK AT ME OR HAVE A SECRET CONVERSATION WITH ME TO GIVE ME SOME SORT OF ...<u>SOMETHING</u> TO LET ME KNOW WHAT IS GOING ON.

To conclude, my hand hurts. I can't remember the last time I wrote—oh real quick, apparently someone is completing my degree, so 'I' might actually graduate with a first. Any who, next time I'd rather record what I'm thinking so emotions are seen and I could move around, but since I'm burning this anyways, I don't think that there's any point in wasting storage.

Chapter 41

Medisa

10/05/2022 (Tuesday)

I've been married for almost three months now.

No one's said anything, in fact I hadn't seen anyone I could lean on for a few days, so I could only assume we're no longer going through with the plan. I wanted to think that Maverick wouldn't kill me, that somehow this was all a game and he'll let me go, but the past two nights and for most of the day, he's kept me close to him. He no longer went away to do God knows what. He stayed inside the Manor and for most of the hours, next to me.

I was going to die before I turned twenty-one and I knew it, but I didn't accept it. Every night whilst he slept, since the start of the month, I stayed awake long after he got into bed. I couldn't push myself to get off the bed and out the room, but I did wait to see if there was a pattern. And there was. When Maverick fell into somewhat of a deep sleep, he whistled. It wasn't annoying enough to keep me awake, or to wake me up if I had been asleep, in fact it's barely noticeable. But I picked up on it and knew it was when I had a chance to make a run for it.

As I laid in bed, waiting for the mattress on his side to drop, sending slow growing ripples to my end—letting me know that he's gotten in—Maverick appeared right in front of me, crouching so that our eyes were on the same level. I've been standing out of his way for the majority of the time these past few weeks, so his sudden innocent smile as he took in my expression was a little 'out of character.'

"You've been quiet for ten days now." He wore an innocent mask, but I could see through to his devilish grin. "Something the matter?" His head slowly cocked to one side as one corner of his mouth raised.

'Cow.'

"No, I just...I don't know." I had no excuse he would buy.

"If it's about your twenty-first, you don't have to worry."

My eyes enlarged a little before going back to normal. Of course he knew details like that, and of course he would reassure me by letting me think that everything will be okay when really, *you don't have to worry* was because he was planning to deal with me way before then.

"Wow. You won't even question or be against it?"

Before I had to deal with a response, someone knocked on the door—unusual, but not too surprising—pulling Maverick away from me and the conversation.

They're given permission to enter.

"Sir, the drinks you requested."

Maverick was visibly confused and slightly frustrated that this was what we'd been interrupted with.

"I asked for them."

I did not.

"Thank you." I hurriedly walked over and grabbed a glass before Maverick could dismiss her.

His expression pressed for an explanation.

"I was thirsty and thought they'd bring it faster if I said that you asked for it." I held my glass up, awkwardly smiling, waiting for him to pick his up and tap it against mine.

"Why'd you get into bed if you were waiting for drinks?" He wasn't buying it.

I took a long sip before responding. "Honestly, I'm so tired that I just got into bed and forgot." Being someone who does not easily turn red is something I've become grateful of.

Maverick picked up his glass, holding the tip of his tongue to the side of his parted lips as he slowly nodded his head.

I couldn't tell if he was buying it.

He took a sip then spoke to the woman as she were about to leave. "You made my wife wait so long, she forgot that she even asked for a drink?" He took a longer sip as he kept his eyes on her.

'Crap.'

"It's fine, really, you can go." I tried to save her as I smiled, letting out a light laugh as if to say *'he's being ridiculous don't worry.'*

"No. No you can't."

Getting goosebumps as I moved before consulting myself, I put my glass back onto the tray and stood in between them. Gently placing a hand on his bare chest whilst looking up to him, I waited for him to stop picturing the woman on fire.

"Hey." I quietly spoke—partly because I didn't want to do this—grabbing his attention. "Is this really necessary?"

"It is."

'You need to get his mind on something else.'

"Okay." I calmly acknowledged his petty feelings. "Let her go and I'll make it up to you." I tried my best to look cute? Desirable even, praying that I'm right about this whole thing whilst also internally cringing. Goosebumps continued to make themselves known by travelling over my body once more.

As worried as I was for her, I was scared for myself.

Maverick heavily placed his glass back onto the tray after downing the drink, dismissing the woman. I smiled a genuine smile because somehow, what I did worked. Before my brain and facial expression connected what was going to happen next *if* I wasn't right, I pecked whatever exposed part of him I could reach when I tip-toed to thank him. He needed to buy the dream I was selling and I needed to stall.

"Let me freshen up." I turned to dismiss myself as I shat bricks.

A few steps towards the bathroom and I'm pulled back.

"There's no need." He held me too close, his eyes blatantly looking at my lips then deep into my eyes.

I had the strongest feeling he knew something was up. The part of his mind that wasn't connected to his dick must've thought of how quickly I changed for a stranger, when over the last few weeks, I tried to avoid even the smallest touch. This had to be a test or a tease…or both. I needed a little more time. I didn't know how much more a *'little'* was, but I needed it.

I put some distance between us, well, as much as his arm allowed for there to be as it held my waist in place.

"I'll be quick, I promise, just give me ten minutes. I need to get myself ready. This is a big thing for me."

When he loosened his soft hold, I took it as an opportunity to move away and not so desperately get into the bathroom.

Double checking I had locked the door, I ran to the shower, turning it on at full speed. Runing over to the toilet bowl, already not feeling like myself, I knew I had to stick a finger or two down my throat, but I couldn't get myself to do it.

After failed hyped-up trials I ran over to where the toothpaste and brushes were kept. Putting a lot of paste on one edge of the brush I jammed it into my mouth in attempts to 'tickle' whatever triggered one's gag reflex.

A few gags later and I'd only managed to get myself to spit out thick saliva. I attempted again but before I could get the toothbrush back in, Maverick began to knock.

'Has it been ten minutes?'

"Sweetheart." Maverick's voice was loving, but threatening. The slight shiver in the way he spoke caused one to run through me.

I held my breath.

'Sweetheart'? He's never called me that before.

"Is there something you would like to tell me?" He was calm—a mask of course—but out of breath, like he was holding in anger. He knocked three more times. Each knock loud, with a dragging sound in between like he was forcing himself to be at the door rather than kick it down.

I moved towards the door, my head spinning and my heart pounding. I knew I didn't want to open it, but I also didn't want to barricade another door.

"If you come out now, I'll forgive you. I promise." It was like his forehead was up against the door.

I didn't even know what was going on myself, but I knew something was at play. I lost a little more balance and reached for the door handle for some stability.

Before I could stand a little more upright, I heard Maverick huff, a loud thud followed after.

He dropped, he must have, it's the only explanation. Getting on my hands and knees, I looked below the door. The gap beneath was so little it was pointless to search for some sort of answer. At first it was dark, so I thought there was some sort of thing that blocked the gap to prevent steam or whatever from escaping—if that's even a thing—but then something got dragged. I could both hear and see it.

Two feet came into view—shadows which I assumed were feet by the way they moved—and I held my breath as I lost some more control over my body.

"Medisa?"

Putting the last of my energy into quickly lifting myself and somehow managing to unlock the door whilst feeling fuzzy, I prayed the drugs weren't making me hear things. Holding onto the wall beside the door, I tried my best to stay awake.

The moment Kade came into view, I moved from the wall to having my grip on his arms as he knelt down. Even if I wanted to express my gratitude, I couldn't.

I couldn't even cry or smile.

"Hey Trouble." He delicately greeted me like I were a baby. "Can you stand?"

I couldn't get myself to talk, could barely keep my eyes open.

"Never mind." He carried me through the bedroom where I managed to make out a drugged Maverick on the floor, tied up and against the bed. My lids closed against my wishes before I could even process what that meant.

Chapter 42

Medisa
11/05/2022 (Wednesday)

I thought I dreamt of someone on a chair facing the bed, watching over me, but as soon as I saw the chair in daylight, I knew it'd been something that happened. I just don't know how long ago since it's 10:30 on a sunny day and in my 'dream' the room was dark, almost pitch black.

When I got to a window, I saw that once again I was surrounded by green. But this green I liked. There were some cows in the distance and some chickens nearby—from what I could hear—we must've been staying at some sort of farm. A positive if you ask me. I could ask an actual farmer if it's worth it, what the pros and cons were and if they could teach me so that I could manage my own farm.

"What d'you want for breakfast? We've got fresh eggs." Kassian was in his version of a farmer's outfit.

"I don't like eggs."

He let out a dramatic—but barely filled with enough care—gasp. "Well thank God because I didn't really have it in me to take them from her."

My face definitely spoke for my mouth, but Kassian didn't need to clear anything up because the next thing to walk in was a chicken. She stopped at where he stood, pecking at his boots.

"The elderly couple who are letting us stay here said that we can have whatever eggs she provides, but after spending some time with her, I don't think that I can do that."

I slowly moved my head up and down in a '*I understand*' way but also a '*I'm keeping my lips together to not take the piss*' way.

"So, I've heard about the chicken, but when are you gonna tell me about what's going on?"

Kassian picked up the chicken then signalled for me to follow him into the kitchen. He pulled out a chair for me then moved deeper into the room, where the cupboards were. I sat with the view of a few hilly fields, some animals and other farms.

When Kassian came back to the table, he came with a drink and my phone. I reached for it but then Kassian put his hand over it, basically telling me '*No.*'

He sat down on the chair opposite me. "It's been a few hours since we've taken you. We're still in Scotland. Kade's on his way to London to get Amana, and Maverick—we assume—thinks that you have also pissed off back to London. Ergo, we stay here right up until the fourteenth *then* we can safely take you to sort this all out. Any questions?"

I thought about it for a second, took a deep breath and lined my questions up. "When did he go?"

"Sunrise."

"Why can't I turn on my phone?"

'*Probably know the answer to this one.*'

"Do you want Maverick to know where you are?"

'*Knew it.*'

"Do you think Kade's being followed?"

"Most likely."

"Can I add to the plan?"

"No."

I chugged my drink, recognising it's flavour. It's one of them vitamin drinks. I couldn't tell if I liked it or not, but my mouth was dry.

After slamming the glass down on the table like some sort of Viking, I continued to talk even with Kassian's '*I don't want to hear it*' face. "We can make this easy for Kade."

"No."

'*What the heck?*'

Ignoring his pointless opinion, I continued. "You stay here with my phone. You turn it on, instantly grabbing your brother's attention. Maverick would come here with his men and I will be far-far away, in London, at Aros, or somewhere out the way. You'd start running laps around, keeping them busy and away from Kade and me. Or at least taking away some heat off of Kade. Then on the fourteenth I'll go and sort this all out."

Kassian looked like he were actually considering it whilst I spoke, but then when I was done, he managed to say the exact thing that I didn't want to hear.

"No."

I sighed. "It's a good plan."

"That's not enough."

"We—"

"Do you think Maverick opened the door for us to come in and waltz back out with you? No. We drugged him, and when that didn't work like it was supposed to, Kade knocked him out then took you—Maverick's *wife*— and in three days you'll have joint ownership over everything. How'd you think he's going to be handling things now? A slap on the wrist? No. Do try and remember that he mutilated a girl's hand because you refused to sit." And with that, he got up and left.

He thought bringing up Olivia would hold me in place, but it had an opposite effect. Maverick reacting more wildly to the situation—which I guess was kind of justified—only meant that we *needed* to go through with my plan.

I've been waiting literal months for us to do something. I've got ants in my pants for at least ten people. We're going through with my plan by force.

Chapter 43

Medisa

12/05/2022 (Thursday)

The journey back to central London was a long one, beautiful, but long. You could tell when you got close to a city when the sites became sticky looking.

Kings Cross was where I got off. The first thing I did was get comfortable on a bench to think things over (because the hours long train journey wasn't enough). Kassian should have the phone on by now, so in theory, he's being tracked and the attention is diverted towards him. I could go to Aros, but it's a risk. I could go to university, but that's also a risk. My parents house isn't an option and neither is Amana's, she wouldn't even be there anyways if Kade had already picked her up.

How should I kill two-to-three days without being caught?

Kade made it seem like one in ten people worked for Maverick, so staying at a hotel *felt* like a risk. But it should be fine because I'm sure they would focus on the sites I would most likely go to; University, Aros, Parents house, Amana's House…that's it.

Amana's hotel is an option. I don't think that it would be a risk. It's not too close to Uni or anywhere near Aros, so they wouldn't have people on the look out there. Also, if Maverick believed I was with the twins, he wouldn't think that they've taken me there. And, I've never really been inside despite doing an architecture degree, so the reasons 'for' continued to grow.

"Yep. That's what I'm going to do."

Picking up some overpriced snacks at the station, I headed over to the grand hotel next door. It stuck out like a sore thumb, all the other buildings around couldn't compete even if they wanted to.

'*St. Pancras Renaissance Hotel.*' I blew out in awe, then waited on the side like some creep for someone decent looking—morally—to show up, so that I could try and persuade them to get me a room under their name. Masks are slowly becoming a thing of the past now, so for a lot of people it wasn't that hard to read their face and assume whether or not they were a good person. I guess you could say them not wearing a mask meant that they're a shitty person anyways, but I wasn't wearing one either. And if I had a reason, surely, they did too.

An old man showed up on his phone—a bit too loud and careless—he had to be the one to let me in, there's no way a character like him would refuse. His clothes weren't dark and grumpy, they were light and layered, quite bold too.

I coughed a few times to clear my throat, mentally pushing myself to do this.

'*Hi hello... Hey—no. Hi, could you please—*'

It was now or never. We were both a few steps away from the main entrance.

Once he put his phone down, I lightly tapped his shoulder.

"Excuse me, sir. Hi." I gave him a friendly smile. Not too wide or big to look like I was on something, but enough for me to look good-natured. "Could you please get a room for me. I have the money. I just don't have my phone or I.D to confirm my identity." I spoke whilst walking alongside him.

At first it seemed like he was going to dismiss me, but then he'd done a double take and agreed to help.

'Ugh he better not be a paedophile or something, I've been told I look young.'

Ignoring my thoughts, I continued to walk with him. I'm sure I could survive in my own room for two-to-three days, and even if he did try anything, he's an old man, I'm sure I could take him.

"What did you say your name was miss?"

"I'll tell you if you get me the room." Cheeky, yes, but I had to make things less suspicious.

He let out a dry chuckle as we walked through the doors. I followed half a step behind as if I was his assistant or something, careful to not show my face to too many people. Once he'd done his thing and got given the key, he passed it on to me.

"Thank you. I'm Azira by the way." I stuffed my hand into my jacket pocket to grab some cash, but he waved it off.

"Nice to meet you, Azira. Stay safe." He tried to walk away, but I stopped him in his path, the money still in hand.

"Thank you for being a good person and doing this for me. But I can't accept you not taking the money so please, take it."

He didn't make a move to take the money, so I shoved it into the jacket that was being held by his shoulders. Awkwardly smiling, I walked off before he could do, or say anything. When he finally moved away, and into an elevator, I waited until it felt right to go up to the front desk.

"Hi, my granddad just booked this room." I passed the key over. "Is it possible for us to change to the room a few doors down from it? He likes the view better from that one."

It was possible.

And just like that, I had the keys swapped and got a room that no one, other than this woman, knew about.

I didn't dare to leave the room during rush hours, I didn't even know when the actual rush hours of this hotel were, so I had rationed my snacks for the day, and planned to leave late at night. Staying in this room, with no phone, or way of communicating was eating me up alive, and now that it was time to restock—if there was even a place open—I was hesitant.

I stood at the door, hand on its handle and waited. God knows what I waited for but, I did take my time with it. Thinking the words '*screw it*,' I was about to yank the door open, but some sort of noise could be heard just outside. It wasn't loud, but since I was so close to the door, I could hear it. I waited a second after the sounds had disappeared to sneak out. I could've ignored suspicions and been on my way, but no, I looked down the hallway. No one was outside, and it didn't sound like anyone had barged into a room.

Just as I was about to let out a sigh of relief as my mind was convinced I had effed up somewhere, the room door that had been previously booked for me, opened. The first man to come out was busy on his phone, so I took it as an opportunity to turn around and walk before he looked away from his screen.

Of course there's a possibility the room was booked after I had it swapped, but I wasn't risking it. Then I heard them walk in my direction at an unusual pace, so I started to run, then seconds after hearing my own shoes heavily slap the ground, I heard theirs.

They would've wanted to deal with me quietly, so I started to hit all doors, walls and chucked whatever I could to the ground. *Someone* in this hotel had to help.

Before turning corners and running down some stairs, I heard one of them give my direction to someone else, which meant there was more than one group looking for me here.

"Crap." I frantically looked around, the hallways giving me vertigo.

I couldn't tell if not being able to hear them was a blessing or a curse. They could be right on my arse and I wouldn't even know it. Or they could be somewhere I'm about to run to, in hopes of getting away, but in actuality I would be serving myself up.

Breathing in and out at a faster pace than usual, reminding myself that I was the one who came up with this *decent* plan and by some sort of anti-miracle, I ended up back at the entrance.

Convincing myself that it could be a blessing as they might not think I would use the obvious front door, I marched towards the doors without looking anyone in the eyes.

And a fat lot of good that did me.

I was grabbed and slightly lifted off the ground, pushed up against a wall, away from the public's eye just outside the hotel.

"I'm going to give you a head start, it won't be much, but it's all I can do."

Fake security guard man.

He held up his hand to stop me from talking. "Yeah, she's not out the front yet. Keep an eye out, she could be anywhere inside."

Whilst he was busy talking to whoever, I tried to catch my breath as I went through a wave of thoughts. Maverick knows my location and has probably figured out I was alone.

Most of his efforts, if not all, would be put into finding me, and since I *am* alone, and didn't actually know what I was doing, I'd made myself the easiest target.

"You have about five minutes to get as far away as possible." He stripped me of my jacket, replacing it with his. As he continued to talk, he emptied out my pockets and passed me what little luggage I carried; Kassian's money, food wrappers.

"There's a mask in my pocket."

I gave him a '*Ew I'm not wearing that*' expression.

"It's a clean one. You need to keep your head down, buy a cap and new shoes if you can. A lot of people are looking for you and I won't be able to get you away next time."

He said '*next time*' like he was sure I would eventually get caught. I'm not one to think I'm invincible, but he could've at least lied to give me false hope, to fuel me.

"Thank you."

A smile glitched on his face before he gave way, allowing me to 'unsuspiciously' speed walk away. I didn't know the area well, but if I could follow the train stations, I would eventually end up outside of Uni, which was near Oxford Street, which was busy. *Someone* there would have a heart and would save me if I were to get caught.

Walking round to where I assumed would follow the Hammersmith and City line, I bumped into the old man who booked me the room. My eyes enlarged—my body clearly knowing a threat before my conscious mind—his eyes however looked curious. To his side, there was another man whose eyes mirrored mine. Without thinking, I punched the man, not caring for how old he was. They obviously knew who I was and sold me out. If one thing were to momentarily delay them, it would be me injuring one of them. And it had to be the new guy. One: because him being hurt would obviously affect the guy who booked the room, and Two: the other guy had this weird calm expression which made me feel weird (scared) and avoidant.

I ran down a path I needed to be the right one, the one that would eventually take me past the next station in line. Knowing that I would be followed, I went in and out of roads, but it still felt like I wasn't doing enough.

The roads were emptying, so I pressed my brain to remember where this one dorm was as I circled around. It was around here somewhere, I knew it, I'd been to it First Year when it'd stormed.

Eventually, I heard some students and I desperately prayed for them to go to the dorm instead of some club. And Thank God, they led me straight to the doors, where I joined and parted before anyone could notice.

I walked into the girls toilets and went straight into one of the stalls before security became suspicious of me. After a good amount of time had passed, no one came to check up on me, so I convinced myself that they thought I'd left when they weren't paying attention. Meaning I wouldn't be kicked out.

So, I stayed for the night, squatting over the toilet seat— in case someone looked under—catching my sleepy head every now and then when I accidently conked out.

"One more day Medisa. Just one more day."

Chapter 44

Medisa

13/05/2022 (Friday)

"I really can't be arsed for today."

"Same. I feel like our course is the only one that teaches on Fridays."

My eyes shot open. I'd fallen asleep in a position that kept my feet off the ground and my butt off the seat. Once I heard them leave, I got down from the toilet and opened the stall door. My leg muscles felt like they were being stretched out too thin as though I wasn't standing in a normal position.

After quickly washing my face and admiring my lash extensions—took five minutes—I put on fake security guy's mask to walk past real security. It was another person now, so they didn't find anything suspicious, but still, I had to take precautions.

Since Maverick knew that I was here, here being near the university, I imagined him putting someone at every station surrounding where I had last been seen, to around the university. I was trapped, hungry and tired, but I wasn't going to give up.

It'd be stupid for me to roam the streets, trying to get to where ever the hell, but then I'd remembered, it was Friday, and my course had a module that was only taught today. If I could get to the university, I could convince someone with a car to take me away. It was a risk, yes, but it was better than waiting until tomorrow where I would have no one to drive me anywhere.

Before leaving, I rummaged through the Lost and Found and wore clothing that wouldn't display me as bait. I swapped out the cap for another and shoved my hair into the hoodie, then left.

I could cut through Regents Park to get closer to Baker Street, but honestly that park is confusing as hell and I would end up spending the day in there because of it. The 'best' thing to do was continue to walk down the main road until I got to the universities building.

My stomach was doing that thing where it felt as though it were eating itself, and the only thing that pushed me to continue this journey was not the amount of people I could save, but the food in the cafeteria. I momentarily stopped outside of the church, debating on whether or not I should take a quick break inside. I convinced myself that they were charitable enough to run a quick grocery shop for me, but before I actually walked up to the giant pillars, one man came out.

He didn't see me straight away, but as soon as he did, his eyes focussed on mine. We both stood still until he decided to play it cool and act as though he wasn't just staring at me like I was a golden ticket. But the thing is, it didn't matter who or what his intentions were, he had a familiar face, and that was all I needed.

The campus was literally ten minutes away if I walked, but I was running. I did not bother to check left and right for any cars, I had no time to, the guy was right behind me. The next few minutes, I wasn't even looking at people, my mind and eyes were focused on the street in front of me. I heard shouts here and there, car horns here and there, but it's London, it's always hectic. If I made a connection to me, I'd just freak myself out and go into 'freeze' mode, and I didn't jack Kassian's money for me to get caught a day before.

The university's building came into view, I was *so* close, but I could also see people on the other side of the road running towards me. I needed to pick up the pace to get in before they could snatch me up. It would be a close call, but I needed to at least try.

Getting to the stairs before the rest of them was scarier than someone being inches behind me. There's just something about being chased up steps that makes me want to curl up into a ball.

Dodging one of their arms, I just about made it in, instantly ripping off my mask as I shouted at security.

"Help me. Help! They're trying to take me!" I slammed my hands—and body since I wasn't able to slow down in time— onto the wall-desk that kept us separated.

Two of the security men immediately stood and looked towards the doors. When I followed their gaze, I saw that none of Maverick's men had entered with me. In fact, most of them weren't even there anymore and the ones that were, were casually smoking with some of the students.

"Look! Look! He's one of them, the man in the black shirt!" I began to aggressively point in his direction, looking back and forth between him and security. "Do you see him!"

"Miss are you a student here? Is everything okay?" The worried man came out from behind the desk-wall, cautiously approaching me as if I were a loony.

Lowering my head as my chest heaved in and out, trying to think of the next thing to do, I took in my outfit and pieced together how it did not help. Nothing I wore made sense or actually fit. And the security men, they were alert, but they were that way because of me. Not the men outside.

I almost gave in.

Taking one last look outside, almost not believing that this was how I got caught, this was how things ended, my eyes met with the main guy outside. He had this sneer type of smile, like he knew no one believed me, and it was enough to both piss me off—boosting my fight—and send a shiver down my spine.

"My name is Medisa Menaal, my I.D is 1758781, *look it up,* and call the police. I'm telling the truth." I spoke closer to a normal volume, but that probably added to how they saw me.

One of the staff approached once me being a student here was confirmed. "Let's get you inside. Maybe you've been given something you're not aware of?"

"No. You're not listening to me! I'm being followed! I've *been* being followed for God knows how long and none of you are taking it seriously. I'm telling you, they are trying to take me away!" I went back to raising my voice, not caring for the scene I was making. I didn't care that the smokers outside peered in, I didn't care that the students in the cafeteria made their way to the entrance to see what the fuss was all about.

I just wanted a break.

The man that had been talking to me, saw the growing crowd. "Okay, okay, let's get you somewhere safe."

Those words should've offered some sort of relief but no, I could sense something being off, and the consistent downplaying was not helping.

"Yes, she's here."

My head snapped to the man making the call behind the desk. Who was he talking to? The head of the university? My course leader? My emergency contact—Amana? The police? Or Maverick and his men?

"Your friends should be here soon. Are you okay to be left alone for a minute?"

I nodded, grateful for the opportunity to get away. I waited about ten seconds—if that—after he left, then left the room myself. The studio had a fire exit. If I could just get there and trigger the alarm, it would force the students to leave, giving me an opportunity to leave unseen.

From what I could see, no one was on the studio balcony and the door for it was left ajar, so I didn't need to steal someone's student I.D. One of my peers must've been constantly moving things back and forth and I thanked God for that.

Walking in and away from the edge of the balcony, I went through my options. '*Should I open the fire exit door, or would it be better to pull an alarm?*' They must've realised by now that I had left the room. It wouldn't take long for them to check the cameras and track where I had gone, so I needed to make a bloody decision.

"She needs to stop running and just accept that she can't escape from this."

I recognised the voice. They were in the studio below.

"I know, but if she has a chance then we should try to help her."

"We are helping her. We're not going to long out the inevitable and be punished ourselves. She's already attracted so much attention. First at the hotel and now here."

They're my friends. We're on the same course and we hung out with people from Amana's classes. I couldn't even begin to process that they knew about Baronial. Was one of them completing my degree for me?

"I'm going to try and get her out of this. You don't have to help me help her, but turning a blind eye would be useful."

"Yara, think about it. All of our efforts would go to waste and we would suffer deeper consequences than her. These burns were for disrespecting a *client*, what do you think is going to happen with something like this? Being showered with flowers? No."

Yara responded, but she was too quiet for me to hear.

"What more do you need to hear for you to know that helping her would not be the best thing to do?"

My breaths were more manual than automatic, weirdly making me feel like I was suffocating. Yara was the second name I said to Kade when he asked about my close friends. She understood that I was a low maintenance mate and never took things personally when I wasn't up for things or didn't text her every other day. She had my back when I wasn't around and defended me when my words weren't enough or heard.

I was shocked, but I wasn't annoyed or angry at her. She obviously has a contract under Baronial, I just didn't understand why. From what I understood, her and her family were well off, so how did she get roped in?

"We've left her in that room for too long. C'mon, we were supposed to put her mind at ease ages ago."

I took the end of their conversation as a sign to pull the alarm. Under different circumstances, it would've been fun. I always wanted to pull one.

There were only two places Architecture students stood when the alarms went off. You're either on the far right of the building, or the far left. And since Yara was in the studio, she would've gone down the left of the building.

She was by herself.

"You said you wanted to help. So help me by driving me away. And don't even think about running, or screaming, I've got a knife aimed at your spine." I moved her Stanley knife to her skin so that she could feel its presence.

From another perspective, our interaction looked normal. I stood on a platform to play with her hair—hair that covered the knife on the back of her neck—whilst she allowed me to.

"It's not parked close by, its more towards the bridges."

"Let's go. You're calling a Taxi." Questioning why she'd parked it that far away was pointless.

The whole way to her car was…something. She wanted to explain herself even after I'd shut her down and there was this sense of guilt, but also relief about her.

I couldn't wrap my head around her being on the opposing side, even if it wasn't by choice. Other than Amana, she'd made my Uni experience fun, so even though I felt somewhat betrayed, I told her I understood that she had no choice in anything she'd done against me. I also let her know that if she tried to do me over right now, I'd fuck her up with no hesitation.

Being in her car was another story.

It was still early in the day—almost 11 AM—so I made her take the longest route to my area to kill more time.

I hadn't been in her car before. I knew that she'd recently

passed so I wanted to wait a few months before willingly getting in. The usual *'let them get used to the roads, before jumping in'* procedure. But, since my life was practically in danger anyways, it didn't matter. We could crash and it would still be a better ending than whatever Maverick had in store.

"Why did she get burnt?" I asked even though we could've sat in silence for the rest of the thirty minutes. Silence being me eating whatever she had to offer.

"She'd insulted a client by not doing what he wanted. Apparently, it was someone important, someone he needed for some sort of deal or something." Yara pronounced her *'th'*s as *'f'*s.

"It's rare for someone to meet him you know. And it's rarer for us to see someone that's fucked up again. But she met him." We briefly locked eyes before she turned her head back to the roads. "She met him and she said that at first, he was nice, but when she was somewhat comfortable, he poured hot liquid on her thigh, then held her in place so that she couldn't grab or comfort herself. She had to wait it out."

There were no appropriate words I could find to respond. Yes, that was on brand for Maverick. Yes, he did that for an important client, but now I was wondering what he would do to us. To Yara.

"Why does she think that you guys would get it worse than me?" The answer to this was obvious, but I needed to know what they knew. Did they think I was under a contract like them? Or did they know about the other legal…marital contract.

"Because she saw you with him."

'What?'

"When?" She wasn't in Scotland.

"She saw you with him around the university, even pointed him out to me."

"That wasn't him, that was *Kade*, his *brother*." I tried not to be too defensive, but the '*are you dumb?*' tone came out.

"I don't know man. She was sure that it was him."

"She probably got confused because they look alike." My words came out as the thought of them formed. "He hasn't worked for Baronial for years." I shook my head, then spoke before she could. "Anyways, if I make it till tomorrow, I could end this all. Whatever *Maverick* owns, whatever he has a say in, I would too. I could help everyone under Baronial."

Yara's polite smile made an appearance before she rolled her window down. I could see her pacing her breaths through a small, almost unnoticeable pout. She either didn't believe me, couldn't wait to be free, or she was handing me over and started to feel bad.

After a few minutes of silence between us, a buzzing noise came from the glove box. My face questioned Yara before I opened the compartment to see the vibrating phone.

"It's my work phone."

"Why didn't you get rid of it the *second* I sat in your car?! They could be tracking us!"

"They won't know that you're with me."

I shoved the phone in her face, frustrated. "*Who's* calling you?"

"I don't know, I've never seen that number before."
Maverick.

It had to be Maverick, who else would it be?—My dad?

I answered the phone and waited for the caller to speak first.

"Feeling homesick? Sweetheart, I hate to break it to you but you're going the wrong way." He was a little humorous. Almost like he had control of the situation, like he had all the cards. "I told you this before Medisa. It won't be hard to find you."

'I'm starting to think he's put a tracker in my arse.'

My breath hitched as I moved the phone away from me, ready to throw it out the window.

"Before you decide to go. Say hello to your friend, will you?"

'Amana? Kade? Kassian? Which one does he have?'

"Being in both Scotland and London didn't make sense, so of course I had both checked."

'It's Kassian.'

My stomach dropped triggering the first round of sweats.

"Am I on speaker?"

"You are."

"Can he hear me?"

"He can."

"Kassian. I'm sorry. I'm so-so sorry. I should've listened to you, I should've stayed still, I'm sorry." Before Maverick or he could cut in, I continued with a little more anger than sadness. "I'm sorry that you have a piece of shit brother, and I'm sorry that I'm going to go against what you want again and come get you."

There's some sort of movement before Maverick spoke in Kassian's place. "Wonderful. We'll be at my pub."

Chapter 45

Medisa
13/05/2022 (Friday)

The last time I came to this pub, the lights were a disgusting faded orange and it had some sort of vintage-Gatsby look going for it. But, since the sun was out, I expected it to be well lit, but it was practically the same, if not a little lighter.

Everyone inside was minding their business. I was so sure that Maverick would be inside with his favourite drink entertaining himself. But I couldn't see him.

"Can I get some water please?" I sat on one of the stools. Usually I would look around to find something to admire, especially when a place had been refurbished, but I was tired and desperately needed something to drink. Even with the dangers of being here, I only thought about how cold the water will be, and how it would feel going down my throat and into my somewhat empty stomach.

"Another please."

I knew that voice.

I didn't bother to lift my head or turn my body towards him. I stayed sat with my head down, ditching the thought of cold water to instead think of Kassian, and how we're going to escape this time.

A glass slid towards him, and it took me a second to realise that I wasn't going to get my water. From the corner of my eyes, I could see everyone was minding their own, he on the other hand, had his eyes on me. From what I could make out, his body was facing the bar—like mine—but his head faced me before facing whatever's in front of him.

He picked up his glass. "Kassian is outside."

The stool I sat on scraped the floor as I got up to leave.

Everyone in the pub stopped being so casual and got up a second after I did.

"Sit. Down."

This felt familiar.

I dropped myself back onto the stool, unintentionally signalling for the rest of the pub to do the same.

I faced the bar as Maverick spoke.

"I admire you. I really do. You seem to have more balls than my brother."

I wondered what state Kassian was in outside. What did he go through whilst I was running around?

"We should drink to that. And to you *almost* getting away." He stopped swirling his drink.

I turned my head to him. His words, though calm, were triggering, even with the undertones.

"Let's play a little game. I'll give you another twenty-four hours. *If* I don't have you in those hours, I'll drop this whole thing. I'll drop everything and you can do whatever you want with what's ours." He slid a phone to me. "But, if I have you in those twenty-four hours, I'm going to do as I please, no more privileges, no more warnings."

He took a sip as I went over what he'd just said.

"You have sixty seconds."

The game clearly wasn't an option, but I still didn't move.

'Was this some sort of trick? Some sort of trap?'

"One... Two... Three... Four..."

I speed walked out to where two men released Kassian. He looked beaten, but it wasn't as bad as I thought—the thought being him dead, or close to it.

"We need to run *now*. I haven't got time to explain."

Chapter 46

Medisa
13/05/2022 (Friday)

Kassian ended up taking us to the pub we'd all been to before, swearing that it would be a safe place. Not pushing my argument too much as the last time I went against his wishes it'd done me a fat lot of good, I instead momentarily thought about how we somewhat mirrored the past. Kassian was literally beaten—but not stabbed, <u>Thank God</u>—and I paced the basement trying to figure out what to do. The big difference now would be that I now knew that this pub was one of his investments.

"Kade should be at Scotland by now, right? Or wherever he planned to take her? They're safe right? When was the last time you heard from him?"

"Would you sit down. Your pacing is making me sick."

I dropped my bottom on the ground besides him, legs somewhat spread and visibly (manually) shaking.

"When did you last hear from him?"

"When I saw him back at the farm. He hasn't contacted me and I haven't had the chance to contact him since you ran off...Thanks for that by the way."

I pulled my legs closer to my chest. I really did screw up their plan.

"Hey." He softly nudged me. "It's okay, we only have five hours till tomorrow."

"Tomorrow's hours are still part of the game and something doesn't feel right." I switched his phone on, risking our location.

I searched for Kade's name in his contacts then clicked on it like it was going to teleport him here.

"It wouldn't make sense if he had his phone on. We're all laying low remember?"

"If it *isn't* supposed to make sense, why is the call going through?" I put it on speaker between us.

Kassian and I shared the same eager but worried expression, either one of us could've ended the call, putting our minds at a little bit of ease, but none of us did.

Two seconds after it went to voicemail, I'd finally ended the call. Then, it began to ring, and like the beg I am, I answered it immediately.

"Kade I—"

"Ah-ah. Guess again."

The phone was no longer on speaker so Kassian had no idea what was being said, although his body language and comments let me know that he wanted to know.

"Where is he?" I chose my words wisely. '*He*' and not '*they*.' Amana might not have been with Kade, she could've escaped, so there's a possibility Maverick doesn't know about the plan to get her.

Kassian tried to intervene, but I held a finger close to my lips as if to say '*shut up*' and '*gimme a second*'. Then I put the call on speaker whilst he joined in on the leg shaking.

Maverick sighed. "Let's make things a little more fun. You can come to me—your husband, in Scotland. Come find out if I just have his phone, or if I have him. Or don't, stay at Kassian's pub—"

Me and Kassian shot the same look at each other. He knew where we were. Of course he did.

"—and go through with your original plan, leaving me to

have fun with whatever's in my possession. The ball's in your court darling—"

"It's not really though, is it? You prick." Words ran out my mouth the moment I thought of them.

"You have five hours." He continued.

"*Five* hours? Five hours isn't enough!—"

He hung up, leaving me to deal with not only my mind running but Kassian's too. He never mentioned a girl, only Kade. So it's okay to assume Amana was safe, hell, she might still be at home, which just left Kade. I could wait till tomorrow, have things in my control, then find Kade with my new contacts and resources. It's not like Maverick's going to kill his own brother.

But I wasn't as willing as I should be to risk it.

And he said '*in my possession*' and not something along the lines of '*leaving me to do whatever I want with Kaden,*'… Did he know what Kade was supposed to do? That he was supposed to get Amana? Did he purposely say '*possession*' so that I assumed he had more than one person?

"How the hell is he going from Scotland to London so fast?" I felt like kicking something.

"You think that he's driving? No. He's flying."

"A plane?" Of course these guys own a frigging plane.

"No, he has wings." Kassian's sarcasm was still intact.

"We need to go. Now." When I noticed Kassian moving stupidly slow, I turned back around. "What is wrong with you? Kade's your brother!"

"Maverick knows where we are. Why don't he just come get you himself? It has to be a trick."

"What if it's not? Are you willing to risk that?"

"Kade wouldn't want you to."

"I don't *care*. And how would you know what he wants,

you guys didn't even speak or see each other for years. And why would Maverick risk leaving me here if he didn't have him back in Scotland? I'm going. I don't care."

Kassian stood between me and the door.

"Do you still have my money?"

I scoffed as I tried to move past him. "I'll pay you back after I've got your brother."

My body is pulled by its arm to be back in front of him. "No, we have five hours to get back. A car wouldn't be fast enough but a plane is. Do we have enough money for a ride?"

"You couldn't have this conversation while dragging me to the airport becauseeeeeee?"

His shoulders dropped, then he flicked my forehead and before I could even say anything, he announced '*let's go*' as if I were the one holding us back.

Chapter 47

Medisa
14/05/2022 (Saturday)

We got to the estate ten-to-fifteen minutes before our five hours were up. We still had the road to run down but we were basically there.

It was dark now, and the trees in the distance blew with the wind. Not the type where one would think *'oh this is nice,'* no, it's the type where one would think *'when the hell did I agree to be a part of a horror movie?'*

The beige road ahead was clear, there were no cars parked on the side to ambush us, there wasn't even anyone standing around to take us in. It was just us and this barely lit private road.

We both stood silent until one of us—Kassian—broke away and began moving towards the manor. At first, we were treading lightly, but then we began to pick up the pace which then just turned into full blown running.

You would've thought the manor was abandoned or something by how dark it was. No lights were on except for two dim front garden lights, and they barely brightened the area in which we stood.

"C'mon." Kassian opened one of the large front doors, then led us to another part of the manor.

I would say that he knew what he was doing and where to go, but it felt like we were being led by Maverick. It was kind of like I was in a game, like we had all this space to explore but we couldn't move forward unless we went in the direction the game makers wanted us to. In games, they make which way to go obvious by making an area lighter or darker, or by having some sort of checkpoint or bush out of place or something. But here, in this manor, our pathway was made with candle lights placed here and there. It was obvious we had to follow them.

We ended up in the ballroom me and Kade danced in. The room, like the rest of the manor was dimly lit as if Halloween had come early. Even the balconies that looked into the hall had candles on them. From the looks of it two balconies were at the second floor, two from the third and one from the fourth (or fifth) but all in different areas so it looked random. The fourth or fifth floor balcony was placed at the 'head' of the room.

'I wonder who's going to come out from there?'

The moment we got to the middle, the two doors we came in from, slammed shut, and all balconies but one began to fill themselves with Maverick's men. I recognised some of them from the past few days, including fake security guy and the guy who chased me into the university.

I stuck my middle finger up at him.

Finally, Maverick came into view on the highest balcony. I took a few steps back to have my head raised at a comfortable level to properly view him. At this point my thoughts were, *'just jump.'*

"You all know my wife, Medisa. The girl you've been running after for days."

A few sounds of agreement, wolf whistles and other noises were made.

"If only you knew that all you had to do was set a trap." He continued with a playful tone.

The men and some of the women that filled the crowds

let out some sort of hushed laughter.

"Maverick enough of this! Where is my brother?"

"Patience. You're ruining the surprise." Maverick didn't even bother to spare Kassian a glance. His eyes were on me, before he went back to entertaining himself and his crowd.

"Now we all know that she ran away, but does anyone know why?" The question was obviously a rhetorical one but he still looked around, waiting for a response. "No? Well let me fill you in." He brought his crazed eyes back to mine. "The boys and Medisa had it in their silly little heads that I would kill her before our anniversary, if not on the day... How daft is that?" His question came out a little more serious and daring than the way he delivered our assumption. "Anyway, she's back now, and although she gave quite the scare running off like that, I got her a gift. It is our anniversary after all."

Maverick disappeared into the room his balcony was attached to, then came out with someone with a bag over their head.

My breaths switched to manual as my brain rushed through all outcomes.

Maverick moved himself and the person in his grip to the edge of the balcony. "Everyone, give it up for..."

I held onto my poker face whilst my insides did all sorts of jumps, skips and dives.

He tugged the bag off, revealing his victim, his gift. "Amanaaa!"

The crowd cheered.

They were the loudest they had been. And whilst I had my breath taken from me, Kassian growled then pleaded, summoning the true intensity and fear of the situation within me.

He ran up to the doors. Banging, punching and throwing

himself at them, trying to force them open but they wouldn't budge.

Amana's eyes were red with both anger and fear. She held herself well, all whilst I was stuck in some sort of denial.

Maverick stroked her hair with the back of his fingers, staring deep into her eyes, before pulling her closer by the rope wrapped around her neck, an accessory I'd noticed after his action. I followed the rope to find its end, only to discover that it's already been tied to his stone balcony railing.

"My gift to you, is to spare your life. But make no mistake, a part of you *is* dying tonight." He pulled out a knife.

Suffocation isn't enough to describe what I was going through. I knew that I needed to be logical, be quick, but the more I looked between Amana and Maverick, the more I felt myself losing it.

"Kassian." I choked on his name as I tried to call out for some sort of help, some sort of support. But he was too busy taking his frustration out on the doors which didn't seem to budge.

Between being confused at what was going on with Kassian and not being able to accept what was going to happen to Amana, I felt myself breaking down some more. Things were happening too fast for me to figure something out.

When I looked back to the balcony, Maverick held a sinister smile as Amana kept her eyes closed. Even the crowd quietened down as he angled the knife towards her face.

"No-no wait! Maverick *wait*! Kill *me*! Kill me." My sight became blurred as my eyes held onto its waters. "Please. Please Maverick, I'm *begging* you." I blinked at the tears that blinded me. "You can do whatever you want to me, I swear it. Just not this. I'm begging you. Not this."

Amana's eyes had shot open as soon as I offered myself

up. She started to argue but her covered mouth prevented any words from being coherent. Frustrated, Maverick pulled on her rope again, this time harder, making her lose balance.

"Maverick, kill me." I offered myself up a little more calmly. "Please, I don't care about what you want to do, just *do it to me*." My temper got the best of those last few words, so I forced some deep breaths before addressing him again. "Maverick, kill *me*."

Maverick swiftly placed Amana's body so that her legs were dangling over the edge of the railing. The top half of her body rested on him as he held her by her waist, burrowing his chin into her shoulder. I ran to the balcony as if her body would drop low enough for me to keep her up.

"Oh." He mocked as though he cared. "But this is for your betterment."

Amana let out some sort of strangled gasp.

My head shot up to see what he had done, only for my face to be met with a few drops of her blood. Ignoring my creative mind of all the options it had presented, I convinced myself that she was okay. Not enough blood had been spilled for it to have been deadly. Amana was going to survive this, she had to. Out of the two of us, she was always going to be the one that would do something for herself, make something of herself and actually change people's lives. She was probably at home continuing to be the person her siblings needed and looked up to, and I just took her away. Deep down I knew that she was always going to be found, we have always been associated with one another, why would this time be any different? From the moment I got involved, she didn't stand a chance.

The last thing I saw before things went slow, was Maverick looking below, gripping her passed out face down to me whilst he appeared insatiable.

Once his smile dropped, so did she.

Medisa's breath hitched as her legs gave out.

She'd dropped to her knees, her head stuck at an angle forcing her to view Amana's lifeless body. Blood from the cut Maverick had given Amana dropped onto Medisa's face, but it didn't seem to faze her.

Continuing to be on her knees through the cheers of the crowd and Kassian's infinite banging and pain-filled roars, she eventually zoned out. Blurring all noises until she couldn't hear anything anymore.

Even with the feeling of acquiring a deep wound, Medisa sat in silence. No noise escaped her mouth as she watched Amana with drowned eyes. She may have been able to ignore the crowd and Kassian's cries, but she couldn't stop her mind from making things worse.

Not allowing herself to move, to talk, scream, shout, cry, or even look away, she made it so her neck felt the presence of a tightly wrapped rope. Even with the added pain, she refused to look away to soothe her throat from the lump of built-up cries, and her neck from the weight of her angled head.

Medisa simultaneously felt and didn't. She'd zoned out even further, the body still in her view, but she could no longer make out the details. It was still there, still dangling just above her, low enough for it to have given Amana a quick death, but high enough for her to be out of Medisa's reach.

In her void, hands grabbed onto her, forcing her to a stand.

It took a few light shakes to get her to come to, and when

she did, sound flowed back into her ears. Gunshots flew through the air, forcing her hands to protect her drums.

"Medisa, we have to go. We haven't got time." Kade tried to both rush and soothe her.

In the second that Medisa found a crumb of comfort in Kade's appearance, she also loses it and becomes a touch worse. As Kade took quick turns in taking in their surroundings then trying to put some of his focus on Medisa, urgently needing her to move, she took in his appearance.

She shook her head, to both address Kade and her accusing thoughts. "No."

It didn't matter what predicament they were in, she didn't care, Medisa was not going to be leaving Amana.

"You're not leaving her. We're going to come back for her." Kade continued to gently try.

Without intending to, Kade was able to summon another emotion from Medisa's void, one that played on humour.

She almost scoffed, but that is put to an end when Medisa puts whatever energy she had left into pushing Kade away.

He didn't move.

"You don't have one scratch..." Her words leaked her thoughts, giving Kade an insight as to what her mind questioned despite Medisa not wanting to confirm.

"I'm sorry Medisa, but we haven't got time for this."

Medisa turned back to face him as his words smothered her, but also because she knew that he was going to take things into his own hands.

What she didn't expect, was her turning around to meet with one end of his gun.

Chapter 48

Medisa

14/05/2022 (Saturday)

Medisa woke up with more than her head hurting

She knew where she was as soon as her eyes opened, Kassian's club. Someone had laid her down on one of the cushioned seats attached to the wall.

Whilst Medisa rested her head on her stretched-out arm, Kade tenderly approached her with a water filled pint glass and a small towel. He crouched down trying to catch her dead eyes but she continued to be in a daze. The only time she showed some sort of reaction was when she moved away from the wet towel in his hand.

The mind was a funny thing. So were emotions. Grief.

How could something intangible have this much control? How could it numb someone to the point they no longer had any thoughts whilst also feeling everything all at once, so much so a deep pit formed within themselves? How was it her mind thought it was okay for her to remember each and every one of her mistakes leading up until this point, whilst also refusing to let her forget Amana's hung body. Why did it split? Why did one part desperately want a break, but not quite as it was aware enough to know it would concretely make her a selfish bad friend? Why did another part want her to use this all as fuel, as an excuse to become angry, reckless?

Medisa's mind was once again at war with itself. It became overloaded, strained and at some point, it even began to blur the images she thought would've stayed with her for a long, long time.

Everyone in Kassian's club knew something had happened, but no one matched the trios energies, they all continued to smoke, drink, dance, laugh and do whatever it was people did when they had no care in the world.

Whenever Medisa felt Kassian's presence or eyes, it didn't take long for a fight to break out between him and someone nearby right after. Eventually Kade kicked everyone out, earning himself a thrown bottle from Kassian. He missed his shot which is how Medisa knew that he'd thrown something in the first place.

Not being able to care for their drama, she too decided to leave the club, or at least the room that they were in.

Grabbing both boys attention as she walked towards the ladies room, she avoided eye contact with Kade, but gave in to observing Kassian for a few seconds. It was enough for her to see that they mirrored each other's looks, the only difference was that he drank himself away whilst her mind couldn't decide what emotion it wanted her to feel.

Once Medisa moved away, confused, annoyed and even a little worried about the way Kassian was and why, Kassian got up with a bottle in hand and left the club altogether, leaving Kade with no choice but to go after him.

Comfort may have been what Medisa needed from others, but she was accustomed to dealing with herself, by herself. So when she heard the doors shut behind Kade, she couldn't have cared less, well, that's what she convinced herself.

The mind was a funny thing. But when unstable, it was scary, and against all.

Chapter 49

Medisa
14/05/2022 (Saturday)

Staring myself down, taking in the drops of blood that seemed to have been perfectly placed on my face, I let myself go knowing that I was finally alone. Tears streamed down my cheeks as I tried my best to prevent any sound from escaping. The pain that had clung to my throat, creating a lump and bringing about throbs, came back almost instantly.

What happened to Amana wasn't a dream. It all may have happened too quick for my mind to take in, for part of my mind to be sure I imagined it, but it was real. I wanted to scream, and to break things, and not being able to just added to the mania. I was going to explode from all these memories and emotions and instead of being able to do something about it, I felt as though they had overexerted my body before allowing me to make a move.

Throwing myself in front of a toilet bowl, I gagged and gagged but nothing came but the pain from my ribs stabbing into my gut

The door to the stall slammed shut and currently being out of my mind, I swore it mimicked the sound of a rope being tugged and a neck being snapped.

My breaths came in quick twos and threes, suffocating me on top of the clogged throat feeling. I tried to cool myself down, but my thoughts wouldn't allow it. Once again, I was punishing myself with her smile and then the way she looked whilst hung. She didn't deserve that.

And I couldn't even get into what Maverick had in store for us. What else he'll do. What else we had to do before finally feeling safe.

Washing my face didn't work.

Pacing didn't work.

Trying to control my breathing didn't work

Every attempt was given a few seconds to cure me, and when it failed, hell, even the attempts to stop being such a little bitch, added to the guilt.

I dropped to the floor, away from the stalls and away from the door, defeated with never-ending tears that ran through what was left of the dried blood, either taking it down my neck, or jumping straight onto my lap.

Sobbing into my hands, I tried to muffle, or at least mute myself in case they had come back inside. A part of me was peeved beyond relief for having the audacity to feel and express these emotions, as though I didn't know my actions always had severe consequences.

My breaths continued to come in quick twos and threes, and despite the feeling of not having enough air to breathe, I was *slowly* calming myself down.

I couldn't stay in here forever. I couldn't try to push the blame onto them when I knew a chunk of it was mine.

"Bad time?"

Hearing his voice instantly put a hold on anymore tears being produced.

Trying to stop my breaths after previously begging for air, I glared at him as he came out from the shadows.

How I felt was too overwhelming and it *drained* me. I couldn't bring myself to move, to fight, and somehow, he knew it.

He sat on the sofa directly in front of me, no weapon in

sight. "All that fire in your eyes and you're still seated."

My mouth may have been shut to prevent the forced gasps for air, but my chest, and the quick two-three forced sniffs gave away my prolonged panic attack.

If he was going to kill me, he might as well get it over and done with whilst I still had some sort of control to make sure he gained no satisfaction from it.

"If you must know, I never took her. She was offered to me." He spoke to me like I was a child having some sort of strop, as if he had no choice but to do what he did and was tired of my act.

But just like that, with one sentence, he had my mind on something else, something other than the constant guilt-trips.

My expression softened, unintentionally giving him a break from the glares.

"The list of betrayals are yet to grow." He leaned back, his arms raised to rest on top of the backrest. "Kaden gave her to me."

My shoulders dropped. Then, my brain with its comical timing reminded me of the way Kade looked before he knocked me out.

"He knew I would have you and would be unforgiving with the stunt that you all pulled, so he offered your friend—"

"*Amana.*"

"Right. Apologies. Amana." Placing a hand over his heart, he bowed his head a little. "Kaden offered Amana in order to fill my satisfaction. And it did, just not all the way. Which is why I am here now."

My head hurt from how hard I had pulled my brows together. "You're lying."

Maverick adjusted his position as he let out a dry chuckle. "Medisa, I'm about to tell you more truths than your so-called friends out there. But please, if you don't believe me, if you don't want to hear it and want revenge on the wrong person, call them in here to do what you clearly cannot."

Looking over him again and again, I knew not to trust a word, but still I asked, "What do you know?"

Maverick sucked in air through his teeth. "I know that Kassian met Amana when she was sixteen. I know that he grew to like her. And I know that Kaden was the one who tricked her into working for Baronial."

A humourless laugh escaped as I got up.

"Get out. Or kill me. I don't care anymore so you can stop with the—"

"He didn't know you or her then, there were no loyalties towards you girls. So why would he care?"

I didn't want to give in. I'd spent time with a charitable, funny, noble person, but I also won't dismiss his past or his alter ego as quickly as I've done previously. There's also what Yara had said that I was so quick to dispel. But Amana's lying abilities couldn't be ignored either, I could see through her. I knew when she lied or when she was upset. I would've caught on.

"Think about what Kade could've done to anger Kassian. Think about what year Amana started to work, what year she took her headscarf off. It all lines up."

My breaths were now deep and heavy.

'*I just feel like I'm disrespecting the hijab and when I stop, I'll wear it all the time again.*' That's what Amana had said when we had a conversation about it years ago. And the day I met Kade, Amana had scrolled so far back to show me the pictures she had been collecting of him. She never took pictures of guys. She could've been trying to build a case on him, or they're from when she's sneaked pictures of Kassian—*if* they really did meet before. There was also the time where she'd said that Kade owed her, what could he have done that was worth giving her friend with no experience a job with that pay? And Kassian, he avoided Amana and looked as though he were picturing her whenever I spoke about her, as though he knew what she looked like and had already witnessed her habits. And when we first met, he knew my name…he knew my name because Amana had told him.

It made sense.

Maverick was telling me the truth.

Peeling the skin off my lips as I went over what he'd said and what I know, I tried to come up with excuses for their actions when they probably didn't even deserve it.

Maverick stood from his seat to approach me.

"I hurt you. I know I did. But you hurt me too, so in some books we're even now. All that's left to do is get back at the one who put us all in this position." He spoke like he understood the pain he put me through, the pain that I continued to put myself through.

"*You* killed Amana."

"Ugh yes and *Kade* helped." His shoulders lowered themselves, already wanting to move on from his part in this.

Maverick pulled his phone out with a video ready. Before my eyes could adjust to the scene, he pressed play. It was a car outside the manor. The driver's door opened and Kade came out. He was angry, the way he slammed his door and made his way to the passenger side made that clear. When he opened the passenger door, Amana is revealed. The video ends with the both of them approaching the door.

"He practically put the noose on." Maverick provoked.

Before I could give an actual reaction, the door to the toilets was knocked on a few times.

"Medisa? Medisa, have you locked the door?" Kade asked whilst Kassian mumbled in the back.

"Spoiler alert. I locked the doors." Maverick stood in between me and the door.

"Talk to me Medisa." Kade continued after getting no response as my mind went back and forth, it may have even jammed a little.

"He signed your best friend into Baronial, making her do things she never wanted to do, then offered her up to me, *knowing* she would die." Maverick continued to rub salt into new wounds.

Something dropped, making Kade tell Kassian off.

"I can't hear her." Kade's almost panicked voice said a second after.

"And I don't think you will anytime soon." Maverick spoke loud enough for the boys to hear.

It didn't take another second for Kade to try and kick the door in.

I tried to stomp my way over to Kade, to confront him, to beat him, to do something, but Maverick grabbed onto my arm and held me away. "Come with me. You'll be my equal, nothing less. What's mine is already yours, and by coming with me, you'll hurt him. Your absence will consume him."

Other than the feeling of wanting to bash everyone and thing in, I was numb. Amana knew and trusted the both of them at some point and it got her killed. I thought I knew and trusted them, but time and time again I'm shown that they will always keep something from me. And I'm tired of giving them the opportunity to come clean.

Moving away from the door, I showed Maverick I was choosing him this time.

He opened the fire exit and waited for me to walk through,

and I did with no hesitation.

When I turned back to get one last look at what I was leaving behind, I took in an unexpected but satisfying sight. Kade couldn't create a gap large enough for him to fit through, but what he could do was watch me walk away with his partner in crime. To add to my satisfaction whilst simultaneously adding to my anger and the want to turn back around, he begged me to stay, to listen.

It took a lot for me to not stay, to not do something here to get it over and done with, but I didn't want to risk Kade being able to talk me out of this, to tell me I didn't need to leave, that I didn't need to come up with the best way to set them all on fire.

Chapter 50
Medisa
15/05/2022 (Sunday)

Pushing the hidden door open, revealing the room, I walked in and past Maverick's inquisitive look.

Picking up a bat, I made my way out the room, not patient enough to wait for Maverick to follow behind. The first thing to feel the other end of the bat was anything on his desk, including the lamp I gifted him. I smashed everything to bits. The first sound of contact called Maverick out of the hidden gym and into the office.

After his office, I made my way down the hallway, throwing and swinging at anything linked to a memory or that I knew he held close to his heart. Once paintings were torn, structures were cracked beyond repair, I moved onto the next place.

Everything but Bellamy's office was attacked.

Cushions were ripped into and thrown across the floor. Plant pots smashed into, leaves and flowers ripped from stems and sprinkled across the floor. I flipped tables, chairs, spray painted anything he mentioned he liked, then finally when I thought I was done, I decided it wasn't enough.

Out of breath and wanting to leave instead of entertaining whatever memories this place triggered, I took the elevator down.

As I took in and released deep breaths, the doors opened, revealing Bellamy. Almost instantly, all extreme emotions dramatically dropped. Whatever hate I had was close to disappearing and I almost felt bad for completely destroying the floors.

"Oh my God. Medisa? Are you okay?" He came close, hands raised as though he were going to inspect and hold me, but I flinched back as if he were a disease.

I followed his eyes as they examined my appearance, then realised I had bought the bat down with me. Slowly circling him so that I was now outside the elevator, in the car park and he with his back towards it's closed doors, I finally spoke. "Did you know?"

That was too broad.

"Did you know about them and Amana?"

He opened his mouth to speak, to lie, but decided against it, nodding his head instead. "I knew, but Medisa, it's—"

That was all I needed. The truth. Months ago. But he delivered it now when it was too late. After tightening my grip on the bat, I swung at him. He dodged it of course, but before he could do anything else, the elevator doors opened once again, letting Maverick out, who sprang into action once he saw the scene.

One thing after another and Bellamy's body was with us in the car.

If Kade could take my person away, why's it unfair for me to do the same?